The Pearl of Wisdom Saga
Volume 1
Two Heads, Two Spikes

Jason Paul Rice

Cover Art by CJ McDaniel
Published by Jason Paul Rice
Copyright 2014, Jason Paul Rice.
All rights reserved.

Third Edition, 2016

Special thanks: Mom, Nandita, Nikola, Ken Scott, Tara Woods, Heidi,

Background information
for
the Pearl of Wisdom Series

POV/VIP CHARACTER INFORMATION

Ali-Stanley Wamhoff-65-Fox Chapel

King of Donegal, old, flabby man, very clumsy, has been king for 30 years, not a warrior or good leader

Ali-Ster Wamhoff-18-Fox Chapel

King's son, battle tested, unmarried, tall/red hair/brown eyes, long freckled face, back in capitol after four years at war

Brehan Castaway-22-Mattingly

Knight, bastard from pearl islands, dark skin/chiseled features/green eyes, close to riceros & in secret relationship with elisa

Edburgh Etburn-26-Waters Edge

Brown hair/blue eyes, son of duke tyus etburn of waters edge, battle tested, seeking vengeance

Elisa Burke Wamhoff-18-Burkeville

Daughter of Duke of Burkeville, tall/pale, long brown hair and eyes, married to heir of the kingdom, Prince Ali-Varis Wamhoff

Emilia Burke Wamhoff-33-Fox Chapel

Lower born member of the Burke family, Queen Of Donegal, married King at 14, frisky, bored with the King and castle life

Jon Colbert-41-Mattingly

Duke of Mattingly, at odds with king because of his father's rebellion, short/stout, green eyes, blond hair

Leimur Leluc-20-Goldenfield

Princess, expelled from castle by parents at 16, rose up the ranks of army, badass, black hair/purple eyes

The Man With The Golden Sword-30

Bastard of unkown parents from blairs beak, believes he is destined to be king, blond hair/blue eyes, had a rough life so far

Mariah Colbert-17-Mattingly

Girlie girl, daughter of Duke Jon Colbert, naive, tall and skinny, light brown hair/gray eyes

Ollor-??

Mysterious man of unkown background, on a mission to save his soul, castle born but rugged

Penrose Ellsworth-20-Fox Chapel

Member of Kingsguard, Haunted by voices, blond hair/blue eyes, Kings right hand guard

Riceros Colbert-11-Mattingly

A scrawny kid, son of Duke Jon Colbert, blond hair/green eyes, mute, genius, expert archer, mysterious past

Russell Seabrook-17-Waters Edge

Knight, bastard, lives in castle as the favorite of the Duchess Ali-Pari, looking for more in life

RULING FAMILIES BY REGION

<u>Fox Chapel</u>

Wamhoff Family Crest: Two foxes addorsed on either side of a crown

Patriarch—King Ali-Stanley Wamhoff-65

Matriarch—Queen Emilia Burke Wamhoff-33   King's 1st Wife—Parys Etburn Wamhoff-Dead

Sons—Ali-Varis-47 (Parys), Ali-Ster-18 (Emilia), Ali-Sundry (Emilia)(Dead)

Daughters—Ali-Terri-45, Ali-Cary-38, Ali-Tiste-34, Ali-Bia-29, Ali-Gare-26, Ali-Sandre(Dead)—All Born To Parys

King's Guard Knights—Sir Penrose Ellsworth-20, Sir Anderley Ellsworth-26, Sir Jermar Lolat-33, Sir Oliver Wedgeword-42, Sir Nate Edgewell-36, Sir Thomas Maron-34

Grand Count Silzeus

<u>Mattingly</u>

Colbert Family Crest: A golden bull on a black field

Patriarch—Duke Jon Colbert-41

Matriarch—Duchess Camelle Etburn Colbert-38

Sons—Krys-18, Ryno-16, Ruxin-15, Riceros-11

Daugter—Mariah-17

Notable Knights—Sir Brehan Castaway-22, Sir Herman Weiham-38, Sir Balthasar Strong-44, Sir Richard Rosebud-40, Sir Jeremiah Elmhurst-28, Sir Ryan Caughleigh-18, Sir Gunnar Pine-36

Count Sproul

Waters Edge
>   Etburn Family Crest: Silver eagle on a field of burgundy
>   Patriarch—Duke Tyus Etburn-81
>   Matriarch—Duchess Ali-Pari Wamhoff Etburn-70
>   Sons—Ben-54, Paul-52, Eliah-50, Rollo(Dead), Edburgh-26
>   Daughters—Camelle-38
>   Notable Knights—Sir Randall Wendell-52, Sir Raymond Stevens-60, Sir Perry Stevens-47, Sir Gary Stevens-54, Sir Lawrence Stevens-50, Sir Russell Seabrook-17
>   Count Priehold

Burkeville
>   Burke Family Crest: Black bear on an argent field
>   Patriarch—Duke Aston Burke-38
>   Matriarch—Duchess Ali-Tiste Wamhoff Burke-34
>   Sons—Butrel-4, Astrid-2
>   Daughters—Elisa-18, Telly-14
>   Notable Knights— Sir Erich Longway-36, Sir Regis Green-27, Sir Barry Bondifer-44, Sir Alexander Applebaur-30, Sir Denny Plumlee-46
>   Count Bidwell

Bottomfoot
>   Malik Family Crest: Silver ram on a powder blue field
>   Patriarch—Edword Malik-41
>   Matriarch—Lucille Malik-41
>   Son—Torvald
>   Notable Knights—Landry Lemon-31, They Claim To Only Have One Knight

Kingdom of Goldenfield
>   Patriarch—King Pascal Leluc-51
>   Matriarch—Queen Harla Leluc-39
>   Sons—Huber-4, Romer-2
>   Daughters—Leimur-20, Leirum(Dead)

SUCCESSION OF
KINGS FROM KINGDOM OF DONEGAL

The calendar of donegal started when the wamhoff family, led by a man named dus conquered a small portion of the kingdom of goldenfield. The wamhoffs named dus the king of the newly forged donegal and gave him a more regal sounding name with ali-dus. The four-season/twelve month calendar with each season lasting 90 days/thirty day months was created in the first year of ali-dus' reign.

1-41(calendar year)-**King Ali-Dus the Great**-(age of rule 22-63)

Led a rag tag bunch from the Androsi isles and fended off the goldenfield army to create a kingdom called Donegal. Known as Ali-Dus the Great because he improved everyones lives and gave them the religious freedom they were seeking. Died of natural causes while fishing.

41-50-**King Ali-Ramuel**-(age of rule 24-33)—first son of Ali-Dus

Died of a sudden fever under very suspicous circumstances. Known as a good king.

50-67-**King Ali-Raven the Dangerous**-(age of rule 18-35)—third son of Ali-Ramuel

He had two brothers ahead of him as heir to the throne. Both died mysteriously, and then his father, the king, died suddenly. It was widely believed that he killed those in his way to earn the title, "the dangerous." he died on a hunt.

67-89-**King Ali-Neron**-(age of rule 13-35)—first son of Ali-Raven

Died in a duel with his younger brother, Ali-Gareth. He had always been jealous of his younger brother and when his queen took a strong liking to Ali-Gareth, he challenged him to a duel. He lost.

89-114-**King Ali-Gareth the brave**-(age of rule 25-50)—second son of Ali-Raven

Good king. Took ali-neron's queen as his after the victory. On a military campaign, he developed a wound that ultimately became

7

infected and died.

114-138-King Ali-Terry-(age of rule 31-44)—second son of Ali-Gareth

His older brother, ali-gareth ii, died of winter fever two weeks before he would take rule as king. Started out as a good king but then gave in to the world of overindulgance. Didn't get along with the ruling nobles. Was expelled from donegal after losing a king's moot to his son, ali-sander.

138-184-King Ali-Sander "The Raging Fox"-(age of rule 12-48)—fourth son of Ali-Terry

Powerful men saw the potential in ali-sander from a young age and they used him to expel his father, Ali-Terry. Great conquering king who increased the size of donegal greatly. Died in battle while searching for the Pearl Of Wisdom.

184-185-Queen Ali-Tiste-(age of rule 40-40)—wife of Ali-Sander

Died suddenly while holding the throne for Ali-Banly. Poison was the prime suspect. Was only holding the throne for a few years until her son's 12th birthday.

185-187-King Ali-Tarrison-(age of rule 40-42)—brother of Ali-Sander
Named king after the death of Ali-Tiste until he was found guilty of poisoning the queen. The trial took over a year but he eventually had his head put on a spike.

187-187-King Ali-Banly the sickly-(age of rule 11-12)—only remaining son of Ali-Sander

The weak Ali-Banly took the throne only a few weeks before his birthday. On his twelfth birthday, he died in his sleep. Most believed he was smothered because he had a broken and bloody nose.

187-187-Queen Ali-Ganoly-(age of rule 34-34)—Ali-Sander's sister

Won a king/queen'smoot against Ali-Sander's cousin. Died two weeks later from a random arrow attack in the king's woods.

187-187-King Ali-Harrison the haunted-(age of rule 52-52)—Ali-Sander's cousin

He was behind the killing of Queen Ali-Ganoly. It haunted him until he jumped off the highest tower on the King's Castle and died.

187-200-King Ali-Brondell "The Forever King"-(age of rule 14-26)—Ali-Harrison's first son

Nicknamed The Forever King after lasting two years on the throne. After five kings in only a little over a year, ali-brondell brought stability back to the throne. Died on military conquest.

200-231-King Ali-Antone-(age of rule 12-45)—first son of Ali-Brondell

Was a good, conquering king who died due to a ship wreck.

231-270-King Ali-Antwelle-(age of rule 28-67)—second son of Ali-Antone

Started out as a good king, but ran the kingdom into a lot of financial trouble before he died of old age.

270-297-King Ali-Antone II-(age of rule 41-68)—second son of Ali-Antwelle

A wise and just king who cured all the problems that his father had caused. Died peacefully in bed.

297-299-King Ali-Antemis-(age of rule 31-33)—fourth son of Ali-Antone II

Became extremely gluttonous after becoming king. Choked on a fowl bone and died.

299-304-Queen Ali-Tomeo-(age of rule 26-31)—wife of Ali-Antemis

Held throne for five years as regent for her son, Ali-Pharell. Only queen to survive her entire rule on the throne.

304-341-King Ali-Pharell-(age of rule 12-49)—first son of Ali-Antemis

Considered the last of the good kings. Successful reign. Went to Gama Traka and never came back. They say he disappeared in the night to live in Gama Traka.

341-364-**King Ali-Baris**-(age of rule 31-54)—1st son of Ali-Pharell

Drunk, whore chaser. Didn't take the throne seriously. Died while having sex in a brothel.

364-384-**King Ali-Baster**-(age of rule 32-52)—second son of Ali-Baris

Another bad king. Died while on the chamber pot. Family told everyone he died on the throne.

384-414(present)-**King Ali-Stanley**-(age of rule 35-65)—first twin son of Ali-Baster

To view the maps, go to:
http://jasonpaulricebooks.com

Pearl of Wisdom
Volume 1
Two Heads, Two Spikes

Prologue

THE STRANGER PUSHED the young boy into the thick shrubbery and marched forward. Three unarmored, sword wielding men appeared out of nowhere, approaching from the front.

"That's far enough right there," said the first man.

"I'm just trying to do a little fishing," the stranger replied as he stopped and put his hands up.

The second man barked, "Perhaps you haven't heard then, the King don't want anybody going near the river today, so you can turn right around now."

The outsider asked, "And the King sent you three to forestall intruders?"

The men raised their swords in response. Ollor had invaded a foreign land, but he realized he was much larger than all three of these boys, who were tall, but not yet men. The troubled man stood tall and muscular, but sin still clung to his soul. He had greasy black hair that cascaded halfway down his back. His long beard and moustache cloaked most of his facial features. Ollor also wore the specially designed armor created by a wizard. But he did not want to kill these boys.

If they don't attack, I can talk some sense into them. Oh Gods, too late.

All three men rushed Ollor from the front. In one swift motion he drew his sword and took the first attacker's left sword arm off along with half of his shoulder. As quick as the sword went down, it flashed upward, the furious metal thrusting between the young man's ribs and into his heart. Like lightning, Ollor pulled out the sword, spun around deftly, and took the second attacker's head clean off. The third boy ran for his life away from the river, down a beaten trail. The warrior reached behind him for the longbow that always graced his back and plucked out an arrow with a broad, barbed head.

He closed one eye, drew back, steadied his hand and said, "Sorry young man, but I cannot have you running off and alerting any real guards."

The arrow sizzled through the air, slicing straight through the third boy's neck, dropping him to his knees immediately. He reached up with his right hand and felt the arrow tip dripping with his own blood. Ollor noticed that the blood coming from the back of the boy's neck was black. The dying boy muttered some incomprehensible words as he gagged. He finally fell flat on his face, splintering the arrow and choking to death. He suddenly dissolved into a black liquid and melted into the ground. Ollor had never seen a coldomore before, but had heard stories of the demon skin changers turning into black blood and sinking into the ground after death. They were known to take over the body of a human or animal. Ollor froze in his tracks, staring at the shattered arrow on the ground. He quickly remembered the closing window of opportunity and focused again. He reached into his pocket to feel for the dragon coin; it was still there.

Ollor hastily made his way back down the path. In the past he had never felt bad after killing but this time he fought mixed emotions. Ollor was searching for resurrection of his buried soul and didn't believe killing the young men would help matters. He knew he had to do it for the greater good of all, but for the first time the confused man felt remorse for his actions. Ollor bent down and pulled back the bramble. The young boy that he called Sunny was still there with both hands covering his mouth.

"You wanted to scream, didn't you?"

The red-headed little boy nodded up and down, still with his hands over his mouth.

"It's alright now, you can take your hands away," Ollor reassured the boy.

He was starving and knew the boy must be too. His dark bluish-grey eyes peered up at the sky as he whistled gently. A huge black falcon with red eyes descended in a circular downward path. It released something from its claws just before landing on the man's shoulder onto its customary perch. Ollor incurred permanent piercing on his right shoulder from the razor-sharp claws. The hairy, grisly man pounced on the rabbit that the falcon had dropped. The King's river guards had left a fire burning nearby so Ollor, along with the boy and the falcon, went over to the swaying flames. He fell to his knees and butchered the meager prey. Shortly thereafter, he served charred meat to the boy and let the falcon feast on the remaining carcass and entrails.

Nightfall approached rapidly, multiplying the difficulties involved in this effort. Spotting a tiny basket in the Rushing River was not an easy task, even in broad daylight. Strangely this sudden burden soothed the hardened warrior's soul. He had never imagined raising one child, let alone two, but redemption can prove a powerful motivation.

He closed his eyes and started to shake wildly as his arm rose up and touched the falcon. It launched itself into the air, rising quickly. It then took flight upstream along the river bank. The long-haired man and boy rushed out of the woods toward the river. The falcon returned quickly, squawking several times upon landing.

She is still on the way, more redemption. My soul may be saved. What kind of king casts away a child? I know it is customary, but still rather cruel. Just because she was born toeless? Now I have to find the third piece.

It was almost impossible to see anything as the sun strayed behind the rolling mountains faster than expected. Suddenly, the big onyx falcon took flight and screeched again. It glided close to the river and hovered over what appeared to be the cradle. The falcon clutched a large branch of the basket with its claws and fought the strong river current to pull it ashore.

Ollor and the boy were waiting. There she was, vanished toes as forewarned, but an innocent looking baby girl otherwise. The man pried the newborn from the makeshift raft. The basket washed back into the river when the boy snatched it. Ollor grabbed it from the boy and inspected the raft. He couldn't understand how the bassinet had made it miles and miles down the extremely powerful river. He tossed it back into the river but a large beast of the water surged up and devoured the basket. The darkening sky made visibility poor so Ollor couldn't figure out what he had just witnessed. It looked bigger than any river creature he had seen. He remembered tales he'd heard while growing up, about the river dragons in far-off lands, but he didn't know what they actually looked like.

This is a real miracle. The first rescue was amazing and this one defied all logic. That raft should have sunk or been eaten by a river dragon within the first hundred feet. I have to find a sympathetic village away from any cities. Sin flows freely through dark city nights. The deep woods are no place for one child, let alone two and the baby will need shelter soon enough so we must move on. WE.

That was a good sensation. Now the man had a family to take care of, a new purpose in life. Ollor peered down at Sunny's upper lip and reminisced about the boy's mystical birth six years ago.

Ollor had been wronged by an evil woman and vowed revenge. He even faked his own death and lay low for a while. Then, the celebrated ex-soldier went on a gruesome and murderous campaign, heading straight for the Capitol of the kingdom. Therefore, he traveled as a marked man in these parts, but he had the most important mission of his life to carry out. Therefore, the outlaw plastered dank mud onto his shaggy face, disguising most of his distinguishable features. Detection spelled instant death.

The wayward drifter had recently altered his image and went by the name of Ollor. He had used a dull dagger blade to cut two self-imposed scars on both cheeks of his face. Ollor thought this would flush the bloody sin and hide his real identity. He had just turned over a new leaf and realized the error in his brutal ways. It took some heartfelt conversations with the wizard who had sent him on this soul-redeeming voyage. Ollor was in his late thirties and he tried to only speak to those necessary for his mission.

It felt like a warm summer day in the Capitol, even under the canopy of the surrounding forest. Ollor didn't detect any danger from the King's Guard as he surveyed the situation. He looked around for the baby boy that the wizard had told him to find. He received very few clues to go upon, so he followed his nose and the unusual smell of burning hair.

What in the Hells could be burning around here?

He reached into his pocket to feel the silver dragon coin. It was almost as big as his palm with a little pearl embedded in the dragon's hand, right in the middle of the coin. He would need to show the coin to the school-master to gain entry for the children. The little wizard had instructed Ollor to find the boy and girl, then take them to the School of the Learned Warrior to learn physical skill and mental will. The wizard revealed to Ollor that the third piece of the plan would find him at the school.

Is this worth it? Is salvation really going to find its way into my polluted soul? I was told this is my destiny, and so it shall be. For betterment or death.

The stench grew stronger by the step, but eerily coupled with the smell of scorched flesh. His pace quickened as he heard the growl of an angry woods wolf nearby. That sound suddenly turned into painful shrieks from what seemed like the same animal. He hopped over a golden snake on the path as he drew closer to some smoke that billowed into the air. Ollor pulled aside a branch with different colored leaves to see the redemption of life.

A naked newborn baby lay alone on the rough forest floor. The tiny creature smiled and gurgled. A closer look showed a cleft palate and a recent cut on his tiny foot caused by a sharp blade.

How cruel can one be? To heave a defenseless baby to the jaws and claws of nature is torture enough without bleeding the poor kid. All because of a missing lip? I hope his father lives long enough for our homecoming.

He picked up the kid and clutched the baby to his chest. The corners of Ollor's mouth curled up, almost smiling, for the first time in years. The area surrounding the child was unimaginable.

There were ten or fifteen charred animal carcasses around the sanguine baby. Most were still smoldering as if the baby was protected by the spirit of a fire breathing dragon. It looked like the remains of giant foxes, woods wolves, boars and a falcon burned beyond recognition.

What in all the Hells happened here? This baby surely cannot have the power to harness fire. I guess the little man warned me, unfathomable events will unfold before me.

Ollor snapped back to the present. He held the newborn close while he rubbed the boy's auburn hair. Now that he captured the first two pieces, Ollor realized the journey was just beginning. As they walked downstream, just inside the cover of the woods, the young boy asked, "Is this my home?"

The stunned man reflected for a moment and replied, "In some time, I think everywhere may be your home."

1
The Happy Couple—Edburgh

BANG! EDBURGH BOOTED open the door to his chambers harder than he wanted to due to his heavy wine consumption. The sudden, rattling report startled the naked being in his bed. The air of his chilly room was heavy with whorish smelling perfumes. He sauntered toward her slowly, sustaining constant eye contact. As Edburgh drew back the see-through bed shade, he noticed his wife's nipples were extremely aroused. Absent spoken word Ed met her crimson shaded lips in passion. He softly kissed her neck and moved habitually to her breasts. The battle-roughened palm of Ed's hand slid up her smooth thigh. Caroline radiated lust-filled heat from between her legs.

Something is not right. What is she up to?

Edburgh Etburn was an angular man of twenty-six. He possessed shaggy brown hair and a dark complexion, but his bright blue eyes still retained a look of innocence. He tried to remember the story book romance he had shared with Caroline Leeson.

They grew up together in Waters Edge as members of separate affluent families. He loved her before he was old enough to know what love was. They fell deeper and deeper for each other as the years passed. However, Duke Tyus Etburn had other ideas. Duke Etburn had fixed a marriage pact for Edburgh with a very powerful family. Ed remembered how thrilled his father was about the match. But Edburgh turned down the marriage of convenience. Tyus Etburn didn't speak to his son for months after the refusal. Ed was shocked when his father broke the silence by sending an assassin to his chambers. At least, he assumed it was his father who had sent the killer. Unfortunately, Ed dispatched the stout, pig-nosed killer before he could question him. But common sense had told him that he better flee Waters Edge until this blew over.

He needed to see Caroline before he left. During their rendezvous, he disclosed to her that he had to go to Mattingly to handle business with the Colberts.

Just before embarking on this trip, Edburgh whispered to his love, "You mean everything to me. I love you. When I return I will swear my allegiance to you by the Gods and take you as my bride."

Caroline hugged Ed tightly. She squeezed Edburgh with a strong, gripping hug. He recalled her warm face pressed against his and the tears of joy he felt from her eyes that streamed down his cheeks that day. He had extracted a sign of love from his pocket and spun Caroline around. He took the long silver necklace that had a crescent moon dangling from it and secured it around her neck. Ed turned her back around and held her like he would never let go, but his vessel was boarding.

The journey down went according to plan, but the return excursion seemed to take ages. An awful sea tempest spun the boat every which way but home. He endured searing heat, starvation and his brain jesting him.

I must return to Waters Edge, for I shall love Caroline like no other man has loved a woman.

Ed's loving thoughts were suddenly captured by a monstrous beast emerging from the murky waters.

It was dark purple and black, like an old festering wound, with a neck that appeared twenty men high. The body equaled four large ships and looked to be protected by its scale-like armor, shingled from top to bottom. The two arms were half the size of its neck, and there were three spikes protruding from the tip of each hand. The beast had a bright blue head with fiery glowing eyes and curved dagger-like teeth. The monstrosity looked up to the sky and spewed green sea water high toward the heavens. The creature then let out a roar that sounded like thousands of men screaming painfully in unison. It rocked the boat with such force that several passengers were tossed into the deep green waters, plummeting to certain death. The monster could have crushed the vessel like a person flicking a bug.

Abruptly, Edburgh looked up directly into the creature's face that threatened impending doom. For a slight moment the humongous beast didn't appear as intimidating and appeared to recede into the horizon.

One of Edburgh's shipmates looked at him and mysteriously said, "Sin lies and dies in the eyes of the beholder, my Lord."

Instantly the beast recoiled, seeming larger than before as it swam closer to the ship. Edburgh stared unblinkingly into the sea creature's eyes and the beast suddenly pulled up short of the boat. Ed's eyes remained locked with the dragon-like creature's flaming eyes as its head came close to the ocean craft. It firmly bumped the front of the boat to set its course and stopped the back end when it swung around. The suddenly docile creature started pushing the boat amidst the bumpy waves. When they were about one day away from the coastline, the heaven-sent creature suddenly vanished. Even though the other men had seen the same thing, Edburgh still thought that he may have imagined the sea creature and that it was an illusion. One thing was certain—he had been displaced at sea for almost half a year.

He had put up with everything the Gods could throw at him, but now he arrived, ready to claim his rightful bride. Unfortunately, he was in for a nasty surprise. Due to the length of time that he had been missing at sea, the prospects of Edburgh's return seemed bleak and it appeared he might be dead, so Caroline was betrothed to another. But soon after Ed's return, the potential groom suffered a catastrophic hunting accident and finally the golden path to love had cleared for Edburgh. Caroline was the only person that he fully trusted since his older brother died. He had been euphoric on his wedding day with his blushing, newlywed bride.

Ed focused back into reality. He now firmly had two fingers deep inside Caroline and could feel the warm rush over his hand. Caroline squealed in pleasure. She was great in bed, but after almost five years she had yet to bear him a child. They once had sex every night for half a year without positive results. Ed even fathered two bastard children during that time to make sure that he wasn't the problem. His father warned him about it and for that Ed hated him. Caroline had two barren aunts that made Tyus

Etburn believe she would never give him a grandson.

Ed was about to shove Caroline onto her back when she stopped him. Ed cocked his head slightly in a questioning manner until Caroline put a finger over his lips and pushed him onto his back. She leaned down close to his ear and sexily whispered, "I have a treat for you."

He felt the heat over his entire body as Caroline lay on top of him, massaging herself up and down.

She is up to something. I can't believe it.

Caroline Leeson, a real beauty, had lived a nice life in the Etburn castle. Ed had sacrificed a lot of family strain with his father because of her. She was short, even for a female, but had a lovely face. Her long blond hair, which was often braided, seemed like sunshine sprouting from her head. Caroline's endearing smile could melt the heart of the most hardened man. Her only problem was that she trusted too many people. Ed's wife seemed perfectly splendid until the short man from the harbor poisoned her head.

Caroline speeded up her lovemaking, leaning down and kissing her husband. In between deep moans she gasped, "I love you." With her husband distracted, she grabbed it from under the pillow. It was colder than she expected. Caroline quickly raised and plunged the knife down toward Edburgh's heart.

"It's over," she thought. Then the voice rang in her head, *"You will rule Waters Edge...You know what you must do,"* it echoed. *"It's all over,"* she thought again as she felt drunker than ever before without even drinking.

Edburgh caught her wrist effortlessly and the knife stopped less than an inch from his chest. Before she realized it, Caroline was flat on her back, nose bleeding, her own knife's blade now pressed firmly to her throat. *"That is* how it feels. *That is* what it feels like to have a knife coming at you," Edburgh whispered. He raised his voice and said, "I've had hundreds of swords pointed at me, thousands mayhaps; knives and daggers not quite as many. And you thought you would be the one?"

He released the pressure of the blade slightly from her neck.

"Was it my father?" Ed questioned.

"No," Caroline squeaked.

Ed pressed the knife down again and his usually innocent visage took on the look of a madman, "Are you certain?" he growled.

"I swear it," said Caroline delicately, fearing the slightest flinch may cause her throat to be slashed. Ed leaned back and removed the knife entirely from his wife's throat.

"He wouldn't tell me his name. He...he said he was going to usurp Waters Edge and if I didn't comply he was going to rape and kill me." Caroline cowered as Ed stared right through her eyes. Her bright-blues were open windows that let him look straight into her evil intentions. Only one person's name came into Edburgh Etburn's head. He couldn't believe it.

I can't trust anyone in this world.

The feeling reminded him of when he had heard the news that his brother Rollo died. He still believed his brother was the only family member that had truly loved him. Edburgh had partially snapped that day and right now the same anger resurfaced like a flood rising up. Once again, rage ran cold through the body of Edburgh Etburn.

"How did you know I was plotting it?" Caroline questioned.

"A wise man once told me, 'Sin lies and dies in the eyes of the beholder,'" he responded. "In your case, it was all over your naked body, not just in your eyes. We have been married for ten years, I know when my wife is up to something," Ed told her.

Damn, they are beautiful eyes. How could somebody turn her against me?

But he couldn't afford to get distracted by her looks. "Now what am I to do with you?" he asked while rubbing his pointed chin. "I promise, I will do anything," Caroline chimed in. Edburgh totally lost it now.

"Promise?" he screamed. "You DID promise, remember? You promised your life to me. Now you attempt to kill me. You promised me children. We have no children." Caroline countered by crying uncontrollably. Ed, suddenly soothing her, slowly said, "I do feel for you, let's just make certain this doesn't happen again."

Before Caroline could start to smile, her erstwhile knife entered her body. The cold, hard steel came in under her tongue, through the roof of her mouth, and into Caroline's brain. She quivered as life slowly ebbed away, under her own murder weapon, for several moments before lying still.

"Sorry, but there is only one way to be sure you will not try to kill me again," he whispered while removing the knife. Edburgh wiped the blood off both sides of the blade and stood up over the body. "Mattingly forged steel," he said aloud as he stared at the deep emerald tint of the metal.

It was the greenish blade referred to as Dragon-Steel. The knife had a golden cross-guard and black leather grip with red stitching alternating over the leather to form a diamond pattern. The pommel looked like a silver spiked mace as Ed threw it on the bed.

Caroline Leeson was slumped on the floor as bare as the day she was brought into the world, except for one thing. With a quick motion, Edburgh snatched the silver necklace from her neck and clutched it tightly in his palm. Vengeance now colored his every action.

I just had to murder the only person I loved. Did I really need to kill her? Mayhaps I have drunk too much? Wait, of course I had to, she was going to kill me. But I should have made her give me his name. No. I know the man who put her up to this, and he shall pay with blood.

Ed slumped back in a chair and poured an overflowing glass of strong spirits. He drank it faster than most men should. Edburgh Etburn stared at his wife, dead on the floor, as the room began to spin.

2
THE LITTLE DRAGON—JON

"YOU BOYS OUGHT know, we are only as well-off as the poorest man in Mattingly," Jon Colbert clarified to his sons. Krys, Ryno and Ruxin walked behind their father as he continued, "Just because some people are born into the right family, they don't deserve a lifelong advantage. We need to empower every man that can provide a skill."

Ruxin shook his head, "Father, I have been told by friends that if you put power into the hands of the lowborn, they will behave like barbarians."

Jon Colbert quickly retorted, "Our family used to be considered lowborn. If it was not for your grandfather taking a stand, we might not stand here today. Do WE behave like barbarians? I scarcely think so. It was those who betrayed your grandfather that acted like cold-blooded barbarians. Let us not forget what we come from, boys." His deep voice bellowed over the chattering crowds. Jon Colbert always seemed to remain serene even when he raised his voice. They continued to stroll away from the castle.

Jon Colbert led the way and stood closest to the ground. He was compact, stout and powerful. Jon had closely cut blond hair and a long golden goatee. His bright green eyes lit up in the Mattingly sunshine. An ill-placed lance during a tourney about fourteen years ago had left him with a mangled nose and random headaches.

It had the makings of an exquisite day in Riverfront, the Capitol of Mattingly. The frost had finally tiptoed away for another year and the early harvest danced in the wind. The aroma of lavender wafted through the air, occasionally stopping to tickle the nose. There was a bustle in the city with large crowds traveling in to buy necessities for their homes. The Colbert men continued down the crowded street away from the city.

Along the path there were different shops that sold everything from live, local animals to exotic silks from Gama Traka. Jon noticed a tiny piglet in a pen. The babe suckled on its mother's milk, fresh as early-dawn dew. Across the road, buyers haggled with merchants to negotiate better prices for whatever their eyes fancied. Everyone bowed deeply to Duke Colbert and the boys with great respect as they passed.

"Where is Riceros?" Jon Colbert asked. His son, Ryno, scratched his ear and said, "Last I saw, he was in the library with Count Sproul." "Will you ever reveal the truth to Riceros, father?" Krys challenged Jon.

"Someday, aye. I am just unsure of when the right time will be. You should worry more about your bride to be than your younger brother," Jon slyly reminded him.

Krys had a gawky smile but didn't have a ready response. He was a fierce combatant, but rather clumsy with women. Krys was lanky and extremely nervous about his upcoming wedding in the winter. His father knew mentioning it would draw his thoughts far away from the topic Jon despised discussing.

The Colbert men got distracted as they converged on the forging yard. This big area contained fifty raging furnaces lined up in a giant square. The sweet songs of metal hammers pounding glowing steel sounded melodic to their ears. These noises were offset by the constant smoldering of all the furnaces. The sounds got thunderous as they entered the yard. Jon looked back to see big grins on the faces of his progeny. They all had the brown hair and eyes of their mother, along with the determination of their father.

The forging yard was slightly on the outskirts of the city. Constantly covering the furnaces loomed a large slanted roof that hovered twenty feet above their heads. The enormous wooden structure appeared black from all the smoke it had swallowed over the years. But it did serve to keep out most of the rain, except for the precipitation that came in sideways. Seven Colbert flags proudly hung around the structure at regular intervals. The solid black flag with a golden bull represented the Colbert family that ruled Mattingly.

A townsman walked up, pointed at a furnace, and asked a forger, "Tis thee?"

The craftsman smiled showing several missing teeth, and cheerfully said, "Tis our Little Dragon." The townsman stood in reverence for a moment until the worker said, "They are for forging our blades, good man."

The boys could clearly see the furnaces now. They were stone-based burning furnaces with ornate black metal caps. The tops were shaped like a dragon's head gazing up to the sky with gold painted eyes. Smoke shot out of the opened nose, up to the roof, and filtered into the Riverfront sky. Someone had etched "LITTLE DRAGON" on the base of the furnaces. The metals were melded together in the hot fire for three straight days before crafting the steel. These men were the top blade makers in all of Mattingly. They were the highest quality swords Mattingly produced. Jon Colbert reserved these swords that everyone called Dragon-Steel, for the residents of Mattingly. All lesser swords were sold to other regions or realms. Jon even had a building in which they constantly experimented with different metal contents for maximum results. That was where they came up with the recipe for the Dragon-Steel. He also kept strict records of those who bought every sword to make sure no one was arming for rebellion or re-selling the weapons.

They walked the yard for about an hour before heading back to the castle. While walking home, Jon could feel it setting in. One of his headaches was coming on. The intense pains always arrived randomly. He never knew when the pain would strike, but once it started the feeling was unmistakable. He realized that he only had a little time until light and sound would be his worst adversaries.

I hoped these pains would stop someday. But I suppose I might not be that lucky.

As they walked, Jon Colbert listened to his sons' talk.

"Yes, you were. I saw it in your eyes," Krys mocked his younger brother Ruxin. "I wasn't afraid. Not even for a single moment."

Krys and Ryno gave their younger brother a hard time. It made him tougher over the years, but it still bothered Ruxin. All three boys had gone off to fight for two years on the Donegal-Goldenfield border so they could return as men. It was a common custom in Donegal to help cut a boy's teeth. High- and low-born men mingled with the winning duel criminals to battle Goldenfield. Most soldiers stuck with the men from their own region, but they were all fighting a common enemy.

Jon spotted the castle made of black stone blocks with seven giant circular towers. The towers were constructed with a special gray stone that sparkled and looked like silver in the emerging sunlight. The rectangular base of the castle was seven stories high and supported the towers that soared twenty-one into the sky. The thirty-year-old castle was the biggest in the kingdom. Jon's father had laid the ground work and his uncle Jasine made sure the stronghold was expertly crafted. The size and short amount of building time had infuriated King Ali-Stanley who couldn't believe a usurper could achieve such mastery. Nobody in Mattingly would ever attack this imposing castle, but the stronghold had many additional protectionary measures such as the guarded outer gate and a long line of fourteen-foot-high archer towers to get to the main entrance.

He shaded his eyes and hurried to get home. Jon Colbert was glad they reached the castle as his head was really starting to pound. He excused himself from the boys and headed for his chambers. He unsteadily climbed the steep steps, nodding at his guards as he passed them. He lightly pushed open the door to see his wife and daughter talking.

"Hello father," said Mariah cheerfully. "Hello, my darling daughter," he responded as he hugged and kissed her on the forehead.

His wife took one look at him and shook her head. "You have a headache haven't you?" "A little one, aye," Jon feebly replied. "Well lie down, let me fetch a cold rag for your eyes," Camelle said softly.

The cold rag and bed only made him feel slightly better. He closed his eyes tight, trying to force sleep.

"My dear, I am really worried about these headaches." As he drifted off, Jon Colbert wasn't sure if he was dreaming or if his wife was really talking. "How often do they occur now?" Mariah asked. Camelle looked over at Jon and turned to her daughter, "At least twice a month now, sometimes more oft than that. One day they might only last for an hour or two, other times almost half a day."

Concern flashed through the brown eyes of Camelle Colbert. She was a tall woman with brown hair and a warm smile. Conventional beauty had eluded Camelle, but her other attributes molded her into a great woman. She was four months pregnant and it was really starting to show.

She paced around the room as Mariah asked, "Can Count Sproul prescribe something for him?" "Everything he has given to your father up to this point has either not worked or made it worse," Camelle answered. "Do you think he should chance the Priestess of the Gods? I have heard stories that they can perform miracles," Mariah said.

Seventeen year old Mariah Colbert looked very young and naive. She seemed to have been blessed with all the beauty her mother never received. She had a freckled face with light brown hair that bordered on blond. Mariah was tall and skinny, viewing the world through gray eyes.

"Never," Camelle responded, "That black magic can stay in Fox Chapel. You shouldn't even be speaking about things like that, young lady." "I was only trying to help, mother," said Mariah. "Oh I know. I am sorry, dear. It's just if anything happens to your father, there is no telling what could happen to us," Camelle softly told her.

"If anything should happen, Krys will take over as Duke of Mattingly and we will be safe with him, right?" Mariah always took a simplistic view of life.

"You just do not know what people can do when a powerful man dies. I do not think that will ever happen, but that is why we have to pray to the Gods for your father's safety." Camelle wrung her hands together to deal with the constant stress.

She was always worrying about her husband or one of her children and seemed perpetually tense.

Jon Colbert faded in and out of consciousness. He thought about how he would rather face all the nefarious barbarians of Histomanji than these damn head pains.

"Mother, will I ever get married?" Mariah questioned. "You know what you father says, nobody marries until they are eighteen," her mother responded. "That's what he said for the boys who had to go off to fight. I do not get to go anywhere because father and the King hate each other. I could never marry a boy like Ali-Ster Wamhoff." Camelle's eyes opened wide as she looked over at her husband. "Don't you dare let your father hear you say things like that." "He cannot hear us all the way from here. Besides, I never get to do what I want," pouted Mariah.

Jon Colbert slowly drifted off as the pain subsided. He woke up an hour and a half later to realize his headache was nearly gone. He got up to prepare himself for dinner.

3
Bulls Cannot Defeat Lions, Can They?—Riceros

"WOOF, WOOF!"

The big dog jerked his head around and sprinted away from Riceros Colbert. He usually didn't go this far into the woods with only his dog, Jasper, for company. It stayed cool in the Riverfront woods even though the sun blazed above. Riceros quickly realized he had ventured into the area of the woods known as the Blood Tree Forest. The trees had a reddish hue on their trunks and branches that resembled blood. It was also the site for the dire battle of Riverfront two hundred and forty years ago when Ali-Sander Wamhoff had been pushed back by Goldenfield before defeating the enemy and doubling the size of Donegal. The bloody struggle had proved to be the turning point in the war. Most people around the castle thought the woods remained haunted by the ghosts of the war. Legend had it that the trees drank the blood of the fallen soldiers to obtain their color. Almost everyone avoided the woods but Riceros unknowingly followed his dog right into the Blood Tree Forest. He felt a chill on the back of his neck and started to get nervous.

Riceros clapped his hands to call his best friend. They had a special bond despite the fact that they were polar opposites. Riceros was an undersized eleven year old while his dog was enormous. Everyone who saw him considered Jasper, the biggest of his breed, King of the bulldogs. Jasper stood up to Riceros' neck and could easily lick the boy's face with his long, leathery tongue. Jon Colbert had given his son the dog as a present on his fifth birthday. Riceros promptly named him "Jasper" in honor of his grandfather.

He clapped his hands again, even harder this time. Riceros kicked a brown rock aside as he looked around the shade-laced forest. He was worried now because he hadn't heard Jasper for the past few minutes.

The sun slid behind a puffy gray cloud in the sky, throwing the forest into more shadow and making it harder to see in the dim light.

Riceros spent more time with Jasper than he did with his older brothers. It all started when he began sneaking Jasper into his room until his father told him that he didn't have to sneak the pup in anymore. Duke Colbert even made Riceros build a little bed for the dog. Riceros and the rest of the family loved Jasper equally as much as they loved each other. Riceros heard a panting sound behind him and turned around expecting to see his dog.

Instead, there were two slobbering wild foxes eyeballing the small boy. He drew his little dagger, even though he was smart enough to realize that he stood rather defenseless. The two huge foxes, nearly as big as his giant dog, growled at Riceros. He tried to swallow, but his mouth ran dry.

Please, I will never go this far into the woods again.

Riceros' eyes started to twitch and his knees felt like they were going to collapse but he maintained his composure and stared at the two wild foxes. Count Sproul had told Riceros that it was common knowledge around Donegal that the Wamhoffs bred their domestic foxes until they had got too big and dangerous. Then, they released them into the wild. They had been known to grow to enormous proportions. The foxes started stalking their prey. The larger of the pair licked its lips as the beast stood straight up on its hind legs. The other fox stood up too and Riceros noticed that their eyes turned red as the fearsome creatures approached on two legs.

Oh, no....did coldomores take over the foxes bodies? Please Gods, keep me from the darkness and guide me to eternal light.

Riceros Colbert felt his pants getting warm and wet as he closed his eyes to accept a gnarly fate.

"WOOF, WOOF, WOOF, WOOF!"

His eyes flew open to see Jasper explode onto the scene, just as large drops of rain began to fall sporadically from the darkening skies. The two immense foxes took heed of the warning call, dropped down to four legs, and shot off into the camouflaged forest. Jasper chased them away and returned to Riceros. The boy's heart was pounding. As he stroked his friend he realized that Jasper's chest was pumping too. He put his arms around Jasper and thanked the dog for saving his life. They quickly ran back to the castle.

He gazed affectionately at the dog on the rainy walk back to the castle. The dog's coat canvassed a blend of colors. Black spots blended into brown hair that disappeared into white. His back and tail were brown with black spots and his belly and legs were white. Jasper's face was white with brown patches around his eyes. The round pudgy face housed an enormous tongue and his brown ears stuck up on top of his head. As they approached the castle the dog's tail stuck up in the air in the shape of an upside down J as usual. The dog walked right in front of Riceros, like a true friend, shielding his shame. He led the boy straight to his room so he could change his pants and nobody would know he had soiled himself. Riceros changed quickly, hiding his pants, and then going to the library. When he arrived Count Sproul knew he was wearing different clothes but didn't mention it.

He said to the boy, "Perhaps we shall start with the religions of Gama Traka, if you like?"

"But why must I know about the religion of faraway lands?" Riceros Colbert scribbled on his wipe away "paper".

He had a flat black slab and a white rock shaped like a small quill. He used a hand towel to erase the words and write on it again. Riceros had shaggy golden hair and green eyes that matched his father's, but while Riceros had a scrawny body, Jon Colbert had always been husky.

Count Sproul explained, "Well, my young Lord, knowledge can be a powerful thing. It may aid a man in ways he may not see now."

The Count lived all of his seventy-six years in the region of Mattingly. He articulated with a soft voice and many pauses. He had long white hair that curled up at the bottom. Donegal required the counts to grow a long moustache for identification purposes and Count Sproul's hung over the sides of his mouth and down past his neck. The counts wore them like a badge of honor, each one trying to grow his the longest.

The old man slowly continued, "My little Lord, life in Donegal can be fragile. Bonds that are strong today may be broken tomorrow. Men are inherently evil and unpredictable by nature. Power can be a great thing. When placed in the right hands it can help all the people. But when waved in front of the wrong person, it can have disastrous results. I have heard such sad stories of fathers killing sons, brothers killing brothers, even daughters killing mothers. They did all these things for filthy lucre and power that did not bring true happiness. I plead to our Gods every day that this doesn't happen to Mattingly or any other region for that matter, but if that day should arrive you must be prepared. Do you understand?"

The young boy drafted something on the board and held it up to show the Count. Count Sproul cleared his throat and continued, "You will need that finely forged Dragon-Steel, there is little doubt, but that may be only half the battle, my boy."

Riceros suddenly got up to stretch his legs. He couldn't sit for long periods of time because of the lump on his back that often caused him pain. Right now he was just being fidgety, but because of his physical limitations he spent most of his time indoors, gaining wisdom. He had gained the respect of his brothers as a sharp shooting archer, but most other physical activities didn't suit Riceros' skill set very well.

He sat back down as the Count went on, "You see when death comes knocking at ones door, it is best not to answer. A live coward may help in many more ways than a brave, dead hero in most scenarios. You may even be forced to relocate someday. And extensive knowledge shall aid a man in as many ways as the finest sword in all the lands."

Riceros had attained a wide wealth of knowledge in this library but still retained the impatience and inexperience of an eleven year old.

The Count continued, "Life is as unsure as the sea. We from Mattingly navigate the wild waters better than almost all, but even so the sea has funny, unpredictable patterns. I have known of boys younger than you who left with a great captain never to return to their weeping mothers. And life is much of the same. We can predict matters up to a certain point, but estimating the amount of evil a man possesses can prove a difficult task." The long-winded Count gathered his thoughts, waited several moments, and carried on, "You see, I cannot precisely tell you how knowing the religions of far off lands will help you right now. But if the unsure Sea of Green that we always travel were to hurl you into some unknown land, this instruction just may save your life, my Lord. So what is it you would like to hear?" Count Sproul asked.

The two often sat together at the circular, stone table in the library. Books and documents were on shelves, lined all around the room. Maps were unrolled and fastened to the walls, like fine art covering all the vacant space. The library trained the young boy's mind and had become Riceros' most treasured place in the castle. Riceros learned to read at age three and by eleven he showed quicker mental skills than most grown men. He finished printing on the board and spun it toward the Count.

"Aah," the old man sighed, "I am afraid we may not have enough time to talk about the elusive Pearl of Wisdom. Perhaps you would like to listen to a quick story about your grandfather?"

Riceros eagerly nodded his head up and down with an immense grin on his face.

The old man knew Riceros loved listening to stories about his family. He reflected for a moment before starting, "Jasper Colbert lived in a different time. The Colberts were not exactly wealthy and the nasty Beverly family tried to hold them back even further. Patrick Beverly had a personal hatred for Jasper. He used his social graces to turn people against the Colbert family. But you see my young Lord, there comes a time in a man's life when he has been pushed around just a bit too much. When he has to stand up and fight, not only for himself, but for his family and flag holders. And that is what happened to your grandfather. Everyone said that to revolt would be to die," the Count revealed with a wry smile. "The odds were stacked to the stars against your grandfather. Bulls cannot defeat lions, can they?" The old man played with his moustache as he stared off into the distance.

"Well my boy, willpower, unity and determination can defeat raw numbers in certain situations. After the first few battles, Patrick Beverly quickly realized this was not going to be an easy war. The King even provided reinforcements from the Capitol to thwart the advance of your grandfather. However Jasper Colbert was destined to sit as Duke of Mattingly. They called him the Noble Bull, I'll have you know. You see, there are two ways to obtain power in Donegal. One is by birthright and the other is to wrest it by force. You, Riceros Colbert, have the influence of birth that your grandfather didn't possess. Once he had pinned the Beverly men to their homes in Portview, Jasper made them an offer – more in the nature of an ultimatum. To the detriment of the Beverly family, Patrick refused the offer. The soldiers were slaughtered with ease, and Jasper Colbert obliterated the Beverly name from the lands of

Mattingly. Jasper spared the rest of the city, he was compassionate, the man didn't ravage and rape as most expected. King Ali-Baster still demanded that Jasper move the Capitol of Mattingly to Riverfront. Jasper accepted, recognizing he couldn't defeat the whole realm in battle."

One of the servants entered the library, startling the Count. She said, "Riceros, your father and mother are calling you for supper now."

"Alright my boy, next time I shall finish telling you about how the King's son deceived your noble grandfather in the end."

Riceros sprang up and hugged the Count on his way out of the library.

The Colbert family ate dinner at a simple round, red-oak table that had three square legs beneath. His three brothers, sister, mother and father were present. And Brehan Castaway, a knight sworn to defend the Colbert name, always sat next to Riceros. A lot of chatter bounced around the room until Jon Colbert tapped his silver chalice with a spoon. Everyone ceased talking, bowed their heads, and folded his or her hands over their hearts. Jon Colbert stood while everyone else remained seated.

"Great Gods in heaven, we thank you for this bountiful harvest we are about to partake of. We walk as mere mortals, but we do our best to be righteous in your honor and glory. All we do on earth is in the name of the Gods. Please help us to be forever humble and follow the right path of life. Keep us from darkness and guide us to the light." Jon opened his eyes and sat back down.

Everyone resumed talking, except for one person. Riceros Colbert had yet to speak a word at eleven years of age. He wasn't dull. He could spell and write better than most learned men. He had a peculiar gift for knowledge that was manifested by absorbing everything he heard. He wasn't worried about what he was going to say like most people, he just listened. The Count believed he surpassed every one of his brothers in book intelligence, but for some strange reason he just wouldn't talk.

Mouth-watering smells beautifully intermingled in the dining room. The servants began to send the shared cuisine around. First up was a split roasted pig smothered in mushrooms, apples and spring onions with long green tops. Numbles were served separately and Riceros loved the flavor but hated the texture so the kitchen workers always gave him sliced, crispy bread fried in lard. He would smash the offal on the bread with a clove of roasted garlic and enjoy the crunch and delectable taste.

Next, smoked sturgeon showed up with a brown butter sauce and peppered beet greens over the top. The following course consisted of a salad of dandelion greens, purple asparagus, sliced carrot coins and chopped onion splashed with vinegar. Riceros ate his salad quickly and sat back in his chair.

A huge rack of stag chops came to the table and the head cook sliced down along the bone and passed out the juicy cuts. Gravy made with pig liver reserved from the first course was poured over the meat by a serving girl. Riceros cut off a piece of stag, sopped up some liver sauce with it and enjoyed the hearty flavor. The salted water he sipped made a perfect complement. Riceros enjoyed the fine sampling of what early spring harvest had to offer in Riverfront, Mattingly. He ate his food and listened as usual.

"Family, there are matters we need to discuss. I will need to go to Gama Traka for a few weeks this summer, and Krys, I bid that you go with me. I shall introduce you to the land of my friend, Anders Ahitni. You know him from his visits here," Jon Colbert announced.

His wife immediately responded, "Why, why do you have to go there now?" "I just told you why. You know that Anders has come to Mattingly many times. I have to return the favor, it is practical business. He is our biggest trading partner, helps keep our people happy and is a genuine friend. That is a rare feat in these crazy times," Jon told his wife.

I don't trust Anders for a moment, Riceros thought as the conversation continued.

"What about me?" "And me?" Ryno and Ruxin asked respectively. Jon gazed over at his sons, "I bid that both of you sit in on the council meetings and help make decisions for your future region. Mattingly is going to be under your control someday." The two boys confidently nodded in silence. Ryno was sixteen and Ruxin fifteen but they had been trained for this their entire lives.

I could run those meeting better than my two brothers put together if I could just talk.

"As for you, young lady, I bid that you help your mother in her state," Jon told Mariah. "Aaww, that's all I get to do. The boys get to rule, and I get to brush hair," she said with a snotty look. "If the person who brought you into this world is not important enough...?" Jon Colbert let the question linger. A sour Mariah finally replied, "That's not what I meant and you know it father. Of course I can help my mother. I would just like to help with other family responsibilities too." "Alright Mariah, talk with your mother about these boring council meetings while I am gone. She has sat in on enough of them to tell you all you want to know. When I return from Gama Traka, if you still desire to attend meetings, then we shall find a seat for you at the table," Jon responded.

That's why they call him the Deal Maker.

Riceros' brothers had told him about the many nicknames Jon Colbert possessed but people widely knew him as the Deal Maker because of his sharp negotiation acumen. Mariah concurred, of course; Jon always struck beneficial deals for both sides. Most men of the day were wholly unreasonable and trust was a dying breed in this world.

"And for you, little man, I have a task for you too," Jon said as he looked at Riceros. "I bid that you help Count Sproul run the local arbitration meetings. What be your thoughts? Can you do it?" Riceros smiled with a look of assurance.

Sweet, sugary rhubarb scented air teased Riceros' nose. Excitement circled around the family table as the delectable pastries were placed before them. The entire family enjoyed the rhubarb pie. He would need someone to go to the kitchens with him later to read his thankful words to the cooks. They loved him for what a humble highborn lad he was. Riceros acknowledged those who deserved credit, regardless of birthright. But because they couldn't read and Riceros didn't speak, he required an interpreter. He was already ever gracious at eleven because of his upbringing, even though it could be difficult to communicate. He bit into the pastry and instantly dragons crashed into the imagination of Riceros Colbert as they often did, but they weren't angry dragons. The warm rhubarb filling ran down the side of his mouth as Riceros daydreamed about riding a golden dragon.

4
THE COUNCIL MEETING—ALI-STER

ALI-STER WAMHOFF SAT to the right of the King, across from Ali-Varis. Prince Ali-Varis, his forty-seven year old brother, stood in line as heir to the throne. He occupied the seat of the King's Falconer, working as the top advisor to the King. The Falconer needed to be strong, questioning the King's unwise decisions but Ali-Varis barely even paid attention during the meetings. His mental fires burned dim and the successor to the King spent most of the meetings daydreaming while staring out the window.

In comparison, the eighteen year old Ali-Ster was a solid six feet tall with the fire red hair of a true Wamhoff. Ali-Ster had brown eyes and a chiseled body. He scratched his long, lightly freckled face. The young man known as Crimson-Thunder reveled in bloody battle rather than drab council meetings. But he also understood a king controlled the realm with mind and might. He spoke with a deep, manly voice and acted with equal grace toward a court member and a common man. He paid attention as the meeting progressed.

"Alright, alright, enough about the Gold Bandit. What is happening in the other regions?" King Ali-Stanley Wamhoff asked his Chamberlain of the Realm, Otto Cuthbart.

The Kingdom of Donegal was divided into five regions, all headed by a duke. Bottomfoot was basically a neutral region of mostly mountains that kept to themselves. They sent taxes and men to serve in the army to keep the King happy. The other regions were Mattingly, Waters Edge, Burkeville and Fox Chapel. Each region was further broken down into districts that were run by a high lord. There were also areas called Typhoon Alley and the Frozen Forest, but they were uninhabited.

"Well highness, I shall start with Waters Edge. Payments came in on time as always. However they do not seem to have new ventures in place to bring the crown more coin." Otto, the little man with an enormous amount of arrogance, had risen quickly to his new council position. He tended to annoy everyone but the King, the only person whom Otto showed the proper respect.

The King interrupted, "Same tired story from Old Man Etburn, why won't he just die already." The King spoke with a cranky, high pitched voice that made him sound like he was constantly complaining. He relaxed as he fingered his gold scepter. The top of the scepter had a shining fox crafted onto it with two ruby eyes. The King rubbed the eyes of the fox to calm himself. He wore his silver crown today. He had seven different crowns that he wore for each day of the week. The King tended to speak with some of the old-language words mixed in with the current tongue of Donegal. He also liked to quote the 'Words of the Gods' to sound like a Godly man but he often used them in the wrong instances.

Anyone born to the royal bloodline of Donegal started their name with Ali. The regal offspring used two capital letters in their first names to set themselves apart from others.

The King of Donegal held private council meetings in a spacious room in the north end of the castle. The walls were painted gold with alternating horizontal patterns of red foxes and black falcons. Two immense windows on either side of the room let in the pale sunshine whenever the rays broke through the clouds. The thick, rectangular oak table top was about twelve feet long. The top rested upon six lion-shaped legs that had been sculpted from marble. Four were positioned at the corners and two in the middle of the table. Everyone occupied similar wooden chairs except for the King. The taller King Ali-Stanley's seat was higher and bigger than all the others and had arm rests. A plump purple velvet cushion with gold tassels provided added comfort. There were several smaller tables around the room stacked with rolled up maps, records of the realm's finances and former battle transcripts.

"If they won't make use of it, maybe we can take more coastline from them," said Derich Bonsfogger, Admiral of the Sea.

"I might think it best to take the whole damn region if Duke Etburn cannot get his ass moving on new income," screeched the King. "The annual sea harvest doth not suffice anymore; they must take further advantage of their location. If Fox Chapel had the land and coast of Waters Edge, hah, I would not need concern myself with this insolence. Havest thou the firth?"

I have been gone four years and nothing has changed with you. You are still making excuses and misquoting the Gods, father.

"Enough of this guff, let's move to Burkeville," the King declared. His Master of Finance, Henley Moore, spoke up first, "Highness, they are behind again on monthly taxes. However, Duke Burke sends Ali-Tiste's love and begs your forgiveness."

The King smashed his scepter onto the table in a fury, startling his council. His face turned beet purple and he started shaking.

"Father, calm yourself now, be forewarned what Count Silzeus has told you," Ali-Ster cautioned. "Uh, yes highness, it is best you do not get worked up," Count Silzeus feebly agreed.

King Ali-Stanley took heed of the advice and composed himself slightly, "If he believes he can hide behind Ali-Tiste's dresses, he can sit in that sinking boat with Duke Etburn." Otto Cuthbart meekly said, "I have also been hearing that Duke Burke is no longer attending council, and is drunk most of the time. I think we ought question his allegiance to the realm."

"I have heard these same whispers, your highness," Henley Moore added.

"So, needless to say, Burkeville has not any prospects on the horizon?" the King rhetorically asked. Henley remarked, "If so, that money is not reaching Falconhurst." The King shook his head at Henley. "I shan't let this man sink the realm. Can we still depend upon him to shield us from Goldenfield? Someone prepare to send word."

King Ali-Stanley stood by as Henley flattened the paper on the table. One servant retrieved the inkwell and gave it to Henley. Another servant brought him the quill. A falcon feather crafted from ebony, with an ivory tip, served as the writing tool. Henley Moore dipped it into the inkwell as the King dictated:

5
DUKE ASTON BURKE,

The constant lack of appeasement from
Burkeville, has up until this point, received
a pass because of my daughter Ali-Tiste.
Henceforth, preferential treatment will cease.
All past and future payments must
be paid on time, regardless of situation.
I have also received many unsavory reports
regarding several other fronts. I command you to
clean up this behavior at once.
It is fine to have a little fun but we must
carry out our duties to the realm first and foremost.

—King Ali-Stanley Wamhoff, Defender of Donegal,
Keeper of the Seal and First of His Namesake

THE KING SURPRISINGLY remained calm and cool. Although he was in average shape for a sixty five year old man, father time was nipping at his heels. He walked around the room hunched over with a slight limp caused by falling off his horse. The King, a tall man, looked down at his previously well-toned frame. These days it only disappointed him as his body mostly consisted of loosely hanging skin. He even spoke like an old man, forcing the words out of his weary lips. His red hair had suddenly turned gray twelve years ago, as if someone had set fire to a bright autumn leaf. The King also lumbered around in his old age with a battered, portly figure caused by clumsiness and gluttony. He wiped some sweat from his round head.

"Two heads, two spikes. Shall we go for three?" snickered the King.

"My King," Henley Moore interjected, "I am well versed on your differences with the Colberts, but Donegal is managing to get by in large part due to Mattingly. They have increased tax payments every month and scarcely turned the crown down for a loan. As we sit, Duke Colbert has twenty new revenue plans in progress which will all pay taxes to the realm. Mattingly, it appears, should be the least of your concerns, highness," chuckled Henley.

King Ali-Stanley erupted, "The moment I stop worrying about Mattingly is the day you are kneeling to a bull and my head sits upon that spike." He rammed the scepter into the back of Henley Moore's chair, sending a booming echo through the vast room.

"Leave this room right now. You may return again when you regain your wits," said a shaking Ali-Stanley. Henley Moore rose, bowed in deference to the King, and quickly escaped the room.

"I damn near stopped worrying about Jasper Colbert. But I caught that rascal just in time, and we all know what he was planning," uttered the King as he held the scepter to his chin.

We know what you think he was planning. I was not even born but I've heard enough stories to know.

Much of the time at war involved talking to the other soldiers. A lot of the men didn't know Ali-Ster who had disguised himself without royal attire or any special privileges to blend in with the common soldier. In turn, the men didn't sugarcoat their stories about the King. If Ali-Ster had stayed back in Falconhurst, he would only hear the story told the way his father wished people to tell it. His father had a reputation for dealing harshly with anyone he suspected of the slightest offense.

The soldiers said at the time of "The Attack on Jasper" that his father had bad stomach pains and the solutions Count Silzeus prescribed made him temporarily mad. It coincided with the Ali-Stanley's father dying, making him an emotional wreck. He almost barraged Waters Edge in this fit of rage but luckily refrained.

"Who else would like to counsel me not to worry about Mattingly? For what we know they could be planning to march north as you sit around on your asses. The Colbert family is a bunch of usurpers. They are filthy peasants masquerading as royalty. But they still possess the evil that all peasants do, the greed for more and more, and that will soon come out again. And by the Gods, we will be prepared this time," screamed the King as he collapsed into his chair.

"Regarding Goldenfield? Let me guess, Pascal is still a drunk? The Warrior Princess is still stone walling any forward progress?" the King sarcastically wondered.

Jake Fielder, the Foreign Chancellor, addressed the King, "Yes on all counts, highness."

"How can we let a girl mash us about on the battlefield?" asked the befuddled King. "Your highness, it has been widely recounted that she is as vicious as any polished man. They say she has the teeth of a tiger, and she eats the hearts of fallen enemy to absorb their souls. They say her appetite for blood remains unquenchable," Jake Fielder retorted.

The King peered over at his son, "Ali-Ster, did you see this little Princess bitch on any of the battlefields?" "I did father. She fought about average for a man but she seems to have lady luck tied to her breast right now. She is even arrogant enough to wear a red cape on the battlefield while her troops wear white."

"Perhaps she has a horseshoe stuck up her ass," jested Derich Bonsfogger as the table erupted in laughter.

But Ali-Ster knew that the Warrior Princess was not a woman to laugh about. He had lied. He knew she amazed enemies on the field of battle. Ali-Ster even avoided her when he detected the red cape. His life couldn't be captured by a woman, the Gods would laugh at him, he had thought. Ali-Ster had witnessed her shred through about a dozen of Donegal's elite soldiers with ease.

"Her time shall come father, her time shall come soon enough," Ali-Ster concluded.

"The battle rages on with Harbor Valley, highness. So half of Goldenfield's resources are to be employed on the far side of their realm," Jake Fielder announced. "One spot of luck I suppose," the King responded without enthusiasm.

Just when Ali-Ster thought he couldn't take any more of this drudgery, King Ali-Stanley dismissed everyone. Ali-Ster thankfully popped out of his stiff seat.

"I'd like for you to remain Ali-Ster."

What does he want?

"I do not believe I have ever shown you the Alley," said King Ali-Stanley as he slowly rose to his feet. "I have seen many alleys father," Ali-

Ster smartly answered. The King returned, "If you know not what I speak of, then you have not been down there," he stated with an odd smirk. *Down there, what kind of alley is down there?*

As they left the room, Sir Penrose Ellsworth greeted the King. "Uh, Sir Penrose," the King said, "I was just going way downstairs and I bid you escort Ali-Ster and myself." *Way downstairs?*

"Your highness, it shall be my honor, as always," said Penrose as he led the way.

The three proceeded to walk past the dining hall and through the kitchen all the way to the back room behind the castle cook's closets that nobody ever entered. Ali-Ster was confused when they walked into a normal looking room constructed of stone. Penrose Ellsworth tugged on a certain rock in the wall and a door opened.

What the hells is going on? An alley in the dungeons?

Ali-Ster did not want to go any further but his father shoved him through the door. He had served four years in the war and didn't scare easily, but this raised his heartbeat. They went down a stone stair case. Penrose illuminated the path with a burning torch. Ali-Ster knew they were beyond the dungeons at this point; he had never been this far underground and they were still plunging. It got cold at a rapid pace as they descended even farther. Ali-Ster was behind his father and Penrose so he could barely see. He brushed his hand along the wall and sensed solid ice.

"Right here, Penrose," said the excited King as he took the torch from him. "Ali-Ster, it is time."

Ali-Ster did not want to go with his father. He had heard too many stories about the dead from some of the toughest men he knew. They were haunted by the men that they killed until it drove them mad. He could feel the cold dead air surrounding him like he was wounded prey. The King fumbled with a few keys as they arrived at a locked door. The King finally looked at Ali-Ster with a huge smile.

"Are you ready my boy?" "I...I suppose I am," Ali-Ster nervously responded.

The door creaked loudly as King Ali-Stanley gently pushed it open. The atrocious smell hit Ali-Ster first. He had been around a lot of foul smelling battle sites but this really made his eyes burn and tear up. His father started lighting various torches that were set up around the room.

What in the hells is this? Are we in a frozen hell?

Ali-Ster saw marble altars spread around the room. Regally resting atop the altars were what appeared to be charred corpses. *Death is part of life.*

They were laid out on their backs with hands folded over their hearts. Most of the altars had great swords penetrating them. The swords were just deep enough in the shrines to stand at attention. They were beautifully adorned with impressive gems and golden hilts. The swords appeared stuck in the marble near the midsection of each body.

"Have they been burned to death?" an astonished Ali-Ster inquired. "No my son, what you see is a preservation of the body and soul for eternity. This ensures that the body will never erode and shall be around forever. Do you realize who these people are?" asked the King who seemed to be enjoying himself.

Ali-Ster took a closer glance at the resting spots that featured all seven Gods marvelously carved into each one of them. He also saw names etched into them.

"They are Wamhoffs?" asked a confused Ali-Ster. "They are all family ancestors who shared the royal blood line. These are some of the greatest Wamhoff kings of all time. I am sure you have heard stories of the Raging Fox, King Ali-Sander Wamhoff." The former king's altar housed all the Gods and had an angry looking red fox engraved on it.

"And none of us would be here if it had not been for King Ali-Dus Wamhoff," his father reminded him. King Ali-Dus Wamhoff had a giant war ship carved on his altar.

"Is that truly him? But he died almost four-hundred years ago," Ali-Ster pondered. "That is where you are wrong, young one. He died more than four-hundred years ago. When I said forever, that is what I meant. And soon I shall join my family in the Alley to the Heavens for all of eternity."

6
THE WARRIOR PRINCESS—LEIMUR

HE STOOD DIRECTLY in front of her. Again, she was face-to-face with the man who had violated her. The Princess thrust her ice-hardened sword through the man's midsection. *It did no damage. No blood spilled.*

She stroked again, gliding the steel straight through the well-dressed man's neck. *No blood again? Head still intact?*

The Princess started swinging wildly with reckless rage at her familiar foe. *Why can't I kill him?*

Leimur Leluc's lavender eyes flashed open. The braying sounds of a dying horse had awakened her. The Princess wiped the sleep from her weary eyes. She always slept in armor, and even though her suit weighed much less than most of the men's protection, it caused sleep to be extremely uncomfortable. However, once Leimur awakened, all she needed to gather was her sword belt and daggers. Her handmaiden, Tolaya, offered the Princess a cup of steaming morning water. The Princess eagerly drank the desperately needed liquid. Since taking co-command of the eastern army with General Rigby, sleep had become more and more elusive as the days passed. The tent felt chilly, but the Princess was sweating. *I must have been dreaming that dream again.*

The Princess of Goldenfield, Leimur Leluc, had just turned twenty. She possessed short black hair with straight bangs across her forehead and haunting amethyst eyes. She stood tall for a woman and was in peak physical condition. Her skin glowed like a mix of gold and bronze and she had a jagged scar on her left forearm. Leimur concentrated on battle, but natural beauty shone through her rugged looks.

Dark aubergine lips rippled as she said, "Tolaya, I am off to the front line. Please be ready to send word to my father when I return later today."

"Yes, my Princess. Be careful, my brave Princess," responded Tolaya with a shy smile.

Tolaya pulled open the tent flaps and the Princess emerged into a new day. Either it wasn't as cold as it should have been, or she was still perspiring from her dream. Tolaya fastened the red cape around Leimur's neck. It featured a golden tiger in the center. The cape seemed to wave goodbye to Tolaya, aided by the early harvest wind gusts. The Princess walked toward her strong, obsidian destrier. She had named the horse Marius in honor of her great-great grandfather, Marius Leluc. The charger wore a black saddle and light battle armor. Black linen lined the horse's body with a giant, soaring eagle proudly embroidered on the outside. It only took a few minutes for her to arrive at the front. The lined-up soldiers looked like waves from a sea of humanity as the Princess galloped along the perimeter. Thousands of men chattered and the drums rumbled through the morning air.

Boom, baba ba, boom, boom, boom. Boom, baba ba, boom, boom, boom.

These songs were the sounds the Princess heard on a daily basis now and she'd learned to enjoy the racket. The soldiers were ever prepared for an attack even though it seemed highly improbably given the current situation. The Donegal soldiers had claimed the high ground, forcing Goldenfield to wait to attack. But Donegal didn't want to fight Goldenfield on even ground so the two month standoff waged on.

Never get caught with your pants down, her father used to say. It was one of the few things Leimur remembered from his almighty ramblings. She pulled back on the reins once she spotted General Rigby. The smell of shit, piss and puke permeated the air. But the malodor of dead bodies and rotting horses from the battle six months ago still lingered and overpowered it. Princess Leimur couldn't decide which stench was worse but she knew one thing; she preferred that to the rank perfumes the highborn wore. For someone reared in a palace she oddly felt right at home on the putrid battlefields.

Death is part of life.

Leimur approached General Rigby and shouted, "Nothing still?" "We are still at a standoff, my Princess," the General responded. "Let's convene in the strategy pavilion in an hour's time. Please alert Captain Salina and Tetine and Sir Pierre as well," the Princess returned. "Very well, highness," said the General.

She loathed being called 'highness'. At times she even wished she was lowborn.

Power should be earned, not inherited.

Out of nowhere, a giant pot of purple fire flew through the air. It blasted into a large tree about ten feet from the Princess, instantly igniting everything in its destructive path. She checked her body to make sure the fragments from the pot hadn't hit her. She hurriedly climbed on Marius and galloped away from the burning mass. She passed two men whose primal screams of agony tore at her ears as the hapless soldiers watched the purple fire rip right through their organs. The Princess almost hit a tree branch as she stared in horror at the men struggle while death crept in.

Donegal is still up to these old tricks. Sneaking down the mountain and flinging purple fire is the work of cowards. They have no honor or courage. I have them afraid of a girl.

All the participants arrived earlier than expected to the meeting so the Princess saw no reason to wait.

"First order of interest," the Princess started, "I want the whore wagons and tents gone immediately." Sir Pierre Trommel interjected, "My Princess, I am not particularly fond of the whores personally, but they are necessary for the men's morale."

The Princess quickly snapped back, "Morale? Morale? I watched six men die yesterday, fourteen the day before. Pissing blood was the first sign for all of them. Then their whole body turned green and they rotted from the inside out. They were throwing up and shitting out their insides until they died a painful death. Many of them now ask to be put to the sword after pissing blood. Forty-eight men died after contracting these symptoms last month and every single one of those men visited the whores just weeks before their demise. I don't have to be brilliant to put this together."

"But highness, maybe we can find some new, cleaner whores. I do say this for your safety as well," Captain Leo Tetine warned. The Princess immediately came back, "Hah, I think I am able defend myself just fine Captain." She thought for a moment, and declared, "We bring in new whores under this provision: They will be sampled by our most unproductive men first, pages, squires and the like. If nothing should occur to those men, then the soldiers may start using them again. As for these present whores, they are killing more men than the enemy at the moment. We need them removed immediately. Send them over to the Donegal lines with the message that the Warrior Princess will not allow whores in her camps any longer. These girls can be better killers than most of our men at the moment."

"Brilliant idea, my Princess", said Captain Salina.

"As far as my father, I can't seem to get a response from him about consolidating power in the west. Many letters have gone unanswered and I am afraid we must remain here until we receive word from the Capitol," the Princess told her audience. "They must be fighting a war in Sevring that we do not know about," said an annoyed Sir Pierre. "Look," said Leimur as she raised her voice, "Nobody wants to end this stalemate more than General Rigby and I. If we continue to receive no response I will go to the Capitol myself to handle this problem."

"Would that be wise, my Princess?" asked Captain Rosa Salina. The Princess turned to the woman and smiled, exposing her jagged teeth. "No, but it may be required for a Princess General. Captain Tetine, what words have you received from the Harbor Valley front?"

The older man with a missing left eye said, "Same stalemate that we have here. They take a couple hundred feet, Harbor Valley takes it right back. It sounds exactly like the letters we are sending them." "Perfect. We are exhausting resources on either side of the realm and probably all points in between." She looked around and told the war veterans, "Thank you everyone, you are dismissed now."

General Rigby stayed back and addressed the Princess, "Leimur, I have some unpleasant words I feel are necessary for your ears."

The Princess knew the General had something serious to discuss. He had never called her Leimur before.

"It is about your father," continued General George Rigby. The General had served in the Goldenfield army for thirty-two years. He was forty-six and scars of battle were visible. The General, a gargantuan man, had many battle wounds. His two missing fingers and knife scars across the back of his neck were constant reminders of having been a prisoner in Livingstone for three years. Rigby's shaggy, gray hair and short beard matched each other. His gray eyes and several missing teeth completed the haggard look. The Princess took a seat inside the makeshift mobile office.

"I have received several reports from different sources about your father's behavior." General Rigby squirmed as he uttered the words. Leimur tried to make it easier for him, "I am not a stupid little girl, General. You have seen me kill men all over the battlefield and I have even tortured them in gruesome ways, so do not be shy."

She spoke in a deep bass voice that proved useful when she had to shout orders over the chaos on the battlefield. Conversely, she rarely raised her voice in meetings.

The General fingered his moustache and stated, "Unfortunately, it seems your father is going a bit mad. I am told he is uselessly drunk at all times and he is bringing whores into the bed of his holy union." Leimur hated her mother even more than her father, but even she didn't deserve that humiliation. "That's not mad, just disrespectful really," Leimur responded. "I was not quite finished, my Princess. It also seems as though he thinks he holds a connection to the Gods. He takes on a different moniker for all seven days of the week." The General now sat down. "It also appears that he feels that mortals are here on earth for him to feast on. Not only is he taking on whores, but the wives of his council members and family. He is also sacrificing a virgin girl every day in the palace bailey in a mark of respect to the Gods."

The Princess looked down and shook her head, "Does the public know?" "All of my resources trust very little is known right now, but that shouldn't last for long. One of these husbands is going to talk to someone at some point," the General slowly added. "Or kill someone? Send me to all seven hells. How can my mother put up with this?" the Princess wondered. "Damn, I was hoping you wouldn't ask. I have been told that the Queen has - I am sorry - your birth mother has..." the General corrected himself as he remembered the Princess despised people calling her mother the Queen. "She has become very fond of wine, ale and spirits, I am afraid. They say she wakes to six cups of morning water spiked with heavy spirits and progresses to drink it straight as the day moves on. She is believed to sleep sometimes for a full day at a time. She only wakes to vomit or relieve herself."

A disgusted look came over the Princess's face as the conversation angered her the more it went on. She said sternly, "Our realm sits in peril, ripe for sack by outsiders or the general public, and we are stuck here dealing with this nonsense."

7

THE PRICE TO PAY—RUSSELL

HE ABHORRED DOING this. The stark naked Duchess Ali-Pari slowly stood up and leaned over the bed. Russell knew he had to carry out this burden. The young man settled in behind her. He closed his eyes and envisioned Ali-Gare, the fairest maid in the land, as he inserted himself inside Ali-Pari Wamhoff.

"Ooohh," she moaned in her deep voice. He started slowly until Ali-Pari reached back and pinched his thigh, saying, "Pound me young man."

I guess this is the price I pay for being knighted at sixteen.

Russell's eyes remained closed as the sensual slapping of skin got increasingly louder. Sir Russell Seabrook was a bewildered young man of seventeen. He always thought he had greatness within, but wasn't sure of what his destiny had in store for him. Russell had shaggy, curly brown hair offset by brilliant blue eyes. He was tall and strapping but still appeared younger because he couldn't grow facial hair. He had a slight speech difficulty and tended to stutter when stumped or ruffled. Russell served as one of only a few lowborn knights in the realm. His mother worked in the castle kitchens of Duke Tyus Etburn. Duke Etburn was eighty two and cared little for Russell. When he had refused to knight the boy, Ali-Pari threatened to take the boy to Falconhurst to let her brother, King Ali-Stanley, knight him. Duke Etburn ultimately caved in and carried out the wishes of Ali-Pari.

Ali-Pari Wamhoff had always taken care of Russell Seabrook. Even though she had married Duke Etburn, everyone still called her by the Wamhoff name. He never knew his father and she took him in after his mother died when he was eight.

Russell opened his eyes and looked at Ali-Pari's wrinkled skin bouncing around. She was a dazzling woman, but at age seventy, new shortcomings arrived every day like uninvited guests. Ali-Pari's once vibrant auburn hair now grayed, matching the dull walls of her room. She had been nicely shaped, but those days were only fading memories. Russell focused on the wrinkles and blue marks on her legs. After about ten minutes of rough sex Ali-Pari started convulsing and screamed Russell's name at the top of her throat.

The Duchess of the castle released her taut grip on the sheets and said, "Oh Russell, you are my favorite." Russell was simply glad it was over. He felt grimy having sex with the Duchess of Waters Edge, right under her husband's roof. *I cannot continue this.*

Russell put his clothes back on while Ali-Pari lay back, smiling in the bed. "Oh why are you so sad, Sir Russell," poked Ali-Pari. "I'm not sad, it's just..."

"It's just what?" interrupted Ali-Pari, suddenly annoyed. Russell carefully continued, "Well it just feels wrong to do this to Duke Etburn." A direct Ali-Pari said, "My child, that man is deader than a ghost. He couldn't satisfy me when he was in his prime. And every woman, although she will deny it, has sexual needs just like a man." *That doesn't make me feel better at all.* "As you say, my Duchess," Russell offered. "Oh, Russell Seabrook, I cannot have you mad at me," she said as she got out of bed and walked over to a fully attired Russell.

Russell loved Ali-Pari like a grandmother. She took care of him when no one else was willing, but he still needed to figure out an alternative that would convince Ali-Pari to terminate this adultery. She hugged Russell, kissed him on the cheek and whispered in a raspy voice, "Goodbye, my brave knight."

"My Duchess," Russell bowed and slipped out the door. He withdrew from the castle as fast as he could.

The smell of dirty, salty seawater lofted through the afternoon air. Although Elkridge, the Capitol of Waters Edge, lay inland from the Sea of Green, it still caught some of the ocean smells that drifted in. A huge crowd of people thronged the castle. Some traded goods from the early harvest. Others just drank and exchanged boisterous stories. Food and essentials were the main items traded since luxury goods were somewhat forbidden by Duke Etburn who preached against living in excess as he believed it may burn the soul.

There was a strong belief in the afterlife in the kingdom of Donegal. They called it the forever-life because it was expected to last for eternity.

The worshippers believed that they would be judged by their actions on earth to determine their status in the forever-life. Would it be heaven or hell? After death, a person either ascended into heaven or descended to hell. There were seven steps of heaven and seven gates of hell. A test at each step or gate determined if you went to a better heaven or worse hell as each step multiplied the results. The people called them the heavens and hells. The church had also convinced worshippers to repent their sins on earth to the Faith of Eternal Light with the promise that you may enter the tests of heaven with a clean soul. Usually it took a monetary transaction to have one of the Brothers of the Faith of Eternal Light absolve your earthly sins for the Day of Judgment.

The fiery sun blazed bright with hardly any clouds, but the gusty Elkridge winds kept the day proportionately cool. Russell stumbled around before he spied a familiar face.

The older man laughed heartily and said, "Ha, ha, ha, there he is, my brave knight."

His raspy voice sent a sharp, cold shiver up and down Russell's spine.

"I bet you never had to undress a dead man have you?"

"Never," answered the young man. "How can you call yourself a knight and never perform your war duty?" the old salt chuckled. "I had, uh, other duties that, uh...," stammered Russell. The old man cut him off, "Uh, uh, I am just breaking your stones kid. But if you haven't had to steal from a dead man, you haven't been to war."

Russell wanted to go to war, but Ali-Pari wouldn't acquiesce.

"You probably never seen anything like this neither," sighed the gruff old soldier. He lifted his shirt to show Russell but the stink hit him first. It stung his nostrils in a way Russell Seabrook had never experienced before. He considered himself a tough man to have been knighted at sixteen, but this challenged him. From bellybutton to hip, Terry Underling sported an unsightly gash. The wide cut was purple and black down the center, with a bloody red surrounding. It made the ghostly white flesh next to it even more alarming.

"You are dying?" inquired an astonished Russell. "If that's so, I've been dying for years," joked the war veteran. "Tell me more about war, the bad stuff," suggested Russell.

Terry began, "See right now you swing that sword around the practice yard. Sure, it sings lovely songs and at the end of the day everyone goes home safe. You eat a nice supper, kiss your girl, maybe pat her bottom and go to sleep in a comfortable bed. But that's not real, lad. The first time you feel that sword rip through a man's body, that's when it becomes real." He grimaced as he thumbed the wound but kept talking, "It's said that man is mightier than the sword, but my sword has widowed many a woman."

Russell jumped in, "But you, a man, had to wield that sword."

"Aye, that's true," he continued, "But when you have been away from your home and family for years, taking people's lives from their families, that's when you start to question it. Especially when you see childhood friends sliced straight through the neck and their bloody heads land by your foot. Then you watch your brother take a sword through the stomach and I can tell you it's not pretty to watch any man try to shove his guts back into his body."

Russell's stomach started to stir as the zealous man carried on, "I threw up. I looked like you did a little while ago when I showed you my little cut. And then you realize the sword is a pretty damn close second. Then, once you start to be able to stomach the death, the freezing, the stinking, the starving, you realize that we lose even if Donegal wins. I have seen tens of thousands of men slain in the name of the great King of Donegal. I knew many a man who died for Ali-Baster before Ali-Stanley. They laid their lives down for the King who died on the golden chamber pot. They gave up everything for a man who couldn't survive taking a shit."

Russell interrupted, "What are you talking of? Ali-Pari told me King Ali-Baster died on the throne, ruling the realm."

Terry laughed heartily, "Of course that's what a Wamhoff told you. Fuckin' hells, that's his daughter. The Wamhoffs aren't going to tell everyone in the realm that the king keeled over on the pot, stewing up a stinky shit." He settled down as he continued his story, "Not one of these men I speak of ever saw the king. I have never seen either of my kings nor the Capitol for that matter. I am just a poor sea boy thrust directly into the front lines of a fox king's fantasy war. The great Ali-Stanley waves his magic scepter and men like me die."

Russell was a little distressed, but he'd asked for it. Terry went on with his story, "Most men have no idea why the war is even being waged. And the king uses phrases like WE are at war. King Ali-Stanley is still spending away to glory, having feasts and tourneys. He kisses his wife and family every day. He even sends his own son into the action he never saw himself. He sits in the palm of luxury and has the nerve to speak of sacrifice. Hah!" Terry agonized over his wound as he went on, "I was once gone for fourteen years fighting a war that accomplished nothing. I returned to find my loving wife had passed. She has been gone for five years, but I can still see her face right now, like it was just yesterday."

Terry Underling closed his eyes and had a quick smile wiped away by a very painful look. Russell cut in, "Are you alright my friend?" "Aye," grunted Terry as he kept telling his story, "We ate when rations were available, slept on the rocky ground and I killed more men than I care to count. These men never wronged me. They waved a different flag than me and for that I slayed them like animals. And maybe because I ruined so many people's dreams, the nightmares still haunt me. They all involve the wives of the men I killed. I don't know them, but they know me in these dreams, nightmares really. They show up to kill me every damn night. Now that is sacrifice. For the good of the realm, hah. Have I scared you enough, lad?"

Terry started coughing uncontrollably. Russell was really perturbed when Terry spit a wad of blood on the ground. *Is he dying right now?*

"Are you going to be alright?" a concerned Russell asked. "Oh, I am fine, lad. This happens all the time. That's the glory of the privilege to serve in the Donegal army," smiled Terry, exposing his red teeth. The day was making Russell feel ill.

"I need a drink, kid. I guess I'll see you around," said Terry as he scrambled off toward the tavern. Russell simply nodded his head. He had undertaken digging for answers today but only more questions sprouted up. He noticed Edburgh Etburn moving quickly down the street so he hustled over to him.

Russell tapped Edburgh on the shoulder and asked, "How are you, my Lord?" "Just fine, Sir Russell," Edburgh mumbled as he hurried away. "Fare thee well, my good Lord," Russell yelled. Now Russell knew something was amiss. He was naïve, but Edburgh had never called him Sir Russell before and only gave him respect in the company of Ali-Pari.

Maybe he is just as confused as I am? At least he has Caroline with him to travel life's path. I think I might need a walk in the Frozen Forest to discover some answers. I must tell Ali-Pari I will be leaving for several days. I suppose I will have to perform my duty before I leave.

8

A Lazy Afternoon In The Capitol— Emilia

THE HORSE'S HOOVES thudded along the moist beaten trail, launching mud in every direction. It had rained last night and the Queen's dress paid the price. Most women, let alone a queen, never rode their horse in a dress. The two raced away from the rank odor that flowed throughout Falconhurst. The sewage system had failed again and the residents of the Capitol suffered the inconvenience. It was a bright spring day with the wind howling. Puffy clouds swept in occasionally, stealing the sun's rays. The Queen headed toward the wooded area on the outskirts of the eastern side of the Capitol. The petite Queen sat atop her simple white horse in an amber saddle. Her protector rode alongside, controlling a dark brown horse that wore a black saddle.

They stopped and jumped off their horses. Sir Anderley Ellsworth cinched the horses to a post on the side of the trail. It was a nice early harvest day in Falconhurst as the Queen looked at the flowers just starting to bloom. They strolled off the worn path into some thick brush and spotted the little clearing.

"AAAHHH!" the Queen suddenly screamed as she ran behind the knight.

He pulled a small dagger from his hip and flung it toward the ground. It pierced the red-tailed snake that had scared the Queen, killing it on the spot. The Queen released her tight grip from Sir Anderley but her heart still pounded with fear. She hated snakes possibly more than anything else. Sir Anderley pulled out the knife, tossed the serpent aside and cleared the way. In the middle of the short green grass sat a glowing amethyst plant. The sun perfectly penetrated the trees at that point and made the plant shine. Silly smirks came over the faces of the Queen and Anderley.

Emilia Burke Wamhoff, Queen of Donegal, was petite to the extreme, but a perfectly proportioned miniature woman. She sometimes looked like a child next to the enormous King, but even so most people saw her as a fully grown, sexy woman. Her curly brown hair swept down to the small of her back and her green eyes complemented it perfectly. The Queen spoke with a high pitched, girlish voice even though she was thirty-three. Her bronze skin tone glowed in the partial sunlight.

Sir Anderley Ellsworth took the small flat plank out of his satchel and gripped it in his left hand. He held it over the object of the Queen's fancy. He pulled the lavender bud from the plant with his right hand. Anderley smashed it against the board and ground it in with his thumb.

He offered it up to the Queen. She patted the powdery substance with two fingers and rubbed it on her tongue. Sir Anderley repeated the process and the Queen went for a second taste. She rubbed the amethyst on her gums this time and then on her full, luscious lips. It tasted terrible but the final effects were what the Queen wanted. Her eyes twitched and the Queen started sweating. Her stomach felt terrible and swirled around, churning until she almost threw up. Then suddenly, pleasure spread through her entire body as the plant took effect just in time. She used drugs because she felt very lonely in the castle and they made her feel good. She had never felt accepted by the Wamhoff family, especially the older women. The Queen glanced up at the sunlight through the tree branches and the green leaves oddly turned purple.

Thank the Gods did I need this.

The Queen and Anderley were great friends, but they often spent hours together barely speaking. Balance became extremely difficult and the Queen stabilized herself on a low tree branch. The branch felt funny in her hand, it made her fingers tingle.

"What shall you do today, my Queen?" Anderley wanted to know.

"Huh," the Queen said through her purple haze, "How about...we go to the duels?"

Anderley never denied the Queen her wishes. He lived inside a diminutive, fit body with long brown hair and blue eyes. He wore his hair in a ponytail most of the time. He had forfeited all his lands and titles as heir to Lightview to pursue a life of honor. The knight became a member of the King's Guard four years ago but ironically spent most of his time protecting the Queen.

When they reached the horses, the Queen's eyes seemed to be dancing in her head.

A concerned Anderley asked, "My Queen, will you be alright to ride?"

She focused her vision and replied, "I am fine, this one just hit me a bit harder than before."

They both mounted and took off for the Dueling Yard. The Dueling Yard served dual purposes. If the prisoners won seven duels, which were single combat fights to the death, and served seven years in the army, they became free men again. Wooden benches were built all around the yard for people to sit and watch. The citizens placed bets on the fights and cheered on their favorite criminal champions. Twenty minutes later, the Queen and Sir Anderley arrived at the Dueling Yard. A man ran up to the Queen and Anderley, eager to watch their horses. Anderley gave him two coppers and the pair proceeded toward the yard.

The seats were configured in a horseshoe pattern with one end open for entering and leaving. The tiers of seats around the well of the Dueling Yard ascended toward the back and could hold about seven hundred people. The pair strolled into the yard and felt the morbid excitement in the air. Some of the fans belted out crazy sounding screams and others cheered in the seats. Two criminals battled for their lives in the middle of the Yard. The massive crowd roared like a starving beast. The thirst of blood appeared more prevalent in the audience than on the yard of battle sometimes. Most of the audience members were highborn who gambled heavy piles of gold on the fights. On either side of the yard the future combatants lined up for inspection. The Queen and Sir Anderley sized them up, seeing what match-ups they wanted to gamble on. Everyone bowed to the Queen in reverence as she passed. They knew she came from commoner roots with a lucky last name.

The King had gone to Burkeville to visit his sister after the death of his first wife, Parys. He met Emilia during a walk through the woods and instantly fell for her. Emilia's family, the Burkes, had strained family ties with the Duke of Burkeville. Her father was the cousin of Duke Aston Burke, who wouldn't even let Emilia's immediate family in his castle. She grew up not knowing the cause of the feud. They had lived within an hour of the Duke's castle but her father simply told her never to go there.

But that day she had sneaked into Arigold, the Capitol of Burkeville, to see what the King looked like. They found each other and the King fell in love with the beautiful fourteen-year-old.

A king marrying a woman without family influence ruffled a few feathers, but a determined king always gets his way. He had validated it by saying that the Burke name was good enough. And although the Queen appeared somewhat simple in thought, she remained beloved by the people of the city. She mingled with them and gave them respect in return. Most of the city hated King Ali-Stanley, but the citizens were always receptive of Queen Emilia. She needed little protection around the Capitol, but Sir Anderley still escorted her everywhere.

They were whisked right up to the front row, closest to the action. Two men squared off in the middle of the grassy yard. One man stood almost twice the size of his opponent. Fitted with black armor, the mammoth man held a colossal wooden shield and small war axe that he operated with one hand. The tiny man wore silver armor that hung poorly from his body, leaving plenty of exposed area. It shone in the sunlight, along with his little sword. The little guy had protected his head with a silver eagle-shaped helm as he readied for battle. Both prisoners had won two brawls already, but the Queen and nearly all of the gamblers bet on the giant. *Chop his little head off so I can collect my gold fox.*

The referee screamed, "Battle" as the behemoth rushed his opponent and took a heaving swing with the war axe. The smaller, quicker dueler easily avoided the pain. The immense man rushed four or five more times, swinging mightily without success. *Come on you big oaf, finish this little creep off.*

The giant tired quickly but continued to chase the half man around the Dueling Yard. The tiny dancer silenced the crowd of more than five hundred people who had howled like uncontrollable animals at the start of the match.

The gigantic criminal finally discarded the useless shield that only weighed him down. *Let's go, you stupid criminal, you better beat a man half your size.*

With two hands firmly on his axe, he swung mightily hoping to split the already small man into two pieces. He missed again, only succeeding in deeply jamming his axe into mother earth's body. The huge man struggled to extract the weapon from the ground. The slight man pounced at the opportunity with a mighty upswing through the giant's manhood and into his stomach. The tiny man removed the sword and slipped behind the giant. The colossal man was crouched on his knees, moaning in pain. After he felled the hefty man, bringing him down to his own size, he seized the moment. The pint sized man drove his sword through the back of the giant's neck, down into his heart, sending him straight to a bloody, painful death. *How in the hells did that just happen?*

The stadium fell into shocked silence. The only sounds heard were from the few in attendance that stood to make huge amounts of coin courtesy of the victorious little man. It took three full-sized men to drag the behemoth from the grounds in preparation for the next duel.

Maybe I shall take the smaller man next time. That amethyst feeling is wearing off. I will need something else soon. What else can we do after this to stay away from the smelly city and my self- righteous husband?

9
GO FOR A SWIM?—PENROSE

PLEASE FORGIVE ME *Gods, for I have done it again. The craving for blood runs stronger every day. I try and try to fight it, sometimes I can for a week or so, but then the voices take over. I am up to more than four a month now and the demands are getting louder. I almost killed the King today to quiet the chanting. If his son wasn't with him, I may have done it. They should keep me from King Ali-Stanley. Gods help me as I have little control over my lust for blood anymore. These thoughts dominate my life and I need them to stop. Killing for duty is commanded but this is for amusement now. I just like to see the looks in their eyes as they struggle to hold on to life. Please Gods save me, for I fear my soul is lost.*

Thunder boomed through the chapel, but he didn't remember seeing a cloud in the Falconhurst sky when he had entered the temple.

He knelt, hands folded over his heart, praying. When done, Sir Penrose Ellsworth now sat up in the chapel of The Faith of Eternal Light. The Father and Brothers of the church served the elite of Falconhurst by washing away sins in exchange for a hefty financial contribution. Members of the church signed multiyear contracts that bound them to donate a certain monthly allowance. The Faith was extremely shrewd and they knew that promises of salvation after death sold at a prime premium in Donegal. The church also housed some of the high ranking Brothers and the High Holy Leader. Sir Penrose Ellsworth's main duties were to protect King Ali-Stanley, basically serving as his personal body guard. This meant Penrose had access to any place he wanted to go, no one refused him. He rose, bowed to the totem of the Gods, and walked through a door on the side of the beautifully decorated chapel.

"Hello, Sir Penrose," a short guard greeted him. "Oh, hello Randall, are the children alright?" asked Penrose. "Yes, they uh, recovered like magic, thanks for askin'," declared a smiling Randall. "That's great news. Is his Holiness in right now?" wondered a curious Penrose. "Uh, yes he's down in the bath right now," answered Randall. "Thank you, my good man," added Penrose with a fake smile. Behind the grin, a world of pain circulated inside Penrose.

He went down a stone spiral staircase to get to the High Holy Leader's private bathe. Penrose and Father Enroy were good friends and the Father had told him to stop by whenever he wanted. Penrose didn't agree with the lavish lifestyle most of the high ranking officials led. However, he hoped befriending the High Holy Leader might bolster his chance of salvation. He needed his current sins washed away first. The heat attacked him as Penrose opened the door to the bathe. The gleaming torches on all sides of the water made it easy to spot the smallish Father Enroy squirming pleasurably in the heated water. He looked very surprised and a little disconcerted to see Penrose.

"Penrose, hello," said the Father with wide eyes and a lump in his throat.

Suddenly, two small boys popped up out of the water right in front of the Father. Several seconds later, three more toddlers emerged around Father Enroy. The oldest boy couldn't have been more than eight or nine.

The Father's face turned bright red as he asked, "Care for a swim?"

"No thank you. I believe I shall wait outside your office for you, Father," said Penrose as he scurried out. "I shall be right there," shouted the naked Father as Penrose left the room.

What in the hells? Two men together is one thing, but taking advantage of little boys is reprehensible. I should clean him up for the Gods. I can taste his divine blood already. Maybe that will cleanse my soul? Stop screaming at me.

The voices berated him as he headed away from the bathe, demanding the Father's blood. He made his way upstairs, through the chapel and toward the back, to the High Holy Leader's office. The church made a fine spectacle. Stained glass windows with scenes from the holy writs surrounded the chapel. Diamonds and gemstones gaudily accentuated the windows. Masterfully constructed marble pews filled the room that could accommodate about two hundred and fifty wealthy worshipers. Opulent silk pillows more than ten feet long were secured to the ground for comfort when kneeling during prayer. They had the pattern of the black raven of the Faith on purple silk. The raven represented the brothers of the Faith delivering the messages of the Gods. Jade, ebony and ivory sculptures of the Gods were twice as large as mortal men and stationed up front on either side of the altar. Four stood on one side and three on the other. Penrose sat on the expensive bench and wrestled with his thoughts. The thunder resounded through his head again.

I can kill him; I can kill him right now and it will be easy. Wait, no, I can't kill him. He is the only one who can possibly save my soul. If I kill him nobody will absolve my sins. I can't kill him.

Sir Penrose Ellsworth looked like a guileless twenty year old. With long, curly blond hair past his shoulders and bright blue eyes, the ladies were very fond of him. But it didn't matter because he was sworn to the King's Guard and couldn't marry. He spoke softly and eloquently, hardly ever raising his tone. Penrose's daily activities kept him healthy and strong, but internal demons tore him apart. The knight battled constant stomach pains. Only a year ago, everything had seemed fine, but then he started hearing the voices. Penrose's obedience seemed to feed the voices and silence them, but they always came back for more lifeblood.

Penrose came from one of the most prominent houses in the entire kingdom. His father, Ichibod Ellsworth, was the High Lord of Lightview, the most profitable district in Fox Chapel. They even traded with Mattingly behind the King's back. Penrose had shunned land and money as heir of Lightview to live a life of honor. His older brother Anderley was the original heir and it fell to Penrose after he left for the King's Guard. It had crushed Ichibod Ellsworth to watch Penrose follow Anderley's footsteps straight to the Capitol.

He stood up abruptly when Father Enroy arrived, garbed in a scarlet robe. He wore two gold belts to secure the hanging silk.

He spoke first, "Penrose, I do apologize for that. Please do not think it was what it seemed." "Can we forget about that, I would like to talk with you for a few minutes Father," Penrose quietly proposed. The Father opened his office door and said, "Come in, my son."

Father Enroy offered a chair to Penrose and then sat down himself. The Father looked as though he was well into his sixties, but no one precisely knew his exact age. He lived life as a robust, compact man. Gluttony had fattened the Father and imbued him with a false sense of self-worth. The High Holy Leader, a bald man on top with gray hair hanging down the sides of his head, played with his robe. He had a ridiculous patchy beard that should have been shaved off altogether.

The office gleamed with gold and jewels, like a room fit for a king. The couches and desk were finely constructed and expensive silks covered the windows. The Father had a chair that would rival a throne in some realms. Constructed of jade, its armrests also showcased every imaginable precious stone. There were a lot of gems Penrose had never seen and couldn't identify; he only knew that they all sparkled beautifully. The back support extended up to about seven feet and was fitted with two giant pearls on either side at the top. Two ebony carved ravens held the pearls in their claws as they hovered above the chair with outstretched wings. Father Enroy tried to get the water from his ear as he listened to Penrose.

"Well Father, I wondered, what do you do when you have the urge to sin?"

"I like to think of the day when I am being judged by the seven Gods. What would they say? You must try to fight the urges, my son. However, there are times when primal needs must be met. And the Gods might understand that perhaps."

Penrose heard the answer he wanted but the Father's message was vague. *Maybe this is just a primal need I have to fulfill sometimes. But not right now. I can't kill him.*

A sudden hard knock at the door caught both men unawares. Penrose placed his hand on his sword and slowly cracked the door. There stood King Ali-Stanley Wamhoff with three massive guards.

"Penrose, is the Father in?" asked the King. "Yes, your highness," said Penrose as he stepped aside to reveal Father Enroy.

"Father, I need absolution," the King uttered. "Come in my King, it will be my pleasure to absolve you and Penrose both," returned the holy man.

The King turned to his guards, "You are dismissed. Penrose can escort me back to the castle." Penrose said, "Of course, your highness, I shall be certain no harm befalls you." "Yes, I feel perfectly safe with you. You are the only protector I shall require this evening," the King of Donegal confidently stated.

10
A Call To Arms—Jon

JON COLBERT GATHERED his sons into a huddle so he could talk to them over the commotion and the locusts buzzing. "You know why we have to do this, don't you boys?" he asked as he looked them all in the eye.

Ruxin, Ryno and Krys all nodded their heads in agreement as their father clarified further.

"The Fritz family is harboring other families and garnering support for a rebellion. I have received three different confirmations about a planned attack on Riverfront. You boys ought to know that if an egg is falling, you better catch it before it makes a mess. All the families of Mattingly are like a bunch of eggs thrown in the air. This rebellion is like an egg dropping, so we have to grab it now before it builds up momentum and we have a big mess on our hands. A little problem can quickly become a disaster if we ignore it. We must make quick decisions based on the evidence presented and act with haste. But we also must make sure we are thinking clearly and not out for revenge."

As he talked to his sons, the long-distance siege weapons continued to roll by. Each one proudly flew the Colbert banner, a black flag with a golden bull, ready to attack. The Fritz castle rested atop Locust Hill in central Mattingly. It was an older castle for Mattingly, built two hundred and sixty years ago. The castle had no protective siege wall around it and the Fritz' depended on the steep hill and the protection of the Gods for insulation.

"Duke Colbert, if we set up our weapons right along the tree line, straight down there, the castle will be in firing range and we can move to part two of the plan with ease," said Sir Ryan Caughleigh as he pointed along the edge of the woods.

"Alright, remember that we want the weapons mixed as we go, I don't want to see a line of mangonels followed by all the onagers. We need to evenly attack this castle with as much force as necessary if Lord Fritz doesn't come to his senses. Make sure that the arrow shields are secured and positioned in between the weapons. Fire, cover and wait for my command to reload. Where is Sir Richard with the response?"

Duke Colbert had sent a message to Lord Fritz telling him he knew of the plans for revolt and that he needed to pledge fealty to the Duke in person. He wasn't going to embarrass him and make Lord Fritz bend the knee, just a simple promise was all he wanted. He hoped the Fritz' would come to their senses, realizing that they were grossly outnumbered, totally surrounded, and ill equipped to withstand a heavy onslaught. Jon Colbert was positive they would refuse the offer and he would have to attack. He had conceived a quick plan after making sure that advanced efforts for revolt were definitely underway. Then he went on the offensive mere days later to end the aggression before it started.

Sir Rick Rosebud came galloping down on a white stallion with a black saddle, the sign of peace for negotiation in Donegal.

He jumped off and approached the Duke and his sons. "The news is not good, my Duke." "I didn't think that it would be," replied Jon. "He would like me to inform you that the Gods shall cast you down like thunder. Lord Fritz said that you are letting too many foreigners into Mattingly and you have become drunk with money and power."

Sir Rick cleared his throat and spat on the ground as he continued in his husky voice, "He finally said that if you kneel to him and adopt the Fritz family ideals that he will save your soul for the heavens."

"That is an enticing offer, but he could have just declared outright war against us. Sir Rick..."

"Yes, my Duke," he instantly responded.

Jon spoke firmly, "Prepare the siege weapons. Have everything loaded and four rounds back up on each weapon. Line up the archers as well, just behind the weapons and get the men with crossbows in the trees. If they rush us down the hill, we can pick them off with the archers. If they attack with force too heavy for us to handle with the bows, we will retreat slightly to fight on flat land. Ready the troops to unleash justice."

Riverfront had brought forty high-powered siege weapons to bombard the Fritz castle. It was about three hundred feet to the top of Locust Hill, which was well within their firing range. They used mangonels to fling giant pots of purple fire at the castle. The trebuchet was another catapult device that hurled enormous boulders. The onager launched smaller stones, but at a much higher speed. The ballistae were giant crossbows that spit enormous fire breathing arrows to set the enemy ablaze. When applied in unison, the results should be devastating. In theory they should, but Jon Colbert never had to use these before in actual combat.

Jon looked over at his sons before speaking, "Boys, this is a lesson of history repeating itself. Don't think I have forgotten what side the Fritz' fought on during my father's rebellion. They were best of friends with the Beverly family. You see, power will always cause tension. War is very human, my boys. Almost a natural instinct. It is the nature of the beast. The Fritz family feels that we stole some power from them and they want it back. There will always be someone who wants to take power, or take it back as in this case. I allow the Fritz' to make more than they did when the Beverly family ruled Mattingly. I suppose old grudges tend to die hard." *Try to kill my father. Try to kill me. I will not let you try to kill my sons*.

"I know we shall crush this treachery right now, but let's pray to the Gods for strength," decreed Jon Colbert.

They all dropped to a knee, placed their right hands over their hearts and covered it with the left hand as Jon began the prayer:

"Please Gods, guide us in this battle. We didn't wish for this, but it is our responsibility to take care of it. In the presence of the Gods, we shall put a stop to this treason. Keep us from the darkness and guide us to eternal light."

Everyone removed their hands and readied for the attack. "Are the men in place, Sir Herman?" Jon inquired. "Yes, my Duke, they await your command," he returned.

The weapons and soldiers were spread out over an area spanning two hundred feet, but Jon Colbert's deep, sonorous voice could be heard by all as he boomed, "Alright men, we don't want to do this, but we have to. It is our duty. Now take aim. On the count of three, we'll unleash a fiery trip to the afterlife for the Fritz family supporters."

He started walking toward the trees to get behind the weapons as he slowly counted, "ONE, TWO, THREE."

In one fell swoop the north end of the castle was absolutely rocked. Jon Colbert felt the ground shake as large chunks fell out of the wall with some of it shrouded in a purple blaze. A shower of arrows rained on the Colbert faction, but only plastered the fourteen-foot wooden arrow shields and surroundings.

About sixty of Lord Fritz' men raced down the hill. Jon calmly stayed behind the protection of the shield and screamed to the archers, "NOCK. DRAW...HOLD." Jon stepped to the left and surveyed the situation as screaming soldiers pulled their swords and stormed ahead. He took a quick peek around at his own men and noticed some of the archers' arms shaking. He needed them to be strong for a few more moments that he understood would seem like hours to the archers. "HOLD. TAKE AIM. HOLD. LOOSE!" Jon heard the whizzing sounds of hundreds of arrow fletchings, suddenly replaced by shrieks of pain and dying. He could see the missiles hit most of the enemy, stopping them in their tracks. A few men tried to be heroes and forged on only to give up or die soon after.

The Colbert infantry stayed behind the safety of the thick shields until they heard Jon Colbert shout, "Load the weapons again and take aim." Jon instinctively crouched after seeing a streak of flying purple fire over his head. He made sure everyone was ready he exploded again, "ONE, TWO, THREE."

Another round majestically thundered into the air, connecting with almost every high-powered weapon. The screams of terror and hopeless desperation could be heard by all of Jon's men.

They took cover again under the shields but only half the amount of arrows fired down on them. Jon heard the loud thumps in the wood and carefully looked around the shield to be sure his men were safe. Not even one soldier rushed down Locust Hill to attack the Colbert clan and he called the men back into firing position.

This is for you, father. I know Lord Fritz killed your uncle James during your rebellion. Look down with pride today.

After they repeated the process the fifth time, Jon Colbert bellowed through the chaotic air, "West wall move, west wall move."

In harmony, the troops rolled the siege weapons slightly downhill to attack the west wall of the castle. They went about one hundred feet where they had more ammunition set up and began to reload. Jon Colbert allowed his sons to think that he wasn't watching them, but he never took an eye off them as he orchestrated this beautiful destruction as well. The boys looked in awe of their father and the devastated castle wall. His sons had never seen this side of their father, although they knew it existed. They were accustomed to the father and statesman, but never the warrior. Jon seemed to wear that hat well, the boys seemed to note. There were ignited fragments of the castle that fell rapidly down the hill, stopping harmlessly short of the Riverfront men.

Once again the Duke of Mattingly roared, "ONE, TWO, THREE."

The west wall was instantly destroyed and no arrows were sprayed at them anymore. Jon Colbert only fired one more round. It was the seventh overall round and he thought this rebellion may be crushed. The Duke was impressed by how the siege weapons caused a great amount of damage with relative ease. He had many other weapons like these stashed away and even more being built. The Colbert men looked at the fire brander's castle as the wild, heliotrope flames roared like a lavender lion and smoke spilled from the smoldering embers. Black cloud-like puffs mushroomed up into the clear spring sky and blocked out the rising sun. Jon could smell burning stone and wood and human flesh. He didn't enjoy or relish causing misery to others and only used force as a final resort.

They moved the weapons faster and more efficiently than he could have envisioned. Only twenty minutes had passed and this uprising was already snuffed out.

"But father," said Ruxin, "Can't they escape from the other sides of the castle and regroup again for another rebellion?"

"We have men at the bottom of Locust Hill surrounding the entire castle," Jon assured his sons. "Every man sixteen or older will be put to the sword unless he surrenders. I feel sorry that Lord Fritz subjected his supporters to this death wish. We will take the prisoners to Mattingly with us. We'll divide the women throughout the region and find trades for the men."

Most dukes or lords only thought about winning. Jon Colbert knew exactly what to do after victory. He generally stayed at least one step ahead of his contemporaries.

Jon Colbert gazed with pride at his knights, several of whom were tending to matters near him. He felt that they were the best in the land. They were all battle tested, which was a prerequisite for a Mattingly knight. The same could not be said for knights in other regions. Most men achieved knighthood through merit, but the right social connections also helped some slip through the cracks. It was difficult to determine which region had the best knights because they never entered the same tourneys or skills competitions. Some older knights participated in Fox Chapel tourneys but that was over thirty years ago. Some younger knights served at war with each other, but that was about it. The land was divisive, with only Fox Chapel and Burkeville sharing combatants anymore. The Fox Chapel knights almost always got the better of Burkeville but every region claimed to harbor the cream of the crop.

He looked over his top knights who were gathered about twenty feet away. Thirty-eight year old Sir Herman Weiham talked to the older Sir Balthasar Strong and Sir Richard Rosebud, who also answered to the nickname Rick. The twenty-eight year old Sir Jeremiah Elmhurst and Sir Ryan Caughleigh, who was ten years his junior, listened intently. They were all of good stature with strong loyalty to him and that had helped Jon decide to let his older sons squire for Balthasar, Rick and Gunnar. Riceros squired for "The Wild Bull," whose absence was noticeable today. Sir Brehan Castaway almost always graced Duke Colbert's side.

Mattingly was the only region that knighted men who weren't born there. Several of his knights came from different areas of the world. Still looking at his fine crew, he noticed prisoners being led toward him in the background. Some were burned badly, bleeding or both. Jon wanted his sons to see the damage these actions had on real people to prepare them for the hard decisions that one day awaited them. Krys, the future Duke of Mattingly, would need all of his brothers to help him run Mattingly someday. Jon only had a younger, jealous brother to help him and two uncles who had assisted until he grew old enough to rule on his own.

They need to realize that actions can cause terrible reactions on friends and family. You can't bring a knife to a sword fight either, like Lord Fritz tried to do. That stubborn fool put his selfish, false ideals ahead of his family and I don't want my sons to make that fatal error.

The Colbert sons' attitudes perked up slightly as the female prisoners were being led by. Ruxin walked over to help a young lady with a bloody hand.

11

THE PROPOSAL—EDBURGH

ED WANDERED AROUND the city street on foot, under the cover of his hooded cloak. He was very cautious and aware because his brother Rollo told him, just days before he died, that you could never trust anyone in the Capitol. Edburgh had not been in Falconhurst for about ten years. His trip had taken him across Waters Edge, over Silver Cap Mountain and down the Royal River. He took the same path that his ancestors had when they saved Ali-Sander Wamhoff from sure defeat against Goldenfield.

The Etburn flag bearers had raced down to Riverfront to attack Goldenfield from behind, ultimately causing disarray. The Goldenfield soldiers retreated and ended up signing a peace treaty that more than doubled the size of Donegal. The Wamhoffs of Fox Chapel had claimed accolades for the victory, but the Etburns of Waters Edge still take credit for the win to this day.

A twelve-foot-high wall surrounded the ten-mile area around the King's Castle referred to as the Capitol. Technically, it could be called Falconhurst but that was also the name of the district. Edburgh made it through Prince Ali-Hershell's Gate and officially into the Capitol. This was not the entrance he had taken before. He roamed from one run-down, desolate area to the next. People were starving in the streets and begging for coin from Ed as he passed by. They pulled at his loose cloak as he walked to the stable the King had told him about. He could smell the building from down the street and even though his nose told him to run away, he gave the silver to the stable owner who rode with him. He guided the feisty mare toward the King's Castle and passed towns that were even more derelict than the ones before. Scantily clad whores offered their services by screaming to Ed as he galloped by, bobbing up and down on the horse. He made it to the drop-off stable and gave the horse back to the owner.

Now he walked into the middle of the Capitol. The wondrous landscape and structures he remembered seemed to have dwindled in quantity. The epic street shops were gone and the quality of merchandise had dropped dramatically.

It was a nice spring day, but the crisp air was marred by the smell of feces. Ed heard whispers on the way down that the King had stopped funding the maintenance of the sewage system and had given even more money to the Faith of Eternal Light. As a consequence, sewage had backed up and overflowed into the streets creating an invisible fog of disgusting smells across the city. Everything along the Royal Road, from small castles to houses, had appeared run down and even the market places weren't exempt from this problem.

However, all that changed when he approached the heart of Falconhurst. The first thing he noticed was the reason for the unkempt appearance of the outskirts of the Capitol. The Faith of Eternal Light church was immaculate. It was an imposing concrete building about ten years old. Fox Chapel had tried to build fourteen concrete structures before the Faith of Eternal Light. Every single one had collapsed, which led most people to believe that the Gods helped hold up this structure. A golden dome that vaulted above the main entrance amazed visitors. The building rested atop a wide, steep staircase made of marble. The four outer walls had a sky blue background with intermittent white patches to replicate clouds. In the forefront were gigantic paintings of the Gods floating in the heavens. They appeared to be as tall as ten mortal men combined and the intricate detail was amazing for the magnitude of these images.

The King had spared no expense or resource on the church. The building was a masterpiece of false prosperity. The parishioners paid in gold so they could have a man chosen by the Gods and Brothers tell them that everything was going to be alright when they died. In return, they got an immaculate church of fake worship to attract more money. The biggest church Edburgh could think of in Waters Edge held no more than one hundred people. The King had turned religion into a status symbol as well as a faith in the Gods.

Edburgh began to get a little nervous as he pulled his hood back to look around better. He wore none of his usual Etburn markings. The signature Etburn silver eagle was nowhere to be found on his outerwear. He couldn't think of the last time he'd gone out without the eagle on his chest or shoulder. But he couldn't afford to be spotted as an Etburn because the King had told him not to look like the son of a duke.

I better be right on this or it's my life. Maybe I shouldn't have killed her?

Now he knew he was getting close to the King's castle, as he could see the sculptures ahead on the side of the crooked cobblestone road. The Walk of Kings wound down a gold lined road. Life-sized statues made of bronze with impeccable detail featured every Wamhoff king from the first, Ali-Dus, to the most recently deceased, Ali-Baster. They were sculpted to exact height and likeness, right down to the last hair. Most held great swords, but there were a few that wielded scepters. He walked past four hundred years of kings who greeted him as the castle neared. Edburgh once foolishly wished to be king as a young boy, only to realize that the best he could achieve by law would be falconer.

Being alone was a contrast to what he had been accustomed to with Caroline. She was always right by his side and he knew she would have commented on how the statues gleamed in the sunlight. But now he traveled alone, all alone. He had left his family, whom he felt didn't really love him anyway. Now exacting revenge was of utmost importance. Edburgh had already covered a great distance just to arrive in the Capitol, but he still seemed far from being sure this plan would work. After five hundred feet of regal statues, the castle captured the horizon.

It was multilayered with towers that touched the sky and other parts that were only one or two stories high. The outside appeared to be made of huge, rectangular black and gray stones. Rushing water raced beneath the bridge ahead of him as the Royal River intersected the Royal Road on the way to the castle. Ed stopped for a moment as his heart raced. *He could be trying to lure me in to kill me because he doesn't like my father. No, my mother is his favorite sister. He was never much of an uncle though. He would never miss me. I never thought of that.*

Even though still unsure, he proceeded to the crossing on the path to the castle. The bridge had huge, square wooden posts supporting the frame that held the thick cedar planks, pressed flatly along the top of the bridge. At the end was the first set of guards.

They were an odd couple. A small red head with a smashed nose and dopey look sheathed a sword taller than him. The taller man had armor and donned a long sword. He wore the Wamhoff sigil on his surcoat. The two foxes protecting the royal crown had been the family symbol for four hundred years.

The tall guard pushed his long black hair away from his brown eyes and said, "No one gets past here without a passing paper."

Before he could finish, Ed produced the rolled up paper from inside his pocket. The large protector silently unrolled and read the permission slip while his little partner gave Edburgh dirty looks. He handed Ed the paper, stepped aside and nodded his head. With the creaky bridge now behind, the immense castle loomed ahead. A final little cobblestone path guided him straight up to the front gate. A giant silver fox sculpture stood three men high on its hind legs, ready to pounce on any intruders. The seven guards helped keep out unwanted people as well. Ed approached slowly, fumbling for the paper. He was still in awe of the magical sight even though he had seen it before.

The King's Castle rested just atop a slight hill to avoid flooding. Two kings had tried to relocate the Capitol from Lightview to different districts in Fox Chapel without success. Both castles had crumbled to the ground during construction. King Ali-Antone had a master builder named Ariss Hodell oversee the construction of this castle and the Capitol remained in Falconhurst ever since. The front entrance was a wide four story base with ten or twelve story extensions sprouting up in different extremities of the castle. Each corner on the roof and the tops of the towers housed a giant red fox. The walls were built of perfectly stacked rectangular stones that alternated between black and gray to set an ominous tone. A huge falcon was carved into the vast, black wood front entrance. After the guards inspected the paper, Ed could hear the convergence of straining ropes and chains lifting the door straight up. Edburgh strolled inside as the big door slammed down hard behind him. He shuffled up a set of stone stairs to finally penetrate the castle. He approached a guard with curly blond hair and a fancy looking face.

He went through the same proceedings for a fourth time.

"My name is Sir Penrose Ellsworth and the King has alerted me of your visit. I believe he is in the solar if you will just follow me," the knight welcomed.

They walked through a huge hallway that seemed to be a mile long. Posh decorations hung from the walls and elaborate carpets cushioned Ed's steps even as nervousness shot though his body. His pulse jumped as he neared either a pile of golden fox coins, or a fox trap. He wasn't very religious even though his father tried to force it upon him, so he didn't bother to pray internally.

Penrose broke the awkward silence as they approached a spiral stone staircase, "Where is it you come from?"

"Waters Edge," replied Ed listlessly, trying not to reveal anything. *You can never trust anyone in the Capitol.*

"That's a long, long way from Falconhurst. What brings you this far?" Penrose questioned. "Just have something to discuss with his highness," Ed stated shortly, trying to end the stilted conversation.

Luckily they arrived at what must have been the solar. "Wait here," Penrose told Ed as he disappeared behind the door.

Two men emerged but Ed still waited for several minutes. Then a young man with bright red hair and a red fox stitched across the front of his black leather vest came out and passed him. Ed assumed this to be Ali-Ster Wamhoff and bowed quickly saying, "My Prince." He had been to the castle a few times with his mother, Ali-Pari, but Ali-Ster was never there.

The red-headed man scurried off as if he hadn't heard Edburgh and then the door opened yet again.

This time Penrose invited him in. This was unlike any solar he had ever seen. Upon entering, he noticed that the sun beamed down through many different small openings in the ceiling, creating a series of speckled patterns all over the floor and tables. The room looked dark like it was early dusk, as only solar powered beams lit the room. There were several rectangular wooden tables. At the head of a six-foot table in the center of the room sat King Ali-Stanley Wamhoff. His golden crown hung down over his bushy eyebrows as if it was more of a burden than a reward. The crown had a wide, gold base that wrapped around his head with seven points extending up. Six of the points had giant mother of pearls as big as a baby's fist but the one above his forehead was a golden fox. The King with the crown of Donegal on his head looked anything but fierce.

Ali-Stanley spoke up in his screechy voice, "Welcome my nephew, welcome to Falconhurst again. It is a shame that we don't see each other more frequently. How were your travels?"

Edburgh ripped his hood back and bowed deeply to the King, then kneeled down on one knee. "My King, I am humbled you have accepted this meeting," a soft-spoken Ed uttered.

Even though the King was his uncle, Edburgh never had a one on one conversation with Ali-Stanley. He had heard a lot of bad things about the King from his father combatted by good words about Ali-Stanley from his mother.

The King turned to Penrose, "Please wait outside now." He waited for the knight to leave and continued, "I am sorry to hear about what happened to your bride, you wrote that they found the sick man who did it."

"Yes, your majesty, I found the peasant dock worker with a golden fox in his pocket and guilt on his hands. He admitted that a grander plan was in order and our enemy had put him up to it before he faced the king's justice." Ed's hands were clammy even though it was chilly in this so-called solar. Every solar he had ever seen had a huge opening to permit lots of light. He began to overheat. *Keep it together. You can do this.*

The King spoke solemnly, "Again I am sorry, I too have lost a wife to an early death so I know of the pain it causes. I believe your letter stated that you had inside information about a pressing matter."

Ed unknowingly shot an evil grin at the King and responded, "Yes, my King, it appears we have a common enemy who we may be able to help each other dispose of."

The King had a scowl on his face as Ed began to hash out the plan that made him even more nervous. *Keep calm, come on, you can pull this off.*

12
Transference—Leimur

LEIMUR MOVED DOWN the hall toward her father's drinking room. It had been four years since she'd walked through the royal palace. The King of Goldenfield enjoyed relaxing alone every day after supper in this room. At least he did when Leimur had lived there. She looked back and gave a nod as she entered.

A luxurious comfort room of gaudy couches and chairs greeted her. It also contained an elaborate bar with various wines and ales. The furniture was upholstered in a red velvet theme with gold accentuation, while a large dark blue carpet covered the floor.

She saw a fat, disgusting man sitting in a fancy crimson chair. The obese King, Pascal Leluc, was so drunk that he was almost passed out and his blue eyes were nearly shut. King Pascal was balding with islands of bushy black hair on the sides and back of his head. The fifty-one year old also had a full beard and mustache. He shared his darker complexion with Leimur.

"Wake up," shouted Leimur.

Her father jumped in his seat and groggily looked over at Leimur. "Not exactly what I was looking for, but alright," said the King. He lifted his robe, unknowingly exposing himself to his daughter.

"Never get caught with your pants down. Don't you even practice your own rules? You honestly have no idea who I am?" Leimur asked as she shook her head in disbelief. *It has only been four years, you nasty drunk.*

"I will not have some whore come in here and talk to a king like this," Pascal retorted. "I am not a whore. I am your daughter," she screamed back. Pascal slowly rose and squinted to focus his bleary eyes on Leimur. "What in the hells do you want?"

"It is good to see you too, father…"

"Forget that," he interrupted, trying unsuccessfully not to slur his words, "you were never supposed to return here after what you did." "Well, if you would respond to your eastern army correspondence, I wouldn't have to do this. And that pile of horseshit got what he deserved," she quickly responded. "That PILE was the son of the wealthiest lord in Goldenfield, and you killed him in this palace," the King bellowed at his daughter.

"He raped me," she shrieked. "Ha, a husband cannot rape his wife. She is his for the taking whenever he wishes," the King returned. "He told me he would wait until I was ready, but then he had sex with me while I slept. That is rape, father," she said emotionally.

He shouted, "Don't call me that. In fact leave here right now." "Absolutely not, I am home to stay," Leimur said as she approached her father. "Don't make me call for my guards," he threatened. "Oh, but don't you see, that would be failure number two," she smartly pronounced. "Failure number two? What do you mean?" a leery King queried. "Allow me to remind you of the first failure. It was three years ago when you told General Rigby to force your seventeen-year-old daughter into the fiercest part of the battle, and leave her to die."

"Well, it appears that the General is lying to you," King Pascal responded quickly and nervously. "You will like to know he did take your order. He fed me to the fire but I wouldn't burn. The flames enriched me from within and only fueled me to become stronger. Like a tiger," Leimur said almost in tears.

"Enough of this already, I will not be called a liar in my own palace. Either you leave this instant or I will call for my guards. I brought you into this world, and I will take you out if you force my hand," the King declared with confidence. "Please do, my King, it would be my pleasure," the Princess proudly retorted with a mocking curtsy. "Henri, come in here at once. We have a situation," the King yelled.

The door slammed open and a man's head rolled in and came to a stop in the center of the room. "Well, there is Henri. Would you like any of your other guards to help you? We have them all. And here is failure number two. I am absolutely positive that you would be surprised to know a small disturbance can draw most of your guards outside the palace for easy pickings. Pathetically, you never realized Sevring was so ripe for sack."

Fear flashed across Pascal Leluc's face much to the delight of his daughter as she continued, "All we needed was one of the six protector cities to join our cause. So when two came rushing, begging to join my side, I knew what must be done," she said, smiling to expose her tiger-like teeth.

The King turned and ran as the Warrior Princess pounced on his back. She quickly removed a dagger from her belt and drove it into the side of the King's neck with a downward motion toward his chest. It had about a twelve inch blade that was made of amethyst. King Pascal had given it to his daughter as a gift but it was more of a decoration than a useful knife. Over the years the Princess had transformed it from a ceremonial item into a real killing weapon. It had a dark purple grip that matched her eyes and a gold pommel and cross-guard.

He fell on his stomach struggling to remove the dagger from his neck, but he only succeeded in flopping around like a fish on land. She held the blade for several moments, taking pleasure in her father's frantic pleas for mercy. She almost expected red wine to pour from the wound, but human blood actually spurted from the dying King's wound when she pulled the dagger out. He fell flat on his regal face and two more quick jabs to the back of the neck ended the reign of King Pascal Leluc of Goldenfield. His twenty two year rule slid away, mirroring the moving stream of blood on the floor. Leimur stared at her deceased father for several moments before leaving the room. General Rigby was waiting outside.

"Where is she?"

"She is right down the hallway here. We didn't want to, uh, disturb her," General Rigby stated. "Are my brothers safe?" she asked with concern. "Yes, they are safe with us," he reassured Leimur.

They came upon what used to be a guest room. Leimur heard sounds of passion through the thick walls.

No shame. This is how she did not hear the takeover of her own palace.

Leimur booted the wooden door open, rattling the couple in bed.

"Get out before I have you thrown into the dungeons," her mother exclaimed in a raspy, dry voice.

"The dungeons, that is a good idea..."

Before she could finish, her mother jumped out of bed, completely nude, and rushed Leimur. The Princess responded with a closed right fist to the side of her mother's cheek, knocking the Queen onto her ass.

"GUARDS," howled the Queen. "Don't waste your precious breath mother, you haven't much left, and besides they are all dead."

The Queen peered at her in the sparsely lit room, realizing that it was the daughter she had always hated. Leimur looked at the man in the bed only to see it was her uncle Marcel. A brother of her father's, but that didn't make this situation any better.

"Uncle Marcel, your Queen seems to think that you should spend some time in the dungeon to ponder what you have done." She looked at the open door. "Sir Pierre and Captain Salina, please come in here. Take this man to the dungeons."

Just as commanded, the pair entered the room and wrestled a reluctant Marcel Leluc into submission. They bound his arms and dragged him from the room, naked and unwilling.

"Be careful uncle, I hope the rats aren't hungry tonight," Leimur snidely remarked as her uncle left.

The Princess glanced covertly at her mother and saw the horrified look on her face. The Queen of Goldenfield realized her time was up and started to get desperate.

"What did I ever do to you, my child?"

"You must have a worse memory than your drunken husband. Well, not any longer, I suppose. Don't try to pretend that you didn't ignore me from birth until sending me off to die. You hated me because I wasn't the girly princess you expected me to be. But this is more about what you two did to the realm, driving it into the ground." Leimur moved closer to stand over her mother.

Queen Harla Leluc was a short, bronze skinned woman of thirty-nine. Her brown eyes were now reddened from impending tears. Her black hair looked disheveled and she was overweight, but not as much as her husband. She stared at the daughter who had caused the immense pain to her jaw.

"And what are we to do with you?" Leimur asked. "I don't know exactly what you have done. But you will need strong counsel to rule a realm," the Queen reminded her. "So right you are again. You are wise. I shall heed that advice. General Rigby, come in here please," she commanded.

The haggard General stepped into the room. The Queen didn't even attempt to cover herself.

"General, what should we do with our Queen of Goldenfield?" Leimur wondered. "What are her charges?" calmly asked Rigby. "She is charged with treason, and with putting everyone in Goldenfield in danger of their lives through a rule of ignorance and overindulgence," Leimur clarified. "Why not let the people decide her fate? If she has served them well, they will come to her aid," the General counseled.

"Great advice. Thank you for your recommendation about counsel, my Queen," Leimur sarcastically stated. "Tie her hands behind her back and take her to the front steps."

"Can I at least put on clothes and have some dignity?" her mother begged. "You have already shown your dignity in this room. You are lucky I don't parade you around the city so you may be stoned and beaten with sticks. Father didn't even teach you not to get caught with your pants down. Nothing shall conceal your treason against Goldenfield," Leimur said, raising her voice.

She rushed downstairs to be greeted by hundreds of supporters gathered inside the palace doors. Leimur had brought some from the eastern front and picked up others along the way.

This is amazing. General Rigby could have done this a long time ago if he wanted to. Why didn't he?

They pushed open the ten-foot high doors to expose Leimur. She walked up to the front entrance a princess, and moved outside to her throngs of citizens as their Queen.

A crowd of thousands flooded the city and erupted in elation when Leimur walked out to the top of the marble steps. The rich intermingled with the poor in an extremely rare show of kingdom unity. Goldenfield had been plagued with lots of infighting due to taxes being too high and unreasonable. General Rigby handed the golden crown of the land to Leimur. She held it high in the air as the crowds exploded again. It was too big to fit her head so she just held it in her hand as she orated over the audience.

"My people, the tyranny is over. All citizens of Goldenfield, we must work together to return this realm to greatness..."

Before she could finish, the mob cheered again.

When they calmed down, the new Queen continued, "We have our first decision to make as a new Goldenfield is born. Your former Queen, Harla Leluc has been charged with treason against Goldenfield."

Queen Harla was pushed out to the delight of the jubilant people.

Leimur went on, "We will either put her to death or exile her to another land to live out her days. All in favor of the Queen being exiled speak up now."

A hush fell over the boisterous citizens with no one rising up in the Queen's defense. The crowd remained silent for a few moments and then broke out into pandemonium. She stood disgraced, with people shouting about her fat body, along with any other insult that could be articulated. "Gluttonous whore" seemed to be the phrase most often used.

"Now, all in favor of death..."

Before she could complete the words, the Goldenfield crowd went crazy, clapping, stomping and screaming. The Queen was led over to the chopping block reserved for the king's justice and placed over it. The stinging embarrassment made the Queen welcome a quick death. The headsman drew a mighty sword and held it in the air to the delight of the crowd. Leimur stepped in to stop the man wearing a black mask. She couldn't let him do it.

"I will carry out the people's wish myself," Leimur stated. The people worked themselves into a thunderous frenzy and Leimur fed off their energy.

Dusk started easing in as the purple and blue skyline was being flushed away, like the rule of overt excess at its worst. Leimur pulled her sword and got swept up in the chaotic wailing coming from her people. She understood the pent-up aggression from decades of abuse. Leimur felt like a liberator, walking on air as she approached the former Queen.

"You have been found guilty of treason against Goldenfield. Your people have spoken and now you shall pay with your life," she confidently proclaimed.

The sword gleamed in the last rays of the setting sun. Leimur took a deep breath. She raised the sharp steel above her head and brought it straight down, cleanly taking off her mother's head. Power effectively transferred from the old Queen to the new one with just a single swing of the sword. The moment was surreal for Leimur. She stood, shaking, and looked at her diverse citizens. She thought that her heart might explode from her chest. Everything slowed down for Leimur and her ears fell silent for a moment, but then the roaring returned.

"Put it on a spike," urged the townspeople. More raunchy remarks rose from the faithful citizens. "Where is the King? We want his head on a spike too."

The Leluc family had ruled Goldenfield for the past two hundred and eighty years. While there had been some violent power struggles throughout the years, nothing rivaled this hostile takeover. Leimur Leluc always thought power was best earned. In her mind, she'd just earned it. A broken, wayward Princess had left the Capitol four years ago in disgrace to be sacrificed. But she had now returned, hero to most, Queen Leimur to all.

The people of Goldenfield now started to speak as one. Leimur couldn't make out the message at first, but it grew louder and stronger.

They were chanting, "TWO HEADS, TWO SPIKES. TWO HEADS, TWO SPIKES."

Queen Leimur Leluc turned to General Rigby, "Bring me my father's head. I must give my people what they want."

Death is part of life.

13
A CHANCE ENCOUNTER—RUSSELL

THE FROZEN FOREST generally caused more problems than it provided answers to life's quandaries. As a result, solutions didn't rush into the frosty head of Russell Seabrook. He only knew he was slightly hungry. The trees and bushes were completely covered in ice, which hid their once brilliant colors. The ground was thick permafrost that proved difficult to navigate. An occasional howl of the wind was the only sound to be heard in the deathly silence since animals didn't even go into the Frozen Forest. There was nothing to eat for the animals. Legend said that snow bears hibernated in the Forest, but Russell had never seen one.

The Frozen Forest only thawed for about one month during the height of the summer harvest season. It caused high tides in Donegal when it melted every year. But by and large, it was a frigid, unforgiving, cold-hearted place. Ali-Pari begged him not to go, but Russell felt a strange need to get away. He did not mind being alone and the cold never really bothered him, so it was a natural choice. Russell slipped on the slick surface and fell on his back. After gathering himself, he rolled over onto his stomach to push himself up with his hands.

"OH SHITE," screamed Russell as he quickly backed away.

Russell saw an old, dead man buried beneath the ice. He crept back for a second look. He looked again to see a very ugly, wart-covered small man. The dwarf had long white hair and lay there nude, but appeared as peaceful as could be under the freeze. Russell tapped the ice over the face of the dead man, first softly, then harder. When he finally stopped, the man's eyes suddenly fluttered open and Russell quickly sprang to his feet and backed away. The knight turned to leave when he heard water splashing. A quick glance behind him showed the ancient-looking dwarf sitting in a puddle of water and rubbing his eyes. Russell started to run away.

"Stop. Wait. I am not going to hurt you. Look at me."

Sir Russell Seabrook stopped for a moment. He always ran from his problems. Fear had won his internal battles in the past, but he decided that must end. Russell spun around to look at the little man.

"Don't be afraid," said the shivering man. "What in the hells are you?" Russell asked. The little man smiled, "You should curse less and think more. I am but a man, same as you."

The small guy stood only a little more than half of Russell's height and he slumped over as if his years on earth were pounding him into the ground. He was a hairy creature with gray fur covering most of his calloused body. Then Russell made eye contact. *The fire's in his eyes.*

"My name is Sir Russell Seabrook. What is yours, my friend?" The still sleepy man yawned and said in a slow drawl, "I am known by many names in many languages, my very young knight. I suppose Dragon-Eyes or Imp Wizard are the ones people always tend to recognize." Russell got excited, "I thought so, but I always thought the stories about you were made up. I didn't know you really existed. How old are you anyway?"

"Well, let's see, who is king right now?" Russell quickly answered, "King Ali-Stanley Wamhoff." "Oh, he still is, the old fox. And how old is our great King?" the elder man asked trying to shake the effects of hibernation from his body.

Ali-Pari is seventy, so he is five years younger.

"He is sixty-five years old," Russell quickly told him. The Imp Wizard thought for a moment, "Alright, four, five, six, carry the two and it looks like four hundred and sixty-seven years on earth. Well, including some spent underneath as you just saw." "What? No, you can't possibly be that old. Nobody can be that old," an awestruck Russell awkwardly rebutted. "You wouldn't happen to have any food in those bags, would you?" smiled Dragon-Eyes. "Of course I do," said Russell as he opened the leather sack, exposing the contents.

"What would you like, Dragon-Eyes?"

Russell had a veritable smorgasbord to offer. He had salted beef jerky, pickled pork, dried sausages and different types of fruit. There were spring apples, plums and water chestnuts. Russell also had a half loaf of stale bread at the bottom of the bag.

The old dwarf's eyes lit up and his mouth began to water as he feebly asked a question, "So you would help an old, decrepit, poor excuse for a man and give me some of your precious food?"

"Of course I would," responded Russell without hesitation. "You are but a man, same as me, just slightly smaller," said Russell with a smile. Dragon-Eyes smiled back at Sir Russell, "My boy, how would you like to go on a great adventure with a wise old soul who can show you amazing things?"

They both ate while the conversation continued. Russell wasn't sure how to put this, "It sounds like a great offer, really, but you aren't exactly fleet of foot, I am sorry to say." The Imp Wizard stared at Russell with his fiery eyes. "What if I told you that within an hour's time I can fade back to forty-six and a half years of age? Well, a touch more actually, but what say you now?" Russell smiled at the weary old man, "I would say you have about an hour." "Off we are now," said Dragon-Eyes as he slowly led the way even though Russell knew he was trying to move fast.

It wasn't as cold as Russell expected so he threw his extra fur cloak to the old man.

"No thank you, my boy. It will only slow me down and might make me fall back into a slumber," he said even as he shivered.

Russell took it back and stuffed it into his bag. Luckily, it wasn't snowing right now, but that could change at any moment. The saltwater spray storm from Typhoon Alley turned to ice as it crossed the Frozen Forest, producing treacherous conditions. He had been caught in a few storms out here that threatened to steal his life. The Imp Wizard led him into an area that was foreign to Russell.

On looking at the sun, he figured it had been about an hour, when the wizard proudly stated, "There it is, my friend."

The old Imp breathed heavily but still wore a big grin. They appeared to be in an odd sort of clearing. There were seven rolling glaciers surrounding the pair, meeting in the middle where the two men stood. They were steep, vertical waterfalls, bitten by frost.

The Imp Wizard walked slowly in a circle in front of the frozen springs, staring deeply at each one. After the seventh round, he waddled up to one of the glaciers. With a flash, fire shot out of both of the wizard's eyes, melting the solid ice. The flames retracted and the Imp approached the running waterfall. He disappeared under the water for quite a long time, prompting Russell to get closer and closer to the falling water. He still couldn't see the little guy even when he got about five feet from the rushing water. He turned around to see if this was some wizard's trick, but no one was to be seen anywhere. He turned back toward the waterfall and there was still no sign of the little man. He looked straight down and into the eyes of fire. Russell stumbled backwards, shocked at the stunning sight before him.

The Imp Wizard had told the truth. He looked infinitely younger and like someone who could lead him on a great adventure. Although still very ugly, his gray hair had turned light brown, and his skin wasn't sagging anymore. The new man had muscle tone and the warts were gone. It seemed like the heated waters had washed away the years right before his very eyes, a youthful fountain of sorts.

"So, my hour to prove myself appears to be up," Dragon-Eyes stated in a much deeper, manlier tone than before. Russell just gazed at him with a goofy look, "Should I even ask how that happened?" The Imp returned the grin and shook his head, "Not quite yet, my boy."

"We need to get you some clothes, but in the meanwhile, here." Russell tossed the dwarf the spare cloak again and this time he humbly accepted. "I have some belongings in the Forest. If we could pick them up before we embark on our journey, I would thank you," the Imp Wizard said. "Well, first I need to know what kind of journey you are talking about," Russell said carefully.

He had heard stories of wizards who used tricks to get people to carry out their wishes. "Let me ask you a question first. Do you believe in dragons?"

Russell Seabrook responded without hesitation, "No." Dragon-Eyes peered at him for a moment before he asked, "Why?" "Well, I have heard stories of them. I've seen drawings and paintings of them. Yet no one I know or know of has ever seen one in the flesh," Russell firmly stated. "Aahh," the wizard contemplated for a second, "Until a brief while ago you never saw fire surge from a mortal man's eyes, did you?" "Well, uh, uh, uh, no," stuttered a puzzled knight.

"What if I say I can show you proof that dragons exist?" offered the Imp. "You can show me a live dragon?" asked Russell sarcastically. The Imp sternly retorted, "I can show you proof that dragons exist, yes. And it coincidentally happens to be where my things are stored as well."

Sir Russell Seabrook carried two bags over each shoulder as he followed the little guy. The wizard struggled to keep the cloak from dragging on the ice. He didn't look like a wizard with an almost square head and flat nose, but his long hair and fiery eyes were proof enough for Russell. A light horizontal snow started. Russell pulled his hood up and asked, "So what is our grand adventure? You distracted me with that talk of dragons." The Imp stopped in his tracks, looked up into Russell's eyes, and mysteriously asked, "My young knight, have you ever heard of the Pearl of Wisdom?"

14

ELISA

ELISA STARED AT the lemon honey tarts and glazed apple buns that had arrived from Lightview just before first light. She wasn't interested in the rashers of bacon, uncased sausage patties, eggs poached in vinegar water or the exotic fruits from around the world. She preferred sweets to start her days. Elisa and Telly, who looked like a shorter, younger version of her older sister, minded their manners. However, her two- and four-year-old brothers, Astrid and Butrel, could no longer be held back by Count Bidwell's constant verbal warnings. The Grizzly Bear, a huge, disgusting, odorous, murderous, hirsute ogre who served her family, leaned on the end of the table. He had earned his nickname from his long hair and beard that covered most of his face. Elisa didn't even remember his real name but she had seen him knighted by her father as a child. Her mother, Ali-Tiste Wamhoff Burke, pulled her husband across the reaches of the Princess Hall. Tradition called for the bride and grooms to dine separately on the morning of a royal wedding day.

The retinue from Burkeville filled most of the tables across the hall to give the ruling family some privacy. Elisa looked at the black bear flags and pennants around the hall and wished to be back at home. She would be marrying today, and that was the most dreadful aspect of the celebration.

Her mother gently lowered the muttering Duke Aston Burke onto the bench. The Duke tried to lie down and go to sleep again. Ali-Tiste shook the father of the bride until he slapped her hands away and when the well-dressed lady persisted; Aston kicked her in the stomach and knocked her to the ground. Count Bidwell, Elisa and Telly rushed over to help the Duchess. *The King cannot call himself a man if he lets his own daughter be humiliated in his own castle. My grandfather is no real man.*

The Duke finally sat up, bleary eyed and confused. He reeked like a stale cocktail of wine soaked misery, ale and spiced spirits. The still-drunk Aston Burke wore the same wrinkled gear as the previous night but his silk cloak was missing. His heavy odor quickly killed the pleasant smells of the Burke ladies' perfumes and fast breaking foods.

"Sooo, how excited are you?" Ali-Tiste directed her question to Elisa in an upbeat tone. She gave her mother a dead stare, void of emotion and responded, "I am marrying my uncle who can't even control his bodily functions. Is this a question you really want me to answer right now?"

"Ladies and princesses have married their uncles throughout the history of Donegal and it still remains legal. Stop with all of this, for once. We're not marrying you to your brother, heavens sakes. Now if you prefer to be like that, perhaps I should ask again when you are queen," Ali-Tiste said. Brother and sister unions were also legal although severely looked down upon by society, much more so than an uncle and niece.

Elisa looked at her mother, knowing she was behind the whole marriage arrangement, and said, "If that time should ever come to pass, you are more than welcome to ask how excited I am at that time and that time only." She looked away. Elisa had never gotten on with her mother. She thought Ali-Tiste defended Aston too much and a false sense of love kept her mother from telling her King father about the abuse.

Aston Burke grunted and said, "Keep it down before I have to shut some mouths." He filled his plate with sausage, bacon, eggs and a handful of apple buns before sliding to the other side of the long rectangular table, spilling a filled chalice of wine all the way. *Glad to see you are excited for my wedding day. You might be dead if you didn't have me to throw at the King and still you treat me like a dirty waste bucket. You'd better hope I never take rule as Queen of Donegal. Men like you will be the first to be severely punished. Women will no longer have to live in fear.*

After breaking her fast, she walked around the inner-bailey with Telly. Her sister was only a few years younger than Elisa. "I think you might be the lucky one, going back to Arigold and out of this mess. I'm not so sure about this place," Elisa said. Telly shrugged her shoulders and replied, "Looks better than father smacking us around for no reason."

"It breaks my heart more than anything that you won't be staying with me. I know I could take better care of you than him," Elisa told her. "I heard Lord Eller say father sold you to the King. Who do you think they are going to sell me to?" Telly wanted to know. Elisa tried to avoid the question but finally answered, "I don't know. If it were up to me, you would choose your own husband, out of love. However, I don't have that power yet," she dejectedly stated. Telly shot her a wide smile with white teeth, exposing her youth, and asked, "Did you bring your sword to punish all wrongdoers when you take power soon?"

A horrified look came over Elisa's face as she spotted two whispering ladies across the yard. She pulled Telly in and looked into her eyes and whispered, "Lower your voice when you say things like that. The King is healthy and strong. I won't take power for a great long time." They continued walking and talking much lower. Elisa wasn't sure whom to trust and only knew that spies lurked everywhere. She said, "Father's goon searched my trunks and found the sword. He gave it to father and father had Sir Brentley hit me with the flat of my own sword on the chest so the bruises wouldn't show. Luckily everything has healed or I would have some explaining to do because my attire for the feast would have exposed heavy bruising. No matter, I belong to the Wamhoffs now. Oh Gods, I don't know which is worse!" Elisa laughed halfheartedly. Telly answered without hesitation, "Living with father is worse than anything in the world. Why hasn't mother ever put a stop to that monster?"

Elisa waited a moment and said, "Her choices are limited. If she tells the King and he doesn't do anything it will just become worse. I want to believe she's tried to stop father. When you hear all the stories of King Ali-Stanley killing people for basically nothing, I would expect action against the man who beats your daughter and granddaughters."

"Count Bidwell tried to say that some men don't see a problem with using force to keep their lady in line. Maybe our grandfather thinks like that," Telly mentioned. "That's a great shame that I clearly need to rectify. If only I had my sword," Elisa said and the two girls giggled.

Telly tried to keep up the positivity and said in an annoyed but playful manner, "At least you won't have to smell the Grizzly Bear reeking like death and hovering around the dining table, killing everyone's appetites."

The conversation came to a sudden halt as both girls stopped to stare at the dashing Prince Ali-Ster as he passed. He walked tall and straight with a healthy head of flaming hair. The Prince was strong and handsome, yet fearsome, all the same while being chivalrous. He was considered the perfect Prince. Unfortunately, Elisa was set to marry the other Prince of Donegal. Her direct uncle. This aspect was the most infuriating to Elisa. Interfamily marriages still existed but were extremely rare. Elisa promised herself she would never let her future husband lay a finger on her but the entire situation still irked her. Even if Ali-Varis had only been her half-uncle like Ali-Ster, the situation would have been much more palatable for Elisa and extremely acceptable in Donegal.

It had taken all morning for fourteen maidens to help her get ready as the head seamstress yelled instructions to the girls. Only the hands of virgins were allowed to touch the wedding dress after completion. After the girls were finished primping the bride, she was led to the Chapel.

Elisa tried to mentally block out the entire ceremony and simply go through the rehearsed motions. The plan worked and before too long, seven girls whisked her away to a vanity room to get changed for the reception. The only part of the religious ceremony she remembered was her father forcefully flinging her to the foxes after rapidly pulling her down the long aisle in the Castle Chapel. She also recalled Ali-Varis' inability to repeat the vows back to the High Priest and wondered if the marriage was official as the maidens removed layer after layer of virginal white material from the bride. Elisa became lost in the innocent fabric shades of dove silk, argent crushed velvet, snowflake samite, cream lace and ivory linen underskirts. She smiled as she finally shed the bell skirt, high neck bodice and heavy ermine lined tippets. She almost forgot about the seven-foot train that required seven virgins to carry. They finally took away the veil which was Elisa's least favorite part of the whole get up. She became excited about her dress for the feast because she thought it looked better than this one and would be much more comfortable than the wired underskirt and bone-supported corset she had just taken off.

Only a few underclothes remained as Elisa sent the girls away. She waited in the small powder room and wished for a miracle. She heard a rustling sound in the corner, behind a purple changing screen.

A few moments later, her waiting lover was positioned behind her as she leaned over a pearl-studded chair, tensely gripping the cushioned arm. After several minutes of love-filled passion, she felt a mixture of hot liquid love run down the inside of her thigh and leak into the garter belt. She would need to hide the smell of sex emanating from the lacy undergarment with some perfume before the tossing ceremony at the feast, but that seemed leagues from her mind at this point. Today marked Elisa Burke Wamhoff's wedding and she was being pleasured by the man she loved. The sex felt hotter than usual due to the extreme sin involved, she had convinced herself. Brehan Castaway always made her feel safe in his presence. He knew exactly how to treat a lady, and by all physical standards he was desirable. Everything about Brehan's appearance seemed perfect for Elisa except for his birth station. If only he carried a last name of faint nobility, it could be their wedding day. Instead, it was only her wedding day. Brehan kept driving the new bride wild in ecstasy. *My first, my last, forever my only.*

Elisa Burke, a gorgeous woman of eighteen, had arrived in the Capitol only a few weeks ago. She was blessed with considerable height and a paleness that gave her a virginal glow. Her rosy full lips, high cheekbones, brown eyes and long, oak colored hair were Burke family traits. Her soft locks had been brushed this morn with one thousand and seven strokes by her new handmaiden, a tradition for the bride on her wedding day.

Her mind drifted as the steamy sex continued. *That bespawler took me for his wife and swore to protect me in the presence of the Gods, slobbering and spitting everywhere as he struggled to remember the vows. He can barely walk through a room without assistance, for the Gods' sake. Ali-Varis Wamhoff, give me sons, hah, that is pure folly for everyone but me.* She snarled audibly.

"Alright, my love?" grunted Brehan. "Just fine. Don't stop, don't even think about stopping," Elisa seductively pronounced.

Most women would have returned to their own wedding party or at least looked back to make sure the lock-latch on the door was still secure, but Elisa Burke Wamhoff, who was terribly ambitious, wanted everything and more.

If father elects to marry me to a mental cripple, I shall at least enjoy a small piece of my day of dutiful matrimony. Brehan could carve him up like a pig. She giggled internally, picturing an apple in Ali-Varis Wamhoff's mouth as he turned on a spit.

Aston Burke, the Duke of Burkeville, had delivered his daughter to the King like a hurried sack of market goods. The Burkes were one of the founding families and had ruled over Burkeville since the creation of Donegal. However, a recent succession of awful dukes had taken a once proud region and reduced it to the role of street beggar. The King desperately needed a bride from a family of high status for his son, Ali-Varis, so that he would stop pestering him. The royal family had claimed that his last bride had died in her sleep, but it was widely speculated that the rotund Ali-Varis had smothered her when he rolled over in his sleep. Duke Burke offered up his daughter at once, despite all her objections.

A daughter born to Donegal had no legal say to whom she was betrothed. It was the father's prerogative. Political and monetary alliances dominated matrimonial decisions as true love was tragically stabbed in the back throughout the social landscape. Occasionally, people married for love at the risk of being ousted by their family. Love developed for some matches, but Elisa Burke knew she would never love Ali-Varis Wamhoff.

Elisa had enjoyed the royal treatment since arriving in Falconhurst but wondered how long it would last. She wasn't actually a princess, more like a queen in waiting but nobody would obey King Ali-Varis' commands. Elisa felt that she was being held as a prisoner for the King to keep her father in his place as Duke of Burkeville. From the way her father had been talking lately, she realized the growing tension between her father and the King. Now Aston Burke had literally thrown her into the den of foxes. Elisa wore the black bear pin of Burkeville on her dress with pride, but she realized that only the Queen and a few other Burkes that lived in the Capitol could be trusted. The ravenous Wamhoff foxes lurked everywhere. And in the few places where they didn't, their plentiful spies did.

The silver lining in this torture was that she would one day rule as Queen Elisa. Nobody in any power positions would let Ali-Varis make crucial decisions unless they wished to perish. The King looked like he was soon to die in her estimation and Elisa had a plan for Ali-Ster too. She set out to make the best of this situation. Elisa understood she would see Sir Brehan much less now that she had stationed herself in the Capitol, but she hoped that it only created a temporary inconvenience.

She intended to remedy the situation the moment she took control of the realm.

And even though she hated her match with Ali-Varis, he remained her key to the throne. Ali-Ster was fitter to be king, but luckily for her, Donegal had ruled as a land of primogeniture. The same laws of the land that took personal dignity from her today might also give it back later in spades.

Her skin sizzled like hot dragon's breath and pleasure filled tingles flowed freely throughout her entire body as she climaxed. Elisa's soul was satisfied as she collapsed into the plush, purple chair. The two lovers stared intently at each other, breathing heavily, permanent smiles attached.

"I suppose you will need to get back to your reception?" Brehan asked. "*I suppose*, although I wish I could ride off with you and we could finally be together. Now, I know we can't do that, so I will settle for you to help me get dressed again," she replied as she stood up and kissed him. Elisa knew that Brehan was the man for her. He had amazed her by sneaking into her powder room before she arrived. *How did he get past all the guards and know which room was set up for me?*

15

BREHAN

BREHAN STOOD BEHIND the bride and firmly tied her corset. He then helped the bride into the most exquisite outfit suited for a queen. He helped straighten out a form-fitting long sleeved, crushed velvet gown of brilliant vermilion belted just below her breasts by intertwined golden thread, twisted thicker than a hanging robe. The plunging V neckline was aided by the Empire waistline to show off Elisa's ample bosom gently sprinkled with gold dust. Puffs of golden lace poked out of slashes on her shoulders and cuffs. Her natural rosy cheeks flirted with the mixture of gold, silver and ruby dust under her eyes that made her look more beautiful than Brehan could ever remember. He gently placed a hairnet over her flowing locks. The Master of Goldsmith's gift to the bride was a marvel of craftsmanship, tangled strands of filigree that resembled a perfect web spun by a golden spider. The net was accented with a small red ruby in the middle of the web, standing on top of Elisa's head.

Brehan stared at his lady love and saw only one thing that marred the glamor of his angel. A golden fox pin went from the end table into Elisa's hand and finally affixed to her gown, over her heart. She was a Wamhoff now. Until seeing the symbol on her chest, Brehan's denial convinced him to believe this would never actually happen. He lowered his head and looked down, immediately noticing Elisa's embroidered fabric shoes. Tied with lacy draw strings of silver around the ankles and adorned with precious gemstones, they accentuated the bride's petite feet. The glowing gems only dulled his spirits as he realized that as a foreign bastard, he could never provide Elisa with half these comforts no matter how hard he tried in life. Even as a knight, he didn't have a true house to back him. The Colbert's loved him and treated him like family, but he would never be a trueborn Colbert.

Sir Brehan Castaway searched the small room for his apparel. "I wish you could come with me too. You know Mattingly is a safe haven for many people," he said to Elisa Burke with a clever smile. "Don't tempt me," she returned, "I am in too deep now, but we are meant for each other. I know I married another man today, but it was only out of a sense of duty. You saw me today at my wedding reception. Just the fact that we could be together, today of all days, convinces me that you are the only man for me." *My first, my last, forever my only.*

"Let's just hope I can make it out of this castle alive," Brehan said in a sober tone. "Don't ever say that. You die, my heart dies, and a person without a heart is already dead." Elisa grabbed both of his cheeks and kissed him deeply. "Did you find all your things?" she asked. "Almost," he said and looked for his hat.

Sir Brehan Castaway was a knight of Mattingly. The twenty-two-year-old of average height stood just slightly taller than Elisa. The polished warrior had a body sculpted by the Gods themselves. Muscle definition dripped from head to toe. Green eyes and black shaggy hair provided the perfect foil for his dark brown skin. He had turned down advances from several girls over the years due to his allegiance to Elisa. Brehan Castaway was born on the Seventh Island of the Pearl Islands. One large, main island had eight smaller ones surrounding it. Castaway was a bastard's name but he wore it with pride. Brehan's father had left before his birth and his poor mother worked at the docks but could barely support him. When the wealthy Burke family had passed through, she begged them to take Brehan to work in the castle and live a better life. He served the Burke family diligently for many years. It was a long enough time to know that he loved Elisa, but he also realized he would never achieve a higher status than servant in Burkeville.

He had traveled to a place where merit was accorded precedence over birth status. He sneaked into Mattingly to enter a skills tournament. Brehan, already muscular at thirteen and armed with a fake name, fooled the Mattingly men into thinking that he was older, and they allowed him to enter. He had impressed Duke Colbert to the extent that he invited Brehan to train in Riverfront to become a knight. He lived in nice quarters in the Colbert castle and they immediately treated him like a family member. Brehan achieved knighthood at an extremely young age and took an oath to protect the Colberts, but he was also a son and brother of the family.

Part of Brehan wished he had just put a baby into the woman he loved, but the rest of him wanted to be with her to raise the child. Today, he had dressed himself in the fancy garb of a performer to pass unnoticed on the way out of the castle. A long sleeved undershirt clung to his heaving chest and was tucked into black cuffed, oversized performer breeches pinstriped in gold. Over the shirt, he wore a loud pumpkin colored button-down jacket that diagonally tapered out around the crotch to expose his legs and stopped at his calves. Secured by big black buttons shaped into squares, the jacket looked silly on a knight. He tightened the black belt, slid the two daggers into their scabbards on both sides and hid them with the jacket. Brehan slid on a velvet green hat with a long tip and a jester's bell hanging from the end.

He smiled at Elisa, knowing how ridiculous he looked compared to his angel. They held each other in the middle of the room as Elisa playfully smacked Brehan's hip with her open palm.

He said, "Remember the night I had to tell you I was leaving for Mattingly and you said that you cried all night long." "Yes. I was such a little girl," Elisa quickly answered. "I guess tonight is my turn," said Brehan with a slight smile. "Don't make me cry. I know you're only jesting, but I am emotional right now. I have to go out there and pretend I'm happy to be married to Ali-Varis Wamhoff," Elisa sobbed. Brehan used his thumb to stop her tears from smearing her makeup until Elisa collected herself.

He pulled some shaggy hair from under his hat and pushed it down over his eyes. He grabbed an empty chalice, made of onyx, with seven sections of ground jewels, each containing a different semi-precious gemstone as a keepsake from the makeup table and kicked the lilac chair aside. This exposed a secret door on the floor and Brehan flipped it open. He rose, smiling at Elisa. They embraced one last time.

"Well, this is it. I'll miss you, Lady Wamhoff," teased Brehan. "Stop," whispered Elisa, as she kissed him slowly and softly. "I love you. My first, my last, forever my only," she pledged. Brehan kissed her again and said, "And I love you. My first, my last, forever my only. Now be strong in this dirty Capitol. I must take leave now, my past and future Queen."

He grabbed a torch and slipped into the hole in the floor as he waved farewell to his love. Brehan hoped he would only see a few people on his way out of the castle and the clothes would convince the guards he was here to perform for the Prince. He knew they wouldn't believe that he was an invited guest because his skin was so much darker than those attending the wedding.

Sir Brehan didn't like this marriage in the least. He knew Elisa had no option in the matter, so his anger shifted to Aston Burke. Brehan hated Duke Burke. He felt the leader of Burkeville had treated him like a slave and was a drunken slob.

Brehan now wanted to get back to Mattingly to serve the Colberts. He hoped the family had already squashed the Fritz revolt. It hurt him not to be there to support his brothers in arms. The Duke had realized this trip must be important to Brehan. Jon Colbert never pressed him on the true reason for his absence. The torch was dying and he pushed open a door at the end of a darkening path to watch daylight stream in.

Sir Brehan walked out only to notice that two armored city guards had spotted him coming out of the secret door. He took off in a sprint. He easily outran the two guards and used the crowds to shake them completely. A smile came over the face of Sir Brehan Castaway as he thought about how he would always risk his life for his lady, as she had just done for him. He weaved through the army of guard camps for all the visiting lords. Flags and banners of affiliation hung listlessly in the stale spring air. The raging cook fires full of smoking meat couldn't neutralize the usual smell of the Capitol. This was the side of a royal wedding that men like Brehan usually experienced. The guards and knights were feasting, which was nothing in comparison to what would happen inside the castle walls.

When he got farther from the castle, the severe smell of cack dominated the cool air and the poor begged for coin on the sides of the nasty waste-filled streets. They wore dirty duds of rough fabric, torn and tattered, over bodies that hadn't been washed since the last rainfall. Old, dilapidated wooden structures were everywhere, threatening collapse at any moment. The situation was a stark contrast to the party-like scene at the guard camp, not to mention the prepared feast for the nobles. He found an open spot on a wagon heading south that greatly speeded up his trip.

About an hour later, he hopped off and paid his passage. As he walked south, he finally noticed a familiar path. He reached the outskirts of the Capitol and saw a friendly face. Sir Gunnar Pine, fellow Knight of Mattingly, stood there, waiting for Brehan. He laughed uncontrollably at Brehan's appearance for a minute before finally composing himself. Sir Gunnar held up a leather hold bag for Brehan with a change of clothes and tossed it to him.

"Well then, good Sir? Did you enjoy your first visit to the castle?" Sir Gunnar courteously asked with an over-exaggerated bow. Sir Brehan Castaway unleashed a wide smile and declared, "I certainly did. Did you get to see your love?" Sir Gunnar grinned like a fool in love, and replied, "We shared a secret afternoon rendezvous in the woods that I will never forget." Gunnar Pine had worked in the King's Castle before he went to Mattingly for better opportunities. He would have never been given the chance to achieve knighthood in Fox Chapel.

"I still can't believe I was inside the King's Castle. Perfect directions, by the way. I panicked a bit to get out of there but they were spot on to get to that room. How did you know she would be there?" Brehan asked.

"My lover had a look at the bride's itinerary. You know I would never set you wrong, my good sir," Gunnar answered. Brehan had known Sir Gunnar for five years and never seen the man excited. Getting to see his Princess caused a goofy smile he had never seen before. Gunnar said with hope in his eyes, "We will have our day with our ladies. Soon they will tire of this fancy life in the castle and want to go on a real adventure with men who can show them the world. We just need to find a pile of gold first. Ali-Gare keeps telling me that she will take some gold or other valuables and steal off in the night with me, but I told her she doesn't want to live a life on the run. I will not have my Princess a fugitive in her own kingdom, having to sneak around and worry about being spotted and killed. That's no life for my angel."

As they walked toward the city gate, Brehan noticed the smile disappear from Sir Gunnar's face and he reverted back to his usual brooding self. Brehan needed to find a place to change out of his costume and then they would head for the Raging Fox Gate where Sir Gunnar knew the guard. After that, the two would reclaim their horses and ride south with love filling their hearts.

16

QUEEN EMILIA

THE QUEEN STARED at the hourglass and felt like more than enough sand had tumbled through. "Hurry, we have to get back to Elisa soon. The nosy guests will start their favorite activity, gossiping."

"Alright, here it is, all ready." Anderley had the potion poured into a large cup. He had made a quick fire to boil water for the mushrooms that grew on the trunk of the blue-leaf trees. Anderley knew to boil them for at least five minutes to kill the poison.

"It is still steaming hot, so be careful," cautioned Anderley as he gave her the handle of the thick white cup.

The Queen held it in her left hand and grabbed a large spoon resting on her vanity table. She extracted a spoonful, blew it cool, and drank the nasty nectar. Emilia had become immune to the awful taste over the years. She continued until the mug was half full and handed it to Sir Anderley. "No, your highness, I told you I cannot do that today."

"Just a few spoonfuls," insisted the Queen of Donegal.

He knew it was best to oblige or she would fly into a rage. The Queen always got her way. He took a few warm sips and almost threw up. Queen Emilia snatched the potion back and finished the rest. The mushroom tea brought on euphoric feelings and a distorted sense of reality. Emilia decided she needed it to deal with her so-called friends at the wedding, but right now she just felt nauseous. She didn't even realize she had dripped a few drops of the clear liquid on her dress of flowing samite that looked and felt like soft red rose petals.

She had also unknowingly fallen into competition with the Wamhoff women to be the center of attention. A pleated ivory collar of ruffled lace tickled her shoulders and voluminous full-length dagged sleeves, edged in more white lace, jetted close to the ground. She gave special instructions for her mermaid-style dress to be richly embroidered with so many floral patterns in golden thread that her royal pin would become lost. A caul of long latticed strands of gold and silver sat atop seven long braids, joined together around the middle of her back. Over the caul was a chaplet of seven different woven red flowers with long green stems still attached. The pigment of the petals around the flowery circlet harmonized with her samite dress and still left the stunning glimmer of the caul exposed. The Queen hardly ever wore a crown except at mandatory ceremonies. She also didn't keep a constant flock of giggling ladies at court like most of her predecessors.

"My Queen," said Anderley as he led her from her room.

The Queen grew up a simple girl on a horse farm. Even eighteen years of being pampered and fitted in the finest dresses hadn't succeeded in molding her into a social butterfly. Emilia was a shy girl on the fateful day when King Ali-Stanley had locked eyes with her in Burkeville. The Queen had trusted many people early in her reign, only to be betrayed, causing her to become reclusive in the crowded castle. Only a few people in the Capitol existed that she would tell secrets to, but as for the rest, she just nodded and smiled so she didn't appear rude. She actually liked interacting with the common folk more than the snobby nobility who jealously looked down on her. When they arrived at Elisa's powder room, the mushroom beverage really hit the Queen. Everything looked fuzzy and quick movement left wavy trails in the air. Her mouth became parched, palms began to sweat, and her feet buzzed as they made contact with the ground.

Elisa opened the door, pulled in the Queen, and locked it. The Queen noticed the smell of sex still lingering and smiled at Elisa. *I know it wasn't Ali-Varis because I don't smelled burnt bacon.*

"I need you to make sure my dress and make-up look alright to go back out there," said Elisa.

She had some ruby gel smeared outside her lip-line that Queen Emilia didn't notice due to her mushroom-induced funk. She looked at Elisa and wished she were taller. The Queen hated being so short.

She put her hands on Elisa's shoulders and looked up into her eyes, "You are a stunning bride; you really are. The best I have ever seen."

"I don't know. Are you sure these people are going to like me?" Elisa sounded worried. Immediately the Queen answered, "Of course, everybody likes the wife. The king and lord husband is the one who raises taxes, sends men to war and takes land from the citizens. They hate him, not us."

"But I am referring to the top people of the Capitol and the Wamhoffs. I have heard it is extremely...backstabby around here," said a concerned Elisa. "Everything will be just fine, look at me. I had never set foot in a castle until I arrived here to marry the King. And I have survived eighteen miserable years," joked the Queen.

"Queen Emilia, you have been so gracious. I am so sorry for what my grandfather did to your father and in turn you," Elisa apologized. "Oh, look at you, sweet as your honey hair. You needn't apologize for the actions of proud men. I am sorry for what your father did to you and your family, if my ears have heard correctly," the Queen consoled as Elisa started to tear up. Before it could get any more emotional, Emilia said, "Alright, we're off."

The Queen locked arms with the new bride, and Sir Anderley led them toward the feast. As they approached the wide black staircase, she saw that the guests were waiting for them fifteen feet below in the enormous grand hall known as the Fox Den. A herald and page greeted them. The young page at a high circular table fumbled through some papers, looked at Elisa and asked, "Name please?" Queen Emilia answered in an annoyed tone, "She's the bloody bride. Elisa Burke Wamhoff. You should be working the floor as a fool." "So sorry, highness, I imagined the bride would be with her husband, is all. Thousand pardons, I beg of thee," the page pleaded as he went to one knee. The Queen simply nodded her head once and the page stood up again. The mushroom potion made her moody and she hated these situations.

A gilded trumpet bellowed out, "BOP BOP BA BA BA BOP BA BA." A crier screamed over the murmuring crowd, "With extreme honor, I proudly present the lovely bride, Elisa Burke Wamhoff."

"Escort her down," the Queen commanded Sir Anderley. "Can anyone mind their damn duties with any sort of competency around here? This is a Burkeville bride," Emilia muttered under her breath. Even though she had a falling out within the Burke family, Emilia still harbored love for her home region.

She watched Elisa walk right into the claws of the lady foxes known as Ali-Pari and Ali-Tiste Wamhoff, who wore the red dresses expected of a natural born Wamhoff or wife that married into the family. The sister and daughter of her husband, Ali-Stanley, had been the first to break the Queen's trust and cause her to mistrust all the Wamhoffs.

The Lonely Widows had taken over two weeks to create Elisa's dress and Emilia wondered how long before these animals would tear it apart. *Oh my, why it's none other than Ali-Pari, the biggest bedswerver in the entire realm and her nasty niece, a wind-sucking ambidexter who would rival any that came before her. I wonder how many lies she will spread tonight? Be careful Elisa, those frosty bitches are colder than a castle wall after an ice storm. Of course they would try to upstage the bride.*

Ali-Pari wore a sheath gown of length that was inappropriate for an older lady. Made of triple-layered burgundy wine silk, it had milk-colored ermine tippets that drooped listlessly past her knees. The low sweetheart cut around her chest and a side slit through all her skirts except for a few see-through layers exposed far too many blue veins for Emilia's liking. Her matching fur-lined gold fillet, beset with emeralds and sapphires, featured one giant ruby on her forehead. The precious stone dwarfed the one on Elisa's hairnet and upset the Queen.

Elisa's mother, Ali-Tiste, sported a scarlet gown with a sideless bodice secured by gold- and silver-ended laces of the deepest ocean blue only available to mermaids and royalty. The ankle length cut, edged in fox fur, brought attention to her slippers which were crusted in so many purple gemstones, the Queen couldn't figure out what base material they were made of. Her golden headwear appeared to have been drowned in a sea of diamonds and looked more like a crown. The gaudy item hurt Emilia's eyes and she found it to be insulting to her and Elisa. *You aren't the Queen of anything. You are a Duchess to the worst Duke to ever rule a region. You can tell your little lies and spin the truth, but I hear the facts about you from Anderley. You probably have to sell your whole outfit back after the ceremony.*

The Queen tried to relax and let other people make their entrances while she surveyed the scene and saw fresh spring colors featuring every shade that had ever been created of the royal family's favorite color. RED was everywhere. From gowns to dresses to lips to fingernails to cheeks to gemstones, the sight was blinding. Not a single wall sconce contained an unlit torch even though the flashiness in the room didn't need any additional help. The cooking stations in the corners provided early attendees with immediate morsels and wafted appetizing smells of rosemary and charred pigskin to Emilia's nose. Performers on stilts stood nearly as tall as the staircase and waddled around while pan flutes and drums played in the background. The perfect harmony of light drums and golden shakers made a beautiful background for the female singers. All the love songs of the land would be on display at this royal reception.

She looked across at the gallery as a young female singer started to serenade the audience with 'Love Gives and Love Lives'. She vied for attention with the other performers who mingled with the guests on the lower level. The Queen could barely hear the singer, yet she could hear the constantly ringing folly bells of the jesters and fools through all the commotion. She looked at the twenty-foot high banners hung from two wooden ceiling supports. Ten flags of a black bear passant on a white field lined one beam while a row of red foxes rampant set to a golden field lined an adjacent beam. In the middle was one giant thirty-foot banner of the royal standard, two foxes protecting a golden crown. The rest of the room had flags, pennons, pennants and small banners of visiting house affiliations proudly showing their support for the royal union.

A nearby gilded trumpet with a royal streamer hanging from it sounded, "BOP BOP BA BA BA BOP BA BA." The crier screamed, "I proudly present Queen Emilia Wamhoff." Sir Anderley had returned to guide her majesty down the staircase. The Queen noticed a much less rousing ovation than Elisa had received as she defensively entered the Fox Den. She immediately smelled the intensely scented oils and perfumes which she felt to be strong enough to choke a horse. The servants were clad in dull scarlet robes and served bite-sized morsels of meat on ebony trays to the elite of Donegal.

Most guests had come with their immediate family but the King and Queen didn't give a damn about the public appearance of their relationship. Invited attendees were announced and lead to their assigned tables by a page. Most marked their tables with the lady's purse. Emilia noticed most of the closer tables had similar looking soft leather purses. Nearly all had silver silk cords and the leather sides were richly decorated with common love scenes. *This must be the latest trend of the silly nobles. I won't have any part of that gaggle of followers, thank you.*

As she descended the stone steps, Ali-Pari and Ali-Tiste Wamhoff greeted her. "Hello, my Queen," Ali-Pari acknowledged Emilia with barely a curtsy. "Come with me Elisa, I will teach you how to deal with these animals around here and introduce you to the right people." Ali-Pari's wrinkled right arm dragged Elisa away.

An awkward silence ensued until Ali-Tiste broke it suddenly. "I must get back to both of my boys, my Queen," she said with a smirk and half curtsy. The Queen took it as an intentional slight because they had to cast away her last male child because of deformity. Queen Emilia hadn't even got a glance at her baby's face after he was taken from her body, never to be returned.

At least I have a son that may be king one day and she will always have to live with that drunk. Ali-Varis will never produce a male heir and the throne will fall to my son one day. The townspeople are already clamoring for Ali-Ster to be king, although I know that's the last thing he wishes for. And one day, all that financial help that always magically arrives in Burkeville, will simply dry up and disappear. Wouldn't that just be a great shame?

The royal wedding and feast created the illusion that Donegal had a jam-packed treasury. Unknown to the Queen, who took no interest in foreign affairs, the ceremonious week of festivities was paid for by loans from the banks of Arpeppi and Nowa Basha with promise of quick repayment. They were the only two to accept out of the twenty-one requests for assistance sent by the King. The celebration would have had a drastically different look if they had refused. With public unrest tearing at the social fabric of the realm, frivolous ornamentation with golden thread only appeased a very select few. The King did not care at all and was committed to keeping up a certain reputation. Ali-Stanley saw no issue with spending the last bit from the treasury on this spectacle. He hoped the stories of the tourney and feast would lift and amuse the poor, but even sweet poems or honey-dipped songs only exposed the extreme inequality and further angered the common class.

Emilia was also clueless to the fact that there wasn't a single bank left in the entire known world willing to lend to Donegal. The money had essentially run out. The Queen practiced blissful ignorance concerning the affairs of state. Despite the dire state of affairs for the realm as a whole, Emilia had trouble spotting a neck or wrist on a woman ungarnished by gold or silver. The upstaging spectacle extended to the food as well. Twenty-eight courses with entremets sprinkled in throughout the main meal in addition to the appetizers already in circulation seemed like overkill to the tiny Queen of Donegal. That wasn't even mentioning the wines from all over the world that would be served. Several special blends had been solely created for the wedding and only tasted by the chief butler for quality before being unleashed on the guests.

The extreme cost of the event could have been offset if the father of the bride wasn't a financial disaster. The father customarily paid at least half of the wedding bill. The short and stocky Duke was over his eyeballs in debt. Today, he looked like an evil duke in all black with silver buttons and a matching pin shaped like a bear to clasp his black cloak. A black bear rampant stitched in silver thread over the onyx colored silk stretched from Duke Aston Burke's shoulders to the small of his back. His respectable look couldn't mask his horrendous, widely known reputation as a woman beater and tyrant. The despicable man known as the Grizzly Bear lurked near the family. Nobody other than the royal family had brought their personal guard to the wedding feast, but nobody wanted to tell the giant man, who resembled a brown bear, to leave. He sheathed an enormous, plain sword without significant adornment and carried a strong reputation as a man who used that killing device to do unspeakable things at the behest of the cruel Duke Burke. The enforcer gave the Duke an inflated air of confidence that nobody appreciated.

She noticed her cousins and saw why people hated Duke Burke. The father of the bride had his wine in one hand as always and used the other to mess up the hair of Butrel and Astrid. Telly rolled her eyes at her father and scurried away before he went for her head. Emilia thought he looked like a vulture or crow from the front and Ali-Tiste wasn't with the family she had ostensibly rushed off to tend to, causing the Queen to giggle internally. She hated Ali-Tiste for her betrayal but despised Aston for hitting women. Her anger immediately subsided as usual. *A true Wamhoff woman respects nothing, not even her queen.*

She looked at her table with a sculpted black fox head centerpiece holding ruby roses and tulips. Long, oval rosace windows filtered in the last of the remaining sunlight, but the torches kept everything illuminated. When she looked back, Sir Anderley had vanished, leaving the Queen at the mercy of those who resented her the most. She wasn't the typical highborn queen and the prevailing opinion seemed to be that she had thrown herself at the King, when the reality was quite the opposite. The Queen hated these types of events and scanned the room for someone to latch on to. She had expected a life of travel and adventure after the King had swept her off her feet. Due to massive foreign and domestic debt, the King didn't like to travel very often, which kept his Queen stuck in the Capitol all the time.

Emilia spotted her son and rushed to his side. As she arrived, the music suddenly shifted. The pan pipes, harps and flutes were drowned out by a bugle that ripped through the air. Three men dressed in red robes with black ties ran into the room and stationed themselves in front of the harp players. They started a song called "The Courage of Love" about a knight who fought a dragon for his princess. Their deep voices boomed through the expansive room with high vaulted ceilings.

"Where is your father?" the Queen asked her son. "He is down in the Alley with Penrose," he responded.

"Why does he waste all his time down there?" she wondered aloud. "Forget it. You know pretty soon it will be your wedding day, just as soon as we find you a fit bride."

The Queen's stomach felt like it was twisting and tying itself in knots. That constantly remained a possible side effect of the magic tea. However, the Queen believed the drugs kept her from being a bitter person, so she just dealt with the side effects. She excused herself from Ali-Ster and rushed off to her chamber pot.

17

ALI-STER

ALI-STER WATCHED AS his mother ran off holding her belly. He assumed she had enjoyed too much of the bubble-filled white wine already because her eyes certainly looked like it. He really wished she didn't mention his future nuptials as he tried to mentally block it out. Every female he'd talked to at the wedding had asked when he would be married. He feared women more than war. He had gone off to fight at fourteen and didn't have any girlfriends prior to it, so he hadn't even kissed a girl yet.

Either I am growing plumper by the moment or they measured me too tight again. He pulled at the red-painted pewter buttons of the royal standard on his formal sleeveless black leather jerkin. Parti-colored long sleeves of crimson and gold matched his hosen. He wore a brown leather belt mounted with the same ornate decoration and color as the vest buttons. A preserved fox featuring a life-like head set with ruby eyes sat on his right shoulder with the soft hide and tail flung over his back. The Prince looked like a strong huntsman king, only missing a crown. He hated the fancy garb required around the Capitol. He didn't even care for the scabbard or fully covered chape with highly detailed Wamhoff battle blazonry. The only part of the outfit he liked was his sword.

The longsword belonged to King Ali-Sander Wamhoff, The Raging Fox. Over two hundred years ago, he had taken the sword from the dead hands of the Emperor of Ishii during the last battle of the Second War of Bywater Hold. He took the magical sword rumored to be crafted in the clouds by emerald dragons on a mission to find the Pearl of Wisdom. Countless witnesses saw him die on the shores of Fire Island but no one ever found the highly prized sword. Months later, the sword mysteriously washed up on the shores of Lightview, the Capitol of Donegal at the time. The woman who found the fine blade that was tinted like jade, took it to the nearby King's Castle. Every Wamhoff warrior king had wielded it in battle ever since.

Ali-Stanley had no real use for it and bequeathed it to his son when Ali-Ster left to defend the kingdom at fourteen. The sword instantly felt like an extension of his arm and he could feel something special when he first held the haunting sword. The double-edged blade was shiny like emerald in the optimal light and the worn, supple leather grip fit perfectly in Ali-Ster's hand. The pommel was obsidian based and clustered with seven different red jewels believed to have been blessed and placed on the sword by all the Gods before the green dragons finished the blade and brought it down to earth. When the pommel caught the right shine, the glint was nearly blinding, like a ruby flash of lightning. His cousin, Ali-Samuel Wamhoff, already had the nickname Crimson Lightning so the men at war called Ali-Ster Crimson Thunder for his power. Ali-Ster never believed in magic, but the fact that the sword returned across an ocean after Ali-Sander's demise and no Wamhoff king had lost it in battle gave him extra security while wielding the sword in battle.

"Oh, why hello there, Prince Ali-Ster," Lady Cuthbart said as she waved to him with a diamond-covered black glove. Ali-Ster wondered why she wasn't wearing the gloves and only holding them. She laughingly continued, "When *are* you ever to be married already?" Ali-Ster smiled and nodded. He said, "Soon enough." Lady Cuthbart whispered to her circle of friends as she walked away.

I'd rather be out on the battle field, answering to the general than fielding questions from ladies at parties. I look ridiculous in these tight fitting clothes. I like wearing the same armor every day, not a different outfit for every meeting or gathering. I yearn to be back on a war campaign but I am stuck here at this money-siphoning affair.

He thought he was done with these questions. Ali-Ster was mainly nervous about marriage because he never wanted to disappoint anyone; sealing the union scared him most of all. He had listened to the sexual escapades of the soldiers he fought with and had made up a few of his own to fit in. He still felt destined to fail on his first voyage of love. One captain told a young soldier to practice on whores to gain experience, but the prince in him wouldn't let Ali-Ster participate in those activities.

Another person who seemed sure to disappoint his bride approached. The firstborn son of the King smiled nonstop today. The groom, a rotund man low to the ground, appeared to be having a great time, clapping his hands together and rubbing his enormous ears. His bald head had receding islands of red hair on the sides and back and his oversized lips quivered when he talked. He had deep-set brown eyes and a big, wide nose with nostrils that fluttered when he breathed. Ali-Varis stuttered and also struggled to hold a normal adult conversation. He and Ali-Ster were the only trueborn sons of King Ali-Stanley.

"Are you enjoying the feast, Ali-Varis?" Ali-Ster asked. "Uh, yeah, uh, did you know...did you know we are going to have food here?" his half-brother asked. "I certainly did. I can see some right over there," Ali-Ster pointed. "Yeah," agreed Ali-Varis as he quickly nodded his head and picked his nose. Ali-Ster could tell from the glossed-over look that his half-brother had been heavily medicated today, more so than usual, to keep his unpredictable behavior in check.

The remote corners of the room had different cooking set ups. One had rotisserie suckling pigs and baby cattle being slowly turned on a spit over sizzling red coals that sang sweet staccato melodies as the animal fat dripped down. Once fully cooked, they went to the tables in front and guests ripped at their favorite parts. Some men pulled daggers to cut off some choice pieces of the cow.

Another corner had controlled fires with crossed grates over them that were cooking huge, primal cuts of bull. The cook sliced down the finished product with a big, bloody knife and handed it to the people. This was mainly for the King to enjoy the symbolism of eating his enemy and most spit out the chewy meat after wrestling with the gristle. Spiked bulls' heads around that cooking corner provided a grisly atmosphere.

The other end had bubbling cauldrons of bull heart stew being slowly mixed by the cooks with stirrers as big as boat oars. Tiny bowls with trenchers of wheat bread were lined up on the front serving table. As soon as the stew hit the bowls, the greedy guests snatched them up.

The last corner contained seafood. It welcomed guests with shelled, pickled oysters up front in large buckets. Small dome topped ovens cooked spearfish and speckled-belly blue fish. Perfectly round castle towers were constructed out of smashed salted whitefish. Finely chopped red vinegar pickled onions and parsley were used to make windows and rooftop decoration. Pea tendrils and stemmed flowers surrounded the towers, creating a garden-like yard. Three of the seven towers had already been demolished by the ravenous guests, with the fourth being attacked with vigor.

In addition, the back kitchens were full of cooks feverishly rushing to get the twenty-eight courses done on time. The official supper would start soon and the barbaric frenzy of gluttonous eating would commence.

Ali-Ster saw Elisa sitting next to Ali-Varis, forcing a fake smile. He felt awful for her, forced to marry a man well over two decades older whom she could never love. She was a beautiful young girl who deserved better, he thought. For a moment, he imagined her by his side, in front of the High Holy Leader, taking their vows in the Castle Chapel, under the faithful watch of the Gods. He then shifted to thoughts of his mother being over three decades younger than his King father when he plucked her out of Burkeville at fourteen and impregnated her soon after. *Return to the well before it dries I suppose, father.*

Ali-Gare Wamhoff, his half-sister, considered the most alluring maiden in all of the land, walked around the tables, socializing. Her face was so fair, makeup only tended to mar the natural, radiant exquisiteness. Her hair looked like molten gold had been dropped into scarlet dye and delicately stirred. The flowing locks looked so soft, women swore they must've been brushed by angels. She had gentle, welcoming blue eyes and a smile as sweet as summer wine straight from the Pearl Islands. In her presence, men fell to their knees and thanked the Gods above for sending down such a beauty. Her medium height was bolstered by her luscious breasts and shapely legs that made her an inspirational princess, a muse of sorts. Many men had died trying to win the hand of Ali-Gare Wamhoff in marriage while others used her for battle motivation. Tales of her charm and pulchritude had spread to the far corners of the world and men risked grave danger just for a chance to lay eyes on the lovely Princess. The twenty-six-year-old had been betrothed at a young age to Rollo Etburn. He was much older than her, and she strongly protested the wedding. The mysterious hunting death of Rollo left many people questioning the Princess' role in his demise. Ever since, she had avoided marriage proposals citing one reason or another, causing strong disappointment to the King. Ali-Ster had never gotten along with Ali-Gare; he always felt she resented him for some reason.

Ali-Ster watched as his other three half-sisters joined Ali-Gare. All four and Ali-Varis were born to the King's first wife, Parys Etburn. King Ali-Stanley had married her when they were both eighteen. She was his key to obtaining the throne. Not a stunning woman by any stretch of the accepted conventional standards of the day, but she did produce beautiful daughters. After her sudden death from fever, the King didn't even look at another woman for over a year and a half. Even though twenty years had now passed since Parys' death, the King still visited her preserved body in the Alley of the Heavens every single day that he stayed in the Capitol.

Three trained black falcons were released into the expansive room. They flew majestically, nearly colliding with the banners or each other as they circled the hall. This signaled that dinner was ready, so most guests sat down. The falcons flew around for a few minutes before returning to the three outstretched arms wearing red gauntlets that they had launched from. The falconers took the hawks back to the mews as the frenzy started. Nearly one hundred servants weaved through the room, clearing used dishes and straightening table setups.

Finally, the King arrived, just in time for dinner. Now people would stop asking Ali-Ster about his father. He chose not to tell them that their King would rather spend his time with the dead. It irked Ali-Ster and the Queen that King Ali-Stanley spent so much time in the Alley.

The King of Donegal lurched across the floor draped in flowing robes of gold and crimson, secured by belts of strong woven white silk with heraldic adornment featuring battle scenes. Ali-Stanley's lowest belt, just above his wide hips, held his ruling scepter and a few small daggers. The King didn't even carry a ceremonial sword because he couldn't stand the weight of the large weapon. He wore a white cloak with a huge royal standard stitched in gold- and silver-thread. The protective foxes were filled in with real fox hide and a silver agrafe shaped in the form of a fox's head secured the cloak. The spots on his pean scarf matched his golden robes and the King dressed for comfort in slippers made of perfectly stretched and softened fox skin. Ali-Stanley also wore his most elaborate crown, heavy in gold and jewels. A band went around his head with seven arched points extending up from that and connecting in the middle at the center of his head to create an open frame of a dome. At this meeting point rested the biggest, most perfect diamond anyone in the room had ever seen. The smaller gemstones smashed to the band and extensions were no slouches in their own right, just no match for the diamond. Ali-Ster watched as Penrose helped his father, who looked to be dragging his right leg, get to the table of honor. The old King was out of breath and looked feeble.

Ali-Ster wanted to be back in battle, but he seemed destined to be Prince Archduke of Donegal. He would have to deal with all the trivial problems until Ali-Varis died. He would rather take orders from a commander than give them out to the realm as he loathed the shady underhanded dealings of the Capitol. Ali-Ster had only been back for a short time but he'd already noticed this. Ali-Ster saw Penrose pulling the chair for King Ali-Stanley to sit next to his wife and tried to remember the last time he had seen his parents that close to each other. He went and took his place at the left end of the table next to his mother. He looked across the huge hall at the four hundred guests filing into their respective seats. The smell of sour perfume invaded his nose and blocked out the aroma of the food. He noticed Sir Jermar Lolat and wanted to knock the smile off the huge man's face. Ali-Ster had gotten into a screaming match with his father about being forbidden to compete in the wedding tournament. The Grand Champion had been named two days ago, but Ali-Ster knew he would have won if he had participated. The King lectured his son to focus more on ruling the realm than playing games. The Prince didn't attend the tourney in protest and edged for any chance to test his skills against the best knights.

The rest of the table from left to right sat the King, Elisa, Ali-Varis, Ali-Tiste, Ali-Gare, Ali-Pari, Aston Burke and Father Enroy. The rest of his sisters ate with their families on the lower level. Ali-Ster pitied Elisa having to sit in between the two worst party guests. She could have slouched or pouted, but she sat tall and smiled like a dutiful lady should and it impressed Ali-Ster. The dais was up on a raised support, just in front of one of the walls, looking down over every other guest below. This put the table of distinction in a position that every guest could easily view, which Ali-Ster didn't like. He didn't like being stared at while eating or being mindful of his every move. He rarely drank, but a gulp of the sweet and tangy white from Burkeville's Bushes seemed to ease his shaky nerves from having all eyes on him. The nobility sat on the next level and the guards and help usually ate on the lowest level but grand feasts like this required all the seating on every level for the nobles. The guards had their own small feast outside the castle.

Course after course started to arrive and Ali-Ster could only see one object, mountains of gold coins. He couldn't imagine the exorbitant cost of this extravaganza. He could think of a million ways to better allocate the funds. He already had the spicy eel, roasted chickpeas covered in garlic and lemon juice and cabbage sprouts cooked in bacon, butter and red vinegar. Arriving now was a small plate of crisp diced potatoes fried in lard and heavily spiced with white and black peppercorns. Next, the saffron flavored wild mushrooms in meat broth and set like jelly was served cold. Ali-Ster didn't care for it and pushed the dainty plate away. A serving girl immediately scooped up the dish and another one offered Ali-Ster another washrag soaked in rosewater but he waived her away. *We don't need a rosewater wash with a fresh towel between every course. The seven linens on my place setting should suffice, I would hope.*

He stared at the elaborately designed spice caddy to find something that might have made that last dish taste better. He became lost in the intricate pattern of intertwined swords and heraldic shields carved into the long rosewood structure that contained sections of large flake salt, ground black and white pepper, cinnamon, mace, coarse-ground mustard seeds, grains of paradise, crushed coriander and cumin, cloves and sugar. The King had his own, smaller holder with seven different kinds of salt and used the communal vessels as well. The lowest section of seating normally didn't get these expensive spices on the table, but everyone was a preferred guest tonight.

King shrimp from Waters Edge appeared in front of him. It was drowned in butter, garlic, lemon, parsley and a dry white wine from Duskpoint in Burkeville. The steamy aroma filling the air stimulated his excited palate. He savored the fresh taste of the Sea of Green's fine offerings. Before he could finish the shrimp, it was taken away and replaced with whole ducks, stuffed and roasted with leeks and sage, then drenched in orange sauce for the table to share. He picked at a few pieces like the rest of the table and waited for the next course. He looked down the table and noticed that Duke Aston Burke had stopped eating after about the fifth course. He had got so drunk that he nodded off occasionally, only to catch himself before his head hit the table.

He noticed his father made liberal use of most of the spices on the mixed game pie packed with bone marrow, black peppercorns, honey, onions and a spicy northern red from Blairs Beak. The pie was thickened with egg yolks and almond milk, then wrapped in pastry crust, brushed with whipped egg yolks and baked to a golden brown perfection. A pleasing puff of spiced meaty goodness rushed up as Ali-Ster pushed his spoon down and released a mouth-watering whiff that reminded him of the meat pies from the war. Ali-Ster noted they weren't nearly this fresh on the battle campgrounds. The crust never had a crisp bite or this full, sweet flavor. He didn't have time to reminisce as the whole spring lamb roasted with mint, garlic, onions, carrots and juniper berries was served family style. The table of honor waited as the food taster tried a piece from every section of the animal before getting started. Everyone nibbled at the lamb and agreed the flavors were spot on before the next course came to the table.

He could barely glance at the delicious-looking ham legs that had been cured in brine full of cinnamon sticks for two days and smoked for seven hours before undergoing slow roasting. The spicy pepper glaze coalesced with the salt and smokiness until ending with a sweet finish. He wished he could have eaten more of the delectable meat. Ali-Ster became peeved when the next course arrived. He barely had the appetite to eat more than two bites of slow turned boar ribs smothered in a spicy sugar plum glaze. This was one of Ali-Ster's favorite meats and he wished they had served the boar at the beginning of the meal.

He thought one of his buttons might pop and kill an innocent bystander when it was announced that a short intermission would take place before the dessert courses started. Servers still circulated through the room, offering various one-bite treats to all the attendees. *The common folk deserve at least the leftover food from this disgusting display, if not more.*

Ali-Ster looked at the table overflowing with gifts. From a gilded chalice featuring heraldic etchings and standing three feet tall to matching leather riding saddles encrusted in jewels, any of the gifts would support a struggling family of lower social stature for years.

He looked over and eavesdropped on his mother and father's conversation. The Queen raised her chalice to her husband and said, "You look quite handsome today, my King." The King didn't pick up his goblet and replied, "Today? Today? I look handsome every day. And where is your damn crown? Is it too much to ask for you to at least look like a queen if you won't act it?"

Now I remember why I didn't want to come back from the war campaign. This happens every time they spend the briefest amount of time together. When will it ever change?

The Queen immediately answered, "Are you going to yell at your precious Ali-Tiste for wearing a crown out of order as well? No, it's all fine and good when your little Ali-Tiste does it." Emilia looked at Ali-Ster, and said, "I don't know why I even try." The King started to get agitated and spoke fast, "Try what? To down as many barrels of wine as possible so you cannot stand any longer?"

Ali-Ster noticed his mother getting angry as she slowly said, "I'll drink as much as I like. I'll do what I like." She downed her wine and picked up the drinks on either side of her. "And I'll do it when I like." She drained both goblets of wine. The King turned his back on the Queen and said to Elisa, "One thing you must always remember if you are to be queen is to always mind your manners." Ali-Stanley almost shouted this and Ali-Ster could see his mother seething as she shook her head. Emilia poked her husband in the back and asked, "How dare you? I will not sit here and let you passively embarrass me before my friend." The King started moaning like he was being stabbed in the back.

Ali-Ster couldn't take any more of the bickering and quietly shouted so only the table could hear. He spoke in an angry tone, "Enough of this already. We are the ruling family up on stage in front of everyone. I don't care what happens on the morrow but at this feast we will act like a respectable ruling family." His heart was beating through his chest and he thought his father was about to say something but the King just sat there with his mouth open. His mother stood up and stormed away as he sat back in his chair. Although he could barely hear it, he listened to the conversation between Ali-Tiste, Ali-Pari and Ali-Gare.

"Well, I think he's handsome, much more so than my disgusting husband," Ali-Tiste said and the other two giggled. The Princess Ali-Gare opined, "I think he is as ugly as they come. He's tried to catch my eye, but it will never happen." Ali-Pari spoke in a boisterous voice, "I'd let Jermar the Giant take a run up my skirts with his big lance."

The Princess covered her mouth in shock and said, "Aunt Ali-Pari, I can't believe you said that." The older Ali-Pari replied, "Come now; spare me the almighty act of innocence. We all know where you were this afternoon." Princess Ali-Gare's face reddened and she became quiet.

He saw his mother returning and Ali-Ster hoped there wouldn't be any more unpleasant scenes. The Prince noticed his uncle Ryen seated at the lower level. He wanted to be at that table, talking about swordplay techniques and past hunts. Instead, he got to chastise his parents for acting like children at a royal function. He also learned that the normal conversation of duchesses and princesses centered around the looks of a knight. He felt out of place in the Capitol. He looked past his parents at the new bride and thought she must feel the same way.

18
PENROSE

PENROSE STOOD ON the main stage behind the King, with his back against the wall. He always served at these events, protecting the royal family. The voices in his head had been silent for the past couple of weeks, but of course, they rose within him when he broke his fast this morn. He scanned the room for suspicious characters. The only one to stand out was the man from Waters Edge who had met with the King last week. The stranger appeared to be working as a hired guard for the feast but he looked guilty of something as he stood unobtrusively in a corner of the room by himself and pulled the hood of his cloak over his eyes.

Sir Jermar "The Giant" Lolat arrived to relieve Penrose for a bit. The big man gasconaded, "You can run about now, silver boy. The golden Grand Champion has arrived." Sir Jermar wasn't actually a giant, but he was the closest thing Donegal had to offer. The knight with a bristling mustache and dark look hadn't stopped smiling since he had been named Grand Champion of the Wedding Celebration Tourney two days ago. The bragging rights and seven hundred and seventy-seven golden foxes that went with the title added to the knight's prestige. Penrose had finished second and the winner gave him the nickname 'silver boy'. Sir Jermar had won the three previous tourneys and achieved legendary status as a teen in the Battle of Bear Gate. No man smiled when he drew The Giant in a tourney but he was a braggart in every sense of the word.

Penrose walked over to the rest of the King's Guard by the west wall. Sir Oliver Wedgewood yawned, showing a semi-toothless mouth. He was old, raunchy, and willing to do anything for the King. He lived by a policy of any means necessary. Sir Thomas Maron and Sir Nate Edgewell were about the same size and age, tall and in their mid-thirties. The two were above average swordsmen, but not worthy of the King's Guard until their lord fathers monetarily enticed the King to choose their sons for the honor.

Penrose's brother, Sir Anderley, was already speaking as he approached, "I mean, I shouldn't have to run around, watching after the Queen. This is supposed to mean King's Guard," he said, pointing to the pin on his chest.

It was a silver pin with a depiction of a falcon with its mouth wide open and the image of a fox cub inside the falcon's mouth. The King's Guard represented the falcon charged with protecting the Wamhoff foxes. This was their official badge and emblem. The King's Guard had seven members who, the saying went, had been sent by the seven Gods. The number seven was considered a magical number in Donegal and most people looked at it as a symbol of good luck.

Sir Anderley continued complaining to the rest of the men about having to guard the Queen, but Penrose knew that his brother was in love with Emilia. Anderley would never freely admit it, but Penrose saw it clearly with his burning azure eyes. Members of the King's Guard were forbidden to have families or any property that could be used as leverage in a dispute. The chosen knights were married to the duty and service of the crown and nothing could distract them from this endeavor. The men were permitted to visit brothels or rape after war conquest, but were sworn from having wives or long-term affairs.

That made no difference to Penrose Ellsworth, who had become fonder of a man's touch in recent years, although he couldn't let the wrong person find out or it would cause him instant death. Buggery was punished severely in Donegal and Penrose had seen firsthand evidence that the act or even suspected act was harshly enforced without proper trial. The voices constantly told him that everyone knew about his perversion and it kept him in a state of perpetual paranoia.

Penrose moved back over to the King's stage and looked at the newly-married Prince in a formal peascod-belly doublet of deep burgundy velvet with silver stitched royal crests over both bulging breasts. The front of the handsomely tailored top was stained with food, drink and slobber as proof of the groom's sloppy good time. The groom sported the same parti-colored sleeves and leggings as Ali-Ster but his lumpy body didn't look right in the form-fitting attire. In Penrose's opinion, the brown laces on the front of Ali-Varis' doublet were the hardest workers at the feast. The ties were made exclusively for this event but they already looked like they had been worn one hundred times and threatened to burst at any moment. The unstable Prince was permitted to wear a black leather belt with a shined pewter buckle, but he had been strictly forbidden from carrying knives, daggers or seven Gods forbid, a full sword. Penrose was surprised Ali-Varis hadn't suffered one of his episodes of madness yet today. He had an amorous friend named Broem Endo who confided in him that Ali-Varis had animal-like fits of physical madness almost every day. The overfed Prince smashed more of the red velvet tipsy cake into his mouth, spilling most of it onto his body and the floor. He appeared heavily sedated to Penrose.

Penrose looked around the room and became somewhat jealous. If he had forgone the King's Guard, he would be an honored guest at these types of events. He loved high fashion and wished to participate with the rest. His father had been invited as a courtesy but Penrose knew Lord Ichibod would make up an excuse to miss the event because the gruff man hated the Wamhoffs with a flaming passion. This time the reason was because his gout had flared up so horribly that he couldn't even get out of bed. Ichibod Ellsworth hadn't spoken to Anderley or Penrose after they told him they were joining the King's Guard and neither son expected to ever hear a peep from their father's mouth again, unless they were within earshot of his words directed to someone else.

He espied around again and thought about the uniform of the King's Guard that consisted of an obsidian-colored half-sleeved gambeson under a shining jacket of gold-dipped ring mail that hung to the wrist and knees. A thick, sleeveless surcoat blazoned with the royal arms from chest to belly went over the mail jacket. A powder blue cloak proudly showed the stitched King's Guard symbol. Silver thread was used for the falcon head and golden thread for the baby fox. Red, white and black threadwork was used to add detail to the images. Penrose had secured the silk cloak with a silver morse shaped like the King's Guard standard that matched a pin on his chest. Other than his missing helm, this was his normal look for regular guard detail at most times, unless entering a tense situation where the gold scale full plate armor made more sense.

Penrose smelled the spring pears poached in red wine and cinnamon sticks as the servers carried around tiny cauldrons of the steaming goodness and ladled them over the already set bowls of vanilla and orange blossom custard. The hanging cauldrons aromatized the room as they swung around similar in fashion to the hanging baskets of incense the brothers of the Faith of Eternal Light carried around the churches. The dish looked and smelled wonderful but the guests only took polite tastes or stirred it all together with the pewter spoons etched with floral engravings. The following course looked just as delectable. Apple pie with refined sap from the maple tree, anise, figs and an amber-colored liquid sugar drizzled over the top. Next, a dainty serving arrived consisting of early-harvest strawberries and raisins in pudding with pepper-spiced almonds and two streaks of thick, almost black honey straight from a comb imported from the Androsi Isles. People only pushed the food around to make it look like they had tried it. Finally, the gluttonous feasting came to a merciful end but the drinking became the focus of most people.

Food suddenly flew all over the King's table, as Ali-Varis threw three plates into the air with his hands. The elder Prince slammed his fist on the table and let out a primal scream that sounded painful.

"STOP THIS AT ONCE," screamed the King, only to have Ali-Varis crash both hands on the table over and over again while shaking violently.

The Giant grabbed the Prince from behind in an attempt to wrestle the rotund Prince to the ground, but he shrugged him off by throwing his shoulders back. Ali-Varis possessed amazing strength when he went into these fits. Sir Thomas and Sir Nate jumped on Ali-Varis and pulled him to the ground on the raised stage with pure muscle power.

After several minutes of struggling and guests already gossiping, Count Silzeus slowly walked back in and Penrose rushed over to him. He grabbed the heavy dose of nightshade or sleeping serum that the Count had just retrieved from his quarters. He ran over to the knights who had Ali-Varis on his back and the Giant pried the Prince of Donegal's mouth open. Penrose dumped the vial of liquid down Ali-Varis' throat and yanked his hand away, but not soon enough. He looked down at the tip of his thumb bleeding profusely where Ali-Varis had taken out a little chunk when his jaw clamped shut. Penrose wanted to punch the Prince but he quickly calmed himself and retreated from the scene. He took a linen napkin from a table and wrapped it around his thumb. He looked over to see the Fox Chapel knights carrying an incapacitated Prince Ali-

Varis Wamhoff to his quarters. *That is to be our king one day. Gods, kill us gently before that ever comes to pass. If that is the plan, kill all of us now if you have even a minute amount of mercy.*

As they passed, Elisa Wamhoff appeared from behind the procession of knights. The look of terror on her face sexually excited Penrose in a sick, sadistic fashion. He tried so hard to fight these thoughts, only to have them return stronger every single time.

Sir Anderley made his way over to Penrose, "Are you alright? How bad did the fat half-wit get you?" Penrose looked up to respond but he was cut off by Otto Cuthbart, "Oh, the pretty little boy got himself a little cut on his thumb. Just cut it off you sissy."

He slurred his words since he was terribly drunk. Otto Cuthbart, a small man with a behemoth mouth, couldn't control himself. The Cuthbarts were one of the wealthiest families in Fox Chapel. Since his appointment to Chamberlain of the Realm, his already enormous ego had grown to epic proportions. Penrose didn't respond verbally; he just stared straight into his soul.

Don't push me, old man. The beast is demanding to be fed.

"You didn't mess up your make up now, did you?" said Otto as he laughed at Penrose. Again, silence and a chilling glare was Penrose's answer. *We shall see who laughs last, you drunken bastard. And by all means keep drinking. Drink up.*

He finally spoke back after another offhand comment, "No need to start a kerfuffle. You think yourself to be quite droll, only to be reputed as quite the tedious fellow. Your quips are now tired and worn, used over a thousand times already tonight. I will kill you tonight." Penrose said the last sentence under his breath and turned his back on Lord Otto. The loudmouth thought his friendship with Penrose's father would cause the knight to bow down to him.

Sir Penrose Ellsworth walked away to return to the King's side. The Ellsworth family was even more prominent than the Cuthbarts and Penrose knew that he could smash Otto like a jousting dummy. As he stood behind the King, the voices shrieked in his mind. They wanted blood, and they wanted some now.

Shut up. Not now. Stop it.

The King stood up and Penrose looked down at his sword hilt. He fingered the grip and it felt right. He could easily feed the voices with a king's blood right now. That would surely satisfy the greedy sounds in Penrose's head. He would pay for it with his life but Penrose could slice up the King of Donegal before anyone had a chance to react. Would that cleanse his soul for entrance up to the steps of heaven?

Several performers coaxed the King to move over to the actors' stage. It wasn't really a stage but a corner of the lowest tier in the hall where the dining tables had been removed. Long benches were set up and the King took his spot right in front.

Two dwarves emerged from behind a large tapestry that hid the actors who weren't performing. The dwarves were a blond man with a forked beard and a woman who wore false teeth bigger than those of a horse. Her dark hair was greasy and dirty. The gathering crowd began to boo as it noticed the bull on the man's surcoat. It wasn't gold, but more like a drab, dull yellow to match the rest of the man's ragged look. With mad, beady eyes that looked like they were about to burst out of their sockets, the blond actor stupidly said, "Oh no, I seem to have soiled meself again. Look, oh wife of mine, it done made a bull this time. I think oh no, I think oh yes, I shall make this my eternal crest."

The woman who had been made to look ugly spoke clumsily as the wooden teeth occasionally clacked together, "My love, why yes, the time is now. I'm oft compared in beauty to a cow." The burgeoning crowd erupted in laughter and the actress waited for the noise to die back down before continuing, "You stole Mattingly, a nice, fine jewel, but what comes next, mayhaps Jasper should rule?"

Jasper rubbed his beard greedily and spoke, "Oh yes, one I stole but four remain. I don't care if millions lay slain. Blood shall spill, a crimson rain, sure to leave a burning stain. Eternal pain. That is what I shall cause in vain. Then what is left for me to gain? It is but I, the man more important than rain." The crowd chuckled again and Jasper said in a stupid tone, "But truthfully, tis I, the filthy peasant usurper from the south. Where is that hideous whore of a woman I call my wife?" The dwarf actor looked behind and around the woman as she waved her arms wildly and screamed, "Here I is, here I is."

"Oh, there you is, come now hither, I'll take me a kiss," Jasper said and the two shared a short lip lock. He spoke again as he gazed out into the crowd, "So where do we usurp next, Waters Edge, Burkeville, Bottomfoot? No, yes, that's it, don't you see, only one man can be as smart as me. I is so smart to use my dirty scheming to usurp Mattingly. I can use the same tactics to steal the crown right off King Ali-Baster's head." Jasper tapped his fingertips together in a diabolical manner while looking around the grumbling crowd.

The two actors disappeared behind the tapestry screen and four dwarves dressed like guards now came out and stood in front of a tree branch with green leaves that had been dragged out for this scene. Several of the off-stage actors whistled like birds as the first guard said, "Nice day out here in the King's Woods. You hear King Ali-Baster just brought down another fourteen point stag? Rode the beast down and made a clean death cut with his longsword as he always does." The second guard said, "Best huntsman I've ever known but our gracious and noble King has become tired of using weapons against the animals. Guess that's why he's been using his bare hands much of late, yes, he has, I tell ya."

A third guard went on, "That sounds like our King, the mightiest King this realm has ever known." The fourth guard closed by saying, "I know I'm proud as all can be to serve the greatest King to ever rule."

Wow, this is getting hard to take. What a farce!

Penrose rolled his eyes as the four dwarves exited and a normal-sized man came in dressed in only a loincloth. His ample muscle definition was on display and the crowned man with red hair gave Penrose a suggestive hint about who he was supposed to be. The big problem Penrose saw was that King Ali-Baster had died in his fifties and never looked anything like this handsome actor who couldn't have been older than his late twenties or early thirties.

Suddenly, from behind the screen, a black mass rushed across the stage and smashed into King Ali-Baster's back. A wild boar had rammed its tusk into the King. The bloodied actor turned to face the backstabbing boar. A great struggle ensued with the mighty King choking the beast to death with his bare hands. The tall actor rubbed his stomach and stared gravely at the red liquid dripping from his hands. The dwarf guards rushed over to the King and the first guard asked, "What should you have us do, your majesty?"

They tried to help the King up from his knees but he pushed them away and rose without aid. He said, "Bring my horse, I have a kingdom to rule." The dwarf guards backed away and the big actor looked to the heavens and spoke dramatically, "Now, if I should and if of course, death should come and death should pull, remorse be damned, I'll duel a bull. I shall ride right now and sit my throne, and if to die I won't alone. My kingdom I ruled, the only heart I have known, can be stitched to my vest or flesh of my bone."

Slow, sad music played in the background as the attentive guests started to tear up. A chair that resembled the throne of Donegal was dragged in and King Ali-Baster limped over and collapsed onto the throne. A fire headed actor of about twenty wearing only a loincloth entered the stage. This man was taller and more chiseled than the wounded King Ali-Baster who shuddered on the throne and spoke weakly in broken sentences, "Ali-Stanley, my good son. I am soon to die and though I don't fear death, I must warn you of a few things." Ali-Stanley kneeled at his side and said, "My King father, we should get you to bed and find someone to cure your ails."

In a forceful voice, Ali-Baster said, "NO. I will die ruling the realm on this uncomfortable throne, not in the luxury of a bed." "Oh father, you truly are an inspiration to the realm," Ali-Stanley announced.

Penrose looked around and saw most people crying. He couldn't believe these flocks of sheep were falling for these shadow stories. Penrose had seen some stories stretched thin on the truth before but he compared this play to the sun casting a ten-foot shadow of a dwarf. *Neither of these kings could deliver a message let alone a precisely aimed stroke of the sword. I don't even think the starving commons would eat up this rancid bowl of royal porridge.*

The antics went on as Ali-Stanley said, "This cannot be, noble King father of mine. You have bested countless wild boars with only the strength of your hands. That's not to mention the other horned beasts you've taken down as well. Our raven returned from Mattingly." "And...?" asked an excited King.

"Jasper Colbert has refused your dying wish for a duel," Ali-Stanley reported with his head lowered.

Just as Penrose thought he couldn't take anymore, King Ali-Baster said with fleeting breath, "I cannot even stand on my own feet and the usurper won't face me like a man. He has no honor. Pledge me that you will kill this upstart. I won't have you end him any way but fair. Slay him in a duel, my son." The actor took the crown and placed it on the head of the kneeling Ali-Stanley who held his father's hand. The dying King's eyes closed and Ali-Stanley stood up and stared at the body for a few moments before prying his hand away. Four strong men surrounded and lifted the dead King on his throne and walked sideways behind the tapestry.

The actor playing King Ali-Stanley remained on stage and looked up in the air with upturned right palm as he spoke, "I shall invite this usurper to my father's funeral. If the man has any mind of duty he shall pay proper respect. While he is in the Capitol, I shall challenge Jasper Colbert, Duke of Mattingly, to a duel. I promise to drain every last drop of traitor blood from his body." Everyone clapped and the crying ceased.

The dwarf guards entered again, dragging in Jasper Colbert. The first guard spoke, "Your majesty, we found this rascal hiding in the kitchens." A loud collective sound emerged from behind the screen. "OOOOHHH."

The first guard said, "He was searching for the cook who prepared the king's belly timber." The unseen voices sounded again. "AAAAHHH."

The first guard continued, "We found seven different vials of poison on this treasonous traitor." A collective and drawn out gasp came from behind the tapestry.

King Ali-Stanley stood over Jasper and spoke down on him, "So, I invite you to my father's funeral services and allow you to take part in a royal tourney and you repay me with treason. I challenged you to a duel and you spurned a king's demand like a coward. You didn't win one tilt in the tourney and your anger caused you to try to poison me, a better man. I am nothing if not merciful and you will only die at the hands of the Gods and me. We will fight in a fair duel south of the castle."

Penrose had thought this story to be true until he heard more stories in the Capitol and changed his mind. The amalgamated version from hundreds of tellings caused him to believe Jasper Colbert had been named Grand Champion and the King had become infuriated and craved revenge, so he had his men surround Jasper on his way home to ask the Duke to surrender. Jasper Colbert didn't give in despite being outnumbered tremendously and only died after killing five members of the King's Guard. Penrose knew the King had no issue with stooping to dirty deeds as evidenced by the jobs he had performed over the years. The nature of this play only reinforced his suspicions about the truth.

The duel was set up with both men standing a few feet apart and facing each other. The dwarf barely came up to the other actor's thighs and the whole thing looked somewhat silly. One of the guards handed King Ali-Stanley a huge silver sword that glinted in the dancing torchlight.

Jasper said, "I must warn you, King Ali-Stanley. You are looking at the biggest and best swordsman Mattingly has to offer. My sword is made of the finest materials available in my homeland." He twirled around a poorly constructed wooden sword that was nearly falling apart.

The crowd laughed and it only took three dramatic overhand stokes to kill the cowering Jasper Colbert. Penrose stared intently at the real King, who was having problems just sitting and kept shifting his heavy mass back and forth. The knight of the King's Guard wondered if Ali-Stanley's mind was so deluded that he really believed these lies.

As he lay dying, the dwarf actor said, "I thought I could fool our mighty King but you are much too wise for a silly usurper such as meself." He wiggled around and died. The guards came and dragged the body away.

The actor playing Ali-Stanley spoke aloud, "Because you fought with honor and dignity and despite the fact that you are a known traitor, I shall send your body back to Mattingly to your family."

A call came from behind the screen, "Ambush, ambush, it's a set up. These dirty southerners are up to their usual antics again. Retreat, your highness, we are grossly outnumbered."

King Ali-Stanley held his sword as high as possible in his right hand and poetically said, "Die I shall if it comes to that but I shall never run and hide. For kingdom, family and honor," he screamed. The finale consisted of a swarm of dwarves wearing golden bull markings attacking the King. Ali-Stanley slew the entire bunch, dropped his sword, and raised his arms triumphantly.

I can't believe anyone would believe any of this propaganda. These actors are good, but not that good. Pure rubbish and lies, just like everything else about the King and his Capitol. Everyone except Penrose cheered and clapped as all the actors returned for a group bow. The short play provided a pleasing helping of drama, comedy, poetry and fine acting, but it was poisoned with a heavy dose of truthlessness. Facts be damned to please the King.

Penrose thought the utter audacity was over until the actor who played Ali-Stanly kneeled before the real King and said, "There you have it, oh my, oh me, our only wish is to flatter thee. Kings have come and kings have gone; only some shall forever live on. Ali-Stanley the Great, eternalized in show and song. The honor today was on this stage, attended by he in this golden age. The Seven Gods all bless our King, until he assumes the golden wings. Flying up to the heavens, he shall one day. But until that time our King shall slay. Eternal shall live our King," the actor cried and Ali-Stanley's sheep-like followers repeated the words in a unified chant.

The performance was followed by a poet regaling the audience with the battle exploits of Ali-Samuel Wamhoff in the Battle of Bear Gate. He had already heard a few requiem songs for Ali-Samuel, a tremendous warrior assumed to be dead. These words Penrose knew to be true but they faded into mindless chatter as he helped the King back to his heavily padded seat. He tried to solely focus on the King's safety. He glanced around the room and saw the shadowy figure from Waters Edge still lurking in the corner. The voices were demanding to taste the fluid of vitality tonight and they would love for it to be royal flavored. They never took no for an answer.

19
EDBURGH

AS THE MOON rose, the rosace windows recaptured a faint reminder of daylight, but rolling carts of controlled fires were stationed around the hall to assist the wall torches. Edburgh's mother, Ali-Pari Wamhoff, finally shuffled up the main steps to leave. She hadn't stayed this late at a feast in over ten years. Now Ed could stop standing like a shady guard in the corner and really join the party. He was dressed like a common guard in a hooded cloak with boiled leather beneath and a belt loaded with daggers and two short swords. He couldn't let his mother know he'd come to the wedding or what he was planning. The once close Etburn family now stood divided. At their meeting, the King had told him to attend the party in guise. King Ali-Stanley had promised Edburgh grand rewards after completion of their plan.

Ed had told everyone back home that he needed to get away after Caroline's death to clear his head. He had never really felt loved in the Etburn castle. His brother Rollo had loved him before he died. So did his mother before Russell Seabrook came along, but after four sons, Ali-Pari really wished Edburgh had been a girl. She was in her forties at the time and she loved her fifth son, Ed, until Russell became her favorite. She had even forced Duke Etburn to make the bastard boy a knight. He didn't miss home.

If Donegal was a family, Fox Chapel would be the inept father, Burkeville would be his beggar spouse, Mattingly would be the bread-winning son, Bottomfoot would be the wayward sibling and Waters Edge would be the elderly, stubborn uncle.

His home region of Waters Edge was known for upholding old, forgotten customs and traditions. The region had become complacent under the leadership of Duke Tyus Etburn. Ed's ancient father preached a life of religion and simplicity. The Duke's council and Ed had persistently tried to convince him to keep up with the advancements from around the world but Tyus called most of it the work of the demons. His father believed in some improvements but he thought most of the scholars' ideas were steeped in black magic. He started defunding the efforts of the top minds almost five decades ago and the people of Waters Edge suffered. Duke Etburn had already lived a long full life and didn't answer to anyone except his wife and the Gods. Ed even noticed things around and in the castle that showed Fox Chapel had forged ahead over the past ten years.

Ed had been staying at a rundown inn on the outskirts of town. Due to the wedding, all the good ones were already booked before he arrived in the Capitol. He remained constantly tired from the rag that the innkeeper passed off for a bed and the nightmares that awakened him every night. Even though Ed still believed he had no choice but to kill his wife, she was alive every time he tried to sleep. She brought the knife down, but this time Ed's hands were powerless to stop the cold steel from driving deep into his heart. He didn't want to attend the wedding because he thought it would remind him of Caroline. He was correct on that account, but he had a very important reason for being here tonight.

Edburgh stared at the Lord Pyromancer's gift hanging on the west wall. Two circular metal shields were precisely smeared with purple fire to look like a burning fox and bear. He kept moving his vision from the glowing amethyst flames to his possible future bride.

There she stood, right next to the bride. Ali-Gare Wamhoff looked even more impressive in person than in the stories. He hadn't seen her in ten years but she had aged beautifully, like red wine from Abbey Grove . He remembered a skinny teenager, but this was a stunning woman. Many men had claimed they would marry the Princess and suddenly it appeared Edburgh Etburn actually had a real chance.

She wore a flaming auburn strapless sweetheart gown that matched her hair. The sideless piece was secured with luminous teal laces which continued crisscrossing around her bare shoulders and all the way down her arms. The same colored laces extended up from her shoes and twisted around her seductive legs until disappearing into receding layers of skirts just above the knees. Ed focused on her moonstone-covered shoes and dreamed of being in love again. Ali-Gare could be his saving grace. She wasn't married so she couldn't wear a headdress but liberally sprinkled gold dust mingled about her hair and face. She looked perfect to Ed.

Ed looked back at the flaming shields and hoped no one would recognize him. There weren't many people from Waters Edge and nobody looked familiar to Ed. Ed took a hefty drink from his pewter tankard. The King sat him at the one table reserved for the distinguished guards. He hadn't really talked to any of the men at the table and occupied himself with drinking the tasty wines. He sucked down more of the Honey Burgundy Blend from Androsi.

He peered toward the stage and watched trained dogs and monkeys doing tricks on command. The collared dogs pulled the clothed monkeys around on rolling wooden planks. The Lightview apple mead made its rounds and Ed enjoyed the first sip off a full tankard while the dogs now jumped through flaming hoops. By the time he chugged the Frosty Harvest sweet white from Waters Edge, his vision was hazy. Two monkeys stood on their heads and two others walked up and gripped their ankles. The two interlocked monkeys did somersaults as they weaved around the stage like a rolling wooden wheel. The soft-sounding bells around the animals' necks continuously rang and flirted with the rhythmic drumming coming from the minstrels' gallery. Ed's head began to spin as he looked away from the stage and rubbed his glazed eyes.

He started to sweat profusely and his breathing became erratic. It felt like somebody was inside his body, punching his heart. Ed panicked and thought this picturesque scene suddenly seemed tainted, like a healthy red rose growing from the chest of a dead body. He felt this had to be a trap to lure him in. *Why did the King order me not to tell anyone of my visit? If I were to somehow disappear, not a soul would be wise to the matter.* He wiped his dripping forehead with his hood and took a big drink to calm down.

He slowly regained his composure and confidence as he stared at the huge Etburn silver eagle flag fluttering dangerously close to the wall torches. He looked away and noticed that the King appeared to be retiring for the evening. Ed knew he had to seize the moment to carry out his duty. He moved quickly to catch up with the King; he'd only come here to do this. He walked faster now and was only four feet away. Edburgh closed the gap and put his hand on his hip. Just as he got within reach, Sir Penrose Ellsworth came out of nowhere and planted his forearm in Ed's chest, knocking him onto his back.

"Your majesty," screamed Ed. The King looked down, squinting, and pulled Penrose back. "Leave him be, Sir Penrose. He is my guest," said the King.

"Apologies, your highness, but I don't like anyone to rush the King of Donegal as he just did," Penrose said. "Your due diligence is appreciated as always, Sir Penrose. Now, what is it you want, my boy?" the King asked as he turned his attention to Ed.

Now fully upright, Ed said, "I just wanted to pay my respects for such a lovely wedding and wanted to thank you for everything, your highness. That is all." *You know what I want.*

"The pleasure is mine. I believe manners should still count for something. This is my wife, Queen Emilia." The King had to struggle to get his wife's attention as her eyes were almost closed. "Oooh, who is this big boy?" asked the Queen as she ran a drunken hand across Edburgh's chest.

The King slapped her hand down and said, "You will have to excuse my wife, she is...deprived of sleep so it seems. This is an example of those vanishing manners I just spoke of." He leaned in and quietly stated, "I will call for you in a few days. At the right time you will find somebody wearing this silver fox pin," he showed Ed the pin in his open, wrinkled palm. "He will be standing by King Ali-Dus Wamhoff's bronze statue around mid-day. Say the word "pearl" to him and he will bring you to me for the answer. Now stay safe, my boy."

"Yes, your highness, thank you again." Edburgh bowed. The King grabbed his wife and pulled her away.

With that accomplished, Ed turned his attention back to Ali-Gare Wamhoff. The King had told him if he decided to go through with their plan that he would receive Ali-Gare's hand in marriage. Ed now stared at his prospective bride, stopping occasionally to sip his wine. He felt extremely out of place here. No one wanted to talk to him, not even the guards at the table. He said hello to a lot of guests but never had any conversations. He felt like the King's assassin, not his nephew, lurking at the party. He finally broke his dead stare of Ali-Gare but still thought of her. He hoped she could divert his mind from Caroline and maybe stop the nightmares. Ed knew that if everything went according to plan he would be the envy of every man in the free world.

Sometimes you have to be torn down completely in order to rebuild. Maybe I need to make my own family now with a woman who can bear me an heir.

He knew he shouldn't look too far ahead, but Ed wanted to dream for a moment. He decided it was time to leave and walked out of the castle. Moonlight flickered between the trees as the wind shook their leaves, occasionally brightening different areas. A slight fog dulled the dim light of night, presenting a paradise for thieves. Ed had a long walk to his horse and clutched a dagger in his right hand. *You can never trust anyone in the Capitol.*

He was going back to the inn, getting as drunk as he could, and attempting to stay asleep tonight.

20
ELISA

THE SUPPER FEAST mercifully came to an end and Elisa sat in her new quarters and stared at her husband who lay next to the bed on the black carpeted stone floor. He snored and slobbered but Elisa would rather have him sounding like an out of tune trumpet on the ground than crushing her in bed. She didn't want to go to sleep just yet and went to see her sister in the visitors' apartments. The guard, named Danforth, informed her that Telly had gone to the kitchens. *Leave it to my sister to be hungry after a twenty-eight-course feast.*

The new bride went to track her down but didn't know the exact lay of the castle and noticed a huge man from the King's Guard with his back to her. "Pardon me, sir," she said. Jermar "The Giant" Lolat turned around with a wide grin. "Can you direct me to the castle kitchens, please?" Elisa asked. "Can I direct you to the castle kitchens, ha," Jermar huffed.

She could smell booze on his breath and see the haze over his smiling face as he leaned down closer. He said, "I can do a lot more than show you the damn kitchens. I can give you something no other man can boast. I can help you make the biggest, strongest, bravest prince in all the lands. Look at me, Grand Champion of the last three tourneys, living embodiment of courage and the reason Donegal won the Battle of Bear Gate," he bragged but didn't lie. Elisa knew a lot about the battle. Three men were heavily credited with the victory and Jermar Lolat, not a knight at the time, was on the list. The show-off continued, "Let me know when you come to your senses and realize the clear choice. Your son will be a king one day. Do the right thing for the kingdom, my lady."

Elisa backed away and sternly said, "Only one man will ever give me child." *And that man is certainly not Ali-Varis Wamhoff.* Elisa had dealt with many men coming on to her so this wasn't anything new. She would deal with this the way she had always done.

"Ha, you stand a better chance at sprouting a child out of your backside in darkness than our Prince getting you pregnant," the knight said and guffawed. "And you sir, have a better chance of producing a castle out of your backside than getting me pregnant, and I'll thank you kindly to stay out of my affairs," Elisa said and turned to leave but wasn't sure what direction to go. "The offer stands, my lady," The Giant laughed. She retorted as she turned her back on him, "Brute arrogance might work on some, but not all, good sir."

Elisa scurried away and found the kitchens on her own. As she walked toward the back of the main kitchen, she spied Prince Ali-Ster arguing with what appeared to be the head cook. The Prince's back was to Elisa who stopped and listened. An agitated Ali-Ster said, "The guards had a feast in their own right just today. When's the last time you saw a feast along Rat Shit Road, or in Kimberton?" The cook shook his head and answered, "You got me there, can't say as I have. S'just that the commons, they aint comin' in here wiff ugly blades taller than me, tellin' stories o' what that sword done seen. You gonna be lookin' to employ a new mess o' cooks if I tell any a them no, m'Prince," the head cook pleaded. "I'll take the leftover food myself if it comes to that, but I won't allow our guards to sell it at top price on the streets to stuff their purses. Men are starving and our guards plot ways to gain advantage, sickening it is. What has become of our realm?" Ali-Ster wanted to know.

"I'm just tryin' to save m'neck, Prince Ali-Ster. Something I fear you might not understand," the head cook said. "I served four years of war duty, and you?" Ali-Ster asked. "Two years, highness," the cook meekishly answered with his beet-colored face lowered. Ali-Ster said firmly, "I understand. I understand going into battle and risking the chance to be killed at any time. I also know it can be scary."

Elisa couldn't see Ali-Ster's face but a look of relief washed over the head cook's visage. Ali-Ster said, "I will take leave this moment and talk to the guard camps myself. If anyone is to give you or your staff any trouble, be certain to alert me at once." The head cook bowed and said, "With honor, m'Prince, thank you so much for gracing us with your presence. It's an inspiration to all the staff."

"My pleasure, good man," said Ali-Ster who turned suddenly and came face to face with Elisa. The Prince stopped and both of their cheeks became flushed. His long freckled face had become even more appealing to her after the kind gesture. Her heart fluttered in the same manner as earlier today when she had seen Brehan Castaway. She had never experienced romantic feelings for anyone except her one and only love. She could appreciate handsome men for their good looks but this felt different. Ali-Ster's scent of cloves even pleased Elisa's nose in stark contrast to the Grizzly Bear's off-putting odor.

Ali-Ster stammered, "My lady, congratulations are in order...again." He shook his head but continued while looking down, "You were nothing short of beautiful today." The Prince smiled to cover up the awkward greeting.

I was beautiful? What am I now, I wonder? I'm wearing the same outfit. What is that supposed to mean? "Thank you so much, you are too kind," she said shyly with flickering eyelids. The Prince nodded his head and said, "I'll leave you to your own devices, my lady." He closed with a perfect bow and exited the kitchen. Kings and princes weren't required to bow to anyone but a proper gentleman always bowed to a proper lady.

Elisa watched him leave and laid eyes on a much less attractive man. She asked the head cook, "I'm looking for my sister Telly; someone told me she is down here." He responded, "M'lady, I believe congratulations are in order for the lovely bride and future queen." She thanked him and said, "The food was absolutely perfect today." He humbly accepted the praise and told her, "Your sister, she was down here for some sweets but she left right as the Prince arrived, quite a gallant man he is, m'lady."

I couldn't agree more. "You're quite right, I must say. Thank you again." She curtsied and hustled back over to her family's apartments.

Elisa smelled him as she rounded the corner of the hallway. Guard duty must've changed. She hated the Grizzly Bear and barely ever spoke to him. He and her father represented everything evil about this realm and the Prince personified the definition of honor and chivalry in Elisa's eyes. "Where's my sister?" Elisa asked. The towering man was staggering drunk, sometimes sinking down to about Elisa's height. His long matted beard and crusty hair stunk of month-old sweat that united with rotting particles of food that had escaped his mouth. The cruel hallway breeze pushed the sour smell straight into her nostrils. She held her breath in the dimly lit hallway as he answered, "Sleeping. Everyone is sleeping. Maybe you should be..." The Grizzly Bear was cut off by Elisa who bluntly asked in a disbelieving tone, "My father is sleeping already?" "Sleeping, passed out drunk, dead. Who knows? He's not awake or I wouldn't be standing here, that much I can tell you," the Grizzly Bear told her.

"I'm sorry you didn't win the wedding celebration tournament," she said. Elisa wasn't sorry and only made that comment because the behemoth made her nervous. In fact, she had rooted against him at the tourney. She had never talked to the Grizzly Bear for this long and wanted to get away. "I did win. I won seventy-seven gold foxes for winning the Circle of Strength. Grand Champion would have been nice for the gold but I couldn't give a damn about the rest," he said and unsteadily shook around a leather purse with heavy clanking coins inside. Elisa looked at the man in fear as he came uncomfortably close and spoke, "You're afraid of me."

After a few moments of tense silence, she asked with a lump in her throat, "Is that a question or a statement?" He shook his head and said, "I don't ask questions I already got the fucking answers to."

Elisa turned her head to the side to avoid his rancid breath and noticed well-framed paintings on the walls detailing former Wamhoff Kings in battle. She pretended to scratch her nose to avoid his breath as she stared at what looked like vomit in his mustache. He said, "I know you think me as scary, oh hells your father too, I'll bet. But that pretty little Prince you see prancing about the castle is a killer and I'm certainly not talking about Ali-Varis. Killers, all of them. Every man and I mean every..." the Grizzly Bear stopped. He graciously turned his head to the side and released a loud bass-filled belch. The smell almost knocked Elisa over who pulled her hair closer to her nose but the strong orange blossom scent from earlier had been destroyed by the man aptly named after a wild animal.

He wiped his mouth and continued, "Every man is a killer. Every man..." A stern female voice from behind Elisa stopped his words. Ali-Gare Wamhoff came closer and said, "Late at night after a feast is the worst time to deal with these animals. Don't let this big oaf scare you now. Fighting men aren't so scary once you realize they're all soon to die." She stood next to Elisa and looked up at the Burke family guard. Through the flickering torchlight, the Grizzly Bear smiled at the Princess with his eyes but his lips remained still and shut.

Ali-Gare stared at him and said, "Go get back in your cage while we ladies have ourselves a talk." The Grizzly Bear snapped back, seemingly intrigued by Ali-Gare's feistiness, "Two lovely unguarded ladies all alone should fear men like me till the day they die if not after that. Get a guard like me or its best of luck around the Capitol, sweetlings."

Ali-Gare came back at him but looked at Elisa as she spoke in a bitchy tone, "Pay this man no mind as a lioness would never a sheep. He's just part of a flock; a follower is the best he'll ever be. He looks big and bad but at the end of the day; he's just a little sheep, nothing but a follower, waiting for women like us to tell him what to do. Sheep are slaughtered every day, never remembered and the mighty lioness lives on. This little sheep probably won't be around to see your twentieth year come to pass. My guess is he'll only be rotting bones by that point."

Elisa couldn't see a reaction on the Grizzly Bear and even wondered if he was sleeping while standing up because he remained still for the first time. Before Elisa could figure it out, Ali-Gare pulled her over to her private tower.

The thirty-five floor Princess Tower had only one resident. As they went up a few flights of the circular, winding staircase, she could see why Ali-Gare never wanted to leave this arrangement. They stopped on the seventh floor and Ali-Gare led her into a luxurious comfort room decorated daintily with princess colors of red, pink and white. They sat down on a comfortable rosewood couch, cushioned with goose feathers and covered in ruffled pink silk.

Ali-Gare bluntly asked, "How was your secret visitor today?" Elisa stammered, "How did you know? I mean, I didn't have any visitors today." The Princess shook her head and said, "Liar. And one of the worst ones I've ever seen. Not anywhere near convincing, we'll surely have to work on that. So how was it?" Ali-Gare flashed a perfect smile and Elisa wanted to trust the Princess but her last name was Wamhoff. "If this were to be true, what you think you know, how would you know?" Elisa carefully asked. "Well, we all know I'm not married but that doesn't mean I'm not in love. Some people can be married yet obligated by their own heart to love another and that can be beautiful. I know about it because we both had secret visitors that know each other. I'll start; mine was great, and you?" Ali-Gare pressed, concerning Elisa. She smiled cautiously but distrust showed in her eyes as she said, "It was great." Ali-Gare removed Elisa's head dress and her own before shaking her head and saying, "Oh stop with the details, it's too much for me. Alright, I won't press any further but we have much more in common that you may dare to realize."

The two ladies helped each other out of the outer layers of their outfits and lay down on the wide, long couch and snuggled up together. Ali-Gare grabbed the ermine-lined linen blanket and the slight chill was suddenly quelled when the cover came up to her chin and the two ladies rubbed each other's perfect bodies warm. Elisa could feel her heart beating heavily in unison with the Princess' and got a close face-to-face view of Ali-Gare Wamhoff that nearly all men would kill for. She saw and felt the beauty of the Princess and found one story or song to finally be true. Ali-Gare did live up to the angelic reputation.

"So Prince Ali-Ster seems to be quite the young man," Elisa hinted. Ali-Gare answered in an annoyed manner, "Oh sweet gods, not you too. Every lady from Blairs Beak to the Rocky Sea is infatuated with the boy, boy I said. He must be the male version of me." Ali-Gare laughed heartily, seemingly aware of her reputation. "No, no, it's not that. I just saw him in the kitchens making sure the extra food from the feast would go to the poor inside the city gates," Elisa said. Ali-Gare shook her head and her nose brushed Elisa's as it went back and forth. She could feel the Princess' breath on her chin when Ali-Gare said, "There's always one of them. I suppose he is his mother's son. Lowborn blood tends to love lowborn blood."

Elisa didn't have a response and a few minutes of silence made her think the conversation was over but they talked for two more rings of the castle bells. Elisa Burke Wamhoff's day of matrimony came to a close with her falling asleep with her husband's sister on a couch in the Princess Tower. Elisa woke before first light and struggled to reassemble her clothes without waking up the snoring Ali-Gare. She had never heard a sweeter snore. She gave the sleeping Princess a kiss on the cheek before sneaking back to her bedchambers. Ali-Varis was in the same exact position she had left him, snoring loudly on the floor. *Must run in the family*. Ali-Gare's snoring was cute but the robust Prince's baritone droning quickly became annoying and Elisa tried to lightly kick him to stop the bothersome noise. She looked at him and couldn't fathom how the same set of parents could produce Ali-Varis and Ali-Gare. The effort to silence the noise proved futile and Elisa started pulling off her outer layers while thinking about her strange wedding day and new life in the Capitol.

21
THE SEVENTH DAY—ALI-STER

THE KING HAD told Ali-Ster very little about why they were riding away from the city toward the mountains on horseback. King Ali-Stanley only conveyed that he needed answers. Of course, Sir Penrose tagged along for the ride to protect them on this dark spring night. The moon hung low in the sky but was only a slight crescent and the clouds covered it most of the time. A faint breeze cut through the dense fog but visibility was poor. Ali-Ster followed the sounds of the other horses hoping to avoid tree branches and other pitfalls.

It was the seventh day of the month, so Ali-Ster knew this had something to do with the Gods. It was often said that the Gods opened their ears to humans on this particular day. He had never spent much time with his father before he left at fourteen, so he had never realized how much the King depended on religion. Ali-Ster believed that men relied on the Gods too much for protection. He saw men praying on the ground as they died a bloody death. Quite ironic, he thought, they were basically thanking the Gods for delivering doom.

Death is part of life. Prayers will never protect me.

The fog suddenly lifted like a blanket in the morning. The trio rode up to the base of a hill he had never seen before. An opening appeared in the rock. It measured eight feet high and appeared to have two fangs suspended from the top. It stretched about four feet wide and the King halted his horse about ten feet away. Sir Penrose and Ali-Ster followed suit.

Everyone jumped down as the King said, "Penrose, take our horses and wait right over there, please."

"With honor, my King," he replied. "Alright Ali-Ster, let's go," King Ali-Stanley ordered.

Ali-Ster followed him toward the venomous-looking opening.

As they approached, King Ali-Stanley Wamhoff turned to his son, "We

144

must genuflect, my boy."

The two sank to one knee and three red cardinals flew from the tunnel. An instant later, thousands of red birds flooded through the opening, flying in one steady stream for about a solid minute. After the last bird rushed from the darkness, a rolling cloud followed.

"They are ready for us," asserted King Ali-Stanley. This black-magic type religion wasn't something Ali-Ster understood. He had always maintained that sound reasoning would guide people better than praying for answers.

Dimly lit torches faintly illuminated the cave. Two large wooden totems of the Gods were the first thing they passed on the right and left sides of the tunnel. Just beyond that staggered a spooky-looking man, burning incense clutched in both hands. It smelled like a cross between rosemary and cinnamon as Ali-Ster trailed his father toward the man. The man with a shaven head wore a black robe that hung loosely on his gaunt body. His eyes had black and purple flesh around them as if he had been severely beaten, yet the rest of his face was frighteningly pale.

The King kneeled before him as the bald man held the incense beneath his nose and prompted him to inhale the smoke deeply. The King sucked it in and exhaled heavily. Ali-Ster tried to mimic his father but he choked as he exhaled the wicked concoction. Unfortunately, he had to repeat the process six more times. The smoke made Ali-Ster so dizzy he didn't think he could stand up again. The burning smoke danced in front of his bloodshot eyes, taking the shape of a woman, before it vanished into thin air. His heart raced and though he rarely drank, Ali-Ster felt rotten drunk. His father hooked his hand through Ali-Ster's right arm to pull him up. The young man stumbled, but regained his balance as they headed farther into the depths of the cave.

The path got increasingly narrow and the light became progressively dimmer until it faded to pitch black. Finally some torches ahead provided light for the two. Seven symbolic torches aided in showcasing images of each of the Gods that were carved into the walls. A misshapen, rectangular wooden door waited at the end of this haunting march.

It feels like we are headed for the belly of the beast.

The King immediately opened the door without fear and pulled in a reluctant Ali-Ster. The door opened into a small room with colossal torches in each corner. Under the torches were what appeared to be dragon skulls about the size of a normal man curled into a ball. He had never seen a dragon skull before, but he felt sure that is what they were. Bats hung upside down, covering the ceiling, about eight feet above. There was an altar in the middle of the room that Ali-Ster spotted in spite of his disorientation. It looked about four feet tall and the base was made of human skulls stacked on top of each other. The table had a flat, off-white top that seemed to be crafted of bone. A straight line of assorted colored candles stretched from end to end. Smoke slowly escaped from the apertures of the skulls. It filtered through their eyes, noses and mouths as his father dragged him even closer.

They kneeled down in front of the altar as a figure ascended behind the smoke. When the smoke thinned, Ali-Ster was stunned. A woman with snakes for hair appeared to be floating off the ground. His head was still scrambled but it looked like she wore nothing but her soul as she levitated behind the altar. Her pale skin tone almost glowed in the torch light and white and purple snakes intertwined as she slowly drifted back and forth. Her eyes were rolled back into her head so Ali-Ster only saw the whites. To Ali-Ster's befuddled senses each event was more mind-blowing than the one before it.

The King spoke loudly, his voice on the verge of a scream, "I come again for answers from the Gods about a plan that was posed to me."

Silence filled the creepy room for a minute as the snake haired woman closed her eyes.

"I need to know if I should go through with this plan..."

Instantly her eyes opened wide, totally white again. The snakes stopped moving as she stared deeply at the King with her iris-less eyes before slowly saying:

Maybe not, yet maybe so,
Beware you must, how words will blow,
The fires burn and smokes arise,
Make a choice but first be wise,
If threats you feel shall fill you full,
Break into action, wait not you fool,
But if you may and if you must,

Be forewarned that is to whom you trust

The King turned to Ali-Ster, "I have the answer, my boy. We may leave now."

Ali-Ster didn't have the foggiest idea how his father found an answer in that cryptic message. He felt even more confused than when they arrived. Ali-Ster had heard of the Priestess of the Gods from Count Silzeus, but this was nothing like what he had imagined. He wished his father had never reinstated these rituals of nonsense.

Although that was scary and inexplicable, I wouldn't put any credence into it. Does he really think that mad priestess just spoke directly to the Gods? If he bases an important decision on what just happened here, father must be a fool.

The daze wore off slightly as they exited the cave. They began to walk toward Sir Penrose and the horses when they heard a fiery roar and a blast of heat ran up their backs. Ali-Ster turned to see steam shooting from the cave into the night sky. He looked over to see a smug smile on the face of the King. Ali-Ster did not share the King's sentiment and couldn't wait to get out of this place. As he mounted his horse, the strong fog returned like a thief in the night.

22
INSIDE AND OUT—RICEROS

COUNT SPROUL AND Riceros sat at the circular table in the Colbert library. Jon Colbert placed emphasis on reading and education. He often accepted payment in written records, especially of battles, and other historical manuscripts. He had taken all the ancient documents from the King as payment over the years. They were old papers and books that the Etburns had found in a cave and then instantly turned over to King Ali-Antemis more than one-hundred years ago. But the King's thinking men couldn't build most of the designs correctly so they had been stashed away over the years until King Ali-Stanley got wind that Jon Colbert would accept them as payment. The documents showed Jon Colbert how to build a sewer system and helped line the Mattingly landscape with aqua tracks. The tracks looked like stone bridges but they sent water to all parts of the region. They were the biggest reason for the phrase, 'A Mattingly man never starves'. It had taken Duke Colbert's top men several years to figure out how to use the documents, but once they did, many more advancements followed. The Count read from the second book of *The Gods Words* to Riceros in his soft, soothing voice:

Josevius knew what must be done. He rose to his feet, weak from starvation.

He said, "My brothers and sister, I knoweth what needs done. All of us shall starve and die before our sun rises once again."

Josevius slumped back down in exhaustion, but continued, "I am nourishment. Taketh my body to sup upon and I shall live again through you, my siblings."

He turned to Nunce, "Brother, havest thou the firth to taketh my last breath, to save the race of man from evil?"

"It pains me, but I havest not the courage, my brother," responded Nunce.

Josevius turned to Cleon, "My brother, I favor you, havest thou the firth to accept my offer for the good of all man?"

"I also havest not the courage, my brother," Cleon said.

He now turned to Radial, "My brother, havest thou the firth to taketh my last breath so we may ascend to our home in heaven?"

"I doth not havest the firth either, my brother," Radial said, ashamed.

Josevius now turned to Numa, "Sister of meist, havest thou the firth to taketh my body, for the strength of the sun, stars, oceans and earth?"

"My brother, it will taketh all the strength of my womanly firth but I shall doth justice to our heaven."

Radial, Nunce and Cleon said their final words to Josevius, vowing to reunite in heaven. Then they disappeared into the high brush.

"Brother, are you sure this is your will?" Numa asked a final question.

"Sister, I am divine man. I must sacrifice myself for the good of all mankind and our parents in heaven. We cannot giveth in to Travibero," Josevius weakly stated.

"I understand what needs done, my brave brother."

Numa wrapped the bottom of her body cloth into a ball as tears welled up in her eyes. Josevius leaned back, opened his mouth and said a final prayer.

When they had eaten the last piece of flesh from the bones of Josevius, a bright light shot down from above and turned the night sky into morning for a moment. The bones suddenly jumped into the air and assembled themselves as if Josevius was standing straight up. The God Salius, father of Josevius, appeared through the light.

"My son, I havest arrived to taketh thou home," his father said.

A dark figure appeared opposite Salius. It was Travibero, Lord of the Plades, a gruesome, hairy beast with bright yellow eyes. The Plades were demons that opposed the Gods during the first days of earth. Travibero sported the body of a man and the head of a boar. White foam spewed from his slobbering mouth. He had extended fangs, three horns sprouting from his head and a long black tail that scraped the ground. The demon leader's booming voice howled something in a strange language and Salius shouted back in the same foreign tongue. Salius held his hands high, pointing to the sky. With more screaming from his father, the bones of Josevius started to rise into the air. The beast roared back, dropping to his knees and violently pounding the ground with both hands.

Josevius' bones dipped back down, coming close to the soil.

Salius looked to the sky and screamed, "Evil shall not taketh the soul of my son."

Salius levitated several feet off the ground before shooting straight up, out of sight. The bones started to rise again, higher than before. The demon responded with a blood chilling scream and descended underground. The skeleton sank again. Now the bones shook vigorously as the battle of good and evil between the Gods and Plades raged on earth. The skull started to rise again but the other bones didn't follow. They still shuddered below. The head came back to reunite with the other bones, which slowly started sinking into the ground. Suddenly, a heavenly light beamed down from above and surrounded the skeleton. Try as he might, Travibero was powerless to stop the righteous one from ascending to his home in heaven. The bones of Josevius climbed the seven stairs of heaven to take his rightful place next to his father. He was proclaimed Josevius, God of Sacrifice.

The Count closed the book and spoke, "You see, it is the ultimate story of sacrifice, my boy..."

As the Count glanced over at Riceros, he saw that the boy was fast asleep on the table.

Riceros stood on an island of snakes and six-legged salamanders. He was with a young girl and boy and they were walking barefoot on top of a bed of reptiles. There were skeletons riding horses that didn't have heads. The three kids watched as thousands of the headless horses passed without seeing them. The bones of the body-less riders clanked as the white horses with black spots trotted by. Blood still trickled from the necks of the destriers. The serpents and salamanders snapped at the falling liquid of life.

The boy spoke, "Why don't you talk?" Riceros stared at him but couldn't formulate a response. His tongue had betrayed him again.

The girl now looked at him, "Do you think you will ever talk?" Riceros nodded without confidence.

Both of the kids now talked in unison, "Maybe the words you speak are so important that you must save them until the time is right." He just stared at them as the slimy skins of the reptiles tickled his feet. The boy and girl spoke together again, "You might just be meant to talk to..."

Suddenly Riceros woke up from his nap to see Sir Brehan Castaway and Count Sproul. Brehan had always looked after Riceros.

"Let's go outside. I need some practice with the bow," said Brehan holding out Riceros' arrow launcher.

Riceros grabbed the weapon and they were on their way after saying goodbye to the Count. Brehan stuffed Riceros' black writing stone into a bag he had made specifically for carrying it. He liked to be able to communicate with Riceros even when they were outside. They headed out to a target in the woods next to the hunting grounds.

Jasper appeared out of nowhere, panting and bouncing around. He always found Riceros within a few minutes of his stepping outside the castle.

"Come on little man, keep up now." Brehan was a little hard on Riceros to make the boy tougher.

Jon Colbert had pushed Brehan to the limit to better him and he passed that down to Riceros, while keeping the boy's physical limitations in mind. They came upon the training ground for prospective knights. Most were squires, under scrutiny of their knights, trying to impress. Some practiced with staffs, others with swords.

"No, no, no," screamed one of the knights as he ripped the wooden sword out of his squire's hand. "Like this," he said while demonstrating the correct technique on the other squire.

"This is much more intense than the training in Burkeville. They train hard here. Burkeville would have all the older knights sitting around getting drunk and telling the same old stories while the recruits fended for themselves. Sir Gunnar said the training in Fox Chapel is better, but not anywhere near what it is here," Brehan said.

Riceros saw his uncle Ordrid teaching the young boys about swordplay. Ordrid was Jon Colbert's younger brother and the highest lord in Mattingly. He ruled Greeneville, a vast stretch of fertile lands that extended far enough south to enjoy the bounty of the sea. Ordrid differed from his brother in that he coveted gold and power. Ordrid's twelve- and thirteen-year-old sons listened as their father stressed defensive positioning.

Other trainees rode horses, trying to knock over a wooden dummy with a lance. Some squires just jumped on and off their horses while knights screamed at them. "Up," they would yell until they got on the horse and then, "Down." The exhausted participants did this at least thirty straight times in full armor.

As they approached the forest, several birds began to land around Riceros like they always did. They sang and squawked alongside and behind him. Animals always seemed to like Riceros Colbert. A jealous Jasper tried to chase away some of the competition.

Riceros slowed down to stare at the Ruin Stone of the Ancient Men. The impressive natural artifact had symbols and markings on it that no one had been able to figure out. Count Sproul said he believed it was a directional guide from thousands of years ago. The stone stood ten feet high and four feet wide but it appeared to be falling over at every moment because it sat on a slope. The two could finally see the target that sat upon a slight hill.

They moved ahead to the shooting range and the mark that was shaped like a fox. A popinjay sat on an oak tree branch high above the fox. As they pulled their bows, the birds flew away. Riceros had a small bow made of amber wood that was difficult for him to pull back.

They both unleashed all of their ammunition. Riceros had loosed forty arrows. He hit the popinjay with ten and the fox absorbed nineteen strikes. He only missed the high target once. The loser had to climb the ladder and pull the arrows from the popinjay and tree. When Brehan got back down he said, "Alright Riceros, I believe you have embarrassed me enough for today. The only thing I can be glad of is that you can't tell this story to the rest of the knights." Brehan smiled at the boy.

23
THE PEACEFUL SUMMONS—JON

"WHAT ELSE COULD he possibly want? Ali-Ster returned months ago; he is eighteen, she's seventeen. Neither yet betrothed, and the King always needs money. Seal it with a marriage and he will expect a full share of Mattingly."

Jon Colbert's worst nightmares were upon his doorstep. He stared at the parchment on the table that had arrived a bit earlier. It was now mid-day and he waited for the rest of the family to arrive. Brehan and Riceros walked into the sparsely decorated room. The rest of the family sat at a circular cherry wood table with chairs around it.

Jon had been tempted several times in the past few years to defy the King with the constant increases in tribute payments but he gave serious contemplation to saying no to Ali-Stanley. The thought of his only daughter marrying into the Wamhoffs caused Jon to consider an all-out war with the King. *My daughter doesn't belong in the Capitol. I would do anything to keep her from being forced into our enemy's hands. I will tell the family I am going to mind my duty to the King, but I don't know what to do?*

He looked around at the assembled family. "I have been called to the Capitol by the King. He also asked for Mariah to attend." His wife spoke, "It doesn't say that in the letter does it, about Ali-Ster?"

"No, I am only speculating. But what else could it be?" Jon asked. He played with his goatee nervously as his son Krys spoke, "Maybe he wants to borrow more gold?"

"He has always just asked for it in his letters. This has to be more than that." Jon always remained in control, but this fresh problem caused his mind to wander.

"Maybe he wants to borrow a whole bunch of gold?" Ruxin asked. Riceros wrote something on his slab and showed it to Brehan. The knight relayed, "What if it is a setup? Like your father?"

153

"I can't believe that the King would try anything like that again. My father didn't support the kingdom financially like we do now. That was thirty years ago and the King has five daughters of his own, he wouldn't ask for Mariah I would hope. And besides, how can I ask my citizens to listen to me if I ignore King Ali-Stanley. I will be very cautious, but I still need to honor his authority."

"I will make sure you are safe, my Duke," Sir Brehan stated with a smile to break the tense atmosphere.

Jon looked at the young knight and said, "Yes, I'll take you, Sir Gunnar, Sir Ryan and Sir Richard along with some other guards. But I really don't imagine the King would try anything foolish. Mattingly is the key financial cog in the Donegal political machine. He wouldn't sacrifice his cash cow even to the Gods he falsely covets." He got up and walked around his seated family.

"Are you sure you don't want us to go with you, father?" Ryno asked, referring to Krys and himself. "Actually, I will need you and Krys to go to Gama Traka for me now. Anders will be there to take care of you boys. You will take Lord Alfred along because he has been there many times and he knows what business needs to be handled. He will give you boys the details on the trip over there. There will be only a quick stop in Androsi so you will need to pack heavy. Ruxin, you are to stay here and look after the family. You will sit in the council meetings in my stead and watch over the castle. Your uncle Ordrid will be here to help you handle matters." Jon sank back into his chair and tried to appear confident in front of his family.

The group sat in silence, not knowing exactly what to think. Jon broke the quiet panic, "The King may have realized that he needs Mattingly and needs to unite our families. It should only be for a few weeks at most. We will be back before you boys return." Jon tried to add a glimmer of hope to this situation.

"When do we leave?" asked an excited and panicked Mariah. "In about a week and a half, so you better start packing now if you want to be ready, the way you pack," joked Jon. "Very funny, father," Mariah quickly returned.

"Alright kids, you may return to what you were doing," Jon Colbert told the children.

Everyone left the room except Camelle who spoke softly, "Why, why is it always something?" "Our daughter may have a chance to be Queen Mariah someday, you know," Jon reassured Camelle who always feared the worst. Jon understood she was always more emotional while pregnant too. The Duke and Duchess had been through this four times before, so he knew what to expect.

"But to a family of foxes? No thank you. She yearns for love, I know this. But kings and princes do what they wish without caring for their wives. Many end up miserable like Queen Emilia is right now, if the stories are to be believed," Camelle sadly added.

"How are you feeling, my dove?" Jon wanted to know. "My biggest worry right now is this summons. Just yesterday, all these problems seemed to be so far away. Now they sit at our doorstep," she said with a great sigh.

He knelt next to her chair and put his ear on his wife's plump stomach. He used his right hand to start rubbing her belly. "I can remember doing this when Krys was in here. Those were much simpler times, I know, my sweet dove, but our position now requires more responsibility and that might stretch to all of Donegal." "I don't want you to be responsible for everyone in Donegal, just be responsible for our family." Camelle sobbed, with tears welling up. "Everything I do is for you and the family, for our children's children. If we can build alliances that will insulate our family from attack, I have to do it."

Jon rose and wiped the tears from his wife's saddened face. Her eyes and nose were red and puffy but Jon still saw the beauty in Camelle Etburn Colbert. He kissed her on the cheek as she said, "But what alliances are to be trusted?"

"My sweet dove, we cannot live our lives out in fear. Come here," said Jon as he grabbed her hand and pulled her to the middle of the room. "Do you remember when we danced to "Lover's Island" on our wedding night?" Camelle whispered to her husband as they started dancing. "A goodly length of years has now gone by and it still remains the best day of my life. That set the tone for everything else. Without you, my dove, I am afraid I am nothing," Jon whispered back.

As they slowly danced around the room, a smile finally appeared on Camelle's face. They forgot their sudden problems and Jon remembered their questionable union nineteen years ago.

Duke Tyus Etburn had felt threatened from the King and thought a marriage alliance would ensure safety. Duke Etburn saw potential in Jon Colbert and Mattingly and wanted to depend on them to attack Fox Chapel from the south if he needed. Tyus Etburn was one of the most powerful men in Donegal at the time and the marriage had boosted Jon Colbert's reputation in the realm. Duke Colbert then used the new found connections to build Mattingly into the power it was today.

They softly worked their way around the room, both with eyes closed, taking solace in each other's togetherness. Jon kissed Camelle's lips lightly and rubbed her cheek with his thumb. Jon saw the same sixteen-year-old girl he had married that special day in Riverfront. It had been the biggest wedding celebration in the history of Mattingly and the Etburns even paid for half of it. Jon remembered setting up business partners at the ceremony that had lasted until this day. He tightly held the most important partner he made that day as they moved as one.

"I am going to bid Ordrid to stay at the castle while I am gone," Jon tried to assure his wife. "So he may order everyone about? He had the council members ready to throw him into the dungeons last time. Grace has always escaped your dear brother. Pray tell, how can your own brother be the exact opposite of you?" she wondered. "It was hard for him. He had to watch his brother be handed everything that he always wanted," Jon tried to explain. "He is the High Lord of Greeneville. It is one of the most profitable districts in all of Donegal, but it is never enough with him." She held Jon's body tight and escaped the moment again.

"Whether they like him or not, the men will do as he bids. We will return as soon as possible from the Capitol, but the trip must take place. Not to worry, I will be back in plenty of time for the birth." Jon kissed her and rubbed her stomach, feeling two kicks from the unborn Colbert.

Jon tried to sleep that night but he kept waking up at least once an hour. He couldn't decide what to do about the King's summons. He would rise with a revelation to honor the King's request only to wake the next time with a dream to defy Ali-Stanley. He saw sunlight creeping in and still hadn't made up his mind.

24
A QUEEN'S DEMAND-EMILIA

THE QUEEN OF Donegal sat in a steamy bath. Her handmaidens, Direll and Parata, scrubbed her with exotic soaps. Vanilla scents emanated from the foamy water and floated through the Queen's room. Emilia liked both her simple pleasures and her royal perks. Although she still considered herself a reclusive farm girl, she had become quite accustomed to the luxurious castle life. The girls were getting Emilia aroused as they massaged her breasts and thighs. Once she got started, the Queen would not stop until she was satisfied completely.

Emilia shied away from being an authority figure and took no interest in the ruling aspect of her queenly duties. She firmly believed that she was going to outlive the King, but she also had Ali-Ster to keep her in the castle and away from responsibility. She mingled with the common citizens and received much more respect from them than the nobility of Donegal. Most of high society looked down at the Queen and viewed her as a money hungry low born woman who seduced the King into marrying her.

The candles flickered as the Queen stood up, causing waves in the tub. Direll and Parata helped her out with towels waiting to dry Emilia's body. Direll wrapped the Queen in a red robe, and Parata handed her a black belt to secure it. She dismissed her handmaidens and ordered them to send Sir Anderley in.

The knight entered the queen's room and said, "My Queen, you called for me?" As he gazed at Emilia, she suddenly dropped her robe.

"Let's have a little fun. I am in a randy mood."

"My Queen," Anderley said aghast, "Not here. You know I cannot do that here." "What are you afraid of, *SIR*?" she sarcastically jabbed. "It is not about being scared, my Queen, it is simply a matter of not being stupid," he responded. "Oh, so now I'm stupid, am I? I believe I know what I can and cannot do in my own castle, thank you."

The Queen was really irritated now. *Fine, if he will not do it I know where to find men who are not craven.*

After she revealed her desire to Anderley, he looked like he was going to cry. He agreed to her plan as always, but this time he put up more of a fight to try to talk the Queen out of it. Her handmaidens had the Queen nearly dressed while Anderley waited outside the room again. She wore a small black dress that didn't cover very much of her short figure, along with a matching dark veil. She threw on a long black coat that touched the ground and totally hid her scanty clothing. She opened the door to see Anderley, still angry, but she didn't care. *I gave you the option and you forced my hand, so don't pout about it.*

It was almost a full moon and it seemed like half of Falconhurst had set out to enjoy the city night-life. After a fifteen-minute horseback ride, they arrived at a building on the outskirts of town. Neither had spoken a word to the other since the Queen had told Anderley about her plan. King Ali-Stanley had not satisfied the Queen in over ten years, ever since she gave birth to the castaway son.

Anderley and the Queen had sex quite a few times so she thought he was only jealous. They approached the building and entered to talk to the owner. The man sat behind a desk, counting gold. He shot a quick look at them as they came in. After Anderley had briefed the owner about the Queen's plan, he said, "I would like to help you but we do not use little girls here. So sorry, Sir."

"This is no little girl. I can assure you of that. Do you recognize this?" Anderley pointed to his King's Guard pin. As the two argued, the salacious Queen opened the coat to expose herself in the tiny dress. Despite her height, the owner recognized a womanly body and reluctantly agreed to the deal. The totally bald, obese man led the Queen and Anderley into a small room at the end of a narrow hallway.

When they walked in the room, the Queen started having second thoughts. There was a bed in the small room but that was it. Even with little light in the room, the Queen could tell the mattress hadn't been cleaned in a long while. She rubbed her left nipple to get back into the mood. She started getting excited again. There was a door leading outside that Sir Anderley slipped out of without speaking a word to the Queen. She could hear him pacing outside the room as she nervously waited. After only moments, someone entered the room.

"Hello," the man said in a gruff voice. "Hello, there," said the Queen in seductive tones.

The odorous man stripped his clothes off and moved toward the Queen. He tried to unmask her but she stopped him. "Some things must remain a mystery," she said.

As the large man mounted the Queen she could hear Anderley vomiting outside the brothel.

25
EDBURGH

ED FINISHED PACKING the last of his items from the room at the inn. He still had one thing left to do before he left Falconhurst. The King had given Ed his answer yesterday, or was it the day before that? The days were beginning to blend together seamlessly for the sleepless Edburgh. He was still having nightmares about Caroline. He now tried to always stay awake, only to drift off and wake soon thereafter. He would rise, sweating and clutching his chest from the dreams.

Ed hoped that once the King approved the plan, he would finally be able to get some rest.

He could not.

He left the inn and took off on horseback in an attempt to solve his problem of insomnia. Edburgh was not sure how long he would be on this trip, but he was under the King's orders, so he should have felt safe.

He did not.

He seemed to be even more nervous after the King had accepted his offer. The plan was just an idea in his head but now reality crashed down on him. He had to execute the plan precisely or it would be his head and that began to scare him. The King gave Ed a crew of four men to carry out his end of the deal. He was to set out on the morrow.

Ed had already had enough of the Capitol. The retribution that had engulfed his mind just weeks ago drifted away like the sleep he was chasing. Ofttimes he was so delirious, he couldn't even remember what he was doing in Falconhurst. Ed thought about going back home, but quickly dismissed that notion. He had put his neck on the line and knew that the King would have him killed if he tried to back out now.

He arrived at his destination, hopped off his horse, and tied the mare to a tree. The silver in his pocket clanked as he hit the ground. He glanced up at a full moon as he entered. A fat, bald man greeted Ed. He wore a mauve robe and had a red tie wrapped around his neck.

"I require the services of a woman, my good man," Ed said. "Well, what kind of girl are you looking for?" the owner asked. "A faceless whore really, nothing particular," said Ed, looking at the ground. He had never been in one of these establishments before.

"Well then, I think I have the perfect girl for you," chuckled the owner. Edburgh wasn't sure if that laugh was a good thing or not. The owner looked at the red-headed hostess, "Raguel, please take this gentleman to Room Twelve." "Of course, my Lord," she responded immediately with a smile and led Ed down a grungy hallway. *Is all of Donegal going downhill? Even the brothels are filthy. This woman better be worth it.*

Raguel led him up to a door, "Here we are, enjoy yourself but don't disrespect the lady." She pointed out the numerous guards lining the hallway at various points. Still smiling, she gestured to Ed to enter the room.

"Thank you," Ed said, as he entered the barely lit room. Ed thought he heard a man crying in the next room. The whore was lying on the bed wearing nothing but a veil as far as he could see. *Perfect, no face to even look at.*

Ed stripped off his clothes, suddenly questioning this move. Fully nude, he apprehensively approached the silent woman. The tiny woman welcomed him with open legs. He settled on top of her and rubbed himself on her warm vagina. She writhed under Ed for a moment or two; she seemed ready to go and Ed was too. He looked at the black veil and pictured Caroline's face, hoping to make it disappear from his nightmares as he inserted. The whore moaned, "Ooh, you are a big boy."

That voice rang like a bell in Ed's brain. But where was it from? After a minute or so, his mind flashed back to the royal wedding. *There is no way it could be her, could it?*

Caroline disappeared as he opened his eyes again and the face Edburgh Etburn saw belonged to the Queen of Donegal. As she writhed in the throes of passion, her veil slid off of her face and exposed her identity. *What in the hells is the Queen doing? Is this treason? I had no idea before I started. This is mad.*

After Ed finished inside the Queen, he rose without a word and dressed himself while she remained on the bed. He badly wanted to speak to her, but he wondered if she even remembered him. The room was very dark and the Queen had appeared quite drunk when they met at the wedding. It didn't seem likely after thinking about it because it was only a brief introduction from the King. He left the brothel expecting to sleep like a baby that night.

He did not.

Ed slept the same as he had for the last few weeks, terribly. He met his travel companions the next morning and took off on his journey.

26
A THRONE OF SORTS—RUSSELL

"SO YOU ARE saying that not only do you have to find the Pearl of Wisdom, but you must be the chosen one. Well who chooses?" Russell asked the wizard. "You are correct about the Pearl and I believe it is the dragons that choose whether the holder is worthy. I apparently, was not worthy."

"What do you mean?" an intrigued Russell asked. Dragon-Eyes had a happy look on his face as he stated, "I once held the Pearl in these very hands, or at least I thought it was the Pearl. It was nearly as big as my fist." He held a closed hand up to show Russell. "It was white, like a normal pearl, but it was also speckled with gold particles that seemed to float throughout it. It had a rare iridescent luster that glowed when looked at in the proper light. But the fact that most people do not understand is that it can only be used to defend, not conquer. I found this out the hard way."

"I have heard it has magical powers, from the stories about Rockarius, that is. He fought off Damian Doome and his legion of demons with it. Count Tisdale also said that many men hunt it so they can take over the world," Russell added.

"As did I. About two hundred and forty years ago, I lusted over it as I wanted to use it to slaughter all those who laughed at me so that I could rule the world. But I learned that it only existed to even the odds in the eternal war against evil. It is said to be the great equalizer, but it cannot be utilized for non-pure motives. That is why only Rockarius has been permitted to use the dragons. It is reserved to fight off the demon hordes of Damian Doome that can coexist with us as normal men in disguise. They are going to launch a new attack soon like they did five hundred years ago. And the Pearl and dragons will resurface to defend us. I am pretty bullish about it."

Russell butted in, "Bullish?" "Yes, bullish. Confident, stubborn, stern-minded, unwavering, headstrong, adamant. Get the meaning now?" the little man asked. "Yes, except for ada-what?" Russell laughed. "Adamant, it means bullish. Now if I may continue. Most men do not realize that the Pearl can only be used for the most important of tasks. That is why wars are being waged in the Pearl Islands and beyond. Everybody wants to ride the dragon that sets fire to the world and claim a throne of ashes."

It was mid-afternoon in the Frozen Forest as Russell and Dragon-Eyes neared the cave that apparently contained the proof of a dragon and the wizard's belongings. Flurries flaked down on their heads as they continued their conversation. Russell noticed that, for the first time, the Imp shook from being cold and shivered as he went on.

"I have fought on many sides of many battles in my illustrious lifetime to secure the Pearl of Wisdom. It was two hundred and forty years ago that I searched for the prize on the Pearl Islands. It was said to be in the possession of a rival company. Well, we ferociously attacked and thanks to our ruthless band of Prograggers, we drove them back into the Sea of Green. The man with the Pearl jumped into a boat and before we could sink it, the vessel had already drifted out. Then we all saw the gleam in the air as he hurled the Pearl into the emerald waters."

"And it has been there ever since," Russell interrupted again.

"Not in the least, if you would allow me the chance to finish. I can tell patience is something I will need to teach you. So everyone stood flatfooted and watched as I jumped into the choppy waters. I swam out to the area where the soldier had thrown the Pearl. I could always hold my breath for long periods of time so I inhaled and dived deep. I saw turtles, sea horses, blue and red fish as I dropped farther into that olive abyss. I went down about forty feet to the moss covered bed of the sea and I spotted the Pearl. Its brightness hurt my eyes when I first saw it. Then an oyster came out of nowhere and snatched the Pearl from right in front of me. This gigantic oyster was bigger than me but I managed to chase it down. I swam over to the oyster and positioned myself to open it. I had my foot on the bottom shell and my hands on the top. With all the strength of the Gods, I pried it open, kicked it up and grabbed the object as she floated by, finally swimming to daylight. I barely made it to the top before passing out."

"Wow, that is incredible," Russell interjected.

"I would probably not believe it if I had not done it myself. But immediately the Pearl grabbed hold of me and I started lying. I told the mercenary company that I couldn't find the damn thing. I secretly hid it and tried to summon the dragons when opportunities arose. It drove me mad, thinking that every last person was out to get my precious Pearl. I ended up burying the cursed jewel on the beach. It was not until hundreds of years later that I realized you do not find the Pearl, the Pearl finds you. It is reserved for a higher purpose than ruling over the world. I suppose it is funny how a couple hundred years can mellow a man," the wizard chuckled as he finished.

"Here we are then," Dragon-Eyes stated while pointing to a small opening in the ice. Russell wondered why the ice hadn't closed in that spot and pondered if he would be able to fit through it. He followed Dragon-Eyes into the opening. He barely squeezed through, but it opened up once he got inside. The ground wasn't frozen; he could feel the dirt move under his feet. A quick flash of fire sprang from the wizard's eyes, lighting a big torch. Startled, Russell jumped back with widening eyes. He saw the biggest skeleton he had ever laid his blue eyes upon.

"*This* is your proof that dragons exist?" Russell pessimistically asked. "What more do you need?" Dragon-Eyes quickly retorted. "This could be man-made or it could have been here for over a thousand years," Russell said again in a disbelieving tone.

"Question and fact..."

"What?" Russell interrupted. "Listen young man, *patience*. Now, question and fact. Question: What man is going to sneak into this cave in the Frozen Forest to construct that? Fact: I know that until fifty years ago this was not here."

The Imp wandered around the cave collecting his personal items. The shimmering light showed the dragon bones, arranged perfectly, like the beast had just sat down and died. When alive, it must have been as big as a small boat. The teeth were half the size of the little man.

The Imp stopped and said, "They were all I heard about growing up. Dragons. Almost all the older men claimed to have helped Rockarius and swore they saw the dragons. Every story and book told the tales of either

Rockarius or the dragons, or both. Every single person back then undyingly believed that dragons existed and only a few of them, if any, ever really saw one in the flesh. Dragons."

"How did it get in here?" Russell questioned. "I do not know that. I am just happy I wasn't present when it was here or I would have made for a nice little snack. So Sir Russell, how is it that you can walk away from your vows of knighthood?" Russell paused for a second, "I am not a true knight, I know that. It was given to me like a gift on harvest day." "Oh, I am sure it was well deserved," the Imp said in a consoling voice. "Some of it, aye, but Ali-Pari pretty much forced Duke Etburn into it. Now she forces me to do things in return," he softly said as he lowered his head.

Dragon-Eyes didn't say a word, but he knew from Ali-Pari's insatiable reputation what Russell was referring to. Russell continued, "My life wasn't meant to guard a family of nobility. I was born a simple man and I shall likely die that same way, but my life was meant for more. I shall serve you proud on a test of true honor." The wizard stared at him for a moment and said, "I humbly accept. Do you need to at least go back to the castle to gather your belongings and say fare thee well?" "No, I have all the things I need and I shall scarcely be missed at Elkridge. I feel that we have met for a reason. You can help me and I can help you," Russell said with a sudden look of confidence.

"As do I," replied the wizard with a glimmer of hope in his smile. The Imp kept gathering and packing his necessities for this trip. "Alright, now that is settled, I have to warn you of the sacrifice straight away. You must forget about everyone you know and love. You may never see them again. There will not be any fame or someone to crown you at the end of this journey. You may find a woman to love, but it is very improbable. This will be the truest test of who Russell Seabrook really is."

"Then why me...?" Russell wondered. The wizard quickly responded, "You need to develop the attitude of 'why not me'? Why not you, Russell Seabrook? I can generally read a person shortly after meeting him. You have virtue; I could see that plainly and immediately. You showed kindness by sharing food; and patience when following my slow legs around the Forest. I have also seen humility when you denounced a lofty knighthood. I warned you of the drawbacks on our mission and you remain diligent on this quest." "Thank you," said Russell graciously.

"You are certainly welcome. And I have only seen slight sinful tendencies that I can help you break in time. We will be tested by the seven gates of hell. Sin will follow and tempt us at every turn, but we must remain honorable. You must accept what comes our way, good or bad. Some people believe they are smitten by the Gods because they don't receive every little thing they wish for. Now we need to take you to a small school of sorts. We must make your mind as sharp as that sword of yours. Oh, I nearly forgot my own sword," he said as he went over to a large rock and reached behind it. He produced the hilt of a sword.

"What is that?" asked Russell. "It is my sword. What does it look like?" the wizard asked back with a smile. "It looks like only a sword handle to me," Russell answered.

The hilt had tiny emeralds and rubies encrusted on the pommel. The grip was black leather bound with golden strings. The Imp Wizard pointed it toward Russell before holding it above his head and shooting fire from his eyes at it. The flaming sword suddenly took shape. It was nearly as big as Dragon-Eyes with a blade of constant fire. The flames were more of a blue-green than the traditional orange and red.

"Hit it," said Dragon-Eyes as he held it out. Russell pulled his sword and lightly swung it at the fire sword. "CLANK." It stopped his sword as if it had an invisible metal center in the blade of flames. Russell did it again. "CLANK." The wizard had a huge smile on his face. "I call it Soul-Burner. When you look like me, you need all the intimidation you can muster." "So where is it?" Russell questioned.

"Where is what?"

"The school to sharpen my mind," Russell answered. "It lies up in the far north where the Frozen Forest thaws along the Salty Sea. It will take several days to get there. Once there, your training will start."

"Can I ask you something?" Russell asked. "Surely," the wizard replied. "You said that one of your main nicknames was the Imp Wizard. Don't you take offense to being called an imp?" Russell queried.

"As I said before, I wanted to kill all those who made fun of me until I realized that I couldn't just kill everyone. Aah, weaknesses and shortcomings. Wear them like a badge of honor. Make them your strength, not your weakness. Shove them in someone's face before they can tease you about it. Show them it doesn't bother you. Do something that those who make fun of you cannot. Do something that you thought you could never do. And remember only you can make yourself feel down, not others. Think independently of other's thoughts. Measure yourself figuratively and literally by your own standards. Do this and no one can make fun of you. Call me imp all you like because life is too short to hold grudges over name calling."

Russell's laughter stopped the wizard's lesson.

"What?"

Russell answered, "That is just funny because you are really short, but your life has been anything but short. You are like five hundred years old." "I'm not that old. I am only four hundred sixty seven. I am dreading the big five-zero-zero," the Imp said, pretending that he was mad about the age joke.

"Can I ask you something else, Dragon-Eyes?" "Of course, you may ask me anything," the Imp reassured the young man. "Did King Ali-Baster really die on the throne?" Russell asked curiously.

"A throne of sorts, I would suppose," said the wizard with a smirk. "So it is true," said Russell. "Sometimes we try just a bit too hard. Ofttimes you cannot force something. One must allow it to happen. And unfortunately our former King Ali-Baster tried to push just a little too hard. "

27
THE CORONATION—LEIMUR

SHE WALKED DIRECTLY toward her new throne. The royal hall was packed to capacity with the elite lords and ladies, who were lined up to salute their new Queen, Leimur Leluc. Everybody dressed to impress, except for Leimur. She strode down the path in black leather riding pants and matching laced boots. She wore a sleeveless argent and gold patterned side-laced doublet over a boysenberry-colored shirt that hung to her wrists. The samite doublet was studded with beads of amber and tiger eye. Gold tigers with sparkling amethyst gemstone eyes were sewn onto each of the silver shoulders. She had always hated women's clothing, especially gowns, and this was about the extent of her dressing up. A thick golden necklace looked like a loosely coiled snake wrapped around her neck.

The newly selected regime cared little about fashion and much more about control. Respect had seemed to follow as fast as word could spread of the new Queen's murderous takeover. Those in the room respected her out of fear, which sat just fine with Leimur.

The rest of the hall was quite a spectacle even though the Queen had demanded simplicity. The original plan involved a parade through the streets and men to carry the Queen down the aisle on the throne. She had nixed that idea right away.

Trumpets adorned with the new family flag featuring a tiger, were blown in harmony. A red carpet with gold edging rested below her leather boots as the Queen approached the steps. The wide marble staircase led Leimur straight to the throne. Seventeen guards with spears planted into the ground stood on either side of the path as she passed them and climbed the steps.

Leimur stood in front of the throne and saw the troubadours, jesters and singers in the back waiting for the ceremonies to end so they could entertain the guests. The new throne made liberal use of gold and demonstrated quality craftsmanship. The arms looked like eagle wings, extending out, replicating the bird in flight. On the front of the throne's arms were tiger heads with red ruby eyes. The feet resembled silver clawed tiger paws. A red velvet cushion seemed to float over the seat and a tiger's face was painted on the back of the golden throne.

The walls and decorative pillars were painted a gold, light purple and black pattern. Black silk curtains hung in front of the large windows to shield the guests' eyes from the sun.

Leimur already longed to be done with this stupid ceremony. She yearned to be back on the field of battle, not dealing with ceremonial nonsense that had existed for the sake of spending money to look financially secure. All the high lords and ladies of the land had turned up to bend the knee and pledge their undying support to a new queen. They wore the fanciest of fashions and reeked of the awful perfumes that she hated. Queen Leimur Leluc's sympathies lay closer to the common man than to families of nobility. But the Queen knew she needed their backing to run a successful kingdom.

The Queen had ruffled some feathers already by changing Goldenfield's official religion. Leimur wasn't really interested in the subject, but General Rigby talked her into changing it to the Partnership of Gods. The basic structure was a male and female God of equal power. The idea was that Mother Earth and Father of the Sky and Sea live in harmony when the worshippers uphold their values. General Rigby thought it best to choose a religion that had a strong female presence to reinforce Leimur's position.

She more than made up for the religious issues with the highborn by burning all the spy records her parents kept of the lords and ladies of the lands. She had done it in public and the implicated citizens were elated. The people didn't know that Leimur had made copies of all the records before the burning ceremony.

The Grand Priest stood next to the Queen with the crown in his left hand. The man was a tall, skinny individual. He wore a black robe tied securely with purple and white belts. His concave hat was purple with white lining and had a massive ruby jewel above his forehead.

"Lords and ladies of Goldenfield, we are gathered here to witness the coronation of a new queen. I bless thee, Leimur Leluc, protector of

Goldenfield. May you be wise in your decisions and guided by the Gods. It is with both of our Gods' blessings that I crown thee, Queen of Goldenfield. Long shall live the rule of Leimur Leluc."

"LONG LIVE THE RULE," the entire crowd chanted in unison.

He placed the crown atop the head of the new Queen to make it official. It was more of a golden battle helm than a tiara. The new symbol of power in Goldenfield fit her head snugly with face guards on the sides over her cheeks and a giant tiger-eye gemstone planted in the middle of her forehead. It was a proper crown for a Warrior Queen. The new ruler of Goldenfield took her seat on the throne. She looked like she had been born to sit there. The Queen's mind drifted as the guests came up, one by one, to pledge their honor and support. She looked out to see an artist, painting her as she sat on the throne for the first time.

After the ceremonies, the Queen retreated to her room only to find General Rigby waiting outside. "Hello, my Queen. We fashioned a surprise for you to commemorate your coronation," he said with a slight smirk. "You know I expect nothing, General," she said, although she wondered what this could be.

He opened her door for her and pointed the way. Leimur entered her room to see a great sight. It was a set of golden armor fit for a queen. It had a tiger's head crafted into the cuirass with two red gemstones stuffed into the eyes for the Tiger Queen. She had wondered why they were measuring her so carefully for the coronation doublet. Now she realized that they had been fitting her for the greatest suit of armor she had ever laid eyes upon. The vambraces shone in a way that entranced the Queen. Leimur closed her eyes and envisioned herself on the battle field, slaying the enemy in her new suit. There was also a new battle axe next to the armor. It stood about six feet tall with a silver blade and spike that blended into a golden handle. She wanted to use her gifts immediately but she contained herself.

"I thank you, General. I am not sure what to say except you have my sincere gratitude, good sir. I will be certain to take that shine away soon enough. I do not want to look like a Queen in shining armor."

She smiled at the General and saw him as the father she never had in Pascal Leluc. She still couldn't figure out why he had never sacked the Capitol before. *Why did he wait for me?*

The next day the Queen decided she wanted to see her family inspiration. She put on her new armor and walked across the city. Her great, great grandfather, Marius Leluc, had been a great King. He had the unwavering respect of the lords and commoners equally. He ruled with an iron fist, but also showed compassion where it was due.

Right down the road was the Leluc Mausoleum. It was a monument dedicated to the deceased members of the Leluc ruling family. Leimur refused to have anything associated with her parents make it into the Mausoleum. The big domed building housed relics and possessions from the former kings and queens of Goldenfield. As she entered the white stone building, a strange sensation came over her. She felt a tingle over her head and her heart suddenly raced. She could feel the power of the huge burial room as she walked into the middle. Leimur looked around at the air tight coffins that her ancestors eternally rested in. She spotted the bright red casket with a golden, soaring eagle on it.

Marius Leluc had an epic shrine surrounding his coffin. Clothes, weapons, armor, crowns, gold and jewels were laid upon the tables around the stunning tribute. Leimur could identify with Marius because he was called the Warrior King and he had conquered foreign lands and brought treasure back to Goldenfield. His weapon of choice had been the battle axe also. He was also known for his clever and unexpected strategy of traveling down the Rushing River through the Animal Kingdom on the way to attack Harbor Valley. It had completely taken Harbor Valley by surprise and Marius pummeled them into submission. It was a move the Queen currently reflected on as she knelt in front of the casket. Instead of praying to the Gods, she attempted to talk to the spirit of King Marius.

"Great, great grandfather, I wish to follow in your steps when I attack Harbor Valley. Please guide me on the correct path. I am attempting to resurrect our once proud Goldenfield to its glorious days akin to when you ruled. I will conquer and loot, just as you did before me. I regrettably had to dispatch my parents, who tried to do the same to me, but they failed. I did not. I have learned a great deal from their mistakes and I do not plan to repeat them. I will humbly rule until Huber is ready. He is only four years old, but when the time is right I will step aside and respect the laws of the land. I am going to care for Huber and Romer as if they were my own children. I will make sure they respect and cherish the

Leluc family traditions. But first I have to conquer Harbor Valley in your honor, King Marius Leluc of Goldenfield."

She stood up and stared at the red coffin. Her attention suddenly shifted to two battle axes lying on one of the tables. She picked them up and they seemed to match the axe she had received yesterday, except they were shorter. The Queen noticed they could be used in unison as she swung them around. They whizzed smoothly through the air and the Queen really liked the feel of them. She decided immediately that she would take them on her trip to Harbor Valley for protection and good luck. Leimur went back to the palace and put the axes in her room next to the larger one. She then looked around for her brothers to spend some time with the boys before she had to leave for the Harbor Valley attack.

28
ELISA

THE TWO LADIES laughed like children. Excitement rippled through the room as the women sat together having their hair braided.

"Are you sure they don't understand us?" Elisa asked. Ali-Gare replied, "Yes, stop worrying. These handmaidens are from Gama Traka."

The Gama Trakan handmaidens worked on the pair's hair that they had arranged in a figure-eight pattern. Elisa had found an odd ally in Ali-Gare Wamhoff. They had a secret connection that made Elisa feel secure around her.

"I can't wait to kiss him, touch him, feel him inside me," Ali-Gare happily pronounced. Elisa smiled back and said, "It is going to be such a wonderful day. Finally, some *real* men in the Capitol." They both enjoyed a laugh as the handmaidens continued to work on their hair.

"When did you and Gunnar fall in love?" Elisa asked. "The first time our eyes met. I had looked at many boys before that and felt nothing, but this was a man, a *real* man. This time my heart fluttered and I felt nervous. I had never felt nervous before, but when we kissed two days later he said that he was nervous too. I knew when our lips touched, that those lips would be the only ones I would ever need. Soon after that my father tried to betroth me to Rollo Etburn, but I would have none of it. I wasn't going to live in Waters Edge. My father is a king, but he is still only my father. A princess can get her way if she really wants to," Ali-Gare informed Elisa.

"My aunt explained to me what love was on my eighth birthday. That was when I knew I loved Brehan. He left when I was only nine. The first time he came back from Mattingly was the day I knew he loved me too. We didn't fully act on our love until I was fourteen though," Elisa innocently said.

"You beat me," said Ali-Gare. "I beat you, what?" asked Elisa. Ali-Gare explained, "I didn't have sex until I was fifteen. So you have me there."

"I didn't realize it was a contest," Elisa responded. "It's not. I am merely joking. Is he the only one you have been with?" Ali-Gare questioned. Elisa immediately answered, "Yes. Is Gunnar the only man you have been with?"

"Absolutely, and he will be the only one I will ever sleep with," Ali-Gare firmly said. "Is it strange that not very many people in the castle know about the Mattingly arrival?" Elisa wondered. Ali-Gare answered, "My father is always worried about his reputation. He probably wants to make sure that Duke Colbert will accept the marriage pact before making a formal announcement."

"It will be so great once Ali-Ster and Mariah marry," gleefully stated Elisa. She realized that the marriage would open up opportunities for her and Brehan to see one another a lot more. She had experienced feelings for Ali-Ster and felt cheated in having to settle for Ali-Varis, but she still loved Brehan who had informed her that Mariah Colbert was a wonderful person.

"We won't have to sneak around and worry anymore," said Elisa. "I don't know. I kind of like that part. It makes me feel even naughtier," said Ali-Gare. Elisa replied, "Yes, I suppose it sort of does."

"Sir Gunnar and I are going to get married and travel the world. We want to see as much as we can before we die, old, gray and wrinkled. Together. Time seems to stand still when he and I are together, but we also realize no one can avoid aging. I can smell his breath already and I can feel that he is getting near," said Ali-Gare as she deeply inhaled the air through her nose.

"That is beautiful. Brehan and I haven't figured out all of our plans yet. We just know that we want to be together until the end," Elisa said. "That is all that matters. I've forgotten myself at grand parties just thinking about Gunnar. When I am with him, it doesn't matter what the surroundings are. I lose myself in him. But we knew that we would have to leave Donegal to marry and that we wouldn't stop until we saw all that the world has to offer. And we would do it all together," Ali-Gare said with a smile.

The ladies were even more excited now. The handmaidens finished their hair and the two inspected each other's designs. The long braids had been woven into artful patterns all around the girls' heads.

"Yours is just lovely now," joyfully stated Ali-Gare. "Well, if mine looks half as good as yours, I should be grateful," Elisa replied as she blushed. "Oh, I bet it looks twice as nice as mine with your beautiful hair," Ali-Gare complimented.

"You are too kind." Elisa accepted the kind words and couldn't wait to see her man.

Comments like that made Elisa wonder why everyone had warned her about Ali-Gare's mean streak. Elisa now understood her better than others. Ali-Gare was happy today because she was going to see her one and only love. When she didn't see him for long periods of time, she probably had mood swings. Elisa acted the same way when she didn't get to see Brehan for long stretches. However, today the two girls couldn't have been more ecstatic and consequently, more courteous.

29

JON

THE COLBERT POSSE rattled up the Royal Road in search of Falconhurst. The Royal Road was a smooth dirt road that extended throughout most of Donegal. The road in this area was narrow and could barely provide enough room for two wagons to pass each other. Jon knew they were getting close now. They were twenty men and one girl, Mariah Colbert. She rode in a carriage in the back alongside the other wagon filled with supplies. Everyone else trotted along on horseback. Jon Colbert had brought some of his best knights and guards to escort him on this journey. But he was really trying to figure out how he would react when the King asked for his daughter's hand to give to Ali-Ster. The matters he had to deal with in the running of Mattingly did not need the complications of this fresh tension. Jon had ordered Sir Brehan to stay in the back to look after Mariah.

Jon rode in front with his armored knights, Sir Ryan and Sir Gunnar, by his side. He had brought six other armored knights and the rest were Riverfront guards armed with an array of weapons from maces to war axes to different swords. Jon just wanted to get this over with and get back to Riverfront. He wondered how his sons were doing on their voyage. He worried about everyone at home until the blazing sun broke his concentration by nearly blinding him. They were about twenty minutes from the castle. It was visible on the skyline and Jon still felt the stress.

Sweat dripped down his face, off his chin, and onto the horse's saddle. Suddenly a twang vibrated through the air. Six guards fell from their horses. Faceless men lurked in the trees, loosing arrows at the Colbert group. The wounded men fought the good fight for a few moments before succumbing to the Gods' will.

"AMBUSH, AMBUSH," screamed Jon Colbert as he jumped down from his horse. He calmed the horse to stop it from bolting and tried to use it as a shield against the hidden archers.

He grabbed Sir Herman, "Go tell Brehan to get my daughter out of here, NOW. If he cannot do it, you will, alright?"

"Yes, my Duke," said Sir Herman as he took off for the back of the group.

Jon Colbert held his hand in the air to block the sun so he could see the approaching foes. Through the bright golden rays he saw about thirty armored knights marching toward them. They didn't have flags or banners that identified them. It was obvious the Fox Chapel knights didn't want the Mattingly men to know they were coming. As the Fox Chapel knights got closer, he could see the surcoats of the enemy. He recognized the emblem of two foxes protecting the crown that represented the Wamhoff family of Fox Chapel. The exposed silver armor shone in the sun's rays as they quickly marched toward Jon. The opposing knights wore the full metal helm covering their entire heads with gold accents around the eyes and straight down the center of the mask to make a cross. The archers stopped when the Fox Chapel ground crew approached. A few of the Mattingly knights stayed on their horses, but most jumped down.

The Fox Chapel knights screamed for Mattingly to surrender. "In the name of King Ali-Stanley Wamhoff of Donegal, I order you to lay down your arms."

"NEVER," bellowed Jon Colbert and his contingent rushed the enemy.

A tornado of violence erupted. Extreme metal rang through the hot, dry air right along the Royal Road. The conveniently located woods on either side of the road prompted several Mattingly guards to run into it, trying to lure the Fox Chapel men in.

Jon was already in a battle for his life with a man who looked as big as a giant. Jon and the giant traded blows only to repel each other time and again. It was a fight of contrasting styles, the giant moved slowly and powerfully but Jon was lightning-quick without any armor to slow him down. As they jousted for position, Jon was identifying the compromising gaps in the giant's armor. He blocked an overhand swing with his huge sword and backed away. Jon used a long sword that stood almost as tall as he. It had a green tinted blade referred to as Dragon-Steel. The cross-guard was silver as well as the rounded pommel with spikes coming out to resemble a mace. The grip had been constructed of black leather with a golden diamond pattern. He had received his father's sword when he was eleven, but the Dragon-Steel was much stronger and sharper. He called it Green-Fury.

He came back with a quick jab to the giant's knee and the big man started to drop. Jon swung his sword upward as the behemoth was falling and he slid his sword right under the giant's helm, through his chin and out the top of his enormous head. It popped the defeated knight's helm off as the Dragon-Steel broke through the giant's skull. He struggled to pull the blade from the resistant bone and spun around to see at least fifteen Fox Chapel knights lying dead on the scene. One lay still on the road with a spiked mace stuck through his metal helm that ultimately rested deep inside the knight's head. Unfortunately, he saw many of his own fallen men as well. He knew they were still badly outnumbered, but they were starting to close the gap. Mother earth kicked up dry dust around the battleground creating a lingering smoke effect. She greedily drank the spilled blood of the men and seemed to demand more. The clanking of swords and death defying primal screams sent a warning to others to stay far away.

Jon took another Fox Chapel knight's head clean off and saw Sir Gunnar sneak under another man's armor and put him to eternal rest. The clanging of weapons and the screams of dying men continued to cut through the sultry late-spring air. Then Jon Colbert took a great swing and Green-Fury bit hard, breaking through his opponent's armor. It hit the knight in the arm but easily cut through the armor. His sword lodged in the man's arm until Jon quickly pulled it away. He reached back and landed a mighty swing of the sword through the knight's skull. His sword broke right through the helm, jamming halfway into the man's head.

Through all the smoke and hullabaloo, Jon Colbert spotted the King of Donegal.

He was screeching, "Kill everyone. Kill the girl. Kill them all."

Jon recognized his opportunity. He climbed over several bodies in the direction of Ali-Stanley. The King stood next to a black stallion, watching his ambush from a safe distance. Jon Colbert now ran at top speed as the King tried to get on his horse. When he got about fifteen feet from the King, Jon felt a strange pain in his shoulder. Looking down, he saw an arrow sticking out of his left side. It staggered Jon. He gathered himself and stumbled forward as the clumsy King continued to fumble with his foot in the stirrup. Jon saw the fear of the Gods in the King's eyes as he stared directly at him. Jon stopped in his tracks when another arrow planted itself into his right thigh. Still determined, he took one more step until a third arrow burrowed into his other thigh, dropping him to his knees.

I must get back up. Please Gods, for my father.

The blood leaking from Jon Colbert's body seemed to absorb all the dust in the air as the smoke cleared. A knight with blond curly hair spilling from his falcon-head helm approached rapidly. The man turned his sword around and the last thing Jon Colbert saw was the pommel. It was a golden pyramid that crushed Jon right between the eyes. The world went black for Jonathan Colbert. Strangely, he didn't feel an oncoming headache. All of his stress and problems escaped in the dark red blood that spurted from his forehead.

"HE'S DEAD," yelled the knight to the King after he checked Jon Colbert's pulse.

30
BREHAN

BREHAN STRAPPED THE leather sack around Mariah's neck. They were off into the woods, away from the violence that had just erupted.

He spotted a huge bush and said, "Mariah, get behind this, over here on this side. I need to go back and get your father."

"No, you cannot leave me alone," Mariah said with concern. "I took an oath to your father to protect him. I will be right back before you can even get scared."

Brehan took off before Mariah could object again. On his way back to the road he thought about how he was supposed to see Elisa. *Maybe the King found out about Elisa and me? Is this all my fault?*

He saw the carriages and rushed toward the road in rage. Just up ahead heavy grunts and songs of aggressive metal on metal engulfed his senses. Everything slowed down for Brehan Castaway as it always did during violent conflict.

Brehan easily saw that they were heavily outnumbered right now, but Mattingly refused to surrender. He drew his long sword and engaged with a knight he knew to be Thomas Maron. He had a nice sword but Brehan came equipped with Dragon-Bite. Jon Colbert gave him the sword after he had knighted Brehan. Sir Thomas was a skilled knight, but not as quick as Brehan. He caught Maron a couple of times under both arms and the crimson tide trickled out. An attempted block by Sir Thomas only guided Brehan's sword directly into his helm, knocking him silly and the helmet from his head. Seizing the opportunity he sliced his razor sharp blade through Sir Thomas Maron's head. It went in on one side right above the ear and shredded its way out the bottom of the other side. The top half of the head hit the road and the rest of Sir Thomas dropped. Blood sprayed all over Sir Brehan's face and the fighting suddenly died down.

He heard Sir Gunnar yell to Sir Ryan, "Duke Colbert is dead."

Those words resonated and chilled Brehan's soul on this sweaty day. His one oath was to protect the Colberts and he had failed. He went back to find Mariah with his heart in his boots. For the first time in his life he could feel tears forming. *I must take solace in protecting his family now.*

He finally got back to the spot where Mariah should have been. *Where is she?* Brehan scanned the area looking for a clue. He saw nothing in every direction so he blindly walked one way. There were still no signs of Mariah after about two hours of searching. With nightfall imminent, he approached a farm. He now believed he would never see Mariah or Elisa ever again. *I have failed again.*

Brehan's mind flashed back to the Colbert table where he had boasted that he would keep everyone safe. Everyone had looked reassured. Now he had just let them all down. Tears started again as he tried to figure out how to get back to Mattingly.

Sir Brehan found a farm and quietly looked around for a horse. He snuck up behind a stable boy and hit him with a big rock. With the boy incapacitated, he found only one horse with a saddle and hopped on. He trotted out of the barn and into pitch darkness. Brehan didn't know where he was going until he felt the massive pain in his head as he fell off his horse.

Brehan awakened to a fading fire. His hands were bound and tied to a foundation post in a horse stable. He was naked, but Brehan could see his clothes in a pile just a few feet away. He realized this was the barn that he had tried to steal the horse from.

A big ox of a man wearing tattered rags entered the barn, "Oh, you finally woke up. Thought you was dead." "What are you doing with me? I am a knight of Mattingly. The Colberts will pay more than anyone for my return." He felt awkward using the name of the family that he had failed to protect, to bail him out of this situation. "Nobody done pays more for Mattingly knights in Fox Chapel than the King," the farmer said with a cruel smile, "That's where you goin' as soon as my daddy get back in a couple days."

The big man's grin revealed his gums. It looked like Brehan had only a couple of days to figure a way out of this gloomy situation. He could try to outwit the slow countryside man since that looked like the most viable option. *I cannot even protect myself from being captured by a farmer.*

And I call myself a knight.

As the farmer left the stable, Brehan began to think about everyone he had loved and ultimately let down.

31
PENROSE

THE FIGHTING FINALLY died down after reinforcement arrived for Fox Chapel and overwhelmed the Mattingly men. Sir Anderley and Sir Oliver led three captured Mattingly knights to see their fallen leader.

The King of Donegal still screamed, "Kill them all. Even the girl. Kill them all."

He kicked his horse and rode off with four knights. Three men came in from behind to thrust their swords down the back of the Mattingly knights' necks and into their chests, execution style. Blood spattered from Sir Ryan and Sir Gunnar's mouths as they cursed at the killers.

"Is that everyone?" asked Penrose. "They are either dead, halfway to Riverfront, or dying in the woods somewhere. How many of our men did they take out?" Sir Oliver wondered. "Twenty three before backup arrived. Those were some tough bastards," Sir Anderley answered. "Dead bastards," Sir Oliver reminded him as the three knights headed back to the castle.

Chaos reigned in the castle. Sir Penrose found the King in his meeting room with family and council.

"I don't know, we went to greet the Mattingly men and they just attacked us. So we had to put them down. It is as simple as that," King Ali-Stanley explained to the bewildered observers.

"What did you do? What did you do, you murderer?" Ali-Gare screamed at the King as she burst into the room. "Settle down my darling. I only did what needed to be done. Besides, I have a surprise for you. I have found a husband for you finally, his name is..."

The King's daughter had eye makeup running down her face, aided by the waves of tears. Before King Ali-Stanley could finish, Ali-Gare ran out the door.

"Penrose, please go after her and bring her back."

"Yes, my King," Penrose responded and took off. The Princess was already far ahead of Penrose who was slowed down by his heavy armor, but he noticed that she was heading for the horse stable. Penrose still trailed her as she galloped away from the barn and down the Royal Road. The knight grabbed a horse and followed the trail of dust that hung in the air above the dry, dirt road. About fifteen minutes later, he was back at the site of the scuffle. *No one even moved the bodies off the road after we left. There were at least ten men here to clean it up.*

There was Ali-Gare, right up ahead. She leaned over Sir Gunnar Pine's dead body. Anderley had told Penrose that Sir Gunnar used to be a servant in the king's castle before he went to Mattingly. She caressed his bloody face as she bawled, "My love is dead. My heart is dead."

Penrose could hear her as he jumped off his horse. Ali-Gare took a tiny bottle hanging from her neck. Penrose tried to run to her as fast as he could, but the armor really prevented that. She pushed her other hand into Sir Gunnar's boot and pulled out the exact same red, transparent bottle. *No, no, no. Don't do it.*

Penrose screamed, "STOP."

Ali-Gare Wamhoff drank both potions as Penrose came within three feet of preventing her. He stopped just short to see the Princess slump down on top of the only man she had ever loved. *How am I to explain this to the King? This is quite ironic. It was the King who just ordered the death of his enemy's daughter.*

Her face already turned an odd shade of green that made Penrose realize he didn't have to check for breathing or rush her back to Count Silzeus for revival. The sound of a man coughing startled the knight.

He turned around to see the blood-covered face of Jon Colbert as he sat up on the edge of the Royal Road. *I thought surely he was dead. Luckily he didn't get away or the King would really have my head.*

Penrose hurried over to Jon and drew his sword. Jon just sat there unable to defend himself. *The King ordered me to kill everyone and so shall it be.* Penrose readied himself to take off Jon Colbert's head and return it to the King.

32
THE ISLAND—EDBURGH

ED PACED UP and down the docks, wondering if they were ever going to arrive. The King's goons were back at the house, so Ed waited alone. It seemed well past midnight, but he had to keep a constant watch. The ship should have been here yesterday, but the sea can change travel plans quickly. A full moon bloomed above, but Ed had no interest in its beauty. He was still barely sleeping.

The sex he had with the unknowing Queen was supposed to stop the sleeplessness. It did not.

The King agreeing to move forward with his plan was supposed to end this weary cycle. It did not.

His deceased bride still haunted him every night. He even tried to sleep during the day, but he couldn't do it. Edburgh thought he had known exhaustion when he served military duty, but this was hard to deal with. Ed had now started hallucinating, seeing people who weren't actually there and someone could talk directly to him for minutes but he wouldn't remember anything. All he did now was drink until he couldn't stand up straight in hopes of erasing the bad memories that haunted his thoughts.

The King had promised the hand of Ali-Gare to Edburgh and thinking of her kept him motivated. He remembered her radiance from the wedding and often envisioned his prospective life in the king's castle, Ali-Gare Wamhoff constantly by his side. Whenever he wanted to abandon the job and go home, he took refuge in his dreams of this life. He really hoped that when he completed the plan and returned a hero that the nightmares would finally dissipate. A ship pulled up, bobbing along the dark waters.

He stood about one hundred feet away at the end of the docks. All the passengers would need to pass by Ed to get to the island. It was a small vessel and Edburgh only saw about a dozen men disembark. Luckily it was a bright night so he could identify the men easily. He was pretty sure he recognized them as they approached.

"Edburgh, is that you?" a tall, skinny man asked as he approached.

"Yes, it is me."

"What are you doing here? I haven't seen you in what, six years has it been?" the young man asked. "Sounds about right, I am just passing through, doing some bidding for my father," Ed said. "That's strange, that is the same thing we are doing," the tall man chuckled. "That is strange indeed," repeated Ed, forcing a laugh.

Ed started sweating and had trouble keeping everything together. Three big men stood behind the two boys like they were protecting them.

"Hey, it has been a long time. I have something back at the place I am staying at on the island that you guys should see," said Ed casually. "What is it?" the young man wondered. "It is right up this road at the place I am staying. You really have to see it. But it's a surprise. Have your friends head down to the tavern and we will join them shortly." Ed could feel his hands starting to shake as he put them behind his back and smiled nervously.

"Alright, I suppose we have some time to spare. Are you coming too?" he said to the other young man, who agreed. The two gave their bags to their associates and proceeded with Edburgh.

"So how is your wife?"

It sliced straight into his heart, applying pressure. *They had to have heard the news of her death. It must've made it around the kingdom by now. So he wants to play dumb, well, let's play.* His eyes shot open as vengeful blood again rushed through his veins. His pulse jumped and he perspired even more.

"Oh, I suppose you haven't heard. She is the surprise. She has asked to see you," Ed said. "Asked to see me? Why, I barely knew the girl from only a few visits to Elkridge," the man said. "That is strange indeed," said Ed.

They chattered back and forth during the five-minute walk. He drifted out as retribution burned at the core of Edburgh Etburn. He focused on his goal again, without the aid of sleep.

"Here we are," proclaimed Ed leading the two gentlemen into the house.

He took them into a small room and pretended to look shocked. "She is supposed to be here. Hold on, let me go fetch her." Ed left the room and rounded up the King's men, quickly and quietly. Ed and his men stormed back in with swords drawn to trap the boys.

"What in the hells is going on here, Edburgh?" the shorter man asked with alarm. The two young men were both taller than Edburgh, but skinnier. Edburgh promptly punched the taller man square in the nose, sending him back a few feet. Pain shot from his knuckles up past his elbow but the adrenaline soon took over.

"Call me uncle. And just admit that you tried to have her kill me," shrieked Ed. "Look, I don't know what is going on here, but my father will..." Ed cut him off, "Your father," Ed released an evil laugh, "Your usurper father is dead...your usurper sister is dead. And your mother and three usurper brothers...are about to be dead. And as for you, my usurper nephew, there doesn't seem much hope for you either."

Ed took satisfaction from the blood running from his enemy's nose, but he wanted more.

"Put his hand on the table."

Three guards dragged the kicking, screaming man over. Against heavy resistance they put his hand on the wooden table. Ed pulled the dagger made of Dragon-Steel and shoved it straight through the back of the man's hand and stuck it in the table. "OOOWWW," screamed the injured man as he wiggled around with his hand attached to the table.

"Tie them up and secure them to the post over there. I am not done having fun with them yet."

The King's men sprang into action as Edburgh went to chase some sleep. *Maybe this is what I needed.* Ed saw a blond haired woman waiting for him in his makeshift bed. It was Caroline. She suddenly disappeared as he reached out to touch her. Ed really needed to get some rest.

33
WICKED DREAMS—RICEROS

THE CASTLE WAS eerily quiet with most of his family gone. Riceros Colbert, although mentally strong and very intelligent with words and numbers, was still emotionally fragile at eleven. He hadn't realized that he would miss his father so much after only a few days. Riceros knew that children with his limitations were cast away in most families and he loved Jon Colbert for embracing his shortcomings and accentuating his strengths.

His mother had asked him to sleep in her room and he agreed on the condition that Jasper could too. The fire had almost burned out and a few candles flickered in the late-spring breeze that blew gently through the window. Riceros lay in his parents' bed with Camelle and felt his eyelids slowly getting heavier.

He wondered what the king's castle looked like and how Mariah felt about it. She liked to dress elegantly and Riceros thought she would enjoy the grandiose nature of the Capitol. He pictured his father and Brehan. He knew they would not appreciate the wasteful nature of the King's ways. Riceros wished he could have gone to see the Capitol firsthand. He had heard many stories about it and Count Silzeus had sketches of the castle and other monuments but he wanted to experience it in reality. Riceros' mind shifted to his brothers on the high green seas. He had journeyed up the coast to Waters Edge, but never been anywhere even close to Gama Traka. Riceros Colbert started to doze off.

Mariah danced with a red-headed man he presumed to be Ali-Ster Wamhoff. His father talked with Camelle and Duke Etburn. This seemed like a wedding. Riceros stood next to his brothers and Sir Brehan Castaway. Beautiful dresses and outfits were on display in a lavishly decorated room in a castle. Everyone seemed to be having a great time. Riceros spotted the King. He was a large man exactly as the stories went, but he walked hunched over and had several chins. His body was covered with a series of different colored robes twisted into a black, red and white pattern. King Ali-Stanley reached into the capacious robes and pulled out a large dagger from within their folds. He started to walk straight toward Jon Colbert, who had his back turned to the King. Riceros tried to scream but only silence sang out. He tapped his brother Krys and then Brehan only to have them ignore him. The King walked slowly and purposefully, but nobody seemed to have seen what Riceros was seeing. He tried to run to his father to warn him of the impending danger. He wanted to move but something grabbed him from behind. He turned around to see a giant, rabid fox with a tight grip on his shirt. The King closed in and still no one could see what was happening. Riceros tried to shake loose but he couldn't get free. The King of Donegal raised the knife high in the air behind Riceros' father. The party continued and everyone was still having a good time. The cowardly King buried the shining blade into his father's back. Riceros could see a huge, vile smile on the King's face as he tried to struggle out of the fox's grip to help.

"ROOF, ROOF, ROOF, ROOF."

Riceros shot up in bed. Through the dim, shimmering light that the remaining flames had to offer, he could see his mother grappling with someone. He saw the same shiny blade he had just seen in his dream. Jasper jumped onto the person's back. Suddenly Camelle kicked the shadowy figure back and Jasper took the tall person to the ground. Riceros saw a glimmering silver blade fly through the air and hit the ground with a clank. Without hesitation, he ran over and grabbed the knife. The assassin had gotten back to his feet with his back to Riceros as he fended off the dog. He rushed up and stabbed the person in the back of the thigh.

"OWWW," bellowed what sounded like a man.

The man spun around and smacked Riceros right in the ear, causing him to crash into the stone wall. Dizziness wouldn't let him rise to his feet as ringing vibrated in both ears. He quickly refocused and saw someone jump onto the assassin and throw him to the ground. They wrestled around for a few seconds until the killer was on top, in control. Riceros grabbed the knife and ran over swinging blindly. His first thrust struck hard and deep into the left side of his back.

"Bastard," screamed the man in the hooded black cloak.

The second and third swing hit the shoulder and upper arm respectively. Riceros took one more stab and stuck the blade in right next to the initial wound. In an instant, the assassin had been flipped on his back and three hammer-like punches shattered the would-be killer's face. The sparse light revealed that it was Riceros' brother who had ended the man's life.

Ruxin Colbert said, "Close the door and lock it, hurry."

The man who lay dead on the floor had pale skin and a very big nose. Ruxin pulled back the cloak to expose his bald head with black stubble trying to break through. He was bald by choice. Riceros noticed his near-purple lips and busted pinky finger that looked like the number 7. He was a big man who had gotten through all of the Mattingly security measures. *How did he get into Mattingly and then into our castle? Someone on our side must be betraying us.*

Ruxin rushed over to his mother, "Are you alright, mother?" She couldn't respond through the hysterical crying but Ruxin could see that she was bleeding from numerous cuts on her forearms. He went and lit a few candles on the table so he could further inspect the wounds. Riceros looked on, head throbbing, while Ruxin checked his mother's forearms. They had both been slashed several times while deflecting the killer's murder attempts.

Through all the commotion, Riceros didn't realize that his dog was still lying on the floor. He moved over to Jasper and the dog barked in pain. Riceros lay down next to his friend and started to feel for a wound. He found it right behind the back of Jasper's neck. It wasn't bleeding terribly, but Riceros wanted Count Sproul to take care of his mother and dog. He ran to the door and started to unlock it.

"What are you doing? We may still be in danger," Ruxin yelled at Riceros. Personal safety meant little to Riceros as he pushed open the door and rushed to the Count's room. Riceros had to put his life on the line for a friend that had done the same for him countless times. He got to the Count's room and pounded on the wooden door. He heard rustling from inside the room as the Count finally woke and responded. Riceros knew that his mother would be alright but he worried about his dog. He rushed into the Count's room and hurried over to his desk. He picked up a candle and used it to light two more. The waxy glow revealed paper and a quill that Riceros picked up and used to write a message to Count Sproul. The Count read it and moved over to the dresser he used to house his medicine. He grabbed two little bottles and the two of them quickly went back to his parents' room. Camelle had stopped crying but his dog still lay motionless on the floor.

The Count approached Camelle first. "My Duchess, what may I do to help?" "I am fine. The knife didn't cut me deep. Look at Jasper, he is in pain," she said in a low tone. "As you wish," softly said the Count while he painfully got down to his knees to tend to Jasper. Riceros hovered over the dog as the Count inspected the wound.

"It is rather deep. I must clean the wound first. Hold on to our friend as I pour this in," the Count said to Riceros.

He hugged his dog's body as the Count opened one of the bottles. He poured its contents into the wound. Jasper jerked around yelping in pain, taking Riceros along for the ride. After a few moments, the dog calmed down.

"Now we will dull the pain," stated Count Sproul.

Why didn't you dull the pain first, and then clean it?

The Count poured the other bottle into the gash. The dog only moved a touch before staying still.

"Now even though we have numbed the pain, he will still feel the next part when I seal the wound," Count Sproul warned.

Ruxin carried over a flat piece of metal he had been holding in the burning embers of the fire for several minutes and gave it to the Count.

Count Sproul instructed Ruxin, "Hold the cut closed, but be very careful with your fingers." Ruxin had to be nervous as the Count held the red-hot metal, shaking, over his hands. The Count finally zeroed in on the mark and pressed the burning seal onto Jasper's flesh. The dog bounced up and knocked Count Sproul onto his back as he let out a cry of pain.

"What is the matter?" asked Ruxin. "I dropped that fiery metal on my foot when I fell back," the Count yelled. He collected himself for several moments and said, "And now I shall treat you, my Duchess."

The Count limped over to Camelle. A quick survey of her cuts revealed to Count Sproul that they were superficial.

"Now this will sting just a bit," said Count Sproul as he cleaned and bandaged Camelle's cuts. The Duchess appeared to be in shock and didn't seem to feel a thing. Riceros still held on to his friend. The dog was calm now and the wound appeared to be sealed up. It looked like everyone would be alright, but who had sent an assassin to kill the Duchess? Riceros walked over to the window and noticed that there was a grappling hook hinged on the sill. He pulled it to find a roped attached that extended to the ground. Riceros thought it could have been someone who came down the Royal River and bribed or murdered enough men to get to the castle. Then he got in through the window of his parent's second-story bedroom.

Riceros remembered his mother and father arguing about moving up to the fourth floor for better protection. Camelle was afraid of heights and preferred to stay on the second floor. Jon had thought they would be safer on the fourth floor. It was the only time he could recall that his parents had ever fought.

This must have been a skilled assassin who commanded a hefty price. Only a few people in the realm could afford someone like that.

If he was so skilled, why couldn't he finish the job? Are more men on their way?

Ruxin found a coin-purse on the assassin filled with gold bulls and foxes. More than one hundred pieces, to be sure. Ruxin looked over the rest of the body for any clues that could tell them who this man was and who had sent him. He found nothing else on the dead man's person.

"I am going to have the guards get rid of the body. I will have some servants in to clean up the mess in here. We can all stay in my quarters until the morrow," Ruxin said.

Nobody slept the rest of the night and Ruxin called a first-light meeting to revamp castle security. Riceros attended the meeting, but it only made him feel a touch safer. He wanted his father, Brehan, sister and brothers back in Riverfront now.

34
MOVING SOUTH—ALI-STER

"I WANT TO shut down the duels immediately," announced the King at the meeting he had called. "Why, your highness?" asked Henley Moore. "Because we need more men to fight these usurpers. Wait a week and the jails will be full again. We just need to make sure that we are looking for lawbreakers this week," the King said with an evil smile and a wink.

Ali-Ster didn't grin. He wanted to go into battle but his father wouldn't allow it. Ali-Ster had almost left without permission. He thought that by the time his father found out, it would be too late to bring him back. Eventually, however, he chose to stay in the Capitol.

"Next, we take men out of that clustered stalemate along Goldenfield. I want to crush Mattingly quickly," the King stated. "I'm not sure that is the right move, your highness," replied Leo Braunshaur. "That's fine because I didn't ask you, *Lord Braunshaur*. A king orders, he does not ask. Havest any of thou the firth? Oh, and has anyone found out who killed Otto Cuthbart?" he asked, tapping his scepter on the table.

A hush fell over the room until Henley Moore broke the silence, "It could really be anyone with the mouth on that man, your majesty."

"But Penrose found him with his thumbs cut off and shoved into his mouth," the King said with a look of concern. "Again, that would cast a wide net as well, my King," added Derich Bonsfogger. "Well, I need to tell his wife something, so start pressing harder on this one. I still must figure out a price to pay her off. He was the High Lord of Fox Woods. Back on the topic of Mattingly, we will pull almost all resources from the Goldenfield border," said the King.

"I would be certain to keep a close eye on the Warrior Queen right now. New kings and queens can act in very erratic ways. You never know what she could be plotting after putting her mother and father's heads on spikes," Dirk Eller added cautiously. "I kind of like her myself. She is a new ruler and I know a thing or two about being a new ruler. You have to worry so much about consolidating the inside of your realm that it takes months or years just to look outside. Anyway, my whisperers tell me that she is planning a different move right now." The King got up and wandered around the table.

Everyone at the table wanted to object, but nobody had the intestinal fortitude. They didn't agree with pulling necessary troops and releasing criminals to fight a tough, and probably unwarranted, civil war. Even without its leader, Mattingly would stand up to defend itself until the bloody, bitter end. However, everybody's tongues became twisted when attempting to stand up to their King.

The King broke the brief silence as he meandered around the room. "A raven from Waters Edge arrived earlier with word that Duke Etburn is sending men. We can use their old bald heads for battering rams if need be. They might even die on the way down, but we will find a purpose for the elderly knights. We also received a letter from Burkeville."

The King's face flushed bright red and a rare, fierce look flashed into his eyes. His size was the only thing intimidating about the physically awkward King as he continued, "It appears we have a traitor on our hands. Duke Burke has refused to send any help for the war effort and has become entirely useless to the realm of Donegal. He is forcing my hand and he shall not be pleased with the outcome. He might change his tone when I send him the head of his daughter. He forgets that I have her here more as a hostage than a bride for Ali-Varis. We need to handle this problem quickly and quietly before he can bring Burkeville to ashes. I have one Duke ambush me and another who refuses my orders. It is time to teach this realm who is in control," shouted the King angrily. *You show your strength by having someone else kill an eighteen year old girl. You are a coward, father.*

Ali-Ster felt that the whole Colbert ambush story didn't add up. He was positive that his father sent him hunting the day of the already-infamous ambush so Ali-Ster wouldn't see the truth. *He didn't want me there for a reason; he knows I act with honor. He didn't even tell anyone around the castle that men from Mattingly were coming.*

He felt his father was spinning a web of lies. Ali-Ster found it hard to believe that Jon Colbert would attack the King in Falconhurst with his daughter along for the ride. Nothing about this story made sense. The

King would never leave the castle to greet the Mattingly men. He had never done that for anyone in the past. Ali-Ster hardly ever spoke at these meetings, but it was getting harder to hold his tongue with each outrageous statement his father made.

"Lord Bonsfogger, what are the chances we can take the coast?" the King questioned his Admiral of the Sea. "Extremely unlikely. They have five times as many war-ships and they will know we are coming," the Admiral said.

"So straight down on horse and foot it shall be. We will slaughter these mad bulls and offer them to the Gods. We will meet back here in two hours to discuss details about strategy and how to navigate those border mountains. I expect everyone to be here with Count Silzeus as the only exception. You may get some rest, my good man."

As soon as he finished that statement the door flew open with sudden force. It slammed into the wall and shook a few small tables. Two rugged-looking men entered the room in tattered clothes, carrying a large chest. It was an ark with animals carved into the outside. The men staggered over to the King and dropped the heavy chest. The two men bowed and left the room.

A man with long red hair entered the room and shouted, "Uncle." The man known as Crimson-Lightning walked toward the King with an air of confidence. He stepped over to Ali-Stanley and got down on one knee, "My King, I have returned with the spoils from the far east conquest. I do apologize for the length of time it took me. Those nasty seas just would not cooperate."

He opened the treasure chest to expose jewels, gold and silver filled to the brim of the large container. The King's eyes gleamed as they focused on the glowing reward.

"Finally, a soldier who can get things done. I was starting to think I would never see you again," King Ali-Stanley uttered. "I have had many nights filled with terrible thoughts that I would never see the shores of Donegal again. But finally and fortunately, I have made it," the man said.

Everyone just sat at the table, totally stunned. Sir Ali-Samuel Wamhoff had been gone for six years on what started out as a one-year quest. Not many people thought they would see the knight ever again. He was a skinny man who didn't look like a lifelong soldier. Only his stained and broken teeth gave the impression of hardness. His jawline came down in the shape of a V and could be seen under his closely shaved red beard and moustache.

"I lost almost all of the hundred men, but I hope this will make up for their loss," Ali-Samuel said with his head lowered. "We can find more men anywhere. Gold, silver and gems seem to elude us these days," the King said with a big, goofy-looking smile. He didn't smile very often these days and it almost scared people when he did, as it looked sinister. "This comes at a perfect time. You see, we have a little problem to take care of. Sit down and we will talk. The rest of you are dismissed."

The rest of the council walked out and Ali-Ster went over to the training yard, but hardly anybody was there. All of the knights were preparing for the southern advance. None of the squires could keep up with Ali-Ster so he decided to head back to his quarters.

He walked past the throne room and stared at the silver seat. The throne of Donegal had a silver frame with a red seat and back that featured two white foxes protecting the crown. Along the top of the chair was a rack for the crowns of conquered kings. Five crowns hung atop the throne.

As he was walking down the hall, he heard a voice ring out, "Cousin." Ali-Ster turned around to see Ali-Samuel Wamhoff approaching. "Hold on for just one moment. I didn't get to talk to you yet. When did you get back?" He put his arm around Ali-Ster while they walked toward his room. "A few months ago," replied Ali-Ster. "What are you doing right now? Do they still run the horse races in the west woods?" Ali-Samuel asked. "Yes. There are probably a few races left in the day," he said to his much older cousin. "Well, let's go then," smiled Ali-Samuel.

Ali-Ster had only seen Ali-Samuel for brief periods of time before he would embark on another of his many military campaigns. He was considered one of the greatest warriors that Donegal had ever seen. He had set off to conquer for the King on his fifteenth birthday and he had a decorated thirty years of service. Of the five crowns that hung atop the Donegal throne, two were placed there by Ali-Samuel Wamhoff. Small, stealth missions were his specialty. He didn't have any of the noticeable scars or ill effects one would expect from a lifetime of near death experiences. He was shorter and frailer than Ali-Ster, but the soldiers at war had told stories of Ali-Samuel's amazing battle exploits.

The two men rode to the horse racing stadium and Ali-Samuel paid a man two coppers to watch their horses. The racing track looked similar to the Dueling Yard. It comprised a huge, concrete horseshoe for a base. The track featured layered, wooden seating benches around most of the dirt track. A beautiful garden bloomed in the center of the track with flowers of every imaginable hue arranged in artful patterns. The wealthy women of the Capitol loved to stroll around the flower gardens and watch the races. The soil track had a red-painted wooden rail on either side. They ran races of one, two and five laps with the audience gambling on all of them.

Right outside the stadium, the horses were lined up according to their race numbers. Usually seven horses participated in each race unless a last moment problem occurred, in which case they would race with fewer horses if necessary. The jockeys stood proudly alongside their animals, telling the citizens why they should place a wager on their horse. The Wamhoff men walked around placing bets on the rest of the daily races. Ali-Ster never got to spend much time with Ali-Samuel so he was curious to know what the man wanted from him.

"I tried to talk some sense into your father, but he just wouldn't listen," Ali-Samuel said as soon as they sat in a vacant area of the stands.

There were about one thousand people in attendance and the stadium had a capacity of about two thousand.

"We have all tried to tell him that it is a mistake to move on Mattingly. They provide almost everything now. Much has changed since I went away four years ago," Ali-Ster said as he watched the horses start the race.

"Much and more, my cousin, but that wasn't what I was talking about. I tried to get your father to make you heir to the throne," Ali-Samuel lightly said with a blue-eyed wink. "I don't really care about that," Ali-Ster quickly responded.

"Well, every other person in the kingdom does. This place is a literal shit bucket right now once you go outside the castle. If something happens to your father and the simple-witted Ali-Varis takes over, it would be perilous for the realm. If not revolt, then the shores will be overrun by everyone looking for their scoop of the stew. And you are right, cousin, why does the King bite the hand that feeds him and wipes his mouth? He is also lying about that ambush. You can see it in his eyes." Ali-Samuel clenched and pumped his fist as his horse won the first race. "I know. He sent me hunting with uncle Ryen and uncle Tersen. The three people who might actually have been able to stop his lunacy had to be out of the way. He sent us away and none of us had any inkling about a plan to meet the Mattingly men on the Royal Road. He has never gotten over his grudge with the Colberts." Ali-Ster watched as the next race started.

"His judgment is terrible right now, Ali-Ster. What must you do, die on the battlefield to earn your father's respect? What has Ali-Varis ever done for Donegal? He has done as much or as little as your father and King Ali-Baster before him. They made bad decisions because they never served military duty. Sleeping on the throne is a lot like sleeping on your horse. Eventually, you are going to fall off and break your neck. But when you are a king, you break everyone's necks." Ali-Samuel watched as his horse took the lead down the home stretch.

Ali-Ster didn't like anyone talking bad about his father but his cousin made perfect sense. The crowd exploded in excitement as the horses sprinted for the finish line. Ali-Ster winced as his horse lost by only half a length. He opened his eyes to see another big smile on Ali-Samuel's face.

"You won?" he asked. "Of course, I won. And if you follow me, you will always win too. I have won every battle in the past thirty years for Donegal. Things need to change around here to bring this fading kingdom to prominence again. I have been around the world and Donegal is in the position of a fool right now with the exception of Mattingly. In fact, if not for Mattingly, Donegal would be infested with foreign armies, plundering and raping as they go. I tried to explain this to your father in much gentler terms but he didn't want to listen."

The men got up to go collect Ali-Samuel's winnings.

"So what is it you are suggesting, we kill him?" Ali-Ster sarcastically asked. "No, of course not, maybe you could talk to him too. A public affirmation of a change to you as the heir to Donegal will help restore some of the kingdom's reputation. You will be surprised at how the farthest reaches of the world know a great deal about the happenings in Donegal." Ali-Samuel collected a handful of gold. "Thank you my good man, better luck next time." They kept walking as Ali-Ster said, "But I don't even want to be King of Donegal. What do I know about ruling a kingdom?"

"A lot more than Ali-Varis, I would hope. You need a good council, not those shit buckets I saw at the meeting today. I am shocked they didn't attack each other for the riches I brought the King. Thunder and Lightning together. And it just so happens that I have the perfect Falconer for your council," he said with another smirk.

"Let me guess, you?" Ali-Ster said. "No, I think I am a perfect fit for the role of foreign chancellor, don't you?" Ali-Samuel asked with a coy smile. "Then who?"

"*My* father," his cousin said with the biggest grin of the day.

35
TO THE WORKSHOP—RUSSELL

FINALLY, THEIR EXCURSION through the Frozen Forest was almost over. From this vantage point on the hilltop, Russell could see the white, foamy waters of the Salty Sea. Russell and Dragon-Eyes had been walking through the frigid woods for weeks. A short cut turned into a long one when a heavy storm slowed them down considerably. The Imp Wizard told him that they were close to the school. Russell wanted to be done with the frozen trek and cracked a smile when he spotted some fresh grass. Leaving the permanent freeze behind, the pair entered a big open field. Directly ahead of the two men, there appeared a giant snowball in the green pasture. It looked like it was rolling toward them.

Russell dropped the bags, drew his sword, and pushed the Imp Wizard behind him. As the white blob came closer, three black spots became visible on it. They were two eyes and a nose. It was a snow-bear rushing at the two men.

Russell held his sword tight as the wizard spoke, "Just stare him down. Show no fear and the bear will not harm us." "Easy for you to say," Russell uttered as a quick peak behind him revealed the Imp was now backing up. "Look directly at him, not me. Do not swing your sword or it will kill us both," the wizard said as he backed up some more.

It sounded so simple. But with a six-hundred pound beast bearing down on him, every bone in Russell's body wanted to turn and run. His knees started shaking a bit, but he stood his ground. Unfortunately, the bear was picking up speed as it closed in. *RUN. Swing your sword. Do something, anything.*

All of his senses told him to take action, but he just stood and stared into the eyes of the oncoming animal. Suddenly the bear pulled up, and walked slowly toward Russell. "Just stay behind me, my friend."

"Will do," said the Imp from what sounded like a fair distance away. The bear walked right up to Russell, got right in front of his face, and let out a deafening roar. The force snapped Russell's head back. Then the beast opened its mouth, exposing sharp teeth, and licked Russell Seabrook's nose. The bear suddenly opened its mouth again, only to yawn, and then took off into the frozen woods. Other than the soggy tongue and terrible breath, that was the best result he could have hoped for. His heartbeat started to slow back down a bit and the lump in his throat disappeared.

He turned around to see the wizard about ten feet behind, smiling. "You passed yet another test, my boy." "Test? What if that bear had ripped my head off? Were you going to test the bear while he ate me? That's it, I suppose," an irked Russell stated as he breathed heavily from the near death experience. "Oh relax; I had total control of that whole situation," the Imp Wizard cleverly said. "From ten feet behind me?" Russell quickly questioned.

Dragon-Eyes firmly said, "Alright, that's enough. You should be happy. You conquered fear by standing up to the bear. You will be tested by the cruel wench of fear many more times, but you showed courage. Away we go now."

They headed down one mountain but another barred their way to the northern coast of Waters Edge. The Imp said that they were close, but they wouldn't arrive until after dark as daylight was fading fast.

A driving, sideways rain greeted the men as they arrived in the area known as Morningdale. Not many people lived in this area; it was mostly filled with religious refugees called the Daughters of Darkness. The name was originally meant to mock the Faith of Eternal Light but it had given them a stigma of demon worshippers. There wasn't anything worth taking in this land so they didn't worry about invasion. The land was a series of hills and mountains that presented rough growing conditions and most of the inhabitants lived simply.

"There it is," pointed the Imp. Carved into the side of a hill was the school. The façade had doors and entrances that tunneled straight into the giant mass of earth. There were three stories of buildings stacked on top of each other with something Russell couldn't identity, on a fourth floor. The soaked men arrived at the ground floor and Russell knocked heavily.

The door slowly squeaked open and a beautiful woman in a long black dress greeted them. She looked past him and her smile landed on Dragon-Eyes. Russell immediately noticed her lovely looks.

"Hello, old friend, I wondered if we would ever see you again. Then I saw you just the other day in my ball. You were standing in that very spot you are right now."

She had luscious dark lips, and deep-brown skin that looked silky smooth. The sorceress' curly black hair hung past her knees. She wore a snug black dress that seemed to give off a silver glimmer when she moved. She sported an enchanting emerald without any sort of headband and Russell couldn't understand how the gem stayed in place. It appeared to be magically suspended on her forehead. Her matching green eyes twinkled as she spoke, "Who is your handsome friend?" "His name is Russell Seabrook, and this is Gamelda," said the Imp Wizard. It was a quick introduction from Dragon-Eyes at best. Russell extended his hand, Gamelda placed hers in it, and he kissed her hand.

"Did you come for some love potion?" Gamelda playfully asked with a wink. Russell blushed. Other than Ali-Pari he had little experience with women. Gamelda led the guys down a short hallway and into a room off to the right that looked like a work shop. There were candles of many different colors burning around the room. They were as tall as the half man and kept the room well lit. There were thirteen women busy with various activities. When they caught sight of Dragon-Eyes, all of them ran up and surrounded him.

"I can't believe you are finally back." "We missed you so much," a few of the girls excitedly said. The ladies varied in age from about twenty to forty. After only a short interval of small talk, the ladies returned to their duties.

The tallest woman was making more candles. She poured hot wax from a kettle into giant molds. Protective gloves covered most of her arms as she carefully transferred the blue liquid. Another woman sifted through bunches of fresh herbs to burn for their rituals. The Daughters used many different combinations to achieve a variety of desired results. She mixed several blends, while another female scribed the mix of herbs and marked the location of it on her chart. They had a rectangular storage cabinet and a grid on the paper to keep track of the different herbal blends.

Other women were stirring big cauldrons of some steamy surprise that Russell didn't recognize. Off in the far corner, a pale ghostly-looking woman with short hair extracted poisonous snake venom into a clear jar. She grabbed a snake right behind its head and held its mouth up to a jar. The four-foot snake tried to bite the jar and spit the venom right into the bottom. A closer look revealed about ten deadly snakes in the corner. Russell lived in a hot area of Waters Edge so he knew that almost all of those snakes could kill you with just one bite. They weren't even confined but they instinctively stayed near the pale lady. When she finished, she tossed the rattlesnake aside, grabbed a water moccasin and steadily repeated the process. She was fearless in her approach and Russell thought that perhaps the snakes respected that.

"Now if you ever get bit by one of them, we have the antidote to help you survive. Those go for a lot of coin, especially overseas in Gama Traka where there are one-hundred snakes for every man," the Imp Wizard told him.

The walls were covered with a plethora of symbols that Russell didn't understand. They appeared to be chiseled in vertical rows. There were stars, circles, triangles, squares and other shapes he had never seen before.

"Let's go up to our floor," suggested Dragon-Eyes. "Lovely," responded Gamelda and Russell had no choice but to follow. A labyrinth of steps took them to the top floor.

Now this definitely looked like a wizard's quarters. There were book shelves stuffed to capacity and papers were scattered everywhere. Some had only words and others had sketched designs, some even with star patterns and drawings on them. A fire roared off to the side of the room and a cauldron hung above it, brewing some unknown contents. There were tiny, red jars everywhere that may have been the snake venom. He saw a marvelous carpet on the floor with a purple, red and black design that looked like a raven. An owl was perched in the window and went *"who who"* non-stop, seemingly excited about the little man's return.

The Imp Wizard stood on his tiptoes to grab an odd looking amulet from the wall.

"What is that?" asked Russell. "Just a little carrying vessel and good luck charm. It has kept me safe while danger lurked in every corner," he said with a half-smile as he kissed the special container.

It was a sculpted wooden man. He looked like he was hanging from a string with his legs crossed at the bottom, like he was sitting down. His light amber face had a crazy look on it and two mother of pearl eyes with tiny black centers stared back at Russell. The wizard showed him that when you pulled the oversized face, it came apart and revealed a hollow interior that could be used for storage. Dragon-Eyes hung it around his neck and held it to stop it from swinging.

"So how long are we going to be here?" Russell queried of his new mentor. "Well, that depends entirely on you. We will see how long it takes for you to develop the skills needed for this journey. Gamelda and I will try to teach you all that we can before we leave for the Pearl Islands," the wizard said as he leaned back in a small custom-made chair. "Hopefully, I can teach you to see what hasn't happened yet. I will try to pass as much knowledge on to you as I can, Russell Seabrook," Gamelda said with a smile that captivated him.

"Once you reach the point that you are ready for the next step of the journey, we will leave," Dragon-Eyes said. "What if I never do?" Russell asked. "Oh, you will, my sweet thing," Gamelda said in a soothing voice while she stroked his face. "You will, my boy. You need to trust in yourself and understand that you have great gifts already," the Imp reassuringly told him. "Such as...?" Russell hesitated.

The Imp Wizard immediately said, "Bravery and brawn. You take swift, decisive action and you have the body frame to back it up. Bravery and brawn will take you very far, but brains will thrust you over the threshold. I have faith in you, Russell. You simply need to have faith in yourself," the Imp could see Russell already responding from the positive reinforcement.

"Alright, I guess I have always doubted myself," Russell said with slightly more confidence.

He looked over to see Gamelda smiling at him and that instantly made him feel more confident.

"Well that stops now. We shall relax tonight and start when the sun comes over the mountain on the morrow. We only have one final thing to do before we officially start your voyage," Dragon-Eyes said delicately. "And what is that?" Russell pensively asked. "We need to cleanse all your un-pure thoughts. We will do so by shearing your head and face. The face shouldn't present a problem, but those lovely locks will have to go, I am afraid."

36
FAMILY SHIFT—RICEROS

THE REMAINING MEMBERS of the Colbert family gathered in Camelle's room in Riverfront. Word around the city was that everyone from Mattingly had died, even Mariah. Camelle has been inconsolable since the news arrived. Riceros felt terrible, but it was hard to cheer people up with only written words and gestures. The boy tried anyway, only to catch a quick glimpse of a smile that faded back into grief. They sat around a small wooden table on stools.

Ruxin reported, "So we made sure to guard the wall and coastline heavily at today's meeting. Lord Dunston and Lord Kane have a group of men making rounds to gather support for the cause. With soldiers already stationed around the wall and sea, we shall need little back up, we believe."

He was only fifteen but had been handling this situation like a grown man. Riceros noticed that Ruxin had grown up immensely since the ambush and he acted more like their father by the day.

Riceros still hadn't really come to grips about losing his father, sister and brother in Brehan. He cried when he heard the news and a few random times when he saw things that reminded him of them. But he still felt deep down that he should have been sadder. It triggered something in Riceros that he rarely experienced, anger. There weren't a lot of things that fired up Riceros, but he had experienced more anger than sadness over the slaughter of his family. Although he had to deal with his own setbacks, the Colberts rarely suffered strife and lived peacefully. Riceros wasn't sure if he was dealing with the pain properly.

He thought he was dreaming when he saw Brehan enter the room with blood splattered on his face and clothes. He looked as ghastly as expected after being gone over a week.

"Brehan," shrieked Camelle as she ran to hug him.

He looked different to Riceros, almost broken. Brehan spoke in a softer voice than usual, "Hello all, I have failed you." Riceros was giving him a hug from behind as his mother said, "You did not fail us, *OUR* King failed us. The one Jon was paying respect to."

"How did you get out alive? We heard that everyone died," Ruxin said to Brehan. "Well, I wanted to get Mariah out of the action so I took her over into the woods and I should have just left with her right then, but I didn't. I wanted to be the hero and save both Duke Colbert and his daughter. So I went back into the action and during heavy combat in which we were grossly outnumbered, I heard that our father went down. I mean your father, your husband. So I went to rescue Mariah only to find that she was not in the place I had left her. I failed to protect both of them."

"Don't you dare think that way. You are part of this family and we love you. Pray tell, did you actually see Jon or Mariah dead?" Camelle wondered. "Neither. For all I know they are both alive. But the call did ring out that Duke Colbert was dead," Brehan responded as he lowered his head.

"That is some hope, I suppose," Camelle said before breaking down again. After consoling her for a few moments, Ruxin spoke up, "Well, we need to figure out what we are going to do after the incident."

"What incident?" Brehan queried. "We were infiltrated by one of the King's men and he tried to kill our mother. If it was not for Riceros sleeping in her room, who knows what could have happened," Ruxin answered.

Brehan's eyes shifted to Riceros. Just from the look, the young boy could feel how proud the knight was of him.

Count Sproul interjected, "I think all of you should leave Mattingly until these dark storm clouds blow over." "I worry not about the King. Unless he is using tricks, he is powerless," Ruxin stated. "Why don't you take the Duchess to Waters Edge? She has family there that can protect her. And from there you boys should go as far as the waters will oblige," the Count advised the family. "I will go nowhere. I will stay and fight for my father, my family and our flag bearers. But Count Sproul is right, maybe we should split up, especially after the murder attempt," Ruxin announced confidently.

Camelle broke down again, drained from this new possibility of a further breakup of her family. The situation finally hit Riceros like a sledgehammer. No one in the room really knew if they were going to see each other again after a couple of days. About a week ago everything had seemed fine in Mattingly, but seven short days had wreaked intense havoc on the Colbert family.

Camelle drew herself together just enough to say, "Boys, I have to talk to Brehan for a bit in private, please." "If you need me for anything, just call on me, my Duchess," Count Sproul said as he left the room.

On the way out Riceros scribbled something on the black board and showed it to Ruxin. "I need to warn you about something," the board said.

He only hoped his brother's arrogance wouldn't stop him from being receptive to a grown up message from an eleven year old kid.

37
A Normal Mourning—Elisa

MORE THAN A week had passed since the slaying of her one and only love. Elisa was still sitting up in her room, sobbing. Other than mandatory social obligations, she hid from all the backstabbing foxes. She really had only seen the Lonely Widows who stopped in to clean her room daily.

She held a piece of dragon glass in her shaky right hand as she thought about the Queen's warning that nobody can trust the King. She pressed the fang-shaped obsidian onto her left wrist for the twentieth time since sunrise. It was almost afternoon and Brehan Castaway consumed her thoughts. They were supposed to be together until the end, against all odds. Instead he was slaughtered by the King's men on that rotten, sweltering day that had been branded into her memory.

Elisa heard that everyone from Mattingly had died in the scuffle. She couldn't even look at the King or his guards without feeling utterly disgusted.

You die, my heart dies, and a person without a heart is already dead.

That message had been pounding in her head ever since she caught wind of the commotion in the castle and heard the horrific news. She had to pretend that she was sorrowful for the fallen Fox Chapel knights when she really wanted slow, painful deaths for all of them.

This is it, my heart is already dead. Ali-Gare had the right idea. Live with your love, die with your love.

She steadied the glass over her wrist and dug in. It stung hard as blood started to trickle out. A sharp knock on the door made her drop the dragon glass and she watched as it shattered on the floor upon impact. She quickly swept it under her bed and sprinted to the door. It was the Queen and Sir Anderley. She hoped they wouldn't notice that she had been crying.

"Hello there, where have you been hiding?" The Queen playfully asked as she entered Elisa's room and continued, "Are they still taking good care of you?"

"Yes, yes everything is fine. I just thought I should stay out of the way with all that is going on," Elisa said while looking at the ground. "Child, there is always something going on in this castle, but why are you lying to me? You can tell me the truth you know," the Queen stated with a friendly look on her face. "What do you mean? That is the truth." Elisa said with a slight stutter.

"Stop right there. I am an expert in lying. Need I remind you that I am married to the King of Donegal? Listen I am your friend first, family second and Queen last. Tell me what is bothering you," she said as she closed the door and returned to Elisa.

The two sat on the bed and the Queen put her arm around Elisa and started rubbing her back lightly.

"You promise...you will not tell anybody?" Elisa cautiously asked. "I promise, now out with it," smiled the Queen. "Alright, I suppose I must tell someone. I grew up in our castle with a boy named Brehan Castaway. And, well, he went on to be a knight of Mattingly, so..."

It took a minute to click in the Queen's head before she abruptly said, "Oh, oh, no, my dear." She now wrapped both arms around the young lady, squeezing tightly. "Are you sure he was killed? I heard some of them got away." Elisa bounced up from the bed, breaking the Queen's embrace. Hope awoke within her heart as Elisa looked at the Queen and asked, "Who said that?"

"Several people actually, maybe four or five," the Queen informed her.

Energy coursed through the heart and soul of Elisa Wamhoff. It was as if her heart was running again, chasing love. *If anyone could escape, it would be Brehan. I know he could do it.*

Elisa got dressed and went to the Queen's room to play castle cards. The Queen had beautiful, hand-painted cards for different leisure games. A few hours of the card-game called spades buoyed Elisa's sunken spirits.

When she got back to her room, a man with long red hair awaited her. "Hello," she said suspiciously. "Well hello, my lady. Allow me to introduce myself. I am Ali-Samuel Wamhoff." He bowed deeply and returned to normal form. He stood a bit shorter than Elisa and his face was bright red.

"I have heard of you and your return. My name is Elisa Bur...I am sorry, Elisa Wamhoff," she said while shaking her head in embarrassment. Now her face turned as auburn as her visitor's. "I have heard of you as well, my lady. May I have a few words with you?" He exposed his dirty teeth in a smile and Elisa could smell his nasty breath as she opened her door.

"Of course, come in, what is it you would like to discuss?" she cautiously asked her visitor. "I just wanted to meet you and ask you how you feel about your marriage with Ali-Varis," he coolly said.

"Oh, it has just been great..."

He cut her off. "Stop. You are a terrible liar. You really need to work on that if you plan to stay alive in the Capitol. And I plan to have you stay alive." "What, I don't understand...," she was stopped again.

"Shhh, shhh," he shushed, while putting a dirty finger over her lips. "Just listen. Wouldn't you be much happier if you were married to Ali-Ster?" he questioned with a wink for enticement.

A big smile came over Elisa's face, finally prompting Ali-Samuel to remove his hand. Ali-Ster was a much safer option for her to stay in the capitol. She still hoped that Brehan was alive, but if not, she didn't want to return to her father's castle in Burkeville.

He looked directly at her with serious, blue eyes and said, "We have a plan in order. But the first step is to get Ali-Varis out of the way." "How are we going to do that?" she wondered.

"We have to first convince Ali-Ster. We want to have our future King aware of our plans. That is where you come in. You need to paint Ali-Varis as a monster. Tell Ali-Ster about how Ali-Varis hits you, for instance," he said. She cut him off, "But he doesn't hit me," she softly uttered.

Ali-Samuel open-hand slapped Elisa across her left cheek, knocking her down. "Why did you do that?" she asked before bursting into tears. "Oh no, why did Ali-Varis do that? Sacrifice will be needed to pull this off. Here, let me help."

Ali-Samuel held out his left hand. As he pulled her up, he smacked her in the same exact spot, dropping her again. Elisa fell back down, crying on the floor. "Do you believe that damned Ali-Varis? Maybe we should do something about that out of control halfwit, don't you think? I am sorry, but the bruises had to look natural, so I couldn't warn you in advance," he said as he rubbed the handle of his sword. "I am a very serious individual with very serious motives. If you plan to stay alive, you need to listen to me carefully and do exactly as I say."

"Alright," Elisa hesitantly agreed through her sniffling. She couldn't feel the left side of her face anymore. She wanted to run to somebody for help, but who could she turn to? Elisa didn't know anyone who she could really trust in the castle. The Queen was the only one that came to mind. But she didn't even know if she could trust the overly-kind Queen. A trapped feeling came over Elisa as Ali-Samuel started to lay out his plan. Her face throbbed as she paid close attention. This had been a day of lows and highs and lows again. Elisa Wamhoff's plan to rule the kingdom of Donegal with Brehan Castaway was dissolving right before her.

38
Going Away — Penrose

"SO, HE IS mobilizing to move south, huh?" the High Holy Leader posed as he sipped his red wine. "I suppose nobody could talk him out of it," replied Sir Penrose. "I would have tried but it isn't my business to intervene in these matters," Father Enroy said. *No, you only intervene when you want more gold from the King.*

The old man leaned back in his throne-like chair as Penrose stared at the jade. "Are you alright, my son?" "Yes, just tired it seems," Penrose said with a yawn. "Did they find out who killed Otto Cuthbart?" the Father asked as he filled his wine glass again. "No, and it doesn't look likely that they will. He had too many enemies and with everyone present in the city for the wedding, it could be almost anyone in the land. The city watch hasn't a clue to go on," Penrose said.

"Yes he did have a big, nasty mouth for such a small body, that one. Not many spoke a gracious word about him," the Father agreed. *See, he understands too.*

"So do you think it is foolish to rush Mattingly?" Father Enroy sank into his chair a bit more and started showing the effects of the wine. "I think it is a bad move. All the gold comes from Mattingly right now," Penrose stated. "I know," cut in the Father, "Mattingly gold built most of this building we sit in."

"You cannot cripple yourself and expect to walk. The outskirts of Falconhurst are in dire need of heavy maintenance. This war will kill citizens and hurt the upkeep around the castle. War is sacrifice, Father, and I don't believe the people of Donegal are ready for that right now," Penrose pronounced. "I would have to agree. I think it is a terrible idea of misguided revenge," the Father replied. *We know you preach it, but you don't practice sacrifice. Josevius would be ashamed of his High Holy Leader.*

"And now our King is sending you off somewhere?" the puzzled Father asked. "He said there are some pressing problems elsewhere that require my services. I am not at liberty to discuss more than that, but I wanted a blessing for my journey," Penrose said. "Of course, my son," as the Father started the prayer, Penrose's mind shifted to other matters.

He was relieved that the voices in his head had been silent for a while. There was an occasional demand or two but it wasn't the constant badgering he was used to. Penrose was leaving tomorrow and didn't know when he would return. It was part of the demands of being on King's Guard; it didn't always mean just protecting the King. Sometimes it meant carrying out the King's orders and keeping silent about it. Even Father Enroy respected it and didn't pry.

The Father finished his voyage blessing for Penrose and then said, "I have something for your trip, Penrose."

He wandered over to a desk near the corner of the room. He went around behind it and came back after a few minutes.

"This is a piece of the loin cloth that Josevius, our God of Sacrifice, wore. It will guide you if times seem tough and remind you that it takes sacrifice to rise to the heavens," the Father said with a smile. "Thank you, my Father, I shall cherish this relic and remember your message. I shall spread the word of the Faith on my journey when the chance permits. Now I must be off," he stated.

"Alright, my son. Be safe and I will see you upon your return," the Father told Penrose as he left.

He shuffled down the steps of the church, feeling personally protected by the Gods. Penrose liked the fundamental roots of religion, but did not approve of what it had transformed into. Men chose to go into the field for money, not to teach, preach and help others. Penrose headed down the Walk of Kings and noticed a man stumbling around. As he got closer, the man stared at Penrose through the moonlight.

"What are you doing here?" Penrose demanded. "Nuthin' that has nuthin' to do with you, so why don't you piss off," the drunken man exclaimed as he staggered away from Penrose. Something exploded inside Penrose. His entire body overheated and he felt the same anger as the night of the royal wedding.

"Don't you recognize me?" Penrose asked with a clenched jaw.

"I don't know you, pretty boy."

This just further enraged Penrose. "I am the man who is going to kill you," Penrose whispered. "Huh," the drunk responded. "Come closer, you can see and hear me better," Penrose lured him in.

The man stumbled over to Penrose and didn't even notice him pull his knife. Penrose stabbed the man in the stomach.

"I said I am the man who is going to kill you. Look at me. Look into my eyes," Penrose said with a sick smile on his face. The man wailed for help, but not loud enough for anyone to respond. Penrose removed the knife, spun around behind the drunkard, and slit his throat. The body crumpled right in front of King Ali-Terry's statue. Penrose wiped his knife on the dead man's clothes and calmly headed for his quarters. He scanned the area to make sure no one was around. *I should do this to silence the voices, not when people make me angry. What is wrong with me?*

When Penrose arrived at his quarters, he immediately knew something wasn't right. He always hung a small piece of cloth on top of his door, and that linen sat on the ground in front of the entrance. The King's Guard had a free standing building that they shared. It was just outside the castle to the north. He pulled his sword and kicked the door open.

Penrose saw a man waiting inside for him, and he hurried in and closed the door.

The naked man lying in the bed just smiled at Penrose.

"Are you mad? I almost killed you," Penrose exploded, "I should kill you. You could get me killed doing something like this." "Settle down, relax for a minute. I just wanted to do something special for you before you leave. I don't want you to have to visit any whores on your trip," the nude man said in a soft voice.

The man looked a little younger than Penrose with bright crimson hair. He was pale and pudgy, but Penrose thought he was beautiful. The knight was furious, but his anger started to subside as he looked at Neron Wamhoff, nephew of the King.

39
MOVING WEST—LEIMUR

QUEEN LEIMUR ELECTED to keep a small court. General Rigby sat as her right hand counsel and helped her select the new members. The position traditionally called Grand Courtier fell to the war veteran. Her domestic expert was Harold Ritchie and the leader of foreign affairs was Bero Sandway. The only other members were Pippen Mallory and Birney Ferur. She believed that too many council members would provide too many officials to tamper with. Leimur had hand-picked the few straight-fingered people she believed could resist the temptation of bribery.

The group sat on black painted chairs around a circular marble table. An enormous, black rug covered most of the floor and the light purple walls had been painted just a day ago. Large works of art hung around the room presenting scenes of royal family events from the past. Leimur was in the process of redecorating the entire palace as befitted her new realm.

"We received word from Livingstone today that if we attack from the east, they will attack the southern border. They will also send troops into Goldenfield to help with the south-west attack. My forces will hit them further north and that should be too much for them to handle. So, I will be rounding up the soldiers and heading for Harbor Valley in two days. Soon Harbor Valley will be under our control, but I will need all of you to rule the realm in my stead."

Bero Sandway was the first to speak, "Are you sure about this, so early into your rule?"

"There is a reason I specifically chose each of you for this responsibility. Deep down, I am a warrior. I knew I would have to leave to conquer for my kingdom and I knew you were the ones to be trusted."

"We will do the best we can, my Queen," replied Pippen Mallory.

"Now that city security is under control and Donegal is mired in civil battle, the time to strike is right. But we also need to keep a close eye on the city watch. They are notoriously corrupt and I want this to stop on our command." Leimur was ready to get back out on the field. She had already grown weary of palace life. The Capitol attracted unscrupulous people who endlessly thirsted to drink from the chalice of power. So the Queen thought she was in more danger of a knife in her back around the malevolent city of Sevring than on the deadly battlefields.

She thumbed the pommel of her sword and said, "Alright everyone, I thank you. You may leave now." As everyone got up from the table, she spoke, "General, I would like a word with you please."

He quickly sat back down. "So we leave in a few days, huh?" the veteran General asked. "Well, that is what I need to talk to you about. I need you to stay here to keep everybody in line." She looked directly into the General's eyes to let him know that she was serious. "My Queen, I am not well suited for running a palace," the General said as he looked down at the table.

"Of course you are. You run a damn army of cold-blooded killers. This is basically the same thing," she added with a purple-lipped smile. She pulled a small smirk out of the General.

"I would just...much rather prefer to go with you," said General Rigby looking right into her piercing eyes. "Oh General, enjoy it. Find a nice chambermaid to lick your wounds and scrub you in the bath. You need to recover for the next part of the plan," she said as the General shifted in his seat. "Which is?" Rigby asked with a closed eye.

"This stays between us, General. We will conquer Donegal. I will return to get you after we ravage Harbor Valley. By that point Sevring should be stable enough for both of us to leave," she said. "If I must, my Queen," he conceded. "Oh you must, General," she said in a lighter tone. She rubbed the hilt of her purple dagger that she had used on her father.

Unexpectedly, a guard entered the room. "My Queen, it seems you have a visitor. He would not tell me his name. He only said that you would want to see him." "Check him for weapons, then send him in," the Queen decided.

An older man entered the room with a small gold chest in his hands. He set the box on the table and extended a deep bow of respect to Leimur.

"Queen Leimur, let me first congratulate you on your rise to power. I have brought a gift of good faith."

"Who are you?" the Queen instantly demanded. "Oh, how rude of me, I am quite nervous. My name is Ali-Steven Wamhoff," the man revealed. "You are...you are the King of Donegal's twin brother. Are you back in Donegal, and have you been sent by the King?" she asked, sensing a trap. "No, your grace, I no longer reside in Donegal. I was run out of that kingdom many years ago. But I plan to return soon enough," he said with a sly smile. "Open your gift, if you will, your grace."

Queen Leimur Leluc opened the chest to see gold and silver coins with markings from all over the world. "Why are you giving me this? What is it that you want?" "Well I plan to go back home with a welcome party of trained killers. I have people in place right now to actually strengthen Donegal so invasion will only be inevitable and victory all but sure for only me. If it is perceived as too weak, every kingdom will try to invade. I am a man who prefers to be certain that I will succeed. I stand before you to ask Goldenfield to simply cause some trouble along the border to divert attention away from the Sea of Green. I have the numbers and skill to back it up and I would like for us to be civil neighbors," he tactfully stated.

Ali-Steven Wamhoff was a fugitive from Donegal. The fifty-thousand gold fox bounty on his head still stood. The King had ended his public grudge with Ali-Steven after he married Emilia. But Ali-Stanley still had to honor his father's bounty. About two heads or bodies a week were still brought to the king's castle that people claimed to be that of Ali-Steven. The King had never paid the reward because only a few of the dead men over the years had looked a bit like Ali-Steven, and Count Silzeus never confirmed a match.

The Queen of Goldenfield's visitor looked like a big oaf, but she had noticed that he moved rather gracefully given his advanced age and size. His graying hair still held onto a hint of red, but the skin on his face was wrinkled and scarred. It looked like someone had sliced him from above his left eye and down across his nose and through the corner of his mouth. The Queen noticed his injured eye color was gray while the normal one was brown.

"If you think this small pile of gold is worth sending my men to be killed assisting someone I have never met, then you do not know me as well as you think," the Queen sternly said. "I said that was a gift of good faith. Now that we are friends, *RACOO, DERREX*," the old man screamed.

Two men entered carrying a huge wooden chest that could have held a grown man's body. They struggled to get it across the room. The men set the chest on the ground with a heavy thud near the Queen and exited the room. General Rigby monitored the developments as the impromptu meeting continued. Ali-Steven flicked open the lid to show an amazing cache of gold, silver and gemstones. Queen Leimur looked impressed and instantly realized this was a man of motivation. She knew that a large number of men had to die to collect those riches.

"And more will come from your share of the Donegal pillage; of course after it is complete, your grace." Ali-Steven said with a smile. "When do you believe that will be?" the Queen quickly fired back. "Hard to say," he answered, as he scratched his head, "As you well know war doesn't always go as expected. Our estimation is a little more than a few months. I want the citizens to welcome us as liberators when we arrive. We would like to handle it much like your recent situation, without a big mess. And if not, we will slay them where they stand," Ali-Steven said with an intense look on his face.

His serious tone hinted to the Queen that he was too old and tired to play games. Leimur liked this man's style. He got to the point quickly and seemed ready to rule with brute force. She studied Ali-Steven as he spoke, "Send a representative with me to see our operation and I can assure you that he will come back with a message that we are more than able."

"She..."

"Excuse me?" he interrupted. "I will be sending one of my captains with you, and *SHE* is a woman. Captain Salina will inspect your claims and tell me whether this is a worthy proposition."

"Then so it shall be, Queen Leimur. There is one other matter I need to speak with you about. It is an emerging issue that could come back to upset your rule," Ali-Steven warned her.

"And that is?"

"Your sister, your grace," Ali-Steven replied.

Later that day while she was talking to General Rigby about the strategy for the upcoming attack the guards entered again.

The taller guard said, "My Queen, there is a man here that says you will want to see him." "Again? Is it the same man as before?" she asked.

He responded, "No my Queen, he looks very different from that man." "Alright, check this one for weapons and send him in, I suppose," Leimur stated.

She looked at the General and shook her head with a surprised look on her face. A short man with skin deeply tanned by the sun and blue eyes entered the room. He looked skinny under his loose white and red robes. His head was shaved on the sides and back with a small patch of hair shaped like a circle on top of his head.

He wore a close black moustache and his rotten teeth were exposed as he bowed and spoke, "Hello, your grace. I have come to pledge my undying support for your reign as Queen of Goldenfield. My name is Anders Ahitni." He straightened himself from the bow and nodded at the Queen.

"You stopped. Is that name supposed to mean something to me?" she asked.

"I am a very powerful man from Gama Traka and I believe we can help each other. Right now Donegal is in shambles. I have been involved with Mattingly and Fox Chapel, fanning the flames on both sides of this burning conflict. If we wait a short while, Fox Chapel will weaken Mattingly enough for us to easily conquer the realm," he said with a slight smile.

She had trouble focusing on anything but the man's teeth as the meeting went on. "How do I even know that you are the man you say you are?" she questioned.

"Your grace, you can send an official with me. I will show him our six-hundred war ships, our forty-thousand soldiers, and enough gold to sink all those ships. We have the ways and means to take Donegal, but only if we have your support. We can meet in the middle and split the spoils," he said as he rubbed his hands together.

"Forty-thousand men might not even get you two miles inland," she said.

"These are not just men who picked up the sword yesterday. These are the best of the best, the Prograggers." He made a fist and lightly tapped it on the table as he said, "They are worth at least a hundred men, each and every one of them. If you come in from the west, we can roll over their forces like a plow through the field."

She had heard of the Prograggers and by the look on General Rigby's face he had heard of them too. They were a fierce fighting force of brutal warriors that were plucked from their families at a young age in Gama Traka in exchange for gold. Most of them were called dragon babies because they were born in the year of the dragon. Gama Traka had a seven-year cycle of birth signs and the dragon was by far the most coveted. These babies were tattooed at birth with the dragon symbol on their left hand.

The other symbols for different years were tattooed onto different areas of the body to avoid confusion. Many people had tried to add a dragon symbol to their left hand because the dragon babies were considered to be favored by God. The impostors could be easily identified because they would still have their original birth tattoo. Not a single man with the dragon birth mark would ever put another symbol on his body; it would rival blasphemy.

The Prograggers had no other purpose in life but to achieve glory in battle. The boys realized that they would never have a wife or family and thus dedicated their lives to the spear. Their weapon of choice was a nine-foot double-sided spear. Once the long spear started swinging, it created a natural shield and could attack the enemy from a great distance. Most other soldiers had families to return to after a war, but the Prograggers just went on to the next fight, as that was all they had in life. Their biggest honor was to die a glorious death on the field of battle. Just hearing the name Progragger changed everything for the Queen, who did not like Anders up until this point.

"I can see by your reactions I don't have to waste time explaining who the Prograggers are. I will leave you with a small taste of what is in store." He walked over to the door and shouted, "Bring it in now."

Two men lugged a large blue barrel into the Queen's room. They struggled, but finally got it over to Leimur. Anders popped the top off and an instant gleam radiated from the barrel. It was an odd container, but the gold and jewels inside were double the amount that Ali-Steven Wamhoff had brought her earlier. There were golden crowns, goblets and chalices studded with sparkling precious stones.

"That is quite impressive. And what do I have to do to earn this?" she sharply asked. "Just send your official with me so that he can tell you to accept the plan. Once we take care of that, we can start to talk about the details. If you should decide not to pursue, you keep the offering at no cost or ill will," Anders said with a reassuring look.

"Every time someone says there is no cost, there is always a price to pay," interjected General Rigby. "I agree with my General," added the Queen. "This is just a small chip from the mountain that remains. It will hardly be missed. Enjoy it and I will return on the morrow for your official. Thank you, your grace." He stood and bowed before heading for the door.

She waited for the man to leave the room and looked at the General, "Strange day, I must say."

"I think it may be more normal than not, my Queen. It seems like things just jump out of nowhere around here," he said sadly, apparently realizing this would soon be his problem once Leimur left. "We must be careful here. We obviously cannot agree to both men's plans. We will wait to see who has the better chance of conquering Donegal. What are your thoughts?" she asked Rigby. "It looks as though we must wait to make certain these men tell the truth. Flashing gold and diamonds can add a bit of credibility to any person's story, but time will tell which one presents the better option. And do we even want the better option in power?" he answered.

"I think you will do just fine here, General. I would also like for you to look after my brothers, if you would be so kind. I do not bid you change their soiled linens or feed them, just be sure that they are not mistreated. I remember a rude Senna from my days in this palace. A Senna is a nanny, if you don't know. And although she is gone now, I would just like for you to keep a watch for others like her please," said Leimur.

She had taken an oath to Marius Leluc that she would raise the boys like they were her own. She felt that she had saved the boys from a life of misery under her parents. The Queen had to leave to conquer for her realm, but she would not forget the boys.

"Of course, my Queen. Now are you serious about going through the Animal Kingdom to get to Harbor Valley?" a concerned Rigby asked. "I am fairly certain we will do it, just as Marius Leluc did in his day," she confidently asserted. "My Queen, I fear that is a death wish," General

Rigby firmly stated. "Nonsense, but how can we trust that these men of motivation don't try to invade our kingdom?" she asked, quickly changing the subject.

"This is not my forte, my Queen. Both men sound serious and may be content with only capturing Donegal to start. But they are already taking over one kingdom, so why not two might be the prevailing thought. I never trust anything until I see it with my own eyes. I shall send my spies out to gather information on these two men. Let's give them enough rope to hang themselves. We shall see how this plays out, but the gold and gifts are good signs of faith." He looked at the Queen's eyes, already weary from the responsibility of ruling a realm.

"Anders seemed to promise more of a split of Donegal while Ali-Steven wanted to pay us off and take everything. We need to figure out who will be easier to vanquish as we stick to our plan to take Donegal for ourselves," she said with a yawn. "They seem to think we don't know the value of Mattingly alone. I say we hit that border and just keep on going. They will be weakened from the siege and we will have full forces to crush them. Just don't take too long in Harbor Valley and allow them to regroup after the invasion," he warned.

"I like to think you will do just fine in my stead here in the Capitol, General." *Death is part of life. We will send one or both of these greedy men to the gates of hell if necessary.*

40

THE WANDERER—MARIAH

MARIAH PULLED THE last piece of salted beef from the leather sack and discarded the carrying case. She had been following the Royal River for over a week now. She had spent a couple of days stowed away in a barn, only to be chased out the back door and back on her endless path. Mariah thought the river ran south and following it would get her home. At least summer was knocking on the door and she didn't need to make a fire at night. She wouldn't know the first thing about starting a fire. She was brought up as a duchess, but spending a week alone in the woods can change people quickly. Her father's words kept resonating in her head.

AMBUSH, AMBUSH.

Mariah Colbert's thoughts had been going around in circles trying to make sense of the slaughter. But now she had more pressing problems because she was out of food and had nothing to hunt with. Not that it mattered. Mariah hadn't even been able draw a bow in her only attempt. After her brothers had laughed at her, Mariah never picked one up again. She remembered how her father had yelled at the boys in her defense. Now her father was probably dead and it appeared that she would soon follow him.

She approached a mountain side next to the river and decided to climb it. As she started walking up the hill she heard some voices and rustling. Through the oak trees, she noticed a small group of men. She ducked down, not knowing if they were Fox Chapel guards, sent to find her.

"There is no use in hiding," someone with a deep voice said. She stood straight up in front of a tiny tree.

"Who are you?" asked a rugged, handsome man with a beard and moustache. "Mariah Colbert," she muttered. He gave a sharp grin and looked into her eyes as he came closer. Suddenly, his smile melted in the heat as he pulled his sword and said, "Don't move."

Mariah put her hands in front of her face in a pathetic attempt at self-defense. *How did this happen? Only a week ago I was set to marry the Prince. The Gods can be so cruel.*

She pictured her mother, father and brothers. Mariah tried to be brave as the man raised his sword. She wasn't ready to die, but that decision seemed out of her hands now. Tears streamed down her face as she saw the sword in motion. The world went black as Mariah Colbert lay on the ground, motionless.

The bearded man shook her for a few moments until her eyes fluttered open.

"Oh good, you had me worried that I hit you," the man said as he held the back of Mariah's head. "What just happened?" the woozy girl asked. "I killed a rat snake that was hanging from the tree behind you. And when I swung, you fell right down. I won't tell you that the dead snake fell on your face though," he joked with a big smile. "Oh Gods," Mariah used her hands to wipe away any remnants.

The tall man grabbed her hands and looked deeply into her blue-gray eyes, "You're fine. You look lovely."

Mariah knew that right now she probably looked the least attractive she ever had in her life. She smiled for the first time since being abandoned by Brehan.

"Who are you?"

"Torvald Malik, my lady." "Wait, I am in Bottomfoot?" she asked. "Indeed, my lady. I mean, my Duchess," he said.

The Malik family ruled Bottomfoot which was a peaceful, neutral region. It wasn't financially driven and the many mountains of Bottomfoot kept them safe from attack. Bottomfoot lay along the border of Mattingly to the east and Burkeville to the north. The Capitol, Housemont, was high atop the steepest mountain in Bottomfoot.

"What are you doing so far north?" Mariah questioned. "Making sure those crooked bastards from Burkeville don't steal our trees," he said sternly. "Trees?" a confused Mariah asked. "Yes, they come over here and cut our oaks and spruces and drag them across the border to sell," Torvald said seemingly agitated. "They are lucky we haven't spotted them yet," added Chopkins Haddock.

There were three men with Torvald. Chopkins Haddock was his best friend and his family controlled the docks and ports of south-east coastline. They were the wealthiest family in all of Bottomfoot. They sent Chopkins to live in Housemont about three years ago. He was a short man with a big scar above his left eye from his older brother casting a fishing pole. The hook had ripped a big chunk of skin out and left an awkward-looking scar.

"Wait, how could I be in Bottomfoot? I never crossed the Royal River," stated a perplexed Mariah. "Sometimes, before the Frozen Forest melts down, certain parts of the river can look like a stream or creek," Chopkins revealed. "I guess I did cross some of those," she said. "So the obvious question is: What is the daughter of the Duke of Mattingly doing all alone in these nasty woods?" Torvald asked.

"She is looking for you," laughed Sir Bastion Stonefell and J. Everson Hiles joined in.

J. Everson was a tall dopey kid of sixteen. He was Torvald's squire. The Hiles family rebelled against the royal family having two capital letters in their first name and gave their children a capital letter to start their names. Sir Bastion stood short and stocky and tended to rub his nose while he talked, making it difficult to understand him. He had amazing sword prowess helping him to be considered the top knight in Bottomfoot.

"I am just lost from a family trip," she tried to lie, but she was a horrible liar. "I think not. I see pain behind those enchanting eyes. Tell me what is troubling you. I can help you, my lady," he said softly to her.

Mariah realized this was probably her only option, and confessed, "Alright, I was on my way to Falconhurst with my father and the knights of Mattingly and we were ambushed by Fox Chapel knights. I believe I may be the only one who survived."

Tears welled up in her eyes. The muscular man hugged her and scraped his fingers along the back of her neck several times that sent shockwaves throughout her body. She was now crying because of her father and the knights, but at the same time felt pleasure from being held by this strong gentleman. She could feel his muscles tense as he firmed his grip around her and looked into Mariah's confused eyes.

"Come back to Housemont with us. We will get provisions there and I can take you back home, my lady," he added with a slight grin.

Mariah would have followed him anywhere at this point. "Alright," was all she offered.

She started to have feelings that she had never experienced before. They got even stronger as Torvald framed her face with his hands and wiped the tears from beneath her eyes. He then caressed her cheeks and stared into her eyes.

"You are safe with me now, my lady." He decided to seal this statement with a soft, light kiss. In a few short minutes Mariah went from thinking she was going to die to being in love for the first time. "Ready?" Torvald asked before they took off. Mariah couldn't even speak. She tried, but the words got stuck in her throat and never made it to her lips. She simply nodded like a little girl with a smile that wouldn't go away.

41
SECRET VISITOR—EMILIA

A FIRM KNOCKING awoke the dozing Queen. She got up, stretched, and walked to the door. Emilia opened it to see her guard Ulee standing outside.

"My Queen, you have a visitor," Ulee declared.

Her visitor was neither tall nor short, just somewhere in between. He didn't look like the fierce warrior that he was reputed to be. He was rather skinny and too good looking for a lifetime soldier, the Queen thought.

"Of course, I know this man," the Queen responded with a smile. "My Queen, it has been quite a long time," Ali-Samuel Wamhoff pronounced with a deep bow. "May I have words with you?" "Surely, pray come in," she said as she led him into her room.

The Queen invited him to sit at her small table made of forest oak. She poured out two glasses of red wine and joined him at the little table.

"My Queen, I come to you as a man who can offer you more than anyone else in this Capitol," Ali-Samuel confidently stated. The Queen's heartbeat increased as excitement raced through her body. She stared directly into his eyes and said, "What is your offer?"

"Well, as you know better than anyone else, the King will not live forever. But that is no reason you cannot still be Queen." He flashed a smile and although his teeth were brown and rotting, the Queen did not care. "Go on," the Queen quickly said. "We have to get Ali-Varis out of the way as soon as possible. He is the only man that can keep you from your rightful place," he informed her.

"And how do you propose we do this?" The Queen squirmed a bit in her seat as the discussion went on. "Talk to Ali-Ster, make sure that he sees Ali-Varis must go. I have already put this in motion but it will be reassuring to hear it from his mother," Ali-Samuel added with a wink.

"What is the next step?" The Queen suddenly felt an excitement she had never experienced before. Her boring life as the wife of King Ali-Stanley had just got a shot of excitement. She was sweating now with her body tingling and on fire. Although sober, she was pleasurably stimulated and found it was better than being drunk or on drugs. She felt a strong attraction to Ali-Samuel.

"King Ali-Stanley Wamhoff," he stated bluntly to the small woman. "And why would I want to have that happen?" she replied with sudden nervousness. "Because you will still be Queen of Donegal. We will send Ali-Ster away before he can marry and you will remain Queen, supreme queen. Ali-Ster has a much better prospect of longevity to keep you living in this castle and not back on that goat farm in Burkeville. I simply ask that you allow me a place on the council to rebuild this mess your husband has created," said Ali-Samuel with another ugly smile.

"They will demand that Ali-Ster marry and put a baby inside his wife before he leaves," the Queen snapped back. "'They', that you refer to, will be you and I. I have already talked to Ali-Ster about Falconer and Foreign Chancellor. And with the Queen on our side, no one will be able to stop us, my Queen." He didn't take his eyes from Emilia's during the entire statement.

"I don't want Ali-Ster to lose his father," a concerned Queen stated. "Lose his father? He has had a father for eighteen years. I never had a father. Besides, the King is no father if you ask Ali-Ster. I have never known my father and it has made me a better man for it. But all ill will has been forgotten. I understand my father had to leave and if it wasn't for Queen Tomeo, my head would have been smashed on the castle steps. I lived a life as the little bastard of the castle even though my blood was pure. I was cursed with the last name Wamhoff until I left for the Pearl Islands at fifteen. Well, now is the time for just due," he said.

Ali-Samuel got up, walked over to the Queen and massaged her shoulders. He whispered "We are now involved with very motivated people and I want you to know that you are safe with me."

The Queen felt wonderful, although frozen in her seat. Ali-Samuel ran his fingers under her hair and the Queen arched her back with pleasure. He reached around and rubbed her breasts, softly pinching her nipples between his rugged fingers. Queen Emilia threw her neck back and turned her face up. Ali-Samuel kissed her gently from above.

"I will be going to Burkeville to take care of some business for our King, but when I return we will put the plan into action," he whispered in her ear. "That sounds great," smiled the Queen as Ali-Samuel rubbed her shoulders again.

Then he grabbed her hand and led her toward the bed. When they were almost there, he grabbed her and kissed her strongly. Queen Emilia was now soaked in excitement as Ali-Samuel stooped down and pulled her entire dress over her head. He tore her shift away and placed his palm on her vagina.

"Aren't you afraid of doing this in the king's castle?" the Queen whispered as she breathed heavily. "Nothing scares me, my Queen," Ali-Samuel said cockily.

That thrilled the Queen even more as she grabbed for his pants. For a small man, the Queen noticed he packed a lot of excitement. Sir Ali-Samuel Wamhoff threw the tiny Queen onto the bed and started to undress.

The Queen awoke feeling satisfied and a little sore. She got out of bed naked and saw that Ali-Samuel was long gone. He had brought a breath of fresh air straight from the heavens to revive a lonely Queen's stale life. The Queen of Donegal felt something she had not experienced in a long time, feelings for a man. She had fun with Anderley, but he was more of a convenience and too timid in bed. The Queen loved how Ali-Samuel tossed her around and took control, like a real man. The Queen thought men were too pensive at times, checking their foot in the water instead of diving straight in. She still smiled as she thought about what she would do the rest of the day. Right now, the only things that kept crawling back into her head were the lingering thoughts and smells of the man and his plan. This was exactly what the Queen sought to spice up her boring life.

42
GOING AWAY—RICEROS

BREHAN CASTAWAY PADDLED the canoe slowly down the Royal River. He kept on the Greenville side to protect Camelle and Riceros. They still weren't sure where the assassin had broken through so they wore hoods pulled down over their faces. Brehan had his hanging from the top of his head as he guided them to Middlefont.

It had only been a few days but Riceros Colbert already missed Jasper and Count Sproul. He was used to being away from Ruxin but he spent nearly every day with the Count and dog. He felt nervous as they embarked on a voyage that was to take him much farther away from Mattingly than he had ever been before.

Riceros had been acting the exact opposite of Camelle. He had showed barely any emotion since he'd heard the tragic news. For some reason, he couldn't believe that his father and sister were dead. The canoe floated along with a bare minimum of essentials but Brehan had a satchel filled with gold that would hopefully get them to where they were going.

Brehan and Riceros were taking Camelle to Waters Edge to receive protection from her family. Riceros didn't know where they were going after that and he wasn't sure that even Brehan knew. Riceros only knew that they had to leave the only place he had ever called home. His father and sister might be dead and no one had heard from Krys or Ryno. Soon his mother would be gone and Sir Brehan would be the only familiar face he might see for a long time.

Camelle was still an emotional mess most of the time, red eyed and wan faced. She seemed to have aged years over the past few weeks. Riceros tried his best to lift her spirits but his efforts didn't yield positive results. Her entire family had just been snatched from her bosom and her mother's will was broken. He hoped that her birth family would be able to help her. She would be safe there from the King's reach, whose deplorable actions seemed to have no bounds.

Brehan pushed the canoe ashore. Everyone jumped off and walked inland, a few feet off the beaten trail. Riceros noticed that Brehan finally snapped out of his recent funk. The knight must've understood that he needed to be strong for the woman and young boy.

The sun sank slowly over the horizon as Brehan pointed out the inn where they were going to spend the night. They would have camped out, but the Duchess was too pregnant for that. The trio walked through the door to see a decent-sized crowd of mostly men interspersed with just a few women.

Eight rectangular wooden tables were scattered around the dreary room. It smelled of old beer, wine and vomit that made Riceros retch. They sat at an empty table in the center of the room. Most of the rough-looking patrons appeared drunk. The people slurred words and pointed fingers in each other's faces as they rambled incoherently. Although Riceros was only eleven, he knew that the women were working here. He had heard his brothers talking about what the women who wear yellow hoods at the inns do. Riceros heard two men talking at a table of eight.

"He's but a fifteen-year-old boy, he can't hold off no king?" one man said. "This King is weak right now. Mattingly is strong. Even without Duke Colbert, I will piss on our King," he said as he spat on the floor. "Well it will be my neck that gets slit if this kid don't handle it. I don't wish to gamble my life on the side of a child," the first man said. "I plan to bring back the black heart of the King. And I'll show it to you and your pretty little neck. HAHAHAHA," the second man retorted. The entire table erupted in laughter save the embarrassed man.

The innkeeper arrived at their table. She was short, looked to be about fifty, and had three warts on her nose. Brehan ordered three bowls of the pig heart and liver stew with bread and they watched the lady stumble away to get their meals.

"At least it sounds like most people still feel confident in the cause," Brehan stated as he pulled his hood down a bit lower.

"Ruxin...Ruxin will do just fine. I know he will," Camelle managed to get out before she sobbed again.

Riceros and Brehan tried to soothe her by patting her on the back.

Brehan said, "Everything will be just fine in the end, you will see. We will be gone for a little while and then return to get you and go back home. And it will be good for the little man to get away from home for a bit." Brehan forced a smile for the benefit of the family.

The innkeeper showed up with three bowls of rabbit stew and dropped three spoons on the table. Riceros didn't enjoy the taste but he ate it nonetheless. His mother barely touched her bowl although she did stop crying.

Suddenly, the rowdy man from the neighboring table stood up and raised his mug. Then he started singing.

"Blood and sweat, we shed for the bull," as he sang this line, everyone at the inn joined in.

"His cause is our cause too,
Through the dark nights,
And the cold days,
We march on our enemies,
We lay our lives down,
If we are asked to,
For our families,
And we never,
Will ever surrender,
Then we hail a victory,
We return to our homelands,
Where we sit down,
And have a round,
And hug our family,
For the Colberts, and their houses,
We uphold honor and dignity,
For the Gods' sakes men,
Throw down your rakes men,
And take up arms men,
Will-power and unity."

The men crashed their mugs together and drank as proud citizens of Mattingly. Through all the pain a smile finally sprang to Camelle's lips. This spurred return grins from Riceros and Brehan as they ate the stew.

43
A Late Spring Storm-Russell

RUSSELL HAD BEEN at the school for about a fortnight. The Imp Wizard and Gamelda took turns teaching him a wide variety of new and interesting things. They were showing him how to channel his inner spirit and energy to connect to external spirit guides. Gamelda even taught him how to look into her "ball" as she called it. It was actually a crystal skull that Gamelda claimed to be thousands of years old and filled with great energy and spirits. She could see images in the eyes and had tried to teach Russell to do the same. He felt the power of the skull but hadn't been able to see anything yet.

The two teachers had told him that there are benevolent souls who float down from the heavens to help fight the forces of evil. The angels from above provided help to righteous men and women through mysterious powers, but only if they fully believed in them. Dragon-Eyes had said that different spirits provided various powers if you channeled them properly. Russell had been studying the angels and spirits every day since arriving at the school.

He rubbed his short spiky hair as he waited for the Imp Wizard to come downstairs. Russell sat at a table in the workroom, far away from the hissing snakes. They were ornery, but for some reason they never crossed an invisible line in the corner of the workshop. Hisalia walked in with a cloth bag full of something that moved. She walked over to the corner and flung the little animals inside the bag toward the snakes. Mice and rats met an immediate death, although a few got away and rushed out the open door. Hisalia was the snake-master and they obeyed her like they were her children. It was uncanny. She took good care of them and fed the serpents well, but Russell thought they would yearn for the outdoors again and make a break for it. Everyone thought they were all female serpents, but the rattlesnake had three babies last week. They looked like a cross between the rattler and cobra, quite fearsome looking little snakes.

He had worked every job in the workshop, except for venom-milker, since arriving. He also cleaned and gathered fire wood every morning. Russell really enjoyed his time with Gamelda. She was the most beautiful woman he had ever seen and she made him feel good about himself. When she stroked his face or rubbed Russell's stubble, it gave him feelings he had never experienced before.

As if on cue, Gamelda and Dragon-Eyes strolled into the room. The Imp wore a black cloak with a hood. Gamelda had a long, white dress on that made her dark skin look even more gorgeous to Russell. Her scent instantly found Russell's nose and excitement arose within him.

"Hello Gamelda," said a voice from behind Russell.

He turned to see who it was but the person passed him quickly and hugged Gamelda. Russell saw a thin post of a man standing in front of Gamelda. She stroked his face, just like she stroked Russell's. Anger bit him like a rabid dog and his chest began to tighten. *Who is this skinny little fool*?

"Alright now, we have to go, Russell. Say fare thee well," the wizard told Russell.

Russell walked over to the woman he had grown to experience strong feelings for.

"I will return in a bit, Gamelda," he said with a nod of the head. "Russell, this is my friend Wallyson," Gamelda said. "Russell, it is my pleasure," Wallyson stated with an extended hand. "Likewise," Russell returned as he looked over the smaller man. He wanted to carry the man over to the corner and throw him to the snakes. Instead, he just turned to leave. "Have fun, my sweet boy," Gamelda said in a seductive voice.

Russell stopped for a moment and then stumbled toward the wizard. *She called me boy. She just called me boy.* They exited the Imp's main domicile and set out into the dark and stormy evening.

"Don't be jealous," the wizard stated. "What? I am not jealous," Russell tried to lie. "I am not a young fool. I am well versed in the signs of jealousy. Keep in mind that Gamelda is a free spirit, a free woman. She belongs to no man. You know, the King once had these feelings of jealousy and cursed the very Gods that he now praises. You see, there was a day when the King feared he would never sit on the throne of

Donegal. His brother..."

"He had a brother?" Russell interrupted. "Indeed, a twin brother much more fit to be king. Ali-Pari must have really left you in the dark about her true family history. He was the fiercest warrior in the Livingstone war and brought back the spoils for his King father. King Ali-Baster declared Ali-Steven to be the heir to the throne as long as he married Parys Etburn. But Ali-Steven refused because of allegiance to his childhood sweetheart. After that Ali-Steven was chased from Donegal, not to be seen since. They slit the throat of his wife to be and captured his son before Ali-Steven could rescue them. Just as they were to smash the baby's head on the castle steps, the Queen ordered them to stop. She wouldn't let them slaughter an innocent child and Ali-Samuel Wamhoff was allowed to grow up in the castle and keep the royal prefix. Ali-Stanley agreed to marry Parys Etburn and received our kingdom by default."

"Where did Ali-Steven go?" Russell wanted to know.

"I know many people who know many things, but not a one knows where Ali-Steven Wamhoff went off to. He was reported to be in the Pearl Islands for some time, but from there it is a mystery," the wizard said with a smile. "King Ali-Stanley's jealous nature continues to this day and is exemplified in his latest decision. Our King has declared war on Mattingly and has requested the help of all men from Waters Edge. I will understand if your sense of duty precludes you from pursuing our mission," the wizard informed Russell.

"I have heard much about wars of kingdoms. They are often self-serving tantrums of kings. I do not wish to be a counted number amongst the dead. Our noble cause shall outweigh the King's whims of justice each and every day and night," Russell proudly stated. "I am glad to hear that. I will not rush to the King's aid either. We have a grander war to carry out. Now let us go test your training in Morningdale," Dragon-Eyes said as he pulled his hood over his head.

Dusk set in about twenty minutes into their southward walk through the soggy forest. It started raining as they approached a clearing in the woods. The small opening exposed the haunting skies that growled with rolling thunder. Russell looked over to see a smile on the old man's face.

The rain picked up as the Imp spoke, "I have been teaching you how to come into contact with spirit guides to aid you to do anything you wish. Well, now we test that. Do you see that tree over there?" he asked as he pointed to a giant maple tree. "I do," Russell replied.

The wizard closed his eyes and clenched his fists. The intensity of the storm increased and thunder boomed louder. The Imp was now breathing heavily as lightning flashed through the sky. Dragon-Eyes started shaking and threw his hand up into the air. A bolt of lightning shot down and struck the little man, but he didn't fall. He held out his hands in front of his tiny body and the lightning transferred from him and crushed the enormous tree. It instantly turned into black ashes and started crumbling in the rain.

Russell stood in awe once again. Before meeting the Imp Wizard, the young man's life had been rather mundane in comparison. Since meeting the wizard, it had been one amazing feat after another.

"Your turn," the Imp uttered. "My turn? To do that?" Russell questioned. "Of course, is your mind strong or only your body?" Dragon-Eyes asked. "Both, but, it is just a bit scary," Russell said with slight trepidation. "Being scared is not necessarily a bad thing. It is quite natural actually. It means you recognize the danger or significance of a situation. It is how you react to that fear that will define Russell Seabrook. Believe in yourself. Believe in your spirits. And show me that you can do this," the wizard firmly stated.

Russell pointed to a big tree and closed his eyes. He remembered that Afromenda was the angel of lightning and there was a chant to free her spirit.

Afromenda,
Guide your light through me,
Shine your light through me,
Evil, I shall fight against for ye,

The storm got nastier and thunder resonated through his head as he concentrated.

Afromenda, send your strength to me,
Angel of Lightning become one with me,

239

Let your spirit fly free,
Guide your light through me.

Although Russell didn't realize it, he had been shaking for about the last minute. He repeated the words and tried to conjure up the spirit of Afromenda. Lightning brightened the horizon as Russell shook like the leaves on the trees. He felt something pulsing though his body; an external energy seeped into his system.

He saw a bright white light and, BOOM, lightning struck Russell Seabrook.

He stumbled to one knee, but bounced straight back up and extended his hands toward the mighty tree. He could sense the power run through his entire body and exit out his hands. He opened his eyes to see the tree blasted by the bolt. The blackened tree crumbled to ash, just as the Imp Wizard's had done, and Russell collapsed.

His body was numb and cold after harnessing the lightning bolt. He flopped onto the ground and his eyes couldn't focus on anything.

"So cold," was all he could utter. Dragon-Eyes waddled over to him. "Not to worry, my boy. The same thing happened to me on my first attempt."

Why am I cold? I just had lightning inside my body and it burned me up until I released it.

A small bush located a few feet from Russell was set ablaze by the wizard. The flames raged despite the driving rain. Russell wiggled his way over to the flames and warmed his body that was frozen to the core. Russell still felt physically drained, but he was warm again. He got to his feet and leaned on his little friend as they started the trek back to the School of the Daughters of Darkness.

"I cannot believe you just did that. I was just testing you to see how much progress you had made. I never expected to see that. You are well beyond your years for harnessing lightning. The rest should be quite easy," he said as a proud teacher. A smile came over a still shaking Russell Seabrook as they walked through the storm.

44
DECISIONS-ALI-STER

"WHAT DO YOU mean, there is a stone wall?" the King screeched.

He wore his ruby-themed crown today. It was a golden crown, studded with large and small rubies and a red silk lining. It rested more like a hat than a crown on his head but it still slipped down over his bushy eyebrows from time to time.

"There is a fifteen-foot-high wall that is also ten feet wide, along the entire border of Mattingly. We don't have the weaponry to take out a wall like that. And with a majority of the border on top of the hills and mountains, it is rather impenetrable. From the Sea of Green to the Royal River and then over to Bottomfoot, every last inch seems to be accounted for, your highness," said Dirk Eller as he showed everyone the wall on a huge map.

"Havest thou the firth?" the King rhetorically asked for the tenth time at this meeting. "And we cannot take the coast at any point? Why are we throwing money into a navy if it cannot protect us?"

"Well, then this news will not be pleasant, your highness..." Derich was interrupted. "None of the news is pleasant anymore, get on with it," the King ordered. "Mattingly is causing problems with our imports as well. They are offering better prices for our supplies to be delivered to Mattingly. Word has gotten around. And most of these exporters have no loyalty to you because you aren't their King. Mattingly has also threatened to sink any ship that attempts to deliver anything to Fox Chapel," said Derich Bonsfogger.

"Well, what in all the hells are we going to do?" the concerned King asked his council. *Suddenly you want to listen to everyone's opinion.*

"Could we go down the Royal River en masse?" asked Dirk Eller. "There was an attempt to get into Mattingly by way of the River. It ended in slaughter. It appears to be heavily defended at every possible entrance," stated Henley Moore.

Ali-Ster spoke up, "Why don't we go through Bottomfoot and cross the western border? Surely they cannot have a wall along that side, nor do they have reason to with a neutral Bottomfoot. We pull back so that Mattingly believes we are retreating. Then we can hit them from the western border when they aren't expecting it."

King Ali-Stanley Wamhoff stared intently at the map, trying to find a way to breach Mattingly. "Wait. What about the Royal Road passage? They can't have a wall there," the King thought out loud.

"There was a one-mile stretch where they amazingly built a wall before we could rush the opening," a dejected Henley Moore stated. "Unless anyone else can come up with a better idea, it appears Ali-Ster is correct. Can we make it through the mountains and over the border?" the King asked.

"We must find out, if this is your will, father. We cannot run through the wall, so we shall go around it," Ali-Ster sharply said.

His father stared at him. Ali-Ster had never spoken back to him before. But if the King wanted to attack Mattingly, Ali-Ster knew this was the only viable option.

"We shall send word to Bottomfoot and our Generals after the meeting," the King said softly. "I have one last card to play that can help us while we wait..." he said trailing off so that nobody at the table really understood him. "Your highness, Sir Ali-Samuel has left for Burkeville," said Leo Braunshaur. "Good. I hope he can clean up that mess quickly and we can get more Burkeville men to join our cause," the King stated.

"Speaking of men to join the cause," said Dirk Eller, "It seems four thousand of the soldiers from the Goldenfield stand-off have disappeared. "Come again? Disappeared?" the King questioned. "Were they eaten by dragons? Maybe they mysteriously floated up into the heavens? How do you lose four thousand men?" the King screamed as he slammed his scepter into the table.

"Well, your highness, it seems that the eight thousand men were split into two divisions. And somehow the division in the rear must have gone astray," Dirk Eller weakly stated. "Disaster. Disaster," repeated the King as he shook his head. "What is happening to my kingdom?" *Your rule is what happened to this kingdom.*

Everything Ali-Samuel had been saying about the King was true.

Donegal would be a lot better off without King Ali-Stanley, Ali-Ster finally thought. He realized it may be time to put Ali-Samuel's plan into action.

"What else? What else?" the King queried. "Our sword-smiths still cannot replicate the Dragon-Steel that you had asked them to. They say there is a metal in the mix that they cannot identify," Leo Braunshaur said. "I have an idea of who I can ask about the unknown metal," said the King with a devious smile.

"It also appears that the Gold Bandit is at it again. He struck up along the Fox Chapel-Waters Edge border this time. They hit the Sanders and Aprott castles for over ten thousand gold coins. The pattern stretches from inside Goldenfield almost to the Sea of Green. How he can still get into the castle reserves, I cannot understand. If the reports are correct, he has stolen over five hundred-thousand gold rounds. Who could possibly get away every-single time?" Leo Braunshaur wondered.

"Well, when it rains, it pours. Perhaps the mystery man who made my troops disappear is stealing the gold too," said the King listlessly.

This meeting had exposed to Ali-Ster the sad state of affairs in Donegal. It was terrible news on every front. He had only been home for a few months and every one of his King father's decisions was an epic failure. The kingdom was a sinking ship and Ali-Ster never liked swimming.

He yawned as Jake Fielder spoke, "There seems to be a possible threat across the Sea of Green. It may not present a problem for several years, but it looks as though we have a rising son in the east."

Ali-Ster faded in and out of sleep for the rest of the meeting until his father finally dismissed everyone. As Ali-Ster walked back to his room he thought about Queen Leimur Leluc. He remembered seeing her on the battle field and could still picture her purple eyes. He had heard that everyone hailed her for ending her father's reign. *Would they treat me as the same hero, right here in Donegal? My father might not be the drunk that Pascal Leluc was reported to be, but his decision making is much worse.*

He wondered what Queen Leimur's parents did to push her over the edge. He had been told that her citizens understood that she had killed her parents for the betterment of the kingdom, not for a personal family vendetta.

She has men running to fight on her behalf and our soldiers desert their King, who obviously commands no respect. What must I do to restore MY kingdom? Death is part of life.

45
HARD TO FIND-OLLOR

TRAVELING THROUGH THE cities of the Pearl Islands and Gama Traka had tested his former vices. Finding information about the school had also proved no easy task. He wasn't sure whom to trust in this foreign land. Gama Traka was a dry, dusty desert. It remained hot for most of the year and hardly rained. The large towns and cities were the only habitable areas. He had heard stories of people getting caught in sand-storms and being lost in the desert to die of starvation and thirst. Summer was arriving, which made the conditions even more brutal. But he finally thought that they were nearing their destination.

Ollor looked at the twelve year old Sunny and reflected on how much he had grown recently. The red-headed boy stood extremely tall for his age but he still had to look up to Ollor with his brown eyes. Then he patted Muriel, who had just turned six, on the shoulder. Her dark skin, hair, eyes and lips made her look much more like a native than Sunny. Ollor had trained her as if she were a boy, showing no mercy to the girl. He knew the cruel world would take no pity on a little girl so he tried to prepare her as such. If anything, being a girl made her an easy target for twisted souls. He believed that the children were ready for the school.

He saw a building that was supposed to be the school according to his latest clues. Ollor didn't think that this simple one-story house could be the school. The school had been rumored to train hundreds of warriors. This place couldn't house more than ten people comfortably. Ollor took the kids up to the door and tapped on it. No one answered, so he knocked again a minute later. *I knew this couldn't be the spot.*

As Ollor turned to leave, the door cracked open. A skinny, dark arm came through the crack. A man held his hand out and spoke in Gaman, the native tongue of Gama Traka, "Place the dragon coin in my palm."

Ollor pulled the huge silver coin from his pocket and handed it to the hidden man. The door slammed. It remained closed for several minutes giving rise to slight panic in Ollor.

It cracked open again and the same man asked, "Do they bear the true mark of the dragon?" Ollor stated, "They are not born to Gama Traka, but their blood runs pure I can assure you."

He still couldn't see the man, but the gruff voice spoke again, "You must wait outside this door for our decision. If we open this door and you are not here, the children will be eliminated from the reckoning. I cannot tell you how long it will take."

The door shut in their faces. It had not reached mid-day yet and the heat was already unbearable. Ollor crafted a shade for the children to stay as cool as possible. He used clothes from their bags to construct the makeshift reprieve from the sun. The only thing they couldn't avoid was the lack of food.

The rest of the sweltering day and night passed and the children were starving. Ollor knew that they were hungry but they weren't complaining at all. The kids didn't look happy, yet they kept quiet. Suddenly for the first time since they had arrived at the school, they saw a man walking by.

Ollor spoke in Gaman, "My friend, per chance would you have any food?"

The tall man wore a long white robe and he smiled at the hungry group. He rummaged through his twisted robe and produced a salted perch. The skinny man handed it to Ollor and started reaching around his neck. He pulled out a long skin of water and gave it to Sunny. The welcome stranger reached into the other side of his robe and found what Ollor thought to be dried horse meat. Although forbidden to eat horse in his native kingdom, his choices were limited at the moment. He humbly accepted. Ollor pulled a coin from his pocket and held his hand open.

"What is it I owe you?" he asked. "Nothing. You will pay me when the time is right," the man said as he smiled and closed Ollor's hand. *I would rather he took the coin than have to fulfill some obligation down the road.*

He put it back into his pocket. The mystery man left and another day and night passed. The food had barely got them through the night. They were out of water too.

Ollor thought hard as the sun beat down on him and the children. Unless another miracle man with food stuffed in his robes came strolling by, the kids were going to get very sick soon. He started to pack up their belongings and planned an exit strategy. Just when he had everything in order, the door finally opened.

A dark-skinned man in white and burgundy robes, secured by a gold belt appeared before them. His head and face were completely shaved and he had tattoos on his neck that resembled dragons. His forehead was so severely wrinkled that Ollor believed he must be at least seventy.

His fierce, dark eyes were almost black as he spoke, "Your children have passed the first test. They didn't complain a single time during the wait. Patience is necessary. More tests must occur to ensure admission into our school. You may enter." "Thank you," said Ollor as he led the kids into the building.

The interior was bare, with the exception of a clear tank of fish. The gigantic tank took up almost half of the room. A closer look showed it to be filled with the flesh-eating fish, ramboo. Ollor also noticed that the bottom of the tank was filled with bones, human bones. And they weren't the skeletons of grown men, they were those of children.

Their host, who still hadn't revealed his name, broke the short silence, "Bravery. We cannot teach it. A student must have that trait to enter. The boy will be tested, but the girl can leave right now. We have no room for her."

"No," Ollor sharply said, "She is here to be tested also." "She will die," the man coldly stated. "She will not," Ollor retorted.

The older man looked at the stern look on Muriel's face and seemed to like her determination.

"Her blood will be on your hands. Mine are clean hereafter. Look at the bottom of that tank. It is filled with little girls whose fathers thought they were ready. The ramboo do not discriminate, they actually prefer young, tender meat. The first test is to walk the plank over the tank," he informed Ollor.

Ollor walked over to the fourteen foot long tank that was about seven feet deep and saw the tiny wooden plank that stretched over the water. It was barely wide enough for two small feet, side by side. He started to have thoughts of holding Muriel back. *If this is only the second test, it can only get much harder from here.*

He told them in the native tongue of Donegal and Goldenfield about what they had to do. He expected to see instant fear in the eyes of the children, but they surprised him with looks of confidence.

Sunny decided to go first. He walked over to the ladder at one end of the tank and climbed to the top. The ramboo began to get excited and circled around the top of the tank. Ollor felt a knot in his stomach and his heart fluttered. He knew that Sunny could do this, but he wasn't the one who risked being eaten alive.

Sunny stood atop the wooden board and it started to give. He bent his knees and steadied himself. As he took the first two steps, the plank dipped down and then bounced back up creating an extra variable. Sunny kept his eyes fixed on the narrow board, trying to ignore the frenzied fish below that awaited a fatal mistake. He took several more steps and a ramboo jumped out of the water and bit his exposed calf. Blood spurted out and Sunny lost balance. He stuck his left arm out, but he kept falling.

Ollor's heart sank into the floor. However a few more leans back and forth helped correct Sunny's balance. Ollor thought his heart was going to jump out of his body as Sunny reached the half-way point of the plank. It dipped so low that it sat in the water. The ramboo surrounded Sunny, excited from the dripping blood. He hurried to get out of the water and nearly fell again. He slowed down just a bit as he could see the end only a few feet ahead. Sunny reminded himself to keep his head straight down to concentrate on his steps. He saw the end and jumped off the plank, onto the floor.

Relief washed over Ollor but it was tempered with doubt. He felt happy for Sunny but anxious about Muriel who stumbled often even while walking on flat surfaces. This test was the worst possible scenario for a girl without toes. Ollor didn't know what to do. He looked down at the girl and she peered up and smiled. He immediately felt that his decision to bring her here had been strangely validated.

Ollor's nerves went haywire as she started to climb the ladder. Muriel looked ahead, down, ahead, and down again. Her first several steps were fine, but then she stumbled. She waved her arms in circles and fell forward. Her momentum carried her toward the middle of the tank. She couldn't hold her balance and fell into the tank, immediately surrounded by ramboo.

Ollor fell to a knee, head buried in his hands. He didn't know if they should even continue without the girl. *Her blood is on my soul. I failed to discern the real danger. What did I think? She was only a little girl.*

"Ollor," said Sunny. He had no clue how to explain this to the boy. He looked over to see Sunny pointing at the tank. Muriel swam around the water with ramboo following her. None of the fish even attempted to bite her. She went over to the end of the tank and slowly got out. Ollor saw a look of bewilderment on the face of their host.

"On to the next test?" Ollor asked the man. "No more tests. I have seen all I need to," the man remarked, still stunned.

Ollor couldn't comprehend why the killer fish hadn't eaten Muriel. But he did understand that it had just gained them entry into the School of the Learned Warrior. *I knew she had pure blood, but to spit in the face of death is amazing.*

The man led them down a winding staircase in silence and near darkness. When they reached the bottom, several huge torches welcomed them. They walked through a small doorway and it opened up into something like an underground town. The long, wide road had men trotting around on horseback. There were enormous rooms on either side of the street.

As they walked down the subterranean road, they passed a library that had students studying. The room on the other side had people sitting on the floor, chanting spells. They had their eyes closed and their hands pressed together, in front of their faces. The majority of the students were men with an occasional female visible here and there.

"A mind, when used properly, can cause more damage than a misdirected body. When practiced in unison, with proper training, the possibilities are endless," the host said as he led them down the street.

The next set of rooms looked to be set up for strength and conditioning.

"A body must remain sharp, like a blade. Power, quickness and stamina should be a warrior's closest allies," the old man said.

The rooms at the end of the long, straight road were for battle training. They prepared the pupils by teaching them to use many different kinds of weapons with various fighting techniques. Ollor thought he counted at least two thousand students roaming the underground facility. That didn't include the teachers and trainers. Their guide told them there was a floor below that the school used for food and supplies and which led directly to the outside. The sheer size of some of the decorations and training devices made Ollor wonder how they got them down here. He noticed fifteen-foot high dragon sculptures with ruby and emerald eyes. Some were made of jade, but most were made of marble or ebony.

The man spoke again, "In two days' time, we will swear your children into the school. We need all the help we can get right now. Man, child or woman. Nobody is safe in this world right now. A mammoth danger lurks on the horizon."

46

THE WRONG ISLAND—THE CAPTAIN

THE SEA-BATTERED SHIP finally ran adrift on the ominous-looking island. They had been lost for about a year and only four crew members remained. Captain Wallace hailed from Donegal and the other men from Androsi. They had set out to make a simple run to the Pearl Islands and back, which was generally routine. But an unexpected series of storms rocked the Sea of Green. Nothing the crew did could appease Cleon, God of the seas. Thirty-foot swells pushed the boat into unknown areas. Every time they caught a tantalizing glimpse of coastline, the tides changed and the land vanished before their eyes. Finally Cleon had taken mercy on them and pushed them onto this island. The ground was an ashy gray and there were no trees or grass as far as the Captain could see. There wasn't even sand on the coast. The boat docked itself against the dark, spongy surface. Captain Wallace and Spurgeon Flack decided to go inspect the island.

They jumped down onto piles of snakes, six-legged salamanders and various other little reptiles. The two men headed for a hill that lay straight ahead. Night had just fallen so they couldn't see how many reptiles lined their path. Luckily the men wore long pants that kept them from being bitten by the small snakes and lizards. A red glow appeared at the base of the hill. A huge opening about twenty feet wide seemed to invite the men to enter.

They walked blindly up to it in the darkness and heard people speaking in a foreign tongue. There was a giant boulder about fifteen feet ahead, so the men ran stealthily over and hid behind it. A quick peek showed four men talking with their backs to the sailors.

"We are getting very close, but we still need to wait for the grand signal from Travibero," claimed a man with a deep, booming voice in an unknown language to the Captain. "We should attack now, the human race is so weak at the moment," another man said. "And that is why you are not in control, Laramar. You act with too much haste most times. I have waited over five hundred years for this. I am not going to rush now in the final moments. If we could only locate that damned Pearl of Wisdom, we could end everything already. But we cannot seem to find it," uttered the voice the Captain recognized as that of the first man.

Another quick glance showed that while the other three men looked the same as before, the man talking had transformed into a green demon-like creature. He had a long tail and three ears on top of his head that looked like purple triangles. Red pupils surrounded by big black irises finished the scary look.

The demon spoke again, "Once we erase this bunch of humans from the earth, we can begin to rebuild it for our own purposes. We will finally be worshipped, not all those pretender Gods. Every religion on this earth has it wrong, but we will leave it to their Gods to sort them out after we kill every last one of them. Then we will be free to plunder whatever spoils we want."

"When will that day come? When can we finally come out of hiding to get our just due? When will the humans realize they should have been worshipping us who fight against the false idols who treat them so cruelly?" a third man asked.

"Patience is something you lack, Snake Bite. Rewards at the end of a great battle are much sweeter than spoils received after surrender without fight. We have to be certain we can win. Failure would set the cause back over a thousand years this time and that is not an option. I will not turn and run this time. My life has culminated in this final battle," the demon stated.

Suddenly, the two men heard screams coming from their shipmates. They sprinted out of the cave and battled the serpent-laced trail to get back to the ship. The two sailors had jumped off the boat and were running toward them. In a flash that lit up the early-summer sky, their entire ship went up in flames. The Captain stood motionless as he couldn't believe what he had just witnessed.

A humongous black dragon flew above the ship it had just destroyed and tracked after the men. The dragon caught up with one of Captain Wallace's men and snatched him from the ground, tossed him into the air, and caught him in its deadly mouth. The man's screams were terrible, but the Captain still could not move.

His vision, although hampered by darkness, still clearly showed a fire-breathing dragon. This was something the seasoned Captain didn't think he would ever see. *Dragons disappeared thousands of years ago*, the Captain thought to himself.

This beast was nearly the size of his one-hundred and eighty-man ship. It flew back down with its wings fully extended and blazed his other crew mate to instant ashes. He looked back at the cave and made a dash with Spurgeon Flack a few feet behind him. The Captain could hear the heavy breathing and heat of the dragon as it closed in and tore into Spurgeon. He cursed the Gods for sabotaging him as the dragon stopped to chomp him down. The dragon easily went through the bones like they were porridge. The sound made the Captain feel ill but the delay allowed him time to get into the cave.

Unfortunately, he was greeted by the green demon and his associates.

"What is it we have here?" asked the green demon rhetorically in the tongue of Donegal. Captain Wallace went down to one knee, "I beg forgiveness. My boat ran adrift and I will do anything, please, save me." "What is your worth? You are obviously not a good ship captain or you would never have docked here on Venom Island," said the demon with an evil smile. "I will do anything you say. Anything you want me to do," pleaded the Captain, still on his knees. "Get up, we don't even bend the knee for Travibero around here," the demon responded.

That name sent chills down the spine of Captain Wallace. Travibero was the Lord of the Underground.

"My name is Damian Doome, loyal servant of Travibero, and leader of the coldomores. I am the man who lost the great battle to Rockarius five hundred years ago. I am the man who has been getting ready for the final battle in the long war with mankind. I am the man who plans to rule over the entire world after we wipe away mankind. Then the truly deserving coldomores can escape the underground. Follow me," said Damian.

He led the captain into the cave that descended sharply. It got progressively hotter as they went deeper. Damian Doome put his reptilian-like hand on the Captain to guide him. The path started to widen and level off. A bright light appeared at the end of the long walk way. As he got closer the ceiling and path expanded until they formed an enormous sub-terrain room.

There were huge pens filled with naked human beings. The demons threw bloody pieces of food in occasionally and the humans fought like wild animals for the dripping scraps. They were all terribly skinny and their bones clung tightly to their skin.

"What do you think of your mighty humans now? They don't look very civilized, do they? These are our breeding humans. We need to maintain a steady supply of decoys, if you will. I am certain you know that coldomores can take over a human body, but know this, no human has ever taken over a coldomore body. So we breed humans to serve as receptacles when we need to send our coldomores out among you heathens. You humans are not very receptive to coldomores, I have found. Let's move on," he stated with a wave to show the way to the Captain.

As they walked farther into the depths of the cave, demonic creatures appeared everywhere. There were more huge openings that housed demons of different colors and sizes. Green, black, red, orange, purple and yellow were the major colors of these demons. They all looked like Damian Doome in size and form. Like a cross between a human being and a fox. They walked on two feet, but their bodies were grotesquely skinny and awkward when they moved. There were thousands of them and the farther they went in, the more the Captain realized there had to be hundreds of thousands that just kept coming out of different offshoots of the cave.

"We have been breeding our own men too," said Damian Doome, "We are ready for this battle. But if any doubt still persists, I have one more chamber to show you in our mines."

Captain Wallace saw a giant doorway at what appeared to be the end of their path. Damian Doome stopped and held his hands in front of himself. The huge door started to creak as it slowly opened and Damian lowered his hands. It was even hotter than the already scorching heat outside as the two entered. This enormous chamber had about fifty dragons in it. The Captain saw that they were chained up on either side of the room as Damian walked him through the middle of the room.

There were black, red and purple dragons scattered throughout the quarters. Some were small and others as big as the black one that had greeted the Captain outside. They all had the classic look of a dragon with a long neck, scaly body and slithery tail. And judging by the intense heat in the room, they could all breathe fire.

"Now you see that I have the man- and dragon-power to win. I know what I want you to do for me. Let us return to the outside," Damian said.

As they left the cave, the Captain again saw hordes of demons and pens full of humans, while images of the dragons seemed to be branded into his mind. His head swirled as they got out of the underground lair.

"I am sending you to spread the word of Damian Doome. Let everyone know that I am not prepared for a battle," he told the Captain. "But how will I get anywhere, that dragon burned down my ship," Captain Wallace returned.

Damian Doome screamed up to the sky in the unknown tongue. Within seconds, the black dragon that had eaten his crew-mates landed a few feet from Damian. The dragon talked to Damian in this foreign tongue. The dragon talked! Captain Wallace had heard of dragons, but not talking dragons.

Damian told the Captain, "My friend, Brute, has agreed to drop you off in the Pearl Islands where you can spread the word of Damian Doome and the coldomores. You will tell everyone that we are not prepared to fight and will not be ready for hundreds of years. I will make sure that you will not betray me. You will have to hold onto the scales on the back of his neck and hold on tight. Brute will not have any second thoughts about tossing you off while he floats amongst the clouds."

Suddenly, Captain Wallace felt great pain surge through his body. He was having sensations he never had before and his whole body suddenly went numb. The Captain tried to fight against this bodily invader, but his resistance was futile.

"Good work, Ephesi. Now, let him have control of his thoughts and feelings until you arrive. Then make sure that the message he conveys is only of our weakness. The cause thanks you for this sacrifice," Damian said.

The demon-infested Captain climbed up the side of the dragon, using its leg to help prop himself up onto its back. The scales were bigger than his hands and sturdier than metal. He gripped a couple to pull himself up and now sat on the back of a real dragon. He moved up to the dragon's neck and grabbed on for dear life. Damian said something to the dragon and Brute flapped his wings. Before the Captain could gain the courage to look down he made sure he had a firm hold. He was hundreds of feet above the ground, gliding through the night air, and all he could see was the moonlit Sea of Green sparkling. A quick peek behind showed that Venom Island had already disappeared. He didn't remember where the dragon planned to take him but Captain Wallace was flying. He had never experienced a greater thrill in all of his days.

47
THE STANDING DUKE—RUXIN

THE DUKE OF Mattingly walked toward "Thinkers Tower". To only call it a tower, however, was an insult. The tower stood high but also possessed the size of a small castle. All the wise men of the region lived here. They exchanged ideas and came up with inventions. Ruxin Colbert felt uncomfortable here because he didn't understand what the men were talking about. His father and Riceros used to love hanging around the wise men but Ruxin and his older brothers were usually bored. Ruxin understood that being Duke meant he would have to make appearances at places he didn't like. He walked in and immediately saw Tormel Grainwell, the man everyone called the King of the Scholars.

"My Duke, so sorry to hear about your father. Treachery against a king is punished with death, but what is the punishment for a king who, himself, commits treachery? Not but anything apparently."

Tormel looked like many of the older Thinkers who lived in the Tower. He had long gray hair and an unkempt beard and moustache. He looked to be in good shape for an older gentleman who mostly read and philosophized. The Thinkers gave little regard to appearance and celebrated people for their thoughts and innovations. The smell of body odor ran rampant throughout the stale Tower. *Can they invent a man to fan this stench out of here?*

The ground floor of the Tower looked like a disorganized workshop. There were papers scattered everywhere and people assembling items on the tables around the room. They all wore white robes and sandals. Ruxin noticed two men working on a crossbow and another man fiddling with a mini catapult, but didn't recognize anything else.

"Here, my Duke, you have to see this. This is close to being a major breakthrough for moving water," Tormel said, motioning Ruxin over to one of the tables.

Ruxin followed and saw a little dish filled with water. A long cylinder with grooves had a small channel under it and pointed upward on a slant. The wise man took a cover for the cylinder and snapped it into place, being careful not to hit the crank. The circular wooden cover hid the metal cylinder from view and acted to trap the water as it moved upward. Tormel started turning the little crank at the top. The enclosed cylinder caused water to magically push itself from the bottom to the top and empty into the waiting cup. Ruxin wasn't as impressed as the giddy older man.

"My Duke, this is the screw. This will help us push water over mountains. You could make it as big as a tree trunk and use a system of pulleys to crank it. You need manpower like when we lift large stones for a castle, but this should leave no man thirsty. It could even create a system of running water throughout a castle like the ancient baths," Tormel anxiously stated.

"Where did you learn this?" Ruxin wondered.

"The original thoughts came when Theore Ravotti returned from the Great Library of Ton Abelisy. He consulted with foreign scholars about the idea and collaborated with us to find the best way to construct it. After several years, we are close to production. Most of the efforts now are to create better weapons to ultimately save the lives of our men. It may sound strange but we are looking to create a weapon that will end all future wars," Tormel said as he scratched his head.

It had been common practice for the most intelligent men in Mattingly to go to the Great Library of Ton Abelisy in Gama Traka to exchange ideas and thoughts with the world's greatest minds. The elite thinkers of the world made pilgrimages there to see the thousands of books the library contained. The wise men of Mattingly had a constant rotation of scholars at the library and they would return with ideas to better Mattingly. Jon Colbert had always supported efforts to increase education and advancement.

None of this ever interested Ruxin. He enjoyed swordplay, hunting and archery. He also liked to study battle strategies and former battle results. He often found that the reasons for winning battle were usually pretty simple. He consistently read about the winning side having better numbers, more skilled soldiers or the high ground. There were a few instances involving someone beating the odds but more often than not, it was straightforward. Ruxin liked using the weapons created by the wise men even if he didn't understand how to make them. He stayed for about an hour and realized he needed to return to the castle for a meeting. Ruxin thanked the men for their dedication to Mattingly and rushed back to the meeting.

He arrived on time, but Ruxin thought his uncle Ordrid had started the meeting early.

Count Sproul read the next order of business, "Fox Chapel has retreated all along the northern border."

Ruxin and Ordrid Colbert started to speak at the same time, with Ruxin yielding to his uncle.

"They realized it's foolish to try to invade Mattingly," Ordrid said.

"No, it can't be. The King won't just give up now. He's going to try to figure out another way to get into Mattingly. We need to be extra vigilant along the coast. Send letters to all the lords along the coast alerting them of the security increase," Ruxin explained.

Ruxin and his uncle had been butting heads for several weeks. They couldn't seem to agree on anything. Ruxin wished he would go back to his own castle in Greenville and let him rule the region. The three men sat at the council table located in a small room in the west wing of the castle. They were joined by High Lord Perry of Abalon and Lord Embler of Tarkshin.

Ordrid snidely said, "Where would he plan to enter? Mattingly is rather impenetrable. I will explain to you what that word means later, my young nephew."

Ruxin wondered why his father had asked Ordrid to come to Riverfront. All he had done was undermine his nephew's authority and try to embarrass Ruxin. The teenager hoped someone from his family would return soon so he could send Ordrid home. Unfortunately, the young Duke also understood his father was the only person from whom Ordrid would take orders. Ruxin knew firsthand about taking orders from older brothers.

Sir Jeremiah Elmhurst entered the room. "My Duke, my Lords, a man named Anders Ah...ah."

"Ahitni," Ruxin interjected to help the stammering knight.

"Yes, that's it, my Duke," Sir Jeremiah returned.

"Show him in, if you will," Ordrid said.

The small statured man from Gama Traka entered the room. He got to the table, bowed and said, "My Lords and Duke."

"It's great to see you during these trying times. It seems sometimes you never know who your friends are," Ruxin said.

"My deepest condolences for what your King did to your father. Duke Colbert was the kind of man your kingdom needs. He was a great man but treason from the highest level is often unavoidable and unpunished. Even the crafty spider will cast a web rather than chase his enemy. The weaker opponent will draw the other to him. So what's your plan to stop the King's invasion?" asked Anders. Ruxin noticed that Anders blinked frequently while he talked, much more than a normal man.

Ordrid jumped in, "Well first of many defenses, we have a fifteen-foot wall across the entire Fox Chapel border..."

Ruxin cut him off, "Uncle Ordrid, perhaps this isn't the best place to talk about strategy. A spider could have cast his web in this room. Let's take a walk, Anders. I still know a few places where no ears will possibly hear us."

"I shall come," said Ordrid.

Ruxin knew his uncle didn't want to be left out but he needed to talk to Anders in private. He spoke, "Give us an hour's time and you will be the first man I report to, my honorable uncle."

"Well, I suppose that might be alright. No more than an hour," agreed Ordrid.

"Well if you will excuse us, my Lords," Ruxin bowed.

"My Lords," Anders added with a bow and the two men were out the door. They walked out of the castle and the early summer sun smacked a heavily dressed Ruxin. A few small clouds provided quick relief but the temperature had jumped recently. Ruxin led the way, already sweating from the humidity as the conversation started back up.

"I have news of your brothers, Ryno and Krys. It seems they were kidnapped in Androsi by Edburgh Etburn."

"My uncle? Why would he...?" asked Ruxin.

"I'm sorry; I don't know why your mother's brother would do this. Some have said your mother was involved with the plot but I couldn't imagine why. What caused this rage, I am positively unsure. I have already sent some men to Androsi to find your brothers. Your brothers will return alive, I will make sure of it," Anders promised.

Ruxin forged a path from the grassy pasture into the woods. He made sure to slow down and face Anders while he moved backward slowly. Ruxin noticed he was blinking rapidly again and said, "Thank you, my friend. I will be forever indebted to you. My father was right, you are a good friend."

"It's the least I can do. Your father was a great man and I know his sons will be too. So what is your plan to deal with the King?" Anders asked.

Ruxin felt an odd pain in his stomach as he answered, "It's like you said about the spider. Sometimes people don't even realize they are caught in the web. Let's just say, I am setting a web for the King and his associates." Ruxin kept thinking about what Riceros had told him. The sun tucked itself behind a cloud causing a dawn-like atmosphere in the woods.

"But specifically, how do you plan to stop him?" Anders pressed.

"The King has already stopped himself, my friend. He retreated a few days ago. The war, ha, the fight is over," Ruxin said.

"So you are just going to sit back?" Anders questioned.

Ruxin stopped and looked Anders in his eyes as he spoke, "What choice does he have? Fight an unbeatable opponent and die in shame or simply give up. He got my father. That was his prize. We are still hoping the King will send us the body so he can salvage a scrap of honor."

"I wouldn't hold my breath for that day. You must forge ahead for the honor of your father, bones or not." Anders advised.

"You're right Anders, our good family friend," smiled Ruxin. He took a long look at Anders and scratched his ear for several seconds. He turned his back and walked several feet in front of Anders.

Anders quickly reached into his robe and pulled a glimmering object from it. Ruxin must not have suspected anything because he continued to walk confidently with a smile on his face. Anders approached from behind and raised the dagger marked for Ruxin Colbert, acting Duke of Mattingly.

48

A NORMAL JOB—PENROSE

PENROSE ELLSWORTH AND the other knights finally arrived in Elkridge after a rotten trip. Penrose had seen the struggles of the citizens of Donegal. The King had raised taxes once again, and the people suffered. They were starving in the summer. Penrose had always heard that people were only supposed to starve during winter. The starving turned to stealing and murder. The City and Town Watch throughout the entire kingdom hadn't paid some watchmen for months and that crippled their efforts to curb the lawbreakers. The defunding created a dangerous situation with former watchmen having inside knowledge of how to get away with crime. Ali-Stanley used the money for other purposes, but unknowingly created trained criminals. Penrose had come to understand the King had failed again. Penrose wasn't happy about the nature of this trip either.

Everyone gave the King's Guard and their troupe a little respect as they passed. Penrose remembered the now fading glory that had originally made him want to be a member of the Guard. In his early days, the common folk bowed deeply when they saw the fox and falcon symbol. Now they barely had enough respect to nod their heads fully. He understood the anger. This trip had confirmed that Donegal needed a new leader, a fresh start.

Sir Oliver gave a hand signal and the men jumped off their horses. They secured the animals to a rail post and advanced down a street of nice houses. The voices started to attack Penrose again. *STOP. NOT NOW.*

They wanted to taste blood again. The voices were getting louder with every passing day. Penrose thought about offering the voices his own blood.

What is my life worth? I protect a rotten King, serve an immoral Father and all the while I know I should have stayed in Lightview. I pray to these

Gods that turn their backs on me. Why?

As the men walked down the street, Penrose thought about how his life would have been different if he had listened to his father and stayed in Lightview. High Lord Ichibod Ellsworth hated the Wamhoffs. His father had been crushed when the King snatched his second son for King's Guard. Penrose had several impressive performances in tourneys and the King offered him a spot with the Guard. He had ventured back to Lightview several times since but his father refused to see him every time. His mother, Lady Victoriah Ellsworth, had always made excuses for her husband, but Penrose knew his father was still in a rage over the matter.

Sir Oliver grabbed a man on the street by his throat. "You sure that's the house?"

The cowering man nervously nodded his head.

"It better be or we'll find you," Sir Oliver threatened the man as he handed over some silver. The man grabbed the coin, ran away and the King's men rushed over to the marked house. Sir Oliver pointed at the door and then kicked it in. Two men, a pregnant woman and child stood there frightened. Penrose looked at a tall woman with child and brown eyes. Sir Chanley Hofter dragged another man into the room. "Look what I found. Is this her?"

The man tried to look away. Sir Chanley cracked the man with a backhand fist, knocking him back. "Yes, Yes, that's her, that's her," the scared man sobbingly said. "I'm sorry, I'm sorry," the man screamed to the pregnant woman.

"Then the time has come," said Sir Chanley as he handed the man a small pouch that clanked in the recipient's hand. "Penrose show these people the street. We'll keep this one," Sir Chanley said pointing at the woman.

Penrose shoved the people out of the small house and looked around the street to make sure this wasn't a ruse to set up the King's Guard. A small, skinny boy ran past with something in his hand. Then a grown man raced by and caught the kid.

"Thief," screamed the grown man as he tackled the child. The boy couldn't have graced more than eight years on earth while the man was easily double his size.

"I...I...I'm starving," sobbed the sickly-looking child.

The man showed no mercy as he pounded down a series of blows on the boy's face with his anvil-like fists. Blood shot up like wild flames of fire and spattered the grown man's face. Penrose ran over and stopped the man. Although too late to save the child, he pulled the killer away.

"What in all the hells do you suppose you're doing?" Penrose questioned as he threw the man to the ground.

"This little runt done stole from me. I'm gettin' my justice, the King's justice," said the shaking man.

"He is only but a starving boy."

"And I am only a starving man. What's yer point, good Sir?" the murderous man asked.

Penrose could only shake his head and walk back to the house. He could have arrested the man, but how far would that go after he left, he wondered. He probably had children who would starve if their father were arrested. A somber Penrose heard a woman screaming in terror as he opened the door.

"My turn," howled Sir Oliver Wedgeword as he shoved Sir Winslow aside and began to rape the pregnant victim.

Penrose left the room and wondered about what he was doing with these men. He didn't protect the King and the citizens. He carried out the King's dirtiest of business. He knew this job would be messy when Sir Oliver was involved.

"Penrose, it's your turn. Be careful, she's a feisty one," cried Sir Oliver.

"Can we just finish this already?" Penrose returned.

"You never have any fun, Penrose. Be careful, it'll kill you faster than a sword," Oliver said as Penrose re-entered the room. He saw a partially naked woman with clothes that had been ripped or cut from her body. Penrose saw the scraps of torn fabric as a symbol of the unborn child's hopes and dreams. She lay sniffling, praying to the Gods for mercy.

You are foolish, my lady, if you think the Gods are going to help you now. Unless the Gods strike every man dead in this house, you will be meeting them very soon.

"Now it's time to remove the baby, ha ha ha," laughed Sir Oliver as he pulled a dagger from his hip.

"NNNOOO," screamed the pregnant woman but her desperate plea went unheeded.

"Hold 'er down, men," ordered Sir Oliver.

"No, No, No," wailed the woman until Sir Chanley blasted her with a punch to the right eye. Now she just cried and moaned.

As Penrose gripped her arm and shoulder, he had mixed thoughts about this situation and his life as a whole. He had originally become a knight to act with honor and dignity, but it was the opposite attributes that helped Sir Chanley and Sir Oliver become knights. Numerous dirty favors for the King or a High Lord had been known to result in knighthood. Everything the oaths of knighthood swore to defend against became usual business for the King. All of life seemed to be a farce to Penrose now, a never-ending nightmare. *How did things get to this point?* His mind raced as he held a sexually abused woman down.

"Our King said he wants the baby, so hold 'er steady," Sir Oliver warned.

A shrill scream rent the air as the unethical knight slit her stomach with the blade. Blood spurted a foot in the air as the woman began to flop wildly.

"Watch out," laughed Sir Oliver as he carved her up. He seemed to be enjoying this.

Penrose threw up in his mouth but swallowed quickly. He almost retched again as he watched Oliver sort through her insides looking for the baby. Penrose looked away until his brother from the King's Guard finished the butchery. *Today is the day chivalry finally died.*

"Ha, ha, ha. Feels good to kill a Colbert bitch," Oliver stated as he plunged the knife into her heart. The job was finally over and he looked at the bloody mess of a woman, insides strewn about on the ground, while his associates' faces filled with happiness and satisfaction. This seriously bothered Penrose.

I swear my life and sword to the Kingdom of Donegal. I shall never tire in the quest to defend our King, our royal family and the laws of the land. I swear to protect those who cannot protect themselves. I shall fight against traitors and enemies while acting always with honor, dignity and compassion. I taketh this oath as my brave brothers before me, forever united, in life and death.

Penrose remembered the vows. Every knight had to repeat those words during their King's Guard ceremony. To most, they were only words, soon to be forgotten like a whore's name. Instead of protecting those who could not protect themselves, his knights had just tortured and gruesomely mangled a helpless woman in the name of the King. Penrose had convinced himself that he killed only to quell the voices in his head but these men had enjoyed taking an unborn child from its mother and then had the gall to joke about it.

"This'll make the King happy," smiled Sir Chanley holding up a disgusting, bloody-red object.

"It better, cause she's gonna stink something fierce on the way back," chuckled Sir Oliver.

Thunder boomed through Penrose's head. He had been hearing the sounds of a storm for the past few months and it drove him as crazy as the voices. He hoped the voices would be happy with all the blood he had shown them today but they only scolded him for killing a woman. Penrose didn't know how to satisfy the voices in his head.

49
THE MEETING—EMILIA

"DON'T FORGET TO act surprised when I bring Telly," Ali-Samuel reminded her.

"I promise." Queen Emilia had completely fallen for Ali-Samuel Wamhoff. She kissed him before he left, and lay down in bed again. He had just arrived at the Capitol after his business in Burkeville got cut short. From the second Ali-Samuel had left, she could think only about him. She had felt so starved of attention in recent years, the fact that Ali-Samuel visited her first made the Queen feel very special. Emilia stared out the window into darkness but realized it would be first light soon.

She thought about the adventures Ali-Samuel had promised her. He told her of amazing things she would never have thought possible that existed outside the realm. The Queen enjoyed the comfortable castle life but had rarely traveled outside Donegal. Now she had someone to travel with who could protect her should danger threaten. King Ali-Stanley could only command others to kill and he couldn't even do that right. She also felt sympathy for Ali-Samuel who had been treated like a dog growing up in the King's castle by everyone except his grandmother, the queen. Emilia too had been made to feel like an outcast by the ruthless Wamhoff clan and empathized with the man who had pledged his life to the disrespectful King. Emilia closed her eyes and fell into a slumber.

The Queen awakened in a full sweat. She had again been dreaming of the day they took away her baby boy who was destined to be named Ali-Sundry. The vultures ripped him from her body and tossed the tender baby to the wild. She remembered Count Silzeus trying to comfort her by saying, "We'll let the Gods sort this one out." The Queen didn't even get a chance to see the defect that got him cast away. She had been furious with the King. After years of watching Ali-Varis embarrass the Wamhoff name at every turn, he had the nerve to throw away a mentally healthy, red-haired boy. She even recalled how the King had bragged to his Guard about having a hundred bastards running around the kingdom. *He didn't kill any of those embarrassments to the Wamhoff name.*

She gave up that day. The fire burning inside the Queen smoldered and died. She avoided the King like she would a venomous cobra and the two became more and more distant with every passing day. The Queen even moved a bed into her changing room and turned it into her sleeping room to further avoid the King's company. The dead flames had been relit with a torch by Ali-Samuel.

A heavy knock on the door drove the Queen out of bed. She tied a red robe around her body and walked to the door. She slid the eye slot to the side and saw Ali-Samuel standing outside. A smile curved her lips as she hastily opened the door.

Before she could open it fully, Ali-Samuel said, "My Queen, I bring a guest."

It was a good thing Ali-Samuel warned her because the Queen stood ready to tear off her robe. A young girl she recognized entered with Ali-Samuel.

"Telly, what...what brings you to the Capitol?" the Queen asked.

"My Queen, the kingdom has suffered a tragedy. Duke Aston Burke has been murdered. We believe this is the work of that band of marauders known as Soldiers of the Gods. They claim they will restore true faith in the Gods," Ali-Samuel informed her.

"Oh no, Telly," the sobbing Queen hugged the young girl.

The teenager had cried the entire trip to the Capitol and had finally run out of tears but her face and eyes were red and the poor girl looked physically drained.

Ali-Samuel paced around the room as he talked. "Burkeville is a mess right now. I tried to get over there to assist Duke Burke but I would suppose we arrived a bit late. Only half a day away and this little one wouldn't be mourning. Quite a pestiferous band of outlaws, these ones. The cowards cut his throat in his sleep, very God-like and honorable of them," he noted in a sarcastic tone.

"Next to Ali-Tiste, in their bed?" the Queen wondered.

"No. It would seem the Duke passed out at the supper table. Three guards and the Duke were dead when we arrived. The Duchess Ali-Tiste already grabbed the boys and left. We thankfully found this little one under her bed, scared out of her wits, so we guided her to safety," Ali-Samuel reported.

"Does Elisa know?" the Queen wondered aloud.

"I don't believe so. I bid you tell her, it may be easier to hear from a caring woman," Ali-Samuel answered.

"Of course, good Sir. Telly, would you like to see your sister?"

The Queen saw an awkward look come across Telly's face. It looked like her mouth couldn't decide how to show slight happiness through the sorrow. She unsurely nodded her head and the girl's lips quivered as she forced a smile that disappeared instantly.

"Very well then. Sit down over here while I get ready," said the Queen, pointing to her table designated for card playing. Telly played with the castle cards and Ali-Samuel left as the Queen called her chambermaid to help her dress.

Telly Burke was a smaller version of Elisa. She was tall, pale and her light brown hair accented her similarly colored eyes. At only fourteen, she already stood taller than the Queen. Emilia retrieved a few rings from her dresser and looked at Telly. Emilia Burke had become the Queen of Donegal when she was as old as Telly. She couldn't imagine she had looked that young when she married the King. She actually had looked younger than Telly.

Two guards escorted the Burke women to Elisa's room. They knocked several times but no one answered. As the guard pounded on the door again, the Queen heard a voice from down the hall.

"Hello."

The Queen turned to see Elisa approaching with a strange look on her face.

"Everything alright, young lady?" the Queen asked.

"I just had a really strange interaction with a strange man. Telly, what are you doing here?"

Before Telly could answer, the Queen asked, "Could we come inside for a moment?"

"Surely, is...is everything alright?" Concern showed in Elisa's face and body. She opened her door, let the Queen and Telly in, and followed them over to her table where the three sat down.

"This is hard to say, so I will just come right out with it. Your father is dead," the Queen used a light voice to soften the blow.

Elisa just sat there, staring at the Queen. "What? How did that happen?"

"They believe that it was the Soldiers of the Gods trying to gain control of Burkeville. I am so sorry, my dear," the Queen said sympathetically.

Long tears now streamed down Elisa's powdered cheeks. The Queen had never heard Elisa say a good word about her father. She knew Elisa still harbored resentment toward her father for marrying her to Ali-Varis, but he was still her father.

Emilia thought about her own father and how he had resented her for the death of her mother during childbirth. He had never directly said it, but Emilia had felt the bitterness from the short, stocky man during her years in Burkeville. Emilia didn't have any siblings and had shared a rocky relationship with her father. She had thought bringing her father to the Capitol would help repair their problems, but Garrius Burke had turned down the King's offer to come live in his castle saying, 'The Capitol is not for simple folks like us'. As a result, she had barely seen her father throughout her years at the castle but when he died five years ago, she had wept for days. She went over to hug Elisa and also pulled Telly in.

"If he was always mean to me, why am I so sad?" Elisa sobbed.

"Oh dear, you should be sad, it's so very natural. You too, sweet girl. I cried like a starving baby when my father passed," the Queen said as she rubbed Telly's back.

"Wait, where is our mother? And the boys?" Elisa asked expecting to hear they were in the castle.

"They said your mother took the boys and snuck out while she could. Those murderers probably would have tried to kill the direct heirs next. She must've not had enough time to grab this precious one. Look girls, we all share the Burke name. We will stay together. Remember what we say in Arigold, the only thing that can tear a bear apart, is another bear."

Telly spoke up, "I must tell you something, my Queen."

"What is it, dear?"

"Well, Sir Ali-Samuel told you that he was a half-day away when my father was murdered but I know I saw him the day before father died. I was out in the forest climbing trees when a band of men walked by. It was Sir Ali-Samuel and three other men, but I remember his long red hair.

When they were close I heard one person say, 'Let's take care of this on the morrow'," Telly explained.

"Are you certain? There are many men throughout the kingdom with long red hair, my dear." The Queen wanted Telly to be mistaken. Ali-Samuel wouldn't lie to her. He had told the Queen he loved her and promised her everything and more. *Even if he did kill your father, he did everyone a great favor.* The Queen convinced herself the child saw someone else and wouldn't let it tarnish her shining feelings for Ali-Samuel.

50
ELISA

"SEVEN, RIGHT THERE is seven," claimed Elisa.

"No. That's the same one you've already counted," Anderley argued.

"No it isn't," Elisa shot back.

"Yes it is. It just swam around to the back. Look there are only six," pointed Anderley.

"One of my other fish swam away because it had heard enough of your complaining. You lose, I win," gloated Elisa as she pulled the butt end of a stale loaf of bread out of Anderley's hands. She ripped a piece from the loaf and dropped it into the pond to watch the fish fight for it. The two sat on a fallen tree trunk extending out over the water. They brought the bread to play a game called count the trout. Despite growing up on opposite sides of the realm, they had both played the game as children. The object was to use bait to attract the trout to the top. The winner was whoever counted the most fish around their bait. The results were usually disputed as there wasn't an arbitrary judge to declare a true winner.

Despite their arguments over the game, Elisa and Sir Anderley had formed a recent bond. Anderley had spotted her crying one day and comforted Elisa. After that they became fast friends. The two ran out of bread and made their way back toward the castle.

"I must say, I cannot wait until you are Queen of Donegal," Anderley blurted out.

"Excuse me, Sir?"

"It's only that…it's frustrating to watch our current Queen who doesn't give a good damn about the kingdom. All she cares for is spending every waking second with Ali-Samuel," Anderley snidely said.

"I know. After he struck…I mean…never mind. He rubs me the wrong way, that's all," Elisa nervously said.

"He put his filthy hands on you? I'll kill the bastard," declared

Anderley.

"No, no, no. It's a turn of phrase. It means I don't trust him," Elisa assured him.

"You shouldn't trust him. He is like the green mamba snake, sneaky and venomous. He's the kind that deserves death and nothing less," said Anderley as he held out his arm to stop Elisa. He then pulled a knife from his beltline, threw it sideways and struck a king snake a few feet ahead in the weeds that Elisa hadn't seen.

Anderley pulled the knife from the reptile. "He doesn't love her, you know."

"I know, Sir Anderley," Elisa said sympathetically.

"I did everything she asked of me and well beyond. She treated me like a dog on a leash but she is the Queen. She had me at her mercy. I had to give in to every demand and she took it all for granted. She was so drunk the first time we made love that she didn't even remember it. Each and every day I took chances and risks with her that could have easily landed my head on a spike. The singers would sing about the foolish knight who let the Queen get him killed. Each and every day I took those risks. For what? So she could kick me aside like a dog for Ali-Samuel."

"She kicked me aside, too," Elisa reminded the knight. She knew he loved the Queen but she felt like she handled her situation with Brehan better than this.

"She was the entire reason I accepted the King's offer to become part of his Guard. I saw her for the first time during a visit to Lightview. Never has a lovelier sight ever graced my eyes. I knew the King used me as leverage in the grudge between him and my father, but I cared not. My father still hasn't spoken a word to me since I took the oath. I only knew the King's Guard would get me close to the Queen. I even told my brother, Penrose, how great and honorable the King's Guard was. He would have probably been better off in Lightview. I can even remember the day they assigned me to the Queen's personal guard. It may have been the happiest day of my life. Little did I know the worst day of my life would be a few weeks ago when I saw her kissing that serpent. I wish the King's Guard had smashed his head on the castle steps before Queen Tomeo had a chance to stop them." He shook his head and calmed down. "Alright, my lady, enough of this petty complaining from a knight."

Complaining, more like whining, crying and wishing death on others.

People had told Elisa that Sir Anderley was one of the fiercest knights in the kingdom but seeing him like this gave her doubts. She understood his heartbreak but he was a member of the King's Guard for the sake of the Gods.

They had confided in each other about a plentitude of personal matters in the last few weeks. While Anderley had talked about the Queen before; he'd never blubbered like this. She told Anderley the story of Brehan without mentioning him by name. She only compared her situation to Ali-Gare's and didn't provide any distinct details. At first, Elisa wasn't sure she could trust Anderley but she came to realize he had kept the Queen's trust for years. She felt like Anderley could be fully trusted but she would probably never tell him Brehan's name.

Now she started thinking about Brehan again. She couldn't bring herself to believe he was dead. She thought about the first time they pledged their love to each other. Brehan had whispered to her, "My first, my last, forever my only." It sent chills through her body that memorable day and even today just from thinking about it. *My first, my last, forever my only.*

They got back to the castle after an awkward silence to let Anderley compose himself. "My lady," he bowed and went in the other direction.

As she walked through the front entrance of the castle, Elisa heard someone calling her.

"My lady," the man cried, waving her over toward the throne room.

When she entered the vast, open area lit by many torches, Elisa saw the man's features. Ghost-like pale skin covered the man who stood a bit taller than Elisa. Ivory-colored hair and gray eyes led her to believe he was the albino Wamhoff. Elisa followed him into the empty room.

"How does the lady fare on this fine day?" he asked.

"I am alright, thank you," Elisa nervously replied.

"I am Tersen Wamhoff, High Lord of Cloverfoot and our King's brother and personal councilor," he said with a deep bow.

"And I am Elisa..."

He cut her off, "Wrong, you are soon to be Queen Elisa, look up at your throne."

Tersen pointed to the Silver Fox. "They say it's solid silver with the paintings over it." The arms and legs had the shape of a fox. It featured a curved red seat and the matching back housed intricately detailed white foxes protecting the King's crown. From the top, five golden spikes rose into the air with crowns of captured kings to symbolize their heads on spikes and the world dominance of Donegal. The realm had sent regents to rule the captured kingdoms and empires but they usually only lasted a few years before the natives took back the land. The huge room was wide open with many pedestals containing marble busts of former kings and queens. Red fox tapestries with gold and black backgrounds hung around the room and a red velvet carpet with gold trim led from the entrance to the steps of the throne. On either side of the steps and in front of the throne stood four marble fox sculptures with ruby eyes. Twenty-seven steps led straight up to the Silver Fox. Three beautifully crafted chairs adorned in gold detailing flanked the throne on either side. The lords of the land brought their disputes here before the King's ear to ask for aid. However, most days Henley Moore sat on the throne and decided whether to help the requesting lord.

"I didn't mean to scare you but this kingdom shall soon fall to you," he said in a creepy, scratchy voice. It reminded Elisa of the old kitchen wench from Burkeville named Deona. The albino's voice was as unattractive as the rest of him, including his face and neck that were dotted with pimples. *I'll play dumb with the pale man and let him underestimate me like all the rest.*

"You mean Prince Ali-Varis. It falls to Ali-Varis?"

"I wouldn't give Ali-Varis a puddle to play in let alone a realm to control. My lady, I come on behalf of the people behind the throne to implore you to take active interest in ruling our kingdom. If you are familiar with our history you should know Ali-Varis could be voted out at a king's moot, and where would that leave you? If someone calls one before he is officially crowned, you will be left to deal with a mental cripple for the rest of your days. You can be Elisa of House Burke, wife of Ali-Varis Wamhoff and Queen of Donegal, but you must remember where your support lies, my lady," he added with a wink.

He made Elisa even more uncomfortable as he moved closer, lowered his eyes and continued, "The Silver Fox. Many people think that every king from Ali-Dus to King Ali-Stanley sat on that very throne. And as usual, many people speak from ignorance and spread it like purple fire as if it were truth. The throne was actually designed during the rule of King Ali-Sander, the Raging Fox as most know him. If you know the stories of King Ali-Sander, you will know that he was never really around to sit the throne because he was constantly away at war. Ali-Sander was a smart man who lacked intelligence. He realized his strengths and weaknesses. War was his strength and ruling was a weakness so he put the right men in place to handle the aspects he knew were above his abilities. Smart. A ruler needs to know her allies' strengths and exploit them to the fullest to maintain a prosperous kingdom. At any rate, the men who were to sit the throne in his stead decided their king needed an upgrade. Peculiar how things work sometimes, yes I know. Our first six kings and Ali-Sander actually sat on a simple silver throne without even a back that has since disappeared. Many believe King Ali-Tarrison melted it down to make the coins he would subsequently use to bribe the judges in his murder trial. Each to a man took the bribe and proceeded to promptly vote Ali-Tarrison guilty. People said the smug look that graced his face just before the verdict remained even as his head sat atop the spike in front of the castle. Even in death he couldn't believe that the *honest* men who took his bribe turned on him. Do you know why they turned on him?"

Elisa fumbled, "I...I honestly don't know. Because they knew of his guilt, I suppose." Elisa did know but she played dumb. Count Bidwell had taught her almost everything about the Kingdom of Donegal and the ruling families of the past.

"Aahh, in fairness it has been well documented and discussed that everyone was certain of his guilt. King Ali-Tarrison was quite viperous even to those who helped him. No, the judges found out the King planned to kill them all and take his bribe back after the trial. King Ali-Tarrison betrayed the trust of the wrong men. You must be careful of who you trust. Simply because a man has red hair, he is not divine, contrary to royal belief," softly said Tersen as he stroked Elisa's long hair. The back of his hand rubbed down her belly when he did this, causing her to back up a step.

The persistent albino crept closer again as he continued, "Our King doesn't like the throne at all. He says it hurts to sit on. Do you know why that is so?"

"Because he who sits the throne, should be empty of comfort?" She knew that was right but said it like a question.

"Because he or *she* who sits the throne, should be empty of comfort. Very well indeed. How many of our kings eschewed that credo over the years? You must remember that saying as more than mere words when your day arrives. One look at my brother's belly will show a comfort-filled life, not emptiness. Did you know about the two different thrones?" he asked.

"I didn't know all of it, I had heard of the two silver thrones, I think," she stuttered, looking at the calloused, flaky skin on his face and neck.

"Do you know much of the kingdom you may soon rule?" Before she could answer, Tersen said, "I am sure you know that a man named Dus brought the original citizens of Donegal here from the Androsi Isles because of religious persecution. You probably even heard the stories of how our first King defeated the mighty army of Goldenfield that dwarfed our random army of ragged-clothed farmers. Well, not to shatter your dreams of the perfect Donegal but it never occurred quite like that. King Ali-Dus strategically picked a section of Goldenfield that was of little use to the enemy. Ali-Dus simply made it too expensive for their army to pursue a worthless piece of land in the eyes of the King of Goldenfield. The enemy king retreated to use his resources in a wiser fashion, but ultimately, the king gave up. Most people would like to believe that Ali-Dus the Great pushed the rival king back to his Capitol but that simply is steeped in myth. Now over the years, Donegal has grown and grown, slowly but surely. Now we are nearly the size of the mighty Goldenfield. As for the heroic stories, reality is never as beautiful as the written page, a faeblor's story or a singer's song," Tersen accentuated the last sentence with his hands like a poet would.

Elisa wondered where this history lesson was going and whether this man who seemed cold of heart toward his brother could be trusted.

"I find it quite ironic my brother persecutes those who worship other Gods when that is the exact purpose for which the first men came here. I would never favor this preposterous one God faith either, but as long as they pay taxes, they can worship horse manure if they like. Do you know how many Queens ruled from that throne?" Tersen posed.

"Three," Elisa quickly returned.

"Three, that's right. All were serving as regents until their sons were old enough to take the throne. Two died quickly but only Queen Ali-Tomeo survived the throne. Queen Ali-Tiste was murdered in under a year by the aforementioned King Ali-Tarrison. The red-headed coward used poison on a woman. Poison is the weapon of women and weaklings. She died while holding the throne for her son, Ali-Banly, also known as the Sickly King who suffered a similar fate once he reached that throne. He was indeed sickly and they said he died in his sleep which could have been entirely true, but a broken nose soaking his bed sheets in blood would suggest otherwise to me. After he died there was a king and queen's moot between Ali-Sander's sister and cousin. Queen Ali-Ganoly won the battle but lost the war to the man who would become King Ali-Harrison, The Haunted. Only a fortnight into her rule an arrow attack in the King's Woods expedited the coronation of King Ali-Harrison. No one would oppose the man who had so brazenly murdered a queen. The stories say that the ghost of Queen Ali-Ganoly haunted Ali-Harrison up until the day he dove off the Dragon Tower on the King's Castle. Then we move forward to Queen Ali-Tomeo. She survived for five peaceful, prosperous years until her son Ali-Pharell took the throne at the age of twelve. So how is it one Queen sat the throne successfully and the others failed?"

"I couldn't tell you, honestly," Elisa unsurely answered.

"You should stop saying the word honestly. You should never have to alert someone that you are actually telling the truth. The reason Queen Ali-Tomeo lived to be old and wealthy was because she allied herself with the right people. She made certain she had the high lords of the realm behind her before she accepted the crown. Then she made sure to keep them happy until the day she left the throne. One person sits the throne but many powerful people must stand behind her for a ruler to survive. You should take time to ingratiate yourself to the council and any visiting high lords." He stopped and put his hand on her shoulder. "You should make it a good habit to go far out of your way to please these men."

She pulled back, causing Tersen's arm to fall at his side. He made her skin crawl and she gave him a nasty look.

"No my lady, I don't imply sexual congress. I have a slight habit of touching someone when I make an important point in conversation. The lesson you need to take from this is to be careful whom you trust and align yourself with. Remember, the only queen to live out her rule had the full support of the high lords. My lady," he said with a bow and retreated from the throne room.

Elisa stood alone and thought about sitting on the Silver Fox one day. It would be bittersweet if she didn't have her love there to share it. *My first, my last, forever my only.*

As Elisa turned the corner of the hallway, she saw people outside her room. When she got closer, she noticed the Queen and her sister Telly behind the guards. Her head was still reeling and the next thing she remembered was sitting with Telly and the Queen in her room.

The Queen told her about her father. She could only remember a few conversations they had shared. Most of her memories consisted of her father beating her because she wasn't a boy. He had mostly hit her in the stomach and upper legs so the marks wouldn't show but he snuck in occasional slaps across her face. The Duke was always drunk, and yelled at the girls for no reason. He treated his daughters like a huge burden. Whenever Elisa tried to talk to him, the man shunned her. She hadn't even thought about him once he left the Capitol after the wedding. He treated Brehan even worse than her by having his henchman, the Grizzly Bear, severely beat Brehan when he was only a boy. In a rage she had even talked to Brehan about killing the Duke until he calmed her down and talked her out of it.

Why am I crying? Why do I even feel sad? He was a monster. My father hit me. Ali-Samuel hit me. I'm no better than a sword post. I will have my day soon. Oh poor Telly, I have to take care of her now.

51

ALI-STER

ALI-STER STOOD EYE-TO-EYE, sword-to-sword with the bronze skinned beauty. The pair dropped their weapons and began to kiss passionately. They caressed each other in the practice yard outside the castle. The couple suspended their lip lock and Leimur and Ali-Ster walked toward the castle.

"KNOCK, KNOCK, KNOCK."

Ali-Ster shot up in bed, groggy. He slid on a silk robe and lumbered over to the door, "Yes."

"Sorry to disturb you, my Prince, but the King requires your attendance in the solar," cried a voice from outside.

"Tell my father I'll soon be there." The Prince dressed himself in parti-colored hose of silver and gold with tight shiny black leather boots to his knees. He wore red undershirts to his elbows and tucked into his hose. He put on a sleeveless black leather vest with fox-fur edging that hung to mid-thigh. He secured the last silver button engraved with the royal standard and tightened the gold gilt buckles on his boots. Ali-Ster put on his swordbelt and grabbed his weapon before leaving. He arrived at the solar to find his father waiting outside. "Good day, father."

"Ali-Ster, we must go downstairs to talk, way downstairs," the King stated emphatically.

"You lead the way," an unenthused Ali-Ster returned as he listlessly followed his father down to the Alley of the Heavens. Ali-Ster felt the creepy feelings resurface again as they went deeper into the earth. His stomach started to twist as the two men got closer to the chamber of the dead. Ali-Ster wished he had broken his fast to settle his queasiness. The King opened the creaky door and the smell attacked them like a rabid fox. The men entered the chamber and Ali-Ster noticed two women working on a fresh body.

"Although I did not agree with Ali-Gare's actions, she was my daughter, a princess and she will rest forever amongst royalty," King Ali-Stanley said.

Ali-Ster recognized his half-sister's gray body, but gagged when he realized what they were doing to her. *Death is part of life.* The women stuck long metal hooks up the nostrils of his deceased half-sister and pulled out chunks of brain. They had already dried out the body for weeks with most of the internal organs removed. They removed the brain last. The women used a curing salt to ready the body to survive eternity. He turned away and looked at some of the altars in the room. Ali-Ster noticed his father never once looked in the direction of Ali-Gare. Some of the other black bodies still wore the crown they sported in life. The Prince realized this was a long-standing family tradition but he couldn't understand why one king throughout history hadn't stopped this nonsense yet.

Black magic and praying to the dead won't solve anything. We need to dig our kingdom out of this hole and it just so happens I have the plan of plans.

"Let us move over here to speak," his father said as he led the way to the opposite corner of the room. "I have failed you as a father and King. I have come to realize much of my misdeeds as of late."

"What, come now..."

"Let me speak, my boy. When I took the throne of Donegal it seemed I could do no wrong. Every decision worked exactly in the manner I had wished. There is one thing no one understands about ruling. When you're King, you make hundreds of thousands of decisions. Even if almost all of the decisions are successful, there will be failures. Everyone will focus on your failures, not the great choices that bettered the realm. You too, will make some unpopular decisions but you just have to do the best you can. For me, after an early run of success I thought being a king was easy and took to boozing and whoring instead of council meetings and attending court. I swam in the ocean of gluttony, floated in the clouds of skin pleasures and fathered hundreds of bastards from Blairs Beak to Bear Gate. I mashed loins with any bellibone who caught my eye."

Ali-Ster had never realized he had hundreds of bastard siblings running around. He assumed a few, but hundreds seemed ludicrous. He began to get irritated in the dimly lit, freezing room as his father continued.

"I did what I wished and the people seemed to love me all the same. It wasn't until I saw my first wife lying in bed, dying, that I realized my errors. She died four days later and I didn't leave her bedside until her last breath floated away forever. Parys made me realize the truly important matters in life are family, faith and loyalty. As she fought death with all her might, she made me promise one thing. The Queen said, 'Don't ever turn your back on Ali-Varis. He is the heir for a reason. Do not fight the will of the Gods.' She died shortly after and while I have been tempted to install you as heir to the throne, how would I explain this to her when we meet again in the heavens for the forever life? I realize you are much better suited and even if Ali-Varis should sit the throne it will be in name only. You will truly rule the realm but I need you to take care of Ali-Varis when I should die. Everyone else will turn their back on him, you cannot," the King said by way of reminder.

"Very well, father. Since we are opening up, I must ask about my brother who was cast away," Ali-Ster hinted.

"He was grossly disfigured and looked like a demon. I had met with a Priestess of the Gods and she warned me that one of my sons would try to kill me for my crown one day. I know Ali-Varis wouldn't harm me and you would never come for my life so it must have been that rotten boy sent by the demons." *Or one of your hundred or so bastards you have running around. They count as sons too.* The King lowered his head and continued, "I've come to understand my death is close…"

Death is part of life. Ali-Ster cut off the King, "Nonsense, father. You shall live until you can no longer move. Singers around the world will sing of Ali-Stanley, the Ancient King."

His father labored to draw a half-smile across his wrinkled and weary face. The King did look ready to die to Ali-Ster. The hardships of ruling a realm had steadily added up over the duration of his reign and left Ali-Stanley in a feeble state for being such a large man.

"My father failed me as I have failed you. I have resented you. You would be the perfect son to any father. You are everything I wished I could ever become and so much more. With every accomplishment you achieved I felt the Gods were laughing at my expense. They gave you all the gifts I coveted. Those cruel Gods gave my twin brother the same gifts as you, but they gave me a throne. I took what they gave and tried my best, so here we are. I hope to have the realm more unified and leave matters in a better state for you and your brother. All my decisions that worked in the beginning of my rule are now crumbling before my very eyes."

That is because you don't see the consequences of the decisions. You only see the optimal outcome that is never achieved. Not every action takes place on a level playing field.

"We had better get to the council meeting now," the King told Ali-Ster.

As they walked, Ali-Ster started to feel sympathy for his father.

Being king certainly cannot be easy. He still needs to make better decisions but I see what goes in to those choices. This makes my choice a bit more difficult now.

The Prince followed his father to the council room where everyone awaited them. The King and Ali-Ster took their usual spots at the table.

"My King, we've hit resistance in Bottomfoot," Dirk Eller reported.

"I thought they were neutral. What in all the hells is the problem?" the King wanted to know.

Dirk Eller responded, "Well, highness, the treaty of neutrality states the crown will not send armed men into Bottomfoot. They haven't attacked yet but the people haven't been helpful to our soldiers. Did you contact Duke Malik prior to invasion?"

The King slammed his scepter into the table and threw a fit. "This is my kingdom, my kingdom. I shouldn't have to ask permission to move about my own realm. Why doesn't everyone understand this? My kingdom, my kingdom."

He had sounded so poetic and heartfelt only minutes earlier and now the King pouted like a child who didn't get its way. Ali-Ster thought about how embarrassing the King of Donegal looked and sounded. He then looked over at Prince Ali-Varis playing with the drool coming from his mouth. He stretched it out to see how far it would pull before it broke. He laughed mightily and repeated the process over and over. The future of the realm looked bleak at best through Ali-Ster's eyes.

The ship of sympathy for his father had quickly sailed away and Ali-Ster concluded he would accept Ali-Samuel's offer.

I will do as Queen Leimur did for the good of my realm. Death is part of life. Then we will unite our realms to conquer the world. King Ali-Ster and Queen Leimur.

Almost on cue, Ali-Samuel walked into the room and bowed deeply, "My King, Princes, Lords." He parked himself at the table. Ali-Samuel wasn't an official member of the council but he started to show up for meetings and nobody would tell the war hero to stop coming. Ali-Samuel looked to make sure the door was shut. "Business in Burkeville had to be canceled because of the tragic death of the noble Duke Burke. We were so close to saving him," he sarcastically stated with a chuckle.

Everyone at the table except Ali-Ster either smiled or laughed along with Ali-Samuel. The King's nephew called for wine. "What are we discussing?"

A loud knock at the door prompted Henley Moore to scurry over and slide open the look-through to see who was outside. Henley opened the door, accepted a leather sack from the guards and brought it to the King. "They say this came over from Mattingly on a catapult with instructions that the King would want this."

The King reached into the bag, pulled out an oval object and quickly dropped it. He looked at the thick black blood on his hand and started to retch. He rushed for the door but vomited about halfway to his destination. He swung the door open after fumbling angrily with it and ran out.

We were just standing in a pit of death watching his own daughter get her brains picked out but he cannot handle this. He truly is an odd man. I still cannot figure him out and I suppose I never will.

Ali-Samuel went and shut the door again. He walked back and picked up the severed head from the ground. "Who's this pretty boy?"

Derich Bonsfogger spoke, "That man appears to be Anders Ahitni. Our King sent him to kill Ruxin Colbert, Duke of Mattingly."

"No horseshit. Well, whoever he was, he took at least four arrows to the head," said Ali-Samuel as he inspected the object. "I like this Ruxin's strut. Send the head of the man sent to kill you back to the original instigator. Very nice touch. That takes stones."

"Bigger stones than our fearless King just displayed," snidely remarked Jake Fielder.

"Yes, what are we going to do about that?" asked Leo Braunshaur. "About what?" Ali-Samuel sharply returned. "About that embarrassing display we were all privy to," Leo pressed.

"We aren't going to do anything," Ali-Samuel expressed in a very serious tone as he leaned into the table, "he is our King and we will blindly serve him until his last day. Long may he rule." He gulped down some wine.

"How right you are, Sir. Long may he rule," Leo echoed.

"Another worry is developing in Waters Edge. We seem to have located the missing army and they have been hired as soldiers of fortune," Dirk Eller said.

"Who is employing them?" Ali-Ster asked.

"The Man with the Golden Sword is the only name we have for him," Dirk Eller informed.

"Did you just say The Man with the Golden Sword?" Ali-Samuel asked. Dirk just nodded in return.

"Well I know The Man with the Golden Sword and he is not a man to be trifled with. I never thought he could afford an army of that size. This is not good news. I slaughtered thousands of Goldenfield soldiers with him at the Battle of Bear Gate. If it weren't for that man, these walls would be covered in Goldenfield tapestries. He understood strategy and leadership. The Man would skin you alive just to watch you die slowly if you angered him enough. He had a proper mix of brains, brawn and blatant disregard for human life. That's a dangerous combination. I can't believe you haven't heard of his exploits. *Do not* underestimate this man," Ali-Samuel warned.

Ali-Ster had heard the stories at war about The Man with the Golden Sword, but never met him. He had listened to all the exploits of The Man and Ali-Samuel in the battle of Bear Gate. It was said without those two men, Bear Gate and Burkeville would have fallen to the enemy. After that, invasion of Falconhurst would only be imminent. Ali-Ster remembered how all the Wamhoffs were poised to evacuate when the news came in that Donegal had stemmed the tide and fought back the evil forces of Goldenfield.

"He is said to be moving through Waters Edge," said Dirk Eller.

"We cannot send any men up to Waters Edge right now. We need to send a raven to Duke Etburn to rally his flag bearers and put a stop to this marauder. We then need to retreat from that quagmire in Bottomfoot,"

Ali-Ster said authoritatively.

"We will need the King to verify that, Ali-Ster," said Jake Fielder. "Prince Ali-Ster," Ali-Samuel sternly reminded him. "A thousand pardons, Prince Ali-Ster," Jake obediently responded.

"Send word now. I shall convince my father by talking some sense into him for once," Ali-Ster ordered. Jake Fielder spoke, "Are we any closer to getting Prince Ali-Ster installed as heir?" Ali-Ster jumped in, "I can assure you gentlemen that isn't going to happen." "Look Ali-Ster, I realize you may not want this..." Jake said.

"Ali-Ster cut him off, "It isn't me. I talked to my father as recently as this morning and he told me Ali-Varis shall remain heir."

Ali-Varis responded to hearing his name by repeating it. He clapped his hands then drifted back into his own world again. The meeting ended and as they left Ali-Samuel leaned in and said, "See you in a bit, cousin."

Ali-Ster walked down the castle hall and saw his cousin Neron. "Hello, Neron."

"Prince Ali-Ster," Neron greeted with a bow.

"Let's talk in my quarters," Ali-Ster quietly said.

They sat in Ali-Ster's room. The hot air flowed in through an open window and the absence of wind created heat pockets around the room. Ali-Ster began to sweat as he spoke, "I value your opinion and I believe I may have the best idea of all time. A united kingdom of Goldenfield and Donegal. A super kingdom."

Neron shrugged his shoulders and moved his head back and forth slowly. Ali-Ster could see he didn't like the idea. "What is the problem?"

"I don't believe you can sell the council on this," Neron said.

"Think about it wisely. One giant kingdom. Imagine the lands we could conquer if we worked together. I am going to tell the council I am going on a military campaign in Livingstone. I will tell them I am going for riches, which I will, but I am also going to find the Warrior Queen. Word has it she is going to attack Harbor Valley. I will come up north through Livingstone and meet her at Harbor Valley. I will peaceably talk with her and make her realize this is the greatest plan for both kingdoms," an excited Ali-Ster finished.

"Is this a well thought out idea? Mayhaps you should sleep a few more nights on this matter."

"She is all I think about. I mean, this plan...this plan is all I can think about for the realm," Ali-Ster's face turned red. "See, see, there it is. You love this girl," Neron teased. "I DO NOT. I simply misspoke. This could bail out our tattered kingdom," Ali-Ster fired back.

"Or tear it apart even further?" Neron posed as he left the room.

Later that day Ali-Ster and Elisa walked toward the flower gardens in awkward silence. He didn't have anything clever to say and began to sweat on the cloudy summer day. He wore his red doublet stitched with golden foxes over each breast. He noticed Elisa's fox pin hanging from her pale blue gown. The pin rested against her firm left bosom as Ali-Ster focused in on her physical beauty. He looked at her face and caught a shy smile before she looked away. The King had never taught Ali-Ster about girls. It was another way the King had failed Ali-Ster as a father. For some reason Ali-Ster always got nervous in the presence of potential companions. The Prince saw Elisa as a delicate flower in mid bloom. He knew she had much more to reveal from the few conversations he had with her.

Ali-Samuel scheduled this meeting at the very back of the flower gardens, in a secluded area. Several enclosed outdoor rooms contained tables, chairs and royal decorations along the botanically sweet smelling walk. Ali-Ster didn't know much about flowers but even he could appreciate the natural beauty of these paths. Most of the high-born citizens walked the gardens to bask in the pleasure of nobility. The path had different twists and turns and by summer it housed exotic plants and flowers from around the world. The enclosures popped up randomly and looked like big red pavilions. When they reached the back, a smaller, cozy pavilion appeared. The elegant flowers planted along the sides of the path guided Elisa and Ali-Ster to the meeting spot. The two entered to see the Queen and Ali-Samuel sitting at a red oak table with off-color knots running through it. The top was covered with imported figs, olives, cheeses, oranges and cured meats. Several silver ewers and decanters featured water, ale and red wine. The luxurious spread seemed unusual to Ali-Ster considering the secrecy of the meeting.

"Ah, the Prince and the lady have arrived. Sit, enjoy yourselves," said Ali-Samuel as he pointed at the table spread. "We have worked hard for this kingdom. I have closely dodged death too many times not to enjoy myself. We should take part in the spoils of the kingdom," Ali-Samuel said as he threw a few olives into his mouth.

"Shall I shut these flaps, cousin?" asked Ali-Ster.

"Leave them, it will only draw speculation. That's why I called this meeting in an area where a person wouldn't stop to think that anything sinister was occurring. I have told the servants to come back in half an hour, so be attentive. Now before we cover the final details of our plan, I must be certain where everyone's loyalty lies." Ali-Samuel looked around at each person, stopping to hold eye contact for several moments with his sharp blue eyes. "Tell me now. This is the point of no return. Once we commit, irreversible actions will fall into place. Speak up now if you have any reservations whatsoever."

Silence ensued and Ali-Samuel received the exact answer he had expected. A slick smile shot across Ali-Samuel's lips as he continued, "The ides of the month when the castle bells ring nine." He became serious and said in a deeper voice, "The ides of the month when the castle bells ring nine. That is when we will strike. Now, Ali-Ster and I will handle the physical aspect of the plan and the two ladies must simply stay in your rooms, dressed for bed and ready to weep. In the meanwhile, we must refrain from too much contact with each other. That's not to say we don't exchange pleasantries or ignore each other. Just remain aware of our situation. Any tiny matter that will raise attention to us as individuals or as a group could be detrimental to our effort. Most important, do not speak ill of the King. Resist the urge to do it in the presence of anyone, even those you fully trust. Prince Ali-Ster, stop questioning the King in council meetings. Eat up anything the King is offering and say, 'Thank you, highness. I would love another, my King'."

I wondered why he stood so staunchly behind my father at the meeting earlier today.

Ali-Samuel continued, "I know this all might seem a bit underhanded but this is how it works in this realm. We have to play by the set of rules already established. To fight against dirtiness, you must also get dirty. I would love for a peaceful solution to present itself but it hasn't appeared quite yet. We are involved in a game of the highest stakes and consequences. If anyone suspects us, we are dead because the King won't hesitate to thrust our heads on spikes. Well, I suppose he will have someone do it for him, but it will happen nonetheless. This might seem unfair to the old man, but I grew up as the castle bastard and that wasn't exactly fair either. When the matter is concluded we will call a King's moot and present Prince Ali-Ster as our candidate. Not a man amongst the council would dare back Ali-Varis. Then King Ali-Ster will take Elisa as his queen. We will be your top advisors," Ali-Samuel said referring to the Queen and himself. "All this mess will be soon forgotten. We will be exalted for bettering the kingdom and people will realize the nobility in this act. Look, we must be extremely careful because the bloodhounds will be searching for a scent and someone to blame. I may have found the perfect person to shoulder the blame but we can't leave any loose ends."

Elisa meekly spoke up, "There was this man today. He..."

The Queen cut her off, "She had a strange interaction with Tersen."

"Every interaction with Tersen is strange. That is why he is Tersen the Terrible. Terrible to talk to. What did he have to say?" asked Ali-Samuel.

"He told me that I could be the supreme queen but I must be careful of who I align myself with. He said that the high lords represented the real power behind the throne," Elisa uttered.

"So, the albino snake seizes the field mouse. Leave Tersen to me. Do be certain to tell me if he bothers you again and I will make it stop, permanently. Don't let his empty threats scare you. The high lords are not the power behind the throne. The power behind the throne sits right here. My Queen, my lady, would you be as kind to show Prince Ali-Ster and myself some privacy? We need to go over the gritty details that two proper women needn't hear," Ali-Samuel requested.

The two ladies stood up, curtsied and retreated into the gardens. "Thunder and Lightning will rule this realm," his much older cousin excitedly stated. Ali-Samuel began to lay out exactly how they were going to kill his father. Ali-Ster fought split feelings but he had already fully committed.

Death is part of life. If Queen Leimur can do it, so can I. In a short time we will both be looked upon as heroes. Then we will build the super kingdom to rule the world one day. The Warrior King and Queen will dominate.

52
WAITING FOR A LETTER—EDBURGH

EDBURGH REMOVED AN object from Krys Colbert's mouth, gave a sadistic laugh and held the severed appendage in front of his hostage's face. "Two days, next time we'll go for three," he chuckled.

Ed looked at Krys' left hand, strapped to the arm of the chair, and put the detached bluish pinkie back in place. The naked prisoner shook with enough force to knock it on the ground. The already skinny young man had become even thinner in the past few weeks.

Edburgh had grown impatient of waiting for the King to finally sanction the killings. The last messenger had said the King might need the Colbert boys as bargaining leverage for ransom. This temporary situation had dragged on too long for Ed's liking. He should have been back at the king's castle, resting on Ali-Gare's bosom. Ed found great pleasure in torturing the man he believed had convinced his wife to kill him. After the torture started, Edburgh had been sleeping through every single night. The only problem was the constant nightmares involving Caroline. He wanted to show Caroline that he found the man who put her up to the murder attempt. He wanted to show her Krys' dead body. Ed still had regret about murdering his wife. He kept trying to explain his reasoning in the dreams but Caroline wouldn't hear it. She always blamed Edburgh's drinking.

For the first time, he missed being home in Elkridge. Cramming into this hut of a house with four other disgusting men wore thin on the patience of the castle-bred Ed. He missed the lavish meals and his pleasures and rights as a noble-born citizen of Donegal. His life had become a repeat of tedious exercises. Every day contained torture, drinking and nightmares, torture, drinking and nightmares over and over again. That was it. He didn't even have the right to mingle with the crowds at the harbor and see the imports. The King forbade it in the orders. The only place the men were allowed to go was the tavern or inn to get a meal. The inn required a much longer trip and Ed thought their blashy wine tasted like horse piss but he didn't want another bowl of turtle soup shoved in front of him at the tavern. The last time they had given him the slop he wanted to dump it on the owner's head. The King's guards who came with him were always so drunk that he couldn't stand their company. They rambled unintelligibly and took crudeness to an extreme level.

Edburgh even missed his family but his situation was carved in stone. A sick thought came over Ed as he paced out of the room. He went to his room in the house and picked up a long, thick metal hook. When he returned Krys had fallen asleep. Ed angrily woke him up with a slap across the face.

"Oh, are we awake?" Ed asked while releasing a demonic belly laugh. The blank yet focused eyes of Edburgh made him look seriously disturbed. "So let's see if we see eye to eye. Did you tell my wife to kill me so you could usurp Waters Edge?"

"No, of course not," Krys replied.

"No, what? Or do I need to take another finger to teach you?" Ed reprimanded.

"No, my favorite uncle," said an apprehensive Krys, trying to avoid more punishment. After losing several teeth, two toes and a finger, Krys knew it best to comply with the controlling Edburgh.

"You still got it wrong. It's a shame your eyes don't see clearly. If you don't need them..."

Krys cut him off, "Look, my favorite uncle, I've told you over a thousand times..."

"You told me, you told me the wrong answer," shouted an incensed Edburgh. He paused for a moment and talked softly, "Now you have made me angry. For a person to be as blind as you I have the perfect solution."

Ed pulled the hook from his belt and went after Krys. The prisoner swung his head back and forth as Ed closed in but the captor grabbed his hair to hold Krys steady. Ed took a swipe and scratched the hostage's cheek. He felt like a lion with claws. Blood dribbled down Krys' face as Ed took a second swing and connected with his intended target. Krys belted out a primal scream when the hook punctured the eyeball and his brother

291

desperately screamed from the next room, *"Come attack me, you craven."* An unsatisfied Ed pulled with strength until a chunk of the eye popped out of Krys Colbert's head, still clinging to the bloody hook. Blood filled the damaged eye, flowed down and pooled onto his lap. The disturbing noises coming from Krys were like the dying screams Ed remembered from former battle action. He didn't want Krys to die, not quite yet.

"Now where can I put this piece of your eye? I cannot think of any place to put it. Oh, I have an idea. I know how I can stop your whore-like moaning. Open up," a cruel grin accompanied Ed's statement. "And you better not spit it out or you can taste the other one. You will keep it in your mouth just like the toes and finger or you know what will happen. You know I deliver on my threats by now or at least you should."

Edburgh looked at his battered nephew before he left, smiling. He had cuts and bruises everywhere. A black eye, smashed nose and several missing teeth only highlighted all his injuries.

Ed arrived at the run down tavern and sat with his partners. They were already drunk enough to be incomprehensible and two of the men rubbed whores who sat on their laps. The owner came over to the table.

"You eatin' today?" she asked.

"Yes," answered Ed as she poured his usual red wine and walked away.

The owner was tall, frail and not very sociable. Her rosy red cheeks offset curled black hair tucked into a white bonnet. Ed eagerly drained his glass of red. He had already tortured today, now came the drinking. They had become Ed's only activities. He looked at his tablemates and wondered how it all came to this. He thought a quick killing of a couple of Colberts would precede a life of riches and glory in Falconhurst.

He remembered when his brother Rollo had promised him they would one day save the world from Damian Doome. Rollo had said Edburgh would be exactly like Rockarius and command the dragons. Those noble dreams died along with his brother and here he sat in a rundown tavern in a dreary part of the world.

How did it get this far? Everything I wanted to become has disappeared right in front of me. The only people I have truly loved are dead. Can I love again when I marry Ali-Gare? Did the King send me here to get rid of me?

The last thought started to irk Edburgh. He couldn't believe the King would do that to his own nephew until he realized whom he was torturing.

If I am willing to kill my nephew this easily, the King surely would do the same to accomplish his goals. I'll go back and kill him if he has been using me as a scapegoat.

The owner returned and slapped a sloppy bowl on the table, "Turtle soup," she cried and slowly walked away. Edburgh began to shake. He looked down at his sword and debated whether to bring mass destruction to the tavern. He spotted a blond woman in the corner with her back turned.

Caroline.

Edburgh unconsciously rose and walked over to his bride. He tapped her on the shoulder and lightly whispered, "I got him for you. I got him good."

The woman turned and spoke, "I beg of your pardon?"

It wasn't Caroline.

Ed's head was twisted internally again and the only remedy he knew was to drink more, much, much more. Ed went home later that night and passed out. He slept through the night again and woke up the next day to repeat the process of what his life had become.

53
A Special Young Man—Russell

"WHY, HELLO THERE, what's your name?" Russell asked the young girl. He had left a little later than usual this morning to collect kindling for the fires. He stopped and dropped his pile to talk to the girl. He had seen her being forced into labor by the mean old woman who wore the same long black gown every day. The girl looked malnourished and her skin had been baked in the sun from her daily outdoor work. Her black hair, clothes and body had stains of dirt and blood, but her majestic blue eyes lit up her filthy brown face. She still didn't respond. Russell leaned down closer to her and asked again, "What is your name?"

A cackle came from several feet away, "The girl has no right to a name. She is but a slave."

Russell saw the old lady and asked, "I thought slavery was illegal in Donegal?"

"I am sure many things you've thought over the years differ in reality, boy. All this matters little anyway. The end of days is upon us. The sun surely cannot shine forever. Darkness shall soon reign supreme. You see child, death and suffering will never die. Those on earth who fight against it will die. Those who don't fight back will also die. Not a single soul shall be spared. The demons have spoken and word will soon be put to action, action the humans are not readily prepared for." She cackled again after her statement.

She sounded like the evil witches from the stories Ali-Pari used to tell him. The old lady stood only a bit taller than half Russell's height, but was extremely feisty. She hunched over as she dragged her left leg and labored over to the girl. She took a piece of Russell's kindling and whipped the child fiercely.

"I told you not to leave the house, didn't I? You need to learn to mind your master. Get back. Get back now," the old lady chastised as she continued to swing through the air even after the bloodied girl hastily made her way back toward the house. The old lady slouched along after the girl. Russell wanted to unsheathe his sword and free the slave, but for some reason he didn't. He collected the wood and returned to the workshop.

Russell stopped at the top of the stairs, just outside the door to the shared office. He overheard Dragon-Eyes and Gamelda talking on the other side. He stopped for a moment to listen.

"What are you trying to accomplish with the young man?" Gamelda asked. "I am trying to help the boy achieve his true potential," Dragon-Eyes responded. She quickly replied, "I know you, Dragon-Eyes. It's never that simple. You always have an ulterior motive." "No motives," said the wizard.

"Why are you going to the Pearl Islands?" Gamelda pushed. After a short silence she said, "Exactly. You want him to hold the Pearl for you." "Come on, the spirits seem to love him, you've seen that," the wizard stated. Gamelda returned, "Don't place that burden on him, not at such a young age. Let him be a kid without care while it lasts. You haven't said anything to him, have you?"

"Of course not but you must admit, every skill has come quickly to Russell and I am only taking him to the Islands to further his training. I won't be hunting the Pearl…but if it should happen to find us, well then…" the Imp let the word linger as he shrugged his shoulders.

"No, don't put his life in that kind of danger. Men kill just from hearing the words, 'Pearl of Wisdom'. You have seen the evil it plants in some men's hearts," Gamelda warned.

"What about me? You don't seem to care very much about my life," the Imp stated.

"Not right now, I don't. What do you think? Do you think that you and Russell are going to defeat Damian Doome? With what army?" she asked.

"Nobody believed Rockarius could do it. They said he would die like the ten thousand men sent before him, but he didn't. He got to ride the dragons and became an ageless hero whom I still can't stop hearing about. Russell found me buried in that ice. He could have walked right by and I would have hibernated for another year or two, but he didn't.

And as for little old me, I only want to ride a dragon. I only want to ride a dragon," the Imp Wizard emotionally stated.

Russell readied to knock on the door when Dragon-Eyes continued, "And Russell Seabrook is the best chance I have come across in all my years. The soul is pure in that young man. From all the stories and drawings, Russell looks exactly like Rockarius. Maybe that could be coincidence, but it cannot be solely that. He has something he doesn't even realize yet. He has a gift that most men can only wish for. And that gift will carry a heavy burden."

"KNOCK, KNOCK."

"Welcome, welcome," said Dragon-Eyes as he opened the door, a little red of face.

"Russell, how are you this afternoon?" Gamelda inquired.

"Fine, thank you," replied Russell with a goofy smile at the wizardess. Russell had completely fallen for Gamelda and the two had shared a bed for the last fortnight. She repeatedly told him that she was a free woman and couldn't be tied down to any man. Still, strong feelings persisted. Russell couldn't wait until they left for the Pearl Islands where it would be just the three of them, away from her male suitors in Donegal.

"So, do you remember how magic started on earth?" Dragon-Eyes asked. "I do. I do," coolly replied Russell. "Enlighten us please," the Imp returned.

"From what you have told me, it all started with the First Families on earth. I believe you said that the first people to die weren't quite ready and didn't fully understand death. They still harbored intense feelings for their human families. They asked the Gods for special powers to only use in the heavens. The Gods agreed and they proceeded to prove they had lied, giving their borrowed powers to their earth dwelling relatives. As soon as the Gods found out, they expelled those dirty souls to hell. Those greedy dead souls pulled the same trick on the Lord of the Underground, Travibero. They had disguised themselves as demons and when Travibero figured out the ruse, he fed them all to his dragons to extinguish the problem forever. So there were magical powers that had been given to the humans from the heavens and the hells. Then a supernatural war erupted on earth's surface. The benevolent powers from above combatted with the malevolent force from beneath and it rocked the heavens and hells. The Gods and Plades got involved and Travibero sent his dragons. As the dragons began to hurl fire at their targets, they released the souls from within due to the extreme force. Some of the tortured souls floated up, some sank underground and others simply dissolved into thin air. The souls that went up or down retained their original magical powers. They are still around until this day to be called upon as angel or demon spirits. Mostly the same type of powers can be obtained from either system of angels or demons but both carry consequences."

Dragon-Eyes spoke, "I am impressed. You even remembered malevolent and benevolent. However, in order to master these favors from the spirits, we must practice."

"Alright, let's practice," said Russell as he rolled his eyes, trying to act cool in front of his lady friend.

Dragon-Eyes went off, "What is it? You don't believe you need to practice? Armies and knights, even the squire practices relentlessly. How did you become skilled with a sword? Take an army of men who have practiced for years and pit them against a force twice as large of men who just picked up a pike for the first time. Who wins? If you don't practice now, then when? When your life hangs in the balance, is that when you will want to practice? Now, invisibility is what you will practice."

Russell closed his eyes and concentrated. The old wizard always made Russell angry with the lecturing in front of Gamelda but he came to realize Dragon-Eyes only did it for his benefit. He swept aside his irritation and started to think about disappearing. The Imp had taught him about Carabelle, the spirit of invisibility. Russell remembered that a young Carabelle died after her husband beat her to death in a drunken stupor. She had two daughters whom she watched from the heavens as the children lived a life of constant fear and physical abuse. She borrowed the power of invisibility from the Gods to help her daughters avoid their angry father. Russell tried to summon her help.

He rubbed his eyes and thought hard. Russell Seabrook opened them and clapped his hands twice.

"Dear mother, can you take away the pain?" He clapped three times. "Dear mother, can you break this awful chain?" Russell clapped four times. "Sweet angel, help make me invisible and plain." He clapped three times. "Lend your spirit, and the air I'll surely gain." Russell clapped twice.

He still saw himself but knew he had said the words correctly.

"Aah, very well indeed. I stand impressed. There doesn't seem to be much you cannot do," Dragon-Eyes lauded.

Russell nodded his head to acknowledge this, not knowing his friends couldn't see him. He looked about the room and noticed something awry. Sitting on the wizard's desk was the frame of a body who looked like a ghost. A white cloudy outline surrounded the distinct hollow body of a female with a bruised face. She looked to be very young.

"He sees her too," Gamelda announced.

"Utterly astounding, he has to be too inexperienced for this, right?" the Imp wondered aloud.

Russell had re-substantiated back into human form.

Russell started, "Is that..."

"I believe that is Carabelle. They say the spirits only appear to protect the purest of souls. Neither Dragon-Eyes nor I have ever had one show up when we conjured spiritual help from the angels. You are a special one, Russell," Gamelda said as she stroked his growing hair.

Carabelle floated toward the open window and slipped out into the morning air. As she drifted away, Dragon-Eyes whispered, "Stay close, sweet angel. We may need you again."

"I need to know, if the process to conjure spirits is so simple, just a few secret words, why doesn't everyone do it?" Russell inquired.

Gamelda answered, "They can try, but try as they might the spirits only attend to those who are worthy of their services. How they decide who is worthy or not still remains a mystery. I do know one thing is certain, they favor you, Russell."

Russell gazed fondly at Gamelda. She still wouldn't tell him her age but Russell liked that she wasn't as old as Ali-Pari. Russell believed he could love Gamelda despite her constant warnings against it. A headache came over Russell and his body ached. They were typical side effects of using the magic. After seeing the abused ghost, Carabelle, Russell thought about the slave girl and the way the old lady had treated her like an animal.

54
LOSING CONTROL—OLLOR

OLLOR DID THE secret knock and waited. He had just walked over from the fisherman's wharf where he worked. Ollor had already offered his services to the School of the Learned Warrior only to be spurned by the mysterious man who always answered the door. Ollor had found out during his last visit that the old man's name was Kazu. The old man opened the door and waved Ollor in, "Welcome back, come, come."

Kazu wore all black robes that made his dark dragon tattoos look even more menacing than usual. Ollor came in the back door and saw the kids in class, practicing with spears. The teacher demonstrated an attack and the class would mimic him. The old man took him into another room.

The room contained a small table scattered with carved wooden pipes. Ollor recognized ground cloves, cardamom and black pepper in three dusty piles. The old man mixed all three together and packed two pipes. He handed one to Ollor and kept the other. Kazu had a little pile of uniform twigs to light the pipes. He used a candle to light two twigs and gave one to Ollor who followed Kazu's lead. He decided the blend didn't taste too bad as he exhaled. Ollor had heard stories of the Gama Trakans smoking different spice mixtures out of pipes. This mix had a spicy, minty flavor to it and made Ollor feel drunk. The buzzing in his head only lasted a minute and the old man finally broke the silence, "You know your children are special but I am not sure you fully understand how special they are. The boy is already developing the body of a man and the little girl is beating men twice her size in combat. In all my many days, buried under this sand, I have never seen anything quite comparable to this. Not since the days of Rockarius."

"That is the precise reason I would like to be involved. They wouldn't be here if it weren't for me. I will do any job around the school so I can see my kids more," Ollor pleaded.

"I cannot at the moment, but life is like water, constantly moving and changing. You can always visit on the full- and half-moon. I think at this point it may be better for their development to be away from their father figure," Kazu retorted.

Ollor got angry. He knew what he had to do before Kazu completely blocked him from his children. Ollor had almost been stung by several scorpions in the past few weeks and realized he better tell the kids of their true parentage. Ollor wasn't sure if it was the right move but if he died, they would never know the truth. In Ollor's mind, they deserved to know.

The old man continued, "The best I can do for now is tell you about the noble nature of the school and why the children will remain here. This school was built ten years after Rockarius chased away Damian Doome. I say chased away because the builders knew the demons would strike again. This school dedicated itself to defend the defenseless by teaching superior skills. We took the dragon babies of Gama Traka and turned them into great warriors but they never got to see real battle. With each passing generation, more skills have been added to the School's repertoire. At this point in time, the top level skills possessed by the children are staggering. I have been here since this school was built. I thought the students were ready two hundred years ago, but that pales in comparison to now. They are not just learned warriors anymore. They are lethal devices trained in all combative arts and weapons. They understand languages after only days of study. These children learn and possess magic as easily as a knight sharpens his sword. I believe we are ready for Damian Doome and his legions. This school is connected to six other underground schools of equal size and structure scattered over northern Gama Traka. The others are even more secretive than us and the combined power of the seven should be enough for battle."

"I pray you are right. May I speak with my children now?" Ollor asked.
"I am sorry, the children will work through the night," Kazu returned.

Ollor couldn't understand why the old man kept him from meeting the children again. Ollor needed to tell them about their parents, but that would again have to wait. Being in the lonely, dry desert had made Ollor thirst for booze again. He couldn't do anything for the children at the moment. He wasn't even allowed to talk to them. They were secure at the school and much safer than Ollor out in the open, fully alone. Raising the kids had filled a void in Ollor's heart but he started to empty again. His life had purpose getting Sunny and Muriel to the school. Now he kept a job as fish scaler and gutter just to stay near the kids. Every day he got elbow-deep in buckets of fish parts and his body baked in the Gama Traka heat. Ollor's situation seemed stuck in the solace of knowing his children could one day save the world from the likes of Damian Doome. He wanted to do his share to help. He didn't want to be the guy who dropped off the children he had raised from birth only to be turned away like a beggar. *Come on, old man. Time to prove we're more than just a drop-off man. Time to show we still serve a purpose.*

55

LEAVING DONEGAL—RICEROS

RICEROS FELT SICK again. They had been onboard the boat less than a day since leaving his mother in Waters Edge. At least he knew she would be well protected when she got to her family in Elkridge. Brehan had told Riceros they were going to Gama Traka. Over the years, Count Sproul had taught Riceros a plethora of information about the sun-soaked, sandy oasis and he tried to impart that knowledge to Brehan. He wrote on his black slab and Brehan would talk back to him or ask questions.

The cusp of dusk loomed overhead. Aqua-green waters merged with the horizon and provided a unique foil to the burnt orange sky. Riceros felt the boat rocking back and forth as he tried to embrace the chance to explore new lands but he already missed his family, Count Sproul and Jasper. He looked out at the rhythmic waves as Brehan stopped the lesson about Gama Traka, "Alright, that's more than enough for today."

Riceros wrote on the board and showed Brehan, "Do you believe we'll see Krys or Ryno in Gama Traka?"

"Perhaps, little man, but it is a pretty big place. It would be more than pure luck at this point," replied Brehan.

"How did you get away from the Fox Chapel farmers?" Riceros wrote.

"I outwitted the simple farmers. I waited for my chance and struck when there was an opening. The details will give you nightmares so I won't tell the story," Brehan gently stated.

"Do you think the King will send father's bones back to Mattingly?" Riceros wrote and showed it to Brehan.

Brehan began, "I would like to think so...but I cannot be sure. While we are speaking of your father, there is something I must tell you." He paused for a few moments and looked uncomfortable before saying, "You look much like your father, Jon Colbert, this is true. The good Duke has raised you, that's also certain, but I'm afraid I must tell you *he is not* your real father. You were born on the Pearl Islands, on the seventh island, just as I."

The boat rocked and Riceros felt a tidal wave of shock as Brehan continued, "You are a very special young man and I am to protect you on your travels. I have failed your father but I will not fail you, Riceros Colbert. That is your real name. Your mother simply named you Riceros and Duke Colbert added the surname. Your father chanced upon you while passing through the tiny sea town. Your mother pleaded for Jon Colbert to take and protect you because she knew she couldn't. He happily agreed and took you to raise as if you were his own. He convinced the citizens of Mattingly that you were a miracle baby and Camelle was only pregnant for three months. Only the close circle within the castle knew the truth, but not the whole truth. And from that low number a very select few know the true details of your birth before reaching Mattingly. Duke Colbert raised you as if you were his own and kept the secret even from you so you could enjoy your youth. He always treated you as an equal member of the family."

"He did the same for you too," Riceros scribbled on his board.

Brehan began to tear up but continued, "He certainly did treat me well. Now brace yourself so I can tell you the story of your true father."

A deafening sound of snapping and stressing wood erupted and rocked the boat violently, knocking all the passengers down. Riceros hit the metal burn barrel and his entire forearm and right side were burned badly. The boy didn't feel any pain. He took two steps away and the bubbling wounds healed themselves. Riceros grabbed his black board and looked over at several grappling hooks coming over the port side. He saw a ship hoisting a black flag with two crossed swords on it. The invading vessel put up two ladders and men began to rush aboard, rough and rugged looking men who confidently strutted about the deck. They called all of the ship's terrified guests to the deck and lined them up on either side of the boat. Approximately twenty invaders looked over one hundred fancy looking sea passengers.

A gruff man spoke in a husky voice, "Listen up piss ants and ye just might live to see the sun come up tomorrow. I talk fast and only once. Take anything of value and lay it in front of ye. We be pirateers, so ye know. That means we don't follow no pansy-ass sea laws set forth by any kingdom or empire. We do what must be done so don't be gettin' any heroic ideas. If I even think ye be hiding somethin', ye be sleepin' with the sea monsters."

He looked Brehan up and down. The pirateer was the tallest person Riceros had ever seen and although skinny, still quite imposing. He had long curly black hair and a thick beard with flies circling it as if he had lost a fair amount of food in it. There was a bright blue braid of hair down the middle of his long, straight black beard. He appeared to be about forty and wore a white tunic with slop hose tucked into his calf-high black leather boots. He sheathed long curved swords on each hip but the blades were extremely skinny. The tips of the scabbards scraped the ground ever so gently as the pirateer walked back and forth. They looked similar the scimitar swords that Anders Ahitni used to bring his father as gifts.

The rest of the motley crew wore loose fitting old rags. The torn, mismatched outfits barely constituted clothes and were covered in red wine and blood stains. Riceros didn't see any of the men wearing boiled leather, mail or plate armor for protection. A few pirateers came closer, smelling like stale booze and vomit. Riceros thought they stunk like the grand hall after a big feast before the porters cleaned it. The head pirateer looked back at his allies and pointed to Brehan, "This ox is coming with us."

"No, that's not possible. I am sworn to protect my lord here." Brehan pointed to Riceros.

"He's no lord," the leader laughed. "Ye talkin' 'bout that littl' nipper over there." He and his crew enjoyed a mighty laugh.

"You don't understand. He's a very special little man," argued Brehan.

"Oh yeah, well what's so bloody fuckin' special 'bout ye, boy?" the giant man asked mockingly as he leaned down to look at Riceros' face.

"He cannot talk but he is probably smarter than anyone on this vessel," objected Brehan.

"Oh, he's one of 'em smart ones, is he? Can he lift a bloody sword and kill a man?" the leader asked Brehan.

"He already has killed a man," Brehan smugly stated.

Riceros wrote feverishly on his black slab.

"That's a big load of shit right there," said the pirateer as he quickly picked up Riceros, walked over to the starboard side and tossed the boy in the dark waters. "We don't need to be foolin' with the ransomin' of lords. No. We'll stay at sea to make our way."

Riceros flopped around on the moving tide, holding onto his black board and trying to tread water just to stay afloat. He heard Brehan screaming as the waves began to take him under. *"He cannot swim,"* were the last words Riceros heard as he swallowed some briny water.

Riceros stopped fighting it. The boy held onto the black board as he slowly sank. He thought about joining his father in the heavens, or at least the only father he had ever known. The light of the ship's fires disappeared and only darkness remained. Riceros Colbert gave in to the darkness.

56
BREHAN

BREHAN RAN TO jump in after Riceros but two men took him down and three others had to help restrain him. He had a reputation for being as strong and wild as a bull and the pirateers were finding out why. He would push two men away from his upper body but the other six hands kept him down. The thieves tied Brehan up after he lost his energy and moved him to their ship. He knew it would be a suicide mission to dive in with his arms bound behind his back. Failure filled his heart as he thought about all of Riceros' secrets.

Brehan stood in a daze on the deck of his new ship. The pirateers screamed at him to get out of the way as they heaved down large sacks of coins from the captured ship. The men came back aboard and started to check the take. They opened bags and cases filled with gold and diamonds. If Brehan had known these valuables were onboard, he would never have put Riceros on the ship.

A secret sea fairy must have whispered to the pirateers to attack us instead of merchant vessels stuffed with products. Someone tipped them off.

"Let's hurry our asses up and get all the goods aboard. Then we be the bloody hell outta here," screamed the leader as he landed on his ship and kept shouting orders to the crew. As commanded, the pirateers went back up the ladders and returned shortly with the rest of the food and jugs of wine and ale. The men pulled the ladders down and two men grabbed Brehan and guided him over toward the middle of the deck where a fire burned in a metal barrel.

The Salty Dragon looked like the perfect sea craft for chasing down larger ships. The wooden ship creaked in the waters with a front ram fashioned to look like a dragon's head. It contained many smaller masts and sails positioned perfectly to harness the wind.

Brehan saw about twenty men gathered around the fire, going

through the booty. The pirateers were a crazy blend of men from every part of the world. Most of them looked very different from each other, with skin ranging from ghostly white to the deepest brown. The ship sped along as the men divvied up the bounty, the price of which was Riceros Colbert's life.

"Who's holdin' the hooch?" asked a pirateer, shaking an empty mug.

Brehan stood off to the side and watched the men enjoy themselves. He still hadn't fully processed the recent events. One of the crew members yelled at him, "Kopar."

Brehan shook his head. "I'm sorry, good man, I don't understand that language."

"I speak the common language, my name is Kopar," the pale man returned. He came over and started to untie Brehan's arms.

"Kopar what?" Brehan wanted to know.

"All I answer to these days is Kopar." The man had rough, white skin so Brehan thought he may have been castle reared. He seemed to be somewhere in his mid-twenties, but already looked weathered and worn. Aided by the flickering flames, Brehan saw blond, no, white hair. Kopar looked like an albino with a long crooked nose. Bright red pimples speckled Kopar's face and neck.

"Actually I know my real name, but I hate it," revealed Kopar.

"Could it be worse than Castaway? The common bastard name of the Pearl Islands?" Brehan posed.

"It may. All depends on whom you should ask. My given name was Daerus Wamhoff, son of the honorable High Lord Tersen Wamhoff." Kopar stared away as if embarrassed.

Brehan almost dismissed his claim offhand until he remembered Count Sproul speaking of the Albino Wamhoff, brother of the King. The name Tersen matched up too. He was the High Lord of Cloverfoot, but Brehan heard he spent most of his time in Falconhurst. Brehan knew a little about the man but he didn't often concern himself with learning the members of the ruling families. He believed that type of information served no purpose on the battlefield and was useless to him. Elisa used to tell him about all the high lords and dukes, but he never really paid close attention.

"Yes, our noble Lord warned me that if I didn't take on the look of a true Wamhoff by my seventh birthday I would be sent away. He said my hair better turn the color of his pimples. Tall task for a five-year-old to magically accomplish. Suffice to say, I didn't change in appearance. And needless to say the High Lord is a man of his word. I swung a sword twice as good as that sissy Neron. Ah yes, but he had the red hair. The Gods decided my fate by the color of my hair. My father then decided the value of my life by selling me into slavery but I decided I wasn't going to give up," said Kopar with an odd smile that appeared to cause pain to the young man. Brehan guessed that Kopar didn't get a chance at happiness often.

Brehan noticed Kopar spoke like a highborn of Donegal even though his talk was getting rougher courtesy of another quickly consumed golden goblet of red wine. In contrast, as he eavesdropped on the other sailors' conversations, he could barely understand some of them.

Bilge, hornswaggle, prow, swag, dunnage, hulk, landlubber, scuttle, flying jib, bulwarks, shrouds? They might as well speak a foreign tongue. And they say ye instead of you. I think they are using the common tongue.

"What's wrong with you?" Kopar asked as Brehan stared at the other pirateers.

Brehan quickly shook his head to regain focus. "Sorry, I just watched the most important person in the world get tossed out to sea to die. The *one* person I swore to protect. I have failed again. I am the one who is meant to die for them, I should be dead."

"Can't help anyone if you're dead," Kopar stated. It sounded so stupid yet very apropos and simple.

There are other Colberts still to protect. And Elisa. Can't help anyone if I am dead.

"So is the captain like a king?" Brehan asked.

"No, not really, not at all actually. When we are in battle, Bluebeard has total control over every man. But right now we could vote him out as every man gets an equal vote. I was taken, much like you, but this is truly being a free man with equal rights for every man," Kopar proudly stated.

"Why would you vote out a captain?" Brehan probed.

"Many reasons really. Any man can become a captain if he can get a crew behind him and ships to sail. The captain and crew then draw up articles to abide by or laws to live by. The articles usually contain a section about the overthrow of a dangerous captain that takes a majority vote. I've heard stories of captains being voted out for putting the crew at unnecessary risk or due to silly matters such as jealousy. The last crew I was with went through four captains in one year. The last captain died and that crew disbanded, so I joined this one with Bluebeard. He has been captain for both of my years on the Salty Dragon and his other ships. No one knows his real name but he was in the Livingstone Navy, still grinds an axe for those bastards, no offense. Sorry..."

Brehan didn't care. Being a bastard had never really bothered him. "It's fine, really, go on."

Kopar used the momentary break to down another goblet and continued as if he hadn't missed a beat, "In fact, most of the men are ex-privateers from various kingdoms and empires. The Peace on the High Seas treaty has put most privateers out of work. They trained the men for a life of piracy. A man could earn ten years' wages on only one heist. And the lifestyle, oh the lifestyle. You will see when we get to Shant Island." Kopar threw a piece of wood into the fire pit.

Brehan interrupted, "Shant Island?"

"It is the one true island the pirateers run. They call it that because if you tell anyone who's not a pirateer, you shan't live long. We are welcome in some places for a day or two near the coast. We are going to visit a few of those spots to unload some of this take before heading back to Shant. Ever since pirateers were declared an enemy to every man from any kingdom or empire, we are very unwelcome in most parts of the world. That is until they want cheaper goods. We have no protection from any king, so the brotherhood of pirateers must stay strong. It truly is us against the world and I cannot be certain, but I feel we are winning." Kopar scratched his mouth and Brehan noticed everyone seemed to be crowding around them.

"Pipe down, seagulls," Bluebeard shouted, "I almost forgot we got new blood aboard. Now let's swear him in, or throw him overboard." The drunken men all laughed with the captain.

Kopar grabbed Brehan's shoulder and said, "Just agree to everything and it will be over soon enough."

One of the pirateers came up with a piece of rolled paper and gave it to Bluebeard.

"Drink, boy," one of the older pirateers said as the man shoved an overflowing mug of mulled spirits into his hand. Brehan didn't often drink so he almost spat out the first sip.

"Finish it, ye soft-bellied landlubber," another pirateer remarked. Bluebeard held the bottom of the mug until Brehan consumed it all. Instant dizziness hit hard as he stumbled forward toward the raging flames. Two men quickly grabbed him and held him up for a moment until he regained his balance.

"Now he's ready to become a pirateer. Kopar, get the pledge stone," Bluebeard ordered.

"Yes, captain," answered Kopar as he rushed below deck. They waited until Kopar returned and exchanged something with Bluebeard for the roll of paper.

Bluebeard held up a human skull and said, "If this man should violate his vows in any way or manner, he stands to be haunted by every single man who's ever died at sea. Kopar, read 'em the articles."

Kopar read the articles loudly, "I swear by my own blood to defend my captain and crew until death parts our ways. I swear to uphold the articles as follows:

Article One-The captain holds unquestioned power during times of battle. In peacetime, the captain and all crew members have an equal vote on all matters. A captain can be removed by a majority vote.

Article Two-The captain is to receive thirty percent of all bounty. The quartermaster is to receive twenty percent and the remainder is split equally amongst the remaining crew.

Article Three-All men must remain ready for action with sharpened sword. All disagreements at sea will be settled on dry land.

Article Four-Any man who deserts ship or crew or disobeys any of these rules will be put straight to death."

Bluebeard jumped in, "Do ye solemnly pledge yer life in blood to uphold these articles?"

Brehan agreed, and his hand was pulled away from the skull and placed on a stool next to the fire.

"Hold still, she won't hurt but a bit," Bluebeard said as everyone laughed.

Bluebeard pulled a dirk from his hip, tossed it in the air and caught the exact rotation so he grabbed the handle. With a quick motion, he poked Brehan's index finger. They brought the articles closer to Brehan as he stood up. He noticed a blank area at the bottom with signatures of the crew, in blood. The men steadied the articles on a sworn pirateer's back and Brehan signed it with his blood. Brehan may not have given in so easily if he hadn't been so drunk.

The crew erupted with excitement and fed more spirits to Brehan who didn't fight it this time. Kopar approached Brehan, "Congratulations, you are one of us now. The wonderful world of the sea, where a bastard and the son of a high lord can attain equal status," said Kopar as he rolled his eyes and laughed.

"Why did you pick Kopar for your new name?" Brehan wanted to know after things had settled down a bit.

"When first captured by the pirateers, I was riding on a slave ship headed for Gama Traka. Someone asked me the story of my life and I told him the entire thing. I told him how I hated my name and wanted to change it. He told me he had just learned the word Kopar. He said it meant to rise above in Tantokin. That same day I got picked up by the pirateers and when they asked me my name, I told them it was Kopar."

57

A New Crown Contender—The Man With The Golden Sword

"I HEARD THAT your mother died while birthing you," the drunk man said.

"No, no, no. You're not tellin' it right. They said my mother was dead before I was born," angrily replied an even drunker man at the table.

He had amber blond hair and dull blue eyes with golden brown flecks. A wide scar on his chin looked crudely sutured and his tanned complexion made the white wound stand out in stark contrast. His beard only grew in patches so he was always clean shaven, even at war. Tall, strong and ruthless were three of his best attributes. The Man talked with three friends at a square table in the middle of a tavern. A pitcher of god ale sat in the middle of the table as the men gulped down the strong beverage.

The blond man continued, "What I've been told is my father must've been rather upset with my pregnant mother and cut her throat. Or, if he was trying to kill me, he failed. Sometime later an old man found me, detached the cord from my mother, and kept me at Blairs Beak. Maybe I'll just tell a quick story..."

Even though Benroy, Tucker and Mattrick were probably his closest allies, they still didn't know the full story of The Man with the Golden Sword. No one knew his real name and he was more simply known as The Man. He drank all the time and although he wasn't often drunk, he slurred his words on this night. It must have loosened his lips too, as he scarcely ever talked about himself.

He went on, "The old man turned out to be a thief who taught me the craft of thievery and tried to get me to worship Travibero and the demons. He felt forgotten by the Gods and he cursed 'em on a daily basis. He reminded me of my birthday, the fifth day of summer, every night around bedtime. It was just before he would beat the livin' hells out of me. The old man got stabbed and died while tryin' to pick-pocket the wrong fellow. He may have bled black for all I know. That forced me to live on the streets and beg for everything at just six years old. When I turned seven I tried to see a sorceress. I begged or bartered payment to find out if my future would be as rotten as my life had been on the streets. One sorceress took pity on me and used her crystal ball to see my future."

The Man stopped for a second as he refilled his mug as well as everyone else's at the table.

His friends listened intently as he continued, "She saw a crown in her ball. She said she could clearly see a man in his thirtieth year that set out to conquer a kingdom. She saw a man with blond hair and blue eyes. That crushed me at the time because I had brown hair and gray eyes. The colors changed when I was in my teens. My curiosity had been aroused and I wanted to hear more prophecies. I went to six more of them and they all took pity on me, like the first sorceress. Those six women all saw the exact same images and finished with the same statement, 'Carry a golden sword and the world shall kneel before you.' Soon after that a woman saw me on the street and took me to work at her inn. She put me to work at every job except cook."

The men at the table now understood why the Man with the Golden Sword had been secretly putting together an army of four thousand men. They knew his thirtieth birthday was less than a week away. They also had a strong suspicion of The Man being the Gold Bandit. The Gold Bandit was a mystery man who had raided northern Donegal and stolen entire castle gold reserves.

"One day a knight came to the inn with a real pissy attitude. He said his squire couldn't do anything but complain. After seeing me hustle around the inn, he made a deal with the innkeeper to purchase me. That man happened to be Sir Constador Clybo of Elmsrapt. He taught me to fight, read maps, devise battle plans and strategies." The Man counted on his fingers as he named the lessons.

He continued, "I felt that he had been sent there to prepare me for my foretold destiny. Sir Constador transformed me from a ten-year-old without any skill, into a cold-blooded warrior. He tested me in several district battles and at fifteen I was bigger than most grown men. I met a girl and we fell madly for each other. Life was starting to brighten up for me. Tarasoni Alber will always be my first and only love. Unfortunately, our love, like all love, was not to last. I arrived back at the castle one day to find my lover in tears, telling me to run. The guards arrested me on the spot and I stood accused of murder. Mind you, I had killed seven men in the district fights, but I didn't kill the squire. Everyone knew me to carry a golden sword blade and have a rough past, so it was easy to make me the fall guy. A young Lord of the castle got angry with his squire and killed him. Then he pinned the whole thing on me and everyone believed a noble over a bastard, of course. I thought perhaps Sir Constador would step in to save me at the last moment, but that wasn't to be. The High Lord said a man of my size would be a great offering for the King to use in the duels," The Man said as he took another sip of his ale.

"I can't believe you won seven duels," said Tucker.

"Eight," replied The Man.

"I think our friend may have had a little too much to drink," Benroy jokingly said.

Out of nowhere, a man seemed to materialize behind The Man. He said, "This man is not your friend. He is your future King."

The new man was short and skinny. He had a closely shaved head and bright-green eyes. He wore a torn shirt and ill-fitting britches that were cut off at mid-calf. He looked to be about fifty years old, but no one actually knew his age.

He spoke again, "He could be dead right now. I could have easily killed him. And if I could have done it, another man could as well. You men would have been helpless. What? Are we not drunk enough yet?"

The shoeless man, known as the Crippler, had an air of intrigue to him as well. He had been rumored to have crippled men just by staring at them. Nobody had actually seen the Crippler do it, but no one wanted to test the magical man either. Most people thought that he was a Wizard that used demonic spirits, which some argued were more powerful than angelic ones. For the past few years, he had hovered around The Man, always whispering in his ear.

He never drank, so he spoke clearly to the men, "You can continue your story, quietly. I could hear you half-way across the bloody room."

The Crippler knew the story would only make the men rally around

The Man even more.

The Man with the Golden Sword said, "It's true. I'm drunk. But I certainly remember how many duels I won."

"But people say you only have to win seven duels," Mattrick asked and said at the same time. Mattrick went by the nickname of Mad Dog.

"The guards forgot to mark my first win." The Man slammed two open hands on the table. On seven fingers, right below the nails, he had a black X.

"They didn't brand me after my first win and believe it or not, nobody would believe me. The King was actually there that day. He always walked through the jails to look at the criminals almost every day. Some people said he did it to feel superior over the caged-up men. But when they asked the King if he had remembered me winning a duel, he looked right at me. I saw fear. It stained his clothes and he stunk of it. He looked terrified as he stood surrounded by four armed guards even though all the criminals were locked in pens. The King asked his men what my charges were. When they responded that it was murder, he said, 'Let the bastard murderer fight again, even if he says he already has fought.' Our big, tough King looked at me and walked away. I have been dreaming of a day when I can meet him again. I want to see the look of horror on his face when there isn't a cage to hold me back. I'll take his head and spike it on the highest tower of the castle." A huge smile came across The Man's face. "I cannot wait for that day. The King with the Golden Sword. It has a nice sound to it, don't you think?"

The Man sat back and chugged the rest of his ale. He wiped the escaping liquid from the sides of his mouth and continued to his captivated audience.

"You see, the first two duels were easy. They put me up against a couple of scrawny pickpockets. The next two, well, not so much. I won, but I sustained injuries that didn't have enough time to heal. You fight every seventh day after you arrived, so the winners were there for forty-nine days. I guess some can be there for fifty-six, if they miscount..."

Tucker cut in, "Way better than being there for only seven."

"So very true, my friend," The Man replied as he told his story, "The last three men all won three duels before I had to face them. I cannot remember the details of those fights. The killing and imprisonment, it was all a blur. Strangely, I still remember all the crimes charged against my opponents. Stealing, stealing, adultery, rape, rape, murder, murder, murder." He counted them off on his fingers as he recalled the charges.

"It was in that order too. The crimes seemed to be greater, the further a fighter advanced. Is it mad to say I somewhat miss it? When thousands of people stand and cheer after you end a man's life, well, there are few better feelings in life. I still remember the rabid crowd, begging for blood. The nobility of Fox Chapel acted like animals, and we were the ones penned up. They were like dogs waiting to be fed. And once you fed them a dead body, they loved you but immediately wanted more."

He paused to wipe some sweat from his forehead.

He took another sip and went on, "It's ironic." He turned and winked to the Crippler. "I went to the Capitol falsely accused of one murder. And the only way to eradicate it was for me to murder eight more men."

He turned and looked at the Crippler, "Did I use that right? Eradicate?"

"Perfectly done. Good job," he answered.

"Well, I apparently had put on a great show at the Yard for the crowd. I can recall them hailing me as I was being led away in ball and chains, off to fight as a soldier to defend Donegal."

"That's when you met me," said Benroy.

"Indeed it was. Most people, they know the story from there," The Man said.

Benroy spoke, "About how you killed more Goldenfield men than any Donegal soldier during your service."

The Man said, "I didn't do it for Donegal, or King Ali-Stanley, I can tell you that much. They falsely accused me, forced me to fight in the duels, and then they asked me to defend the kingdom. Kind of an odd sequence, I thought. No, I did it because I like killing. It's the closest you can get to being a God. I chose when those men's lives ended, even if it was backed by the Gods. Now that I have a large army behind me, I will be able to decide many more men's fates. *That* is power. *That* is what drives men. *That* is what will take us to the throne."

"Four thousand men is not exactly a large army," said Mattrick.

"No, it's not. But eight thousand is," The Man said with a smirk.

The last statement was extremely difficult for The Man to make with his current slurred speech. He reached down and rubbed the pommel of his sword. The hilt was almost pure gold mixed with a few base metals to fortify it. The blade was made of ice-hardened steel and painted gold everywhere except the razor-sharp edge. The Man claimed his sword was so sharp that it could shave a lady bug's legs. At eighteen, he had taken the sword off a dead captain from Goldenfield and molded it over the years. The Crippler put a magical blessing on the sword five years ago. He had always had fake gold painted on his previous swords but this one was true gold.

The Crippler had somewhat taken The Man under his wing. He convinced The Man to chase his destiny to sit the throne. The Crippler saw things in The Man that he didn't even see in himself. He tried to clean up some of his bad habits and rough edges. But try as he might, he wasn't able to fully reform The Man who still enjoyed getting really drunk on occasion and regularly visiting whore-houses. He liked fulfilling his base and primal needs without developing emotional attachment. He knew if you had nothing you loved, no one could hold any leverage against you. The Crippler also made him read more, especially old battle records, and tried to clean up his rugged talk. That was a work in progress. The Man with the Golden Sword could speak to many different audiences from soldiers to nobles. The Man seemed to mix his old rough talk with the new things the Crippler was teaching him. He tried to prepare him to be a king.

"Where are the other four thousand men?" Benroy asked.

The Man quickly responded, "They are on their way from the Goldenfield border and should be arriving any time now. The King called all the men from Goldenfield to help with his attack on Mattingly. They split the men up into two divisions of four thousand. Well, one division is on the way to the Capitol and the other is on the way here. Gold and silver can greatly sway a man's decisions, especially when you take men who are owed years of wages."

"So what is the plan after they get here, and how can you afford to pay for them?" Benroy wondered.

The Man pulled up his sleeve to expose a tattoo on his forearm. A black triangle with many random dots on the inside covered a large area of skin. He also revealed about twenty slash-scars all over his arm.

"Do any of you recognize this?" he asked.

All of the men agreed that they did not. The Crippler just smiled slightly.

"Really? It is worth over three hundred thousand gold rounds. It is a treasure map of sorts. It tells me where all that gold is buried. As I said, the thief did teach me how to steal before his demise. Well, ever since my service ended and I became a free man, I have been acquirin' gold," he turned to the Crippler again, "Is that right?"

The Crippler shrugged his shoulders, "You forgot the 'g' at the end, but the meaning was clear."

The Man continued, "I have been acquiring," he accentuated the 'g' and smiled at the Crippler, "gold for many years to save for a rainy day. Well, now it is pouring. It's pouring gold that we will use to make it rain Wamhoff blood."

Everyone at the table smiled and Tucker asked, "So what is the plan after the soldiers arrive?"

The Man looked them all in the eyes and said, "First, we take Waters Edge."

58
GOING UP—MARIAH

MARIAH'S EXHAUSTED BONES wished they had taken the shorter route with the other members of the group. Torvald assumed she would like to see the landscape of Bottomfoot, so they took an extended trip. Sir Bastion and J. Everson had gone ahead on the direct path to Housemont. Mariah could see why no one had ever invaded Bottomfoot. They had been up and down numerous mountains and she saw how it would be hard to march an army through these steep hills.

"What do you mean we aren't going to Housemont?" Mariah questioned.

"Worry not, my lady, we are going to a beautiful place called Ridgetop," Torvald responded.

This trip had made Mariah realize that she loved Torvald. She was almost sure it was true but didn't know what love actually felt like. The seventeen-year-old thought she loved him if all that her mother had told her about the subject was true. She had always dreamed of a rugged gentleman and that characteristic defined Torvald. Mariah rode a donkey up the rough hillside. The steepest mountain in Bottomfoot stood as the final one they needed to ascend. Mariah harbored nervous feelings about meeting Torvald's parents. She knew about the dukes and duchesses from the other regions but Bottomfoot remained shrouded in secrecy. She hoped the Maliks might have good news about her family but realized they seemingly could care less about the problems outside of their region. The mountain plateaued and a little town appeared. Houses made of wood lined the street and continued on a slight incline for several hundred feet. As they walked by, everyone bowed or curtsied in their presence. Mariah liked the respect all the citizens of Bottomfoot had given them during the trip. Almost everyone knew Torvald, and the few who didn't dropped to a knee when they found out his identity.

Mariah saw a family and didn't understand what they were doing at first. As they got closer, she noticed what they were assembling. They were stuffing vegetables into huge blue-tinted jars lined up on a long rectangular table. The family had a cauldron of sour smelling liquid boiling over a fire. The sharpness stung her nose as the stench of potent vinegar pervaded the afternoon air. The father picked up and put on a heavy brown glove that came up to his armpit. He took a moment to get a good hold on the handle of a big metal pitcher and plunged it into the bubbling liquid. With a steady hand, the father carefully filled the jars with red vinegar to pickle and preserve the vegetables. The children followed and sealed the jars after they were filled.

"Summer has barely started. Why do they do this so early?" Mariah wondered. "Do you know the story of the wise ram and the careless ram?" Torvald posed. "I know the story of the wise bull and the careless bull," she smartly answered.

"Do either of you know the story about the wise ass and the careless bull's balls?" Chopkins chuckled as he patted his donkey on the head.

Everyone enjoyed a laugh as they walked through the little town alongside their jacks.

"I know the story of the *animal* that saves throughout the year and the careless *animal* that wastes all year long. Then, when winter arrives, the careless animal has to beg the wise friend to save him. The wise animal always helped out the careless one in our version," Mariah stated.

Torvald smiled, "Exactly, it teaches us to save and be wise about our harvest."

"Does it though?" Chopkins jumped in, "The one animal gets to waste like a glutton all year long and he still sneaks by in winter because of the naïve niceness of the ill-named wise one. So why not just waste away? Isn't that the true message, waste what you wish because your friend will always bail you out?"

"Fool me once, shame on you, fool me twice, shame on me. You would have one glorious winter and then starve the next when everyone figured out your underhanded intentions," Torvald sharply answered with a smirk.

Another foul funk permeated the air and subdued even the sharp vinegar scent. Mariah covered her nose and tried to breathe through her mouth as she spoke in an odd voice, "My goodness, what is that?"

"Someone is boiling leather," Chopkins returned. "Where?" Mariah asked looking around the street.

"Not around here," Torvald answered, "that could be from miles away when the wind gets blowing but it is a foul smelling process indeed."

Chopkins ran over to a metal box with smoke pouring out some of the cracks in the construction. He sucked in the smoke and a smile came over his face. "Tastes like smoked pig," he exclaimed, smacking his lips and biting at the rising smoke. Mariah joined him to cleanse her nostrils of the rank stench. The three stayed for a few minutes and talked to the family. They explained to Mariah how they smoked the meat and packed it in salt for the winter. They told her how they had almost run out of food the previous winter and didn't want to risk it this year. Torvald shot a grin at her when the point of his story was immediately proved. As they neared the end of the road in the small town, they saw something being constructed.

"What are they building?" Mariah asked. "A new church for the town," Torvald responded.

The foundation looked near complete and some men were locking jointed pieces of wood together for the frame. Others stood and argued about the correct direction and height for each wall to maximize sunlight. Long wooden benches were being built and decorated with bright paintings of godly scenes by the women. Two magnificent stained glass windows featuring Josevius' sacrifice leaned against a newly assembled bench. Other women worked on huge embroidery projects for the new house of worship. Everyone looked jovial performing their designated job. Mariah felt Bottomfoot as a whole looked like a good place for anyone to live. She also noticed that most females wore plenty of gold jewelry as they went about their outdoor chores and worked in the dirt. They wore ill-fitting and dirty clothes hanging loosely from their bodies but gold clung firmly to the women's necks and wrists, glittering in the fading sun.

"Is everyone wealthy in Bottomfoot?" Mariah questioned.

Chopkins joked, "Wealthy on cheer, sure."

"No, how does everyone afford all this gold for jewelry?" Mariah pressed.

Torvald spoke after he and Chopkins looked at each other, "The gold mines of Bottomfoot run rich. You cannot tell anyone outside of Bottomfoot or we will be besieged by gold diggers."

"Of course not. I wouldn't dream of telling a soul," Mariah reassured him.

"The truth of the matter is there is no high value on gold in most of Bottomfoot. Nearly everyone can obtain ample amounts so there is no jealousy. It's silly to steal and kill for what one can easily obtain. We mostly use it for decoration, not domestic trade. Goods are mostly traded for independent of gold. We have what we want right here in Bottomfoot and anything else we can bring in by sea. The merchants always accept our gold for goods," Torvald smiled.

She remembered that Chopkins came from the southern coast. The trio made it through the levelled off town and continued the steep ascension on donkeys.

"So Chopkins, will you ever return to live with your family again?" Mariah wondered.

The stout, scar-faced young man answered, "When you run the ports, money and gold consume your life. My parents wallow in it constantly, yet somehow convince themselves they love it. They also think themselves to be enjoyable company as well, but I won't even go into that now. They are blind to the fact that they are quite miserable. Life in Ridgetop..."

"What is Ridgetop?" Mariah asked.

Chopkins continued, "You will find out soon enough, my lady. Life in Ridgetop stresses the enjoyment of life, as stupid as that may sound. They appreciate a good jape or jest. Life in Portville is morbidly serious. No one smiles or likes to have real fun. Those greed-infested mongrels like to count gold and possessions to compare with everyone else to see where they stand. All those people covet is money. They are the black toe of Bottomfoot. And my hilarious humor is much more appreciated in Ridgetop."

"What is this Ridgetop, you must either tell me or stop speaking of it," Mariah insisted.

"Alright enough torture, my lady, it is a Ridge that sits on top of a mountain," Chopkins chuckled.

Mariah looked off the precipice and down on either fog or clouds. She got a bit scared as her donkey bounced along the beaten path.

59
THROUGH THE JUNGLE—LEIMUR

AN INTENSE STORM darkened the bright day to a dawn-like atmosphere. Queen Leimur Leluc's boat rocked along the rising waters of the Rushing River. Her fleet consisted of twenty-five boats containing twenty people each. Harbor Valley knew they were coming but this route could get a force there early and surprise the enemy with an unexpected attack.

She rode in the lead boat as it traveled at breakneck speed, turning to look back at the rest of her fleet. A few moments later, a frantic Captain Tetine pointed ahead and screamed, *"Rocks. My Queen, we must dive in. The boat is going too fast."*

The Captain and rest of the crew dove in and scrambled in the raging tide. The Queen eyed the huge boulders ahead and rid herself of anything heavy including Marius Leluc's battle axes. After lightening her mass, she dove in and fought for her life. Some of the men struggled and several sank in their heavy armor. She passed most of the men and only saw Captain Tetine ahead as the water whisked her toward the oncoming wall of pain. Huge boulders had been placed all the way across the river and only the smallest of canoes could get through the narrow passes. Something or someone had to have put them there if her great-great grandfather had passed through on his trip many years ago.

A few boats managed to get ashore but most of them ignored or never heard the warning calls of the oncoming rocks and jumped out much too late. The ships exploded upon impact, erupting splintering planks of wood into the sky.

The Queen of Goldenfield wildly flapped her arms, slapping the top of the water while her aching legs kicked. She started to get extremely tired and her left calf cramped up. Leimur had never enjoyed swimming. She peeked at the jagged boulders and thought the river was moving too fast for her to make it ashore. She swam mightily and almost touched solid land when her right side slammed into a huge boulder. The river tried to pull her back but she gripped the rock and fought for her life as her hand started to slip. Pulling and scratching, the Queen felt something grab her arm. She frantically pulled and found herself face-to-face with the one-eyed Captain Tetine. Once fully ashore, Leimur collapsed onto the ground. Her legs and arms felt numb as huge raindrops pelted the survivors. She coughed heavily and some river water came out. The Queen finally started to catch her breath. She saw the blood covered rocks being washed clean by the rain and river current.

The Queen looked ahead to see shattered ships scattered everywhere. Amongst the rubble she spotted the gleam of golden armor. It was trapped under a pile of wood but the Queen recognized it. She instinctively felt for the battle axes on her hips, only to remember she had needed to sacrifice them for her life. The Queen stared into the jungle as a fishy smell lingered in the dense air. Shrieking sounds she had never heard before came from the moist, green forest. She assessed the situation and found that they had lost most supplies and more than half of the men. Most of the boats had crashed into the boulders and only one had safely landed on the Queen's side. She looked across the raging rapids to the other side of the river and saw four boats and many more men than she had on her side. She counted thirty six confused soldiers on her side and estimated about five times that amount on the other.

They were deep in the animal kingdom, a place to which nobody went. The searing heat and carnivorous animals were enough to keep anyone out, but the jungles also contained the dreaded Owatowa. They were men and women who lived like savages in the animal kingdom. Nobody had been this far into the animal kingdom for quite some time. Her men meandered around aimlessly, unsure of what to do.

"Everybody listen. Come over here. We have one boat with enough food to barely get through the night. Anyone who still has a weapon, stand over here by me. We will move inland to see if we can find food or a way out," the Queen shouted to the demoralized men.

Leimur borrowed a sword and took about twenty troops into the humid forest. The river had helped to cool things down but that changed as they entered the scary unknown. There were trees and enormous green vines as big as tree trunks with leaves over ten feet tall. The river water they were soaked in turned to sweat after only a few moments and everywhere looked the same. The moist ground supported the small bushes and plant life that thrived in the fertile soil. The crazy sounds intensified and the Queen was understandably frightened. They hacked away at the dense brush and bushes for about twenty minutes without seeing anything except insects and snakes they couldn't catch. She still heard strange sounds and couldn't figure out which direction they were coming from. Everything looked exactly the same.

"Stop, let's get back to the base and regroup," exclaimed the perspiring Queen.

The apprehensive hunters turned and tried to get back to the riverside. Although it took them much longer to return, they finally made it to the river. Leimur and her men were starving. They hoped to see the rest of the troops preparing a meal when they walked up the river bank, but not a man could be seen and even the ship was gone. Queen Leimur ran down the bank and saw her ship speeding away at a great distance down the Rushing River. Screaming would have done nothing with the thunderous waters and eerie sounds of the animals. She looked through the rubble and found they had cherry picked everything of value. She moved the planks around and found her armor. Her heart finally slowed down even though anger still flowed freely from her soul. The men caught up with the Queen. She said, "There they go with all our supplies. You can see where they dragged the boat ashore to get around the rocks. They also took all supplies from this pile over here. Deserters, every single one of them."

The rain finally stopped and the remaining troops set up for the night. After a heated debate, the starving crew lit a fire with the wood from their crumbled fleet to keep the wild beasts away. Some thought it would attract animals but Leimur ruled that animals were usually scared of fire and they didn't even have any food to attract animals. The starving, abandoned crew barely slept during the sultry night. The Queen rolled around on the ground, stomach writhing in hunger pains, trying to get a moment of rest.

The searing morning sun awakened the already sweat soaked soldiers. Leimur pulled her exhausted body up and tried to stretch out her taut muscles. She went over to the remaining planks and located her armor. With the help of Captain Tetine, she put the protection on. The men had no luck trying to fish in the river. They wanted to avoid going back into the jungle at all costs. No one would admit it, but the men were scared. The Queen knew the men looked to her for a solution but nothing flashed into her head. For once Leimur Leluc didn't know what to do. She had to make some decision soon as the men looked restless.

A loud rumbling sound began to build and get louder. Leimur looked up the bank to see an army of gray-looking men and animals bearing down from a distance. The Queen and the men who had them drew their weapons. The gray men were naked and as they got closer, the Queen noticed leopards, monkeys, elephants and jaguars ferociously stomping down the wide river bank. As the horde arrived the Queen killed two gray men with the first swing of her sword. The nude men and women known as the Owatowa had wooden clubs and others attacked with only their hands. A jaguar clamped down on the Queen's left vambrace. The protection stopped the bite and the frustrated animal turned away. Leimur wildly whipped her sword around and dropped two more gray men. An elephant ran directly at the panicked Queen. She froze for a second and ducked down as the elephant ran at her. She quickly flung her sword up into the animal's stomach as it passed. The elephant went down and landed on the Queen's leg. A hobbling Queen struggled to get back to her feet as gray men and women punched, grabbed and kicked the fallen warrior. The armor helped but Leimur couldn't get back up as even more gray men and women surrounded her. She looked over to see Sir Lanely being eaten by a jaguar. A leopard got hold of Blake Amhurst and dragged the soldier over to the other man-eating predators to tear into him. The wild screams of the gray men and all the dying beings created a chaotic atmosphere.

Suddenly a bellow that sounded like a thousand lions roaring all at once tore through the morning air. The gray men and women stopped hitting the Queen and backed away. Leimur saw the Owatowa and their animals continue to back up. The blood drifted down the slanting soil bank and turned the water red as it flowed into the river. Dead bodies and parts were piled on top of each other. Only a handful of her men were still alive. The Queen stood and spun around to a great surprise. A streak of tigers captured her eyes. Queen Leimur Leluc of Goldenfield saw death in both directions. She thought about diving in the river but the rocks would break her just up ahead. Options had run out. The Queen instantly thought about the time when General Rigby had warned her about traveling the river and she brushed his concerns smugly aside. She thought about Huber and how he would be forced onto the throne or killed by her uncle now. So many grand ideas evaporated in the jungle heat that day.

Leimur decided an honorable death for the Tiger Queen would be fitting. She slowly took off her armor, piece by piece, as the tigers and gray men continued a stand-off. She stripped off her clothes and walked toward the tigers.

Being eaten by tigers was the best option she saw. She moved closer as the tigers became even louder and got ready to strike. The Queen stood directly in front of the biggest beast. *Death is part of life.* She smiled and showed the wild animals her tiger-shaped teeth. All thirty tigers darted past her and her soldiers to pounce on the attackers. The gray men and their animal friends frantically tried to escape. The tigers ripped apart their remaining contingent in only a few minutes. Leimur realized the tigers were defending her. Captain Tetine approached the nude Queen with some of her clothes.

"I think it may be safe to get dressed, my Tiger Queen."

The Queen started to get her armor as the tigers ate the spoils of their hunt. She noticed only six of her soldiers remained.

Captain Tetine asked, "Where are we going from here? The Owatowa will attack again. We still need food. Will your tigers share one of those jaguars?"

As if the tiger understood, one went over and dragged the body of a jaguar in front of the Queen. Another tiger followed suit and laid another at her feet. The men hurriedly started a fire and began to feast after starving for a day. The Queen kept expecting the tigers to leave, but they never did. They waited for the crew to finish their meal. The tigers formed together and motioned for the Queen to follow as they slowly crept up the river bank. The Queen instinctively followed the tigers.

"Where are they taking us?" Herbe Lewes asked.

"I couldn't readily say. You can go whichever way you fancy. I'm going to follow my tigers," Leimur returned.

All six battered men followed the Queen and her tigers.

60
NO CHOICE—THE PRISONER

THE HOSTAGE OPENED his eyes. He saw complete darkness again. He smelled and tasted death in the thick, stale dungeon air. How long had it been? Days, weeks, or months? He had only seen light a few times since his expulsion to the dungeon. Lucid dreams and reality became indistinguishable in constant blackness. Without the sun, time became arbitrary in his mind. A day could have been only a few hours in the mind of the confused. Nobody had fed him in a long time but he couldn't figure out how long that had been. The prisoner became feral in the pitch-black cell. He let rats bite at him so he could catch the vermin and eviscerate them with the sharpened blade he had fashioned only by touch. The rats hadn't come around in a while and he starved. Water came more frequently but not enough to sustain life. The prisoner had taken to urinating into cupped hands to recycle the liquid although his shaky arms tended to spill some before it arrived at his mouth. The hungry man closed his eyes and thought he fell asleep.

The starving man opened his eyes and saw light. He moved toward the front of the cell that had a mesh made of thin interwoven wires, leaving only small openings. He saw a large man approach and shove a long stick through an opening and into the prisoner's stomach. He grabbed his gut in pain. It triggered a memory. He heard the man laugh with the screechy sound of an old lady. This had happened before. Every time he had seen light, the same person poked him with a stick and laughed as he hurried away.

Light betrayed him again and darkness persisted. He was starving. How long had it been since he had eaten? Days, weeks or months? He needed to eat something. He found his blade through the obscurity and contemplated the pain. He had to do it.

He pressed his pinkie finger firmly to the top of a large stone in the corner. He held the self-made knife above the bottom knuckle and dug in. He agonizingly worked it back and forth a few times before nearly passing out from the pain. The prisoner caught his racing heart and continued. He worked the crude knife over the finger about ten more times before the appendage came loose. The blade wasn't nearly as sharp as he thought and the enormous amount of pain could attest to that. He felt the blood run out but couldn't see how bad it was. He put tight pressure on the stump using his thigh and couldn't believe what he was about to do.

How did things get to this point? I used to be a warrior, a father, a husband. I won every battle except one. I guess that's all it takes.

It was difficult to think about those things when all he could concentrate on was food. Thoughts of survival dominated visions of the past. He raised the severed pinkie to his mouth and mentally prepared. He steeled himself to continue and bit in. He had to work really hard just to rip a little piece off. He tried to chew quickly and swallow but only gagged. He finally forced it down and used the knife to cut the rest up into manageable pieces while removing some bones. He still shook from hunger pains but at least he wouldn't die tonight. The prisoner never imagined he would have had to stoop to self-cannibalism. He somehow managed to keep the sustenance down and thought he fell asleep.

The man woke up. Had it been weeks, months or a year? The dim light appeared again outside the front of the cell. Like a trained animal he moved toward the light. He got jabbed in the stomach again. The prisoner remembered this cruel trick only too late. The perpetrator laughed again as he walked away. Just before complete twilight the voice smugly asked, "Not so tough now, are we?"

He recognized the voice even in his delirious state of mind. The prisoner knew it to be King Ali-Stanley Wamhoff.

61
TIME FOR ACTION—EDBURGH

EDBURGH ETBURN SAT in the tavern, drinking red wine. He occupied a table in the corner and had been there for about five hours. He reminisced about the past and his thoughts kept coming back to his brother Rollo, and wife Caroline. They were the people who provided the best thoughts. Ed believed that if Rollo hadn't died, Caroline would still be alive. Ed had started his heavy drinking after the death of his favorite brother. He looked at the blond woman he had mistaken several times for Caroline. Ed decided to go back to the house to relieve the other men after a few more mugs.

Ed had always been fond of the drink. He had gotten drunk at about the age of ten but it wasn't bad until Rollo died. After that, he continued to push it to the limit until now. Ed wished he had never killed Caroline. He blamed her at first but now realized it might have been because of how drunk he was that night. Ed only remembered scattered bits and pieces from the night that irreversibly changed his life. He didn't know what he had done until he saw his wife dead the next morning and started to put the pieces together. That was now over and he couldn't change what had already unraveled but his mind kept coming back to the same thoughts about Caroline.

In his red wine-induced inebriation, Edburgh made the decision he would kill Krys Colbert tonight. He already figured out an alibi. He would tell everyone Krys tried to escape and he was forced to kill him. No one would question that, he had thought, over and over again. Ed again found himself staring at the blond woman. The woman turned her back to avoid his creepy looks. Ed did this almost unknowingly every time he came to the tavern.

Ed chugged his last drink and staggered toward the door. He fumbled with it and had to readjust his focus on the task of the night. He lurched from left to right on the straight path to get back to the house. Once there, he told all the other men to go and have a good time. Every guard left and Edburgh walked into the room of his one-eyed prisoner. He had all but forgotten about Ryno Colbert in the other room. He may have starved as far as Ed knew unless the other men had been feeding him. He concentrated his efforts on Krys.

Ed pulled up a stool to sit near Krys Colbert. His nephew struggled in the chair and his already-skinny frame looked like that of a starving beggar now. He labored through every breath and visible wounds and scars covered his beaten body. Ed had already cut off two fingers and two toes. He then made Krys keep the severed appendages in his mouth for days at a time. He still had one in his mouth right now.

"My nephew, I let you into my castle, treated you like family and you betrayed me like a stranger." Edburgh raised his eyebrows. "What? Were you going to say something?" laughed Ed. "It's not your fault, really. I come from a long line of a proud family that will survive forever and you come from a family of usurpers. Your family will fall as fast as it rose. It's your traitor blood, is what it is, don't feel bad. Everyone in Waters Edge knew that your dead father wasn't fit for my sister," Edburgh slurred his words severely and picked a dirk up from the floor.

"Well, what have we here? This looks like it could be fun," he snickered. "I'm going to kill both of you and claim my Princess, the fairest in all the lands, Ali-Gare Wamhoff."

He sat up and thought about the good life that soon awaited Edburgh Etburn. He would be the envy of men around the world. Ed smiled in true happiness for the first time in a while and looked at Krys as he stood. He fell back onto the stool, dizzied, but sprang right back up.

"I should make this last so I can enjoy it too. Now, which arm do you prefer in battle?" Ed tapped his left arm and Krys shook his head. He tapped the prisoner's other arm and the prisoner shook his head again.

"Oh good, the court jester has arrived. I would have you tell jokes but something is in your mouth," he chuckled. "You know what? I believe I shall start with another finger. That toe needs company."

Edburgh moved in toward Krys' right hand. The prisoner spat out the toe, hitting Ed's hand just before he cut him.

"I suppose I should up the prize," Edburgh said as he stood up. "Why are you smiling?"

"Because I get to watch you die," Krys returned, looking behind Edburgh. The prisoner spat a wad of blood in Ed's face.

Ed wiped his eyes and turned around too late to see a figure lunge at his stomach. He doubled over in intense pain, clutching his bleeding belly. The man raised the dagger again and shoved it deep into Ed's back, down toward his heart. The hot, humid night couldn't help the freezing cold Edburgh Etburn. He thought about his brother, wife and even his father. Ed finally realized how shallow his life had become but it was too late and he started seeing visions of rainbows. He shook for several moments as he watched Ryno Colbert untie his brother. The one-eyed Colbert dove on Edburgh like a panther on its prey. The freed hostage ripped at the helpless, dying Edburgh, tearing at his face with the long fingernails on his remaining fingers. Krys' pent up aggression had been released and he smashed his fists into the face of the man who had disfigured him. Ed's perfect life that had seemed so close now dissolved in front of him as Krys found the dagger he had used to kill Caroline. Seven stabs to the heart area officially ended the life of Edburgh Etburn. His body now looked worse than the man he had intended to kill. Ryno pulled his incensed brother away. The mangled body of Edburgh Etburn lay on the floor as the nude, blood-spattered Colbert boys escaped out the backdoor.

RUSSELL AWOKE ALONE in darkness. He could smell Gamelda but he didn't see her around his meager accommodations at the workshop. He put on clothes and followed his nose. The sweet smell of his lover led him up to the office as the scent grew stronger by the step. *She smells like a princess ought to smell.*

She emitted a flowery essence swirled with vanilla. It always put a smile on Russell's face when he caught wind of Gamelda. She still wouldn't budge from her stance about being a free woman. Russell pressed on, hoping the trip to the Pearl Islands would change her mind. He knocked once and opened the door with a smile on his face.

He saw Dragon-Eyes drop a little bottle that cracked on the floor, causing white dust to flow upward.

"NO, NO, NO," the little man screamed, covering his eyes.

"Don't worry, old friend, we're in the process of making more," a calm Gamelda stated.

A frantic Dragon-Eyes said, "I know that, but this may now delay the trip."

"What is that powder?" Russell inquired.

"You might as well tell him," Gamelda said to Dragon-Eyes.

"I will naturally assume you have never heard of Fuji Dust." Russell shook his head, and the wizard continued, "It's a mixture of crushed powders that helps a person remain young. It's the real secret behind how Gamelda and I stay so young," he said with a playful smile.

"Wait, what? How old are you, Gamelda?" Russell quickly asked.

"Oh, you really don't want to know. I feel it might change your feelings toward me," she said.

"Nothing in this world could change the way I feel about you," Russell promised.

"Even if I said the number six hundred thirty seven?"

"I'm the young one," japed the Imp.

"That's a bit older than I expected but it still changes nothing. You can use all the, what is it, funer dust?" Russell fumbled. "Fuji Dust. Just be sure never to get any in your eyes," the Imp corrected and warned. "Why is it called Fuji Dust?" Russell wondered.

"Because the man who developed the exact blend lived east of Gama Traka and his name was Fuji. Not nearly as exciting as one may expect," Dragon-Eyes stated.

"Not exactly, no," Russell agreed.

"My friend, Kazu, will tell you that he came up with the blend and Fuji stole it from him. If we should ever meet Kazu, just agree with him that he came up with the mix first. It will save us a long argument," Dragon-Eyes told him.

"Alright, I am leaving for my morning chores if you will excuse me," Russell said as he left the workshop and went on his early morning search for kindling. He could only think about one thing as he mindlessly continued on his way.

Six hundred and thirty seven years old. And I thought the Duchess Ali-Pari was old.

Russell heard a cackle and looked up to see the old witch laughing. "Why, haven't they claimed your soul yet? That is a surprise. I won't worry. Soon enough the worms will have a meal to enjoy. Ha, ha, ha, ha," the small woman chuckled. Russell remembered Dragon-Eyes had told stories of the evil Queen of Heldoor and this woman reminded him of the tales.

Russell stood tall and stared down at her. She wore the usual black gown and her silver hair waved in the slight breeze that cut through the bright summer day. The cackling witch held a small axe and pointed her bony finger at him.

The young slave girl came up and tapped the old hag from behind. The woman spun around and swatted the little girl in the face with the flat end of the axe. It drew immediate blood and the little girl sprawled out on her back. "I told you never to sneak up on me. This is your fault," she yelled.

"What's the matter with you?" Russell screamed.

"I have much of the same reserved for you, young naïve one," she threatened.

Unafraid, Russell marched toward the old lady. He heard a loud boom of thunder as large drops of rain started to fall. He looked up to see dark skies rapidly obscuring the brightness. He focused back on the old lady and heard her mumbling something. She extended her hands out in front of her face and lightning shot from her fingers to strike Russell in the chest. The impact lifted him off his feet and threw him about ten feet back.

The old lady laughed and screeched, "The demons' time has come. The plan will soon take action and is bigger than any human can imagine. They will rule Donegal in the end. Ha, ha, ha."

Russell sat up, dazed, and looked into the woods to his right to see friendly-looking ghostly figures. He recognized Carabelle and probably could have guessed the names of a few more angelic spirits that he could see in the brush. His scrambled head couldn't put the necessary words together to borrow the spirits' powers. They were all waiting to assist the young man, eager to help. The weakened Russell staggered to his feet only to have the witch use borrowed strength to throw him onto his back again. He tried to remember any of the spirits' words to defend himself but his mind was still warped from the pain. The rest of his body went numb.

The old lady yelled, "When you meet your Gods, tell them the Plades are coming to conquer..."

The old witch suddenly fell quiet, turned to a figure of black liquid and pooled on the dirt path before retreating downward into the earth. Her disappearance revealed the young slave girl behind her with the axe buried in the ground after the girl's mightiest swing. She had the courage to slay her demon master and save Russell's life. Despite the raging pain, he ran over and picked up the slender girl. He hugged her and looked at the gash above her right eye to see how bad it was. Russell carried her back to the workshop as fast as he could. The driving rain cleared up on the way back even as Russell's pain still throbbed. He held the girl tight and came to the front door. Russell went to the workshop and set the girl on a table.

"HURING," he called. Huring the Healer came over and looked at the little girl's laceration. "Leave her to me. I will tend to her wound," the healer instructed.

"I'll be right back," Russell told the girl, not knowing if she could understand him. He had to pry her hands from his leg before he ran up to the office and knocked hard. This time he waited. "Enter."

He recognized Gamelda's voice and opened the door. He told Gamelda and Dragon-Eyes what had happened.

"The demons are looking for him already. We must leave now. They know our location, we cannot stand still," Dragon-Eyes disappointedly said.

"Why me?" asked Russell. "They must see you as a threat. This is bigger than we imagined if the spirits were there to help you too," Gamelda said with concern.

"We have another person to bring," Russell told them. "Who?" Dragon-Eyes queried. "The young slave of the old woman. She saved my life and killed the old hag with the very axe the woman used to cut her forehead," Russell stated.

"How old is she?" Dragon-Eyes demanded. Russell responded, "I don't know, maybe eight?"

"No, no, no, no, no. There isn't any room for an eight-year-old girl on our journey," the Imp contended.

"She can stay here with us," offered Gamelda. "I will keep track of her for you."

Russell's heart sank and he spoke through a lump in his throat, "What do you mean you will be staying here?"

She turned to Dragon-Eyes, "Will you give us a few moments, please?"

"Of course, I will gather my belongings and then we must leave," said the wizard as he walked to the door.

"Before you leave, take this." She handed Dragon-Eyes a full bottle of Fuji Dust.

"I cannot possibly take all of this. It's all we have," the Imp said.

"The girls are making more that will be finished before I need it. You will need this for your great adventure. You can't get old if you are going to save the world," Gamelda conveyed.

"I thank you greatly," the Imp said as he took the small vial, poured the powder into his ornate carrying case and pulled the silk cord to close the wooden face. He smiled and left them alone.

She grabbed Russell's hands and pulled him close, "I told you not to fall in love. I told you many times."

"I tried to fight it, I really did." *She smells like a princess ought to smell.*

She backed up a step and spoke, "What have I told you? There is no such thing as real love. We have a God of sacrifice and war but not love. That should tell you something right there. If the Gods can't even have love, why should we chase it?"

"That doesn't prove love doesn't exist," he argued.

"I've witnessed love stomped by the feet of the Gods so many times in my many years," she playfully smiled at the young man and continued, "It is mostly pain, lightly sprinkled with moments of pleasure. And it's always in that order, my sweet soul. People take stupid chances for those they love and the Gods forgive them not for these noble deeds. You need to learn to love women less and you will live longer. If I went with you it would be out of love and not the best decision for Gamelda. Love your friends but don't fall in love, my sweet Russell. I made a promise to stay with my girls here as you have made a promise to go with Dragon-Eyes. We never made any promises to each other. I will chase that Pearl no longer. Our friend will until his last day, though. Take care of the little man. I have a soft spot for him. And as for you," she moved in on Russell and seized his lips.

They passionately kissed for what could be the last time, before breaking apart.

Her lips taste like what princess' lips should taste like. A bouquet of flowers dancing in a field of vanilla.

Russell Seabrook's mental anguish now matched his physical pain. He hobbled downstairs, gathered his belongings from his room and went to say farewell to the girls. Huring dealt with his injuries and gave him some medicine for the long journey ahead. He limped around and hugged the girls before going up to the slave girl.

"You are going to stay here until we return," he told her.

The girl began to cry and latched onto Russell with all her strength. Gamelda came over, "Everything will be fine, sweet girl."

She tried to pull the skinny girl away from Russell but couldn't. Russell looked at Gamelda and she just smiled.

"Good luck trying to leave her. She has taken a quick shine to you," Gamelda stated.

Dragon-Eyes came up with bags packed, "Everything taken care of? Are we ready now?"

Russell looked at the girl, then looked at Dragon-Eyes and said, "Yes, both of us are ready," as he grabbed the girl's hand.

63

CHANCE MEETING—OLLOR

OLLOR SHOVED THE knife into the bottom of the sea trout's belly and ran it up to the neck. He set the knife down, secured either side of the opening and in one swift motion flung the guts into a metal bucket. The unforgiving sun attacked Ollor and he spotted fish scales being cooked into his arm. He ran over to the water, saturated the scales and rubbed them off with his fingernails. If he let the scales dry, they ripped his skin when he tried to scrape them off. He had become quick to notice the scales by now to avoid the pain. He scraped all the scales off knowing it would happen many more times.

Ollor had cut his hair short and shed the beard and mustache. He had shaved his head bald the first time but the sun burned his head severely. The summers in Gama Traka were legendary for the heat. He wore pants he had cut off above the knee, a rope belt and nothing else. He envied the kids for being in the cooler underground school.

Ollor still had to get used to his simple lifestyle. He worked every day from sunrise until the last boat came in. He went to see the kids and to the local tavern but most nights Ollor went back to his hut and thought about the kids. He wondered what else he had to do for redemption. *Have I cleansed my soul enough? Does this good outweigh all the bad? Do I need to stay with the children any longer?*

As the end of the day neared, Ollor saw the last ship coming in through the falling night. The vessel blocked his view of the night sky but as it came closer, a half-moon appeared. He could visit the children tonight. Temptation had been hounding Ollor for the past few weeks. The urge to drink came around again and Ollor knew bad things usually happened when he got drunk.

He finished up and went over to the school. This time he got to see his kids and they stood in the library and talked. He noticed how big both of them had grown recently and remembered when he could hold each of them in one hand.

"What did you learn today?" Ollor asked. "We learned about how Rockarius defeated the coldomores," Muriel answered. "And how was that?" Ollor probed. "At first he didn't have the numbers or a battle plan but he had the determination. When others saw this, his army grew and men gave up everything to join him. They say several kings vacated their thrones to help Rockarius. He didn't have money to pay an army but the men came nonetheless. It helped that he had the dragons on his side too. Our teacher said that as much as men want to fight with each other, we will always band together when faced with destruction."

Ollor couldn't believe his ears. His six-year-old sounded like a grown woman. He kept staring intently at the children and wanting to be a bigger part of their lives. He couldn't argue with the training and education the children were receiving and knew it was best for them.

Muriel finished her story and he turned to Sunny, "What about you?"

"We learned how to defeat the battle inside ourselves during combat. That you have to be completely focused or you will die. Turn fear to rage. Harness rage to courage. Hatu told us that we have to defeat our own fear before we can defeat an enemy. He said a certain amount of fear is understandable but too much can be crippling. He showed us a giant scar on his belly that he got when he carelessly moved in battle. He said his wife had been killed just before and his thoughts remained with her until the sword hit him," Sunny told him through his lisp.

These kids know more than I do. I cannot believe how they are evolving into Learned Warriors. I need to tell them of their past, it's only fair. Now is the time.

A kettle-sounding whistle bounced around the underground library. The two kids ran off without a word to Ollor. He looked around and found Kazu.

"What is going on here?" Ollor demanded. Kazu said, "Pain tolerance. If they are late, there is extra reinforcement. If you would show yourself out, I will see you on the next moon."

Ollor got angry again. Twice now he had tried to tell the children, only to be blocked by the school. He went to the tavern and sat in his normal seat. Tonight, Ollor ordered a pitcher of ale from the wine wench.

"No need," sounded the voice of a man with a pitcher in hand. He sat across from Ollor and filled a tankard the wine wench set on the table. The man with black shaggy hair and long beard had silvery eyes and a strange smile. "Captain Wallace. Who are you?"

"Ollor. Thank you," he raised his tankard and Wallace met it with his. The two men took a healthy swig as Ollor sized this man up. Something struck suspicion in Ollor who noticed the man wearing long pants and sleeves to the wrist. Ollor sweat through his soul in only short pants and this man barely leaked fully covered.

"What's your trade?" Ollor asked. "Boat captain. I just secured a deal with one of the merchants down at the docks. I'll be 'round these parts for a little while. What do you do, friend?"

"I'm a fish gutter. And you're not properly dressed for this part of the world," Ollor stated.

"Looks like I gotta adjust my clothes. Where you from?" the captain asked.

"Kingdom of Donegal."

"World isn't as big as we may think. So am I. What part?" Captain Wallace questioned.

"Waters Edge," Ollor uttered. The captain quickly responded, "Bear Gate in Burkeville. I couldn't stand those nasty Goldenfield marauders always coming over the borderlines to loot and pillage. I seen our little city torn apart too many times. I lost too many family members to continue there so I took to the waters. When you're on the high seas, nothing can bother you."

"Except pirateers and tempests," Ollor countered.

"Ah, a good captain can navigate around both," the man smiled.

Ollor had finished two pitchers before realizing it. He hadn't been drunk in more than ten years because of the kids. He took the parental responsibility to heart but it appeared the children wouldn't need him as much anymore. Maybe the Gods only needed him to get the kids to the school, he had been thinking recently.

"Here's a doozy. A little bit back I been lost at sea for over a year and you will never believe where I washed up," the captain winked. "Bear Gate," joked Ollor.

"Not quite. A little place called Venom Island. Have you heard of it?"

"Of course, every boy from Donegal has heard the stories of Rockarius pushing the remaining few of Damian Doome's forces back to that island. They say he's been recovering on the island ever since," Ollor said.

"What would you say if I told ya I met the dirty demon? " The captain raised his eyebrows and piqued Ollor's interest. "Still quite broken after all these years. It's been well spoken the demons are craven and, sure enough, Damian ran from me when he saw me. I scoured the entire island for food but only salamanders and snakes would do. When we went back to the ship we found a cave close by. I went over to see about one hundred demons and the leader, Damian Doome. Realizing he was cornered, he came and talked to me," he took a big drink.

"What did he have to say for himself?" Ollor couldn't figure out if he could believe this man he had just met.

The captain continued, "He tried to build a great army to attack the humans again but a plague ran through a few years ago and wiped most of the demons out. He said it will be at least three hundred years before he could rebuild to even present a threat to the humans. He looked ready for death, almost welcomin' it."

The wizard told a very different story than this.

Ollor still maintained his wits during the fog caused from all the ale. "You are certain it was Damian Doome?"

"Positive," replied the captain.

"Green with a long tail?" Ollor asked. "Yes."

"Three pointed, purple ears on top of his head?" "Yes." the captain responded.

"Red pupils?" "If that means his damn eyes then yes, yes and yes. I know who he was and we have nothing to fear, at least concernin' Damian that is. Tell everyone ya know," the captain confirmed.

Why is he referring to this demon by his first name?

"So it may seem," Ollor agreed.

"Listen, if you want to get out of the glorious fish guttin' life, I'll be around. I always need men on the boat. I'm sure I can pay better than those crooks down at the fisherman's wharf," Captain Wallace offered.

"I shall let you know, my friend," Ollor slurred.

64

A CHANGE OF PLANS—QUEEN EMILIA

"WHY WOULD HE change the plan now?" the Queen demanded. "Ali-Ster said someone with devious intentions is on to our plan and he is being watched closely. He said we must do this quickly and meet him at the ports. We have to leave this place for a while," Ali-Samuel whispered.

The pair walked quickly from Emilia's quarters and arrived near Elisa's room. "Stay over here, I'll be brief," Ali-Samuel instructed.

The Queen found herself by a window. A cool breeze came in an open airway but she felt a fire raging inside. Emilia had slept terribly last night and her body was already exhausted. She had listened to her lover snoring all night and wondered how he could sleep so well under the circumstances. She watched Ali-Samuel turn the corner toward the room as her heart raced. This was her last chance to run back to the King and stay safe. She had always felt secure in the castle under the King's protection.

Where are we going? Why would Ali-Ster change the plan? I bet Tersen found out, it must be him. If we get caught it's all our lives. I could still run back to Ali-Stanley and he would believe me. The intense debate swung from side to side in her head before she realized her love for Ali-Samuel would force her heart to follow him anywhere. The plan was in motion and the Queen convinced herself it was too late to back out now.

"Come here," he called her over to Elisa's room. Ali-Samuel took a small flat piece of parchment from his inside pocket. The square object was about a thumb nail in size and had a black 'X' on it. He whispered, "I have a strange feeling about all this. I'm going to place a marker on her door to make sure she doesn't leave." Ali-Samuel stood high to get the marker to rest on top of the door. "If this is on the ground when we return, that means we've been set up and we may already be dead." He pushed the Queen in the back and dropped something but didn't stop to pick it up.

"Alright, quickly, let's get back to your quarters," Ali-Samuel stressed in a serious tone that scared the Queen. He passed her and she followed the quick pace he set. Ali-Samuel opened her door and let Emilia in.

"Here's the situation. Ali-Ster wants us to kill the King and then meet him at the Boar Stone Harbor in Greenville. We can only take what is on our backs so only the important items should come with you."

"What are we doing? Where are we going?" she asked.

"Not to fret, sweet one," he kissed the Queen softly on her forehead and gave her a quick hug while gazing into her pale green eyes. "I have a plan already in place to ensure your safety. You are my top priority."

Ali-Samuel gave her a peck on the lips and moved away. He pulled something from behind her bed and handed it to the Queen. "These are more practical clothes that will serve you better on our journey."

He handed the Queen of Donegal a pair of small trousers and a simple button down long-sleeved shirt. They looked suited for a boy but the Queen knew they would have to conceal their true identities.

"I had the Lonely Widows make these for you as a costume for an upcoming ball but they will be perfect for our purpose now. Use any undergarments of your choice and a grab purse or pouch for small valuables and gold. We will need to pay our way out of Donegal," he told the Queen.

The Queen gathered some jewelry and coins. She stuffed them into a leather purse and pulled the draw string tight. She balled up the clothes into her other hand to change after they left the castle. Nervousness shot through the Queen because she would look suspicious holding clothes and a purse. She thought Ali-Samuel would be able to talk their way out of any trouble and calmed down a bit.

When the Queen was ready, she saw Ali-Samuel move a small carpet to expose a door in the floor that led to the tunnels. Every castle in Donegal had an underground network of tunnels in case of extreme evacuation or emergency. Most castle owners deluded themselves and thought their tunnel systems were a secret known only to the close circle of high nobles inside the castle. Ali-Samuel knew exactly where to go as Sir Penrose Ellsworth had given him a guided tour only days ago. The Queen found a little carrying case with a long shoulder strap and stuffed her new clothes into it. Ali-Samuel grabbed a torch and jumped in to the dark hole. He then helped the Queen lower herself in. She held her long, loose-fitting dress around the knees and twisted it firm to her body with one hand as they embarked on their journey through the tunnels.

The Queen felt the excitement of the adventure immediately as her heart began to pound with trepidation. She had wanted exhilaration but wondered if this might be too much to handle as she started to shake. Her palms moistened with sweat and her trembling right hand shook the bunched up dress, with the resultant rustle echoing through the tunnel. The noise prompted two stern looks from Ali-Samuel. The Queen couldn't stop shaking but didn't want to let the loose black dress sweep the filthy floor. Ali-Samuel grabbed the Queen's hand and they came to a stop. He pointed up with his finger.

She whispered ever so gently, "Are you certain of this? It's all our lives if we're wrong."

Ali-Samuel scrunched his eyes and set his torch down to the side. The Queen took the look as a sign not to question him. He pushed up on the secret door above and caught some resistance. With a flat palm he pushed up a few more times and the door popped open. Ali-Samuel went first and helped Emilia up. She saw a small table knocked over that had covered the secret door.

Her heartbeat quickened to a pace she previously thought unthinkable and she couldn't swallow. Her mouth felt dryer than a Gama Trakan dessert. She tightly squeezed the purse with both hands in fear while she slowly followed Ali-Samuel toward the bed. He whispered, "He couldn't even make it into bed," Ali-Samuel pulled a dagger from its scabbard and moved in closer. He stopped suddenly and the Queen moved up to his side. She saw her husband of eighteen years.

He lay face down in what used to be his white night robe. The robe now showed shiny, dark crimson through the flickering candlelight. Pools of blood had already collected on the uneven floor around Ali-Stanley Wamhoff. A closer inspection revealed numerous stab wounds to the back and neck, without the Queen even seeing the other side of the body.

The King ruled and lived in these quarters for thirty years. I remember the day our eyes locked in the woods of Arigold. Who did this?

She started feeling sympathy for the man Ali-Samuel had convinced her to hate. However, her thoughts quickly shifted to her unseen child whom her late husband had deemed fit to cast away and the well of tears in her eyes dried up.

"Who could have done this?" she asked.

"I know not. I do know something is awry and we had better get to the river, fast," Ali-Samuel stated and grabbed her hand to lead her back into the tunnel. She turned and took one last look at the mess of a man who had brought her to this castle. Ali-Samuel picked up the torch after they dropped back into the maze, closed the door overhead and they were off. She dwelled on the matter for only a heartbeat because the following minutes were a whirlwind that the over-stimulated Queen couldn't process. They arrived outside the south wall of the castle through a secret door and saw two horses tied to a post about twelve feet ahead. Sir Oliver of the King's Guard approached on horseback. The Queen worried this would be where the adventure stopped, but the knight cordially said hello and went on his way.

They jumped on the horses and rode off, with the Queen following Ali-Samuel. He quickly ducked a small tree branch that whipped the Queen on her left cheek. She shifted the reins to one hand and checked for blood with the other. She saw a red stain on her hand in the falling dusk and became more alert. A huge tree branch emerged from the forest gloom and she crouched instinctively to avoid the wooden impediment. Her heart pulsated in her chest and the rest of her body did the same. She couldn't remember the last time she had bled while safe in the castle but also hadn't got this rush of emotion even from the drugs. Ali-Samuel and this new adventure were her drugs now. She hadn't even thought about doing them with Sir Anderley since she had started her romance with Ali-Samuel.

The Queen began to panic as the blood trickled down her cheek and tickled her chin. *Is this the right choice? Is it too late to go back? I had no worries in the castle. Now I haven't any idea of what can happen. How did Ali-Samuel make me believe that everything was so bad?*

The two riders arrived at the Royal River. She could hear the rushing tide that always picked up in summer. When they got near the bank, Ali-Samuel stopped and got off. The Queen did the same and noticed her faithful guard, holding a rope to their getaway vessel.

"My Queen and good Sir, your ship awaits," Sir Ulee said as the Queen took the rope and held the canoe. Ali-Samuel handed the guard the reins to their horses.

"Thank you, you will be remembered for your service," Ali-Samuel said as he leaned in toward Ulee. The tall guard began making gagging sounds and shook wildly as he fought to get away from Ali-Samuel. "Remembered for your sacrifice." Ali-Samuel removed the knife from Ulee's stomach. The horses bolted and her guard fell to the ground before Ali-Samuel came over to the canoe.

The Queen's excitement and anticipation shifted to terror. "Why did you do that?" the teary eyed Emilia asked.

He ignored her and got into the canoe. He washed the blood from the knife in the river. "I asked you a question," the Queen said as she got into the canoe. They started to drift downstream as Ali-Samuel grabbed the long double-sided oar. "I believe I asked you a question?" she raised her voice.

He snapped at her in a low but aggressive voice, "I had to. I respect your affection for him but you have never involved yourself in affairs such as these. In contrast, my entire life has revolved around these types of matters. You cannot leave loose ends in a plan that could cause death. Now keep quiet before we swallow arrows."

After a minute she persisted, "Sir Ulee was a noble guard, he wouldn't have said anything."

"Everyone is faithful until you torture them enough. Some have higher pain thresholds and you may have to get creative with them, but they all crack. Have you ever been tortured, my Queen?" he asked.

"I cannot say that I have," she answered.

He continued in an annoyed tone, "Men will say whatever you want to hear if you torture them enough. If the torturer wants to hear that you and I killed the King, he will eventually hear it. I've seen it happen all the time. Men will admit to killing someone they have never even met. When death or lying are the only choices, only the honorable few will meet their Gods with a clear conscience. You must rid yourself of this soft heart and realize if we come back to rule this kingdom, much more blood must spill. Sometimes it will be the blood of people we care about like Sir Ulee. Other times it will be the blood of the enemy and you must have no mercy on them. My thoughts and actions may seem drastic but everything I do is for you. Take notice that you are on this canoe, not wallowing in your bed. I could have abandoned you but I...I love you," he uttered.

"My love for you is fierce," she responded.

The former Queen Emilia Burke Wamhoff believed this to be the best decision. Her worries and nervousness fluttered away as she stared at crisp moonlight bouncing off the river ripples. Her new found confidence fed off the arrogant man she loved. It had been over fifteen years since the King had told her he loved her. The Queen removed her dress and put on clothes more suitable for a great adventure.

65

PENROSE

PENROSE ELLSWORTH LEFT the castle and walked into near darkness with blood on his hands. Since returning from Waters Edge, he had changed drastically. The voices wouldn't allow him to sleep and he often screamed back at them. He couldn't concentrate on anything other than stopping the blood-lusting voices. He figured out his life was meaningless. He protected a cruel King who caused nothing but hard times and human torture. He served a representative of the Gods who didn't even practice his preaching. His prayers to the Gods had fallen upon deaf ears and his daily pleas were ignored. Penrose made his way blindly toward the House of Eternal Light.

"Are you alright, Sir Penrose?" one of the guards at the entrance asked.

"Fine, just a small accident. I need to speak to the Father."

The two men stepped aside and Penrose entered the building. He could feel the sin floating through the hot, stale air. Penrose headed straight for Father Enroy's chambers.

"Sir Penrose, are you injured?" the Father's guard asked, looking at his bloodied hands. "I'm quite alright, thank you," Penrose responded.

The man knocked for Penrose. Blood was something the guards routinely saw upon devout practitioners who purged the demonic liquid from their bodies, so Penrose didn't raise suspicion. The Father answered the door and concern flashed over his face, "My son, what has happened?"

He grabbed Penrose's hands and saw slash marks on both of the young man's wrists. "Father, I will be fine. I need your counsel," Penrose said in a demanding tone.

"Yes, yes, of course. *Fletcher*."

"Yes, father," the guard quickly responded. "Take the rest of the evening to your own devices. I shall be well protected by Sir Penrose," he replied as Penrose came in and the Father wiped the blood from his hands.

"Father, I have been questioning whether I can reach the heavens given my questionable deeds on earth," Penrose finally shared his concern. Just saying it out loud caused Penrose to feel like half the world had been lifted from his shoulders.

"Sir Penrose Ellsworth of the King's Guard. The King is the first man under the Gods and I am the second. You are among the most honorable men in the entire realm. You hold the highest duty a knight may be tasked and carry it out in the divine name of our Gods," Father Enroy complimented him.

"I must stop you there, Father. It's what you just said that is the problem. I'm not exactly performing any work that would be approved by the Gods. When I heard the songs of the King's Castle and the brave men who guarded it, everything sounded so honorable and chivalrous. The poets, they used pretty words that caused me to see a myth, a mirage. When the King came to Lightview, the scene was so grandiose. It all seemed like a dream and I wanted nothing more than to be a small part of it. All the stories I had heard growing up didn't do justice to the real-life production. It was simply breath-taking to see but it never exposed the seedy underbelly to follow," Penrose emotionally uttered.

"My son..." the Father started.

"You'd be wise to let me to finish, Father," Penrose announced with a mad look on his face, and the Father backed off. "Within the first fortnight I discovered how dirty ruling a kingdom could be. Our King ordered men, women and children to be killed like he was choosing pieces of meat at a feast. The deaths didn't seem to bother him because he never saw the gruesome outcomes. He asked men to do things he could or would never do himself. He recently asked us to rip an unborn child from inside a defenseless woman and return it to him. A sight he knew he could never lay eyes on or he would become ill. That was my Godly business I had to tend to in Elkridge. He is a strange man, our King. He orders death regularly and spends most of his time with dead relatives but the sight of a man dying or fresh blood irks him. I've seen more than a lifetime of horrors with these weary eyes. The atrocities carried out in the name of King Ali-Stanley have been branded into my memory and haunt me every moment of every waking day. You couldn't imagine the murderous visions I've witnessed in only twenty years and you really wouldn't want to, no decent person would. I've carried out orders at the King's behest that will forever reserve a spot for me with the demons and perhaps Travibero himself. Father, have you ever seen a small child killed in front of his mother, an unarmed man slain by Godly knights?" Penrose posed to the fidgeting Father Enroy.

The High Priest became extremely uncomfortable and Penrose noticed him perspiring heavily through his purple robes. The knight stared in great disgust at the gaudy crown Father Enroy wore. Penrose continued, "Honor be cast asunder when you see sworn men rape and murder in the name of the King and the Gods. The only difference is when you wear this," he said and pointed to his King's Guard pin. The voiced in his head were screaming for blood but somehow he continued, "Where was I? Ah, law-breaking becomes forgotten, simply washed away. We are sworn to protect those who cannot protect themselves, all of the Gods' creatures, big and small. Instead, we terrorize the weak for monetary gain that we are strictly forbidden to keep so we have no leverage in times of aggression."

Penrose began to pant like a thoroughbred, primed to race. He tried to calm down for a moment and looked at the frightened expression on the Father's face. The voices demanded more blood and they wanted it now, but he fought them off and pressed on, "When I came to Falconhurst I had a penchant for chivalry that the castle knights quickly cured me of. I found myself to be a personal assassin of the King, not protector of the realm and all of its wonderful creatures. Falconhurst is so rotten it doesn't even smell good. I never heard about that in all the songs and poems, and I can find many words that rhyme with shit."

The old man wanted to interject but the crazy look on Penrose warned the Father to participate with only his ears and eyes.

"What am I doing it for, Father? The Gods have turned their backs on me."

"Now Penrose, just because we don't get everything we ask of the Gods, it doesn't mean they don't love us," he said encouragingly.

"Didn't you just hear my words? Has that crown deafened your ears? Do you think I only innocently witnessed these atrocities and didn't have to commit them myself? Throw aside the naivety, it only insults us both. Look at you with that gluttonous gut. You've used me just like the King has. You know all too well I have no chance to reach the heavens."

"That is positively not true. If you denounce these actions, I can wash the sins away and you can reach the heavens with a clean soul for your day of judgment," the Father promised.

"Just like that." Penrose blew into his open palm. "I can stain my filthy soul for years and years and suddenly after a few words from our Father, everything's forgotten. The man who swims with nude boys will personally talk to the Gods and everything will be fine," he mocked the Father and continued in a serious tone, "I am not a fool like the other citizens who stuff your collection boxes and think salvation can be bought or pleaded for. We are our actions; no more, no less. In life and in death, we are who we are. Judgment day will ultimately arrive. A few words cannot change what has already been done. And I can denounce the sins all I like but our King will remain to give me orders. I have to take these orders or it is my head," Penrose started fighting back tears. Talking about it made Penrose really see how crazy a life he had lived. Delivering death and destruction sanctioned by the King had taken its toll.

"Perhaps I can talk to our King and push for more leniency in these matters," the Father said.

Thunder rang inside Penrose's skull. The voices intensified, trying to shout through the thunder.

How can there be thunder? There wasn't a cloud in the sky when I entered. Why am I always hearing thunder?

"It won't work, Father. You people have no idea. You don't know that someone could mildly anger the King and it's as simple as him saying, 'I don't want him at the next party'. Everyone thinks an ordered death is well debated and voted upon by many lords before the King makes a verdict. It could be a simple nod and men or women die. It certainly isn't the grand production of armored knights proudly riding up the Royal Road, rounding up the outlaws. It is more likely to be a village torched at night in a sneak attack to send a message to pay taxes on time. How can people pay back taxes when their entire village is burned down? He uses the lives of our Gods' creatures to send messages, Father. Innocent people are killed every day in this realm as devices of threat to discourage those debating action against the King. It's a dirty, backstabbing realm and the justice is carried out in the same manner. Our King isn't much for arresting men. His paranoid attitude makes him certain they will escape and kill him, we all think. This life isn't anything like I read in the stories or heard in the songs. It isn't anything like my brother Anderley said it would be. He must have known, but he dragged me into this grime. Why wouldn't my own brother tell me, Father? My own brother even lied to me. This life is a living nightmare that demonstrates the kill or die attitude. People who may pose a threat stand in great danger, usually a lot more than they ever know. And the innocent commoners are used as geese to play the games of the noble born foxes..." he stopped. Thunder rang out again in his battered head. Penrose had tried to cut his wrists earlier to see if the Gods wanted him, but it had seemed that even they rejected him. The thunder was driving him mad while his eyes twitched uncontrollably.

The small, plump father walked over to the corner of the room. A long beam shaped like a round log rocked back and forth like an ocean ship with a small device in the very center that held the log. It evenly distributed the weight back and forth without the log falling off. It intrigued Penrose. Father Enroy picked it up and stood it against the corner of the room in an upright position and the sound stopped. Penrose Ellsworth's blood felt like it had been boiled in a cauldron as he lost all control and exploded, "What is that?" "The thinkers call it a thunder device. They make it so perfectly balanced and something inside causes the thunder to stir as it moves back and forth. I am not certain precisely how it works but it is surely aided by the Gods," the Father explained.

This "device" has been driving me mad. I cannot sleep anymore because of these damned thunder sounds. And this little weasel has driven me mad.

A sequence of memories flashed in Penrose's mind from childhood until the present day. He thought about how simple things had been back in Lightview. He wondered again why his brother had lied about the King's Guard. The voices screamed for death even louder now. Penrose decided to quiet them as he purposefully closed in on the Father, "You very well may see me in the hells, Father, but you will get there first."

Penrose gripped the fleeing holy man who screamed for his guard, and easily flung him to the ground. He jumped on top, got hold of the Father's neck and squeezed with both hands. Despite the lost strength from the slashed wrists and lack of sleep, he pressed sharply with both thumbs to apply pressure to the windpipe. The old man was weak and barely put up a fight. He tried to scream for his guard again but he had already sent him away. Penrose had never killed a man with only his bare hands and he looked at the Father's face turning from the brightest red to a sickly dark bluish purple. Father Enroy shook under the chokehold but couldn't break Penrose's grip. The Father gasped for a breath of air but it wouldn't come and the holy man's head fell back as the lopsided struggle came to a close. Penrose stared at his hands, then looked up and started crying, "Is this enough? Are you happy now? You called for his life many times and I finally delivered. Now you can stop. Please stop."

Penrose left the Father in his chambers and ran to the front altar. He looked at all the sculptures of the Gods around the altar and screamed, "Are you happy now? Is this what you wanted? I did what you told me again. How many more must I kill?"

Nothing made sense anymore. Penrose Ellsworth began to remove his clothes and repeatedly shouted at the statues, "I am a monster. You have turned me into a monster. Are you happy now? I am a monster. I must get rid of the monster inside. You forced me to do this."

Penrose stood naked on the altar and continued to shout at the Gods.

66
ELISA

SHE SHUT THE door and came back into her room. "You can come out now," Elisa said.

Anderley Ellsworth crawled out from behind her bed and warned, "I told you he is a snake. He asks a woman to do his killing for him. Ali-Ster would have never said that. You should go talk to Ali-Ster, I am sure Ali-Samuel is lying."

"I can't kill the King. I can barely kill a fly. I told him I would but I really don't think I can," she stated in a panicked voice.

"I'll do it. Just come along so you can provide the details and I will do it for you. I am a real knight," Anderley bragged.

She ran over and hugged him, "Thank you, thank you so much. You are a true knight."

"It's no trouble. I may take some pleasure in disposing of the man who has caused me mostly anguish with the King's Guard," Anderley revealed.

"When the castle bells ring nine, that's the signal," Elisa informed Anderley.

"I still think he is lying and you should talk to Ali-Ster," Anderley advised.

"I cannot talk to him or several people could die. Do you know these underground tunnels? That is the only place I am to go and I can't remember the directions Ali-Samuel just gave."

"Why are you afraid of him?" Elisa immediately answered, "I could get many people killed if I act suspicious and that's a chance I'm unwilling to take."

"Don't forget me when this is all done. I have a feeling after your plan is realized, you will kick me aside like the Queen," Anderley softly said.

"I will never forget you," she said looking down into his eyes. "You've not only provided me protection but we have become good friends," Elisa reassured the sensitive knight. She was already tired because she hadn't slept the previous night and hoped Anderley wouldn't get scared now. She needed him to be the fierce warrior everyone had told her about, not the lovesick fool.

They sat in silence for a while and Elisa had a mental duel about whether she could go through with this. Ali-Samuel wouldn't take too kindly to her backing out at the very last minute. In the end, the thought of ruling the kingdom with Ali-Ster swayed her decision to carry out the action that would lighten the entire kingdom's burden. She couldn't back out now and she perspired through her chemise and red short-stockings. She had never been involved in a situation like this and didn't know how to prepare. Sir Anderley worried her because he seemed unreliable in Elisa's eyes. While she despised Ali-Samuel, she would still prefer him to Sir Anderley on a mission like this. However, her choice was sealed by the Gods.

Anderley kept throwing a small steel disc with spikes at a board on the wall. The knight flung it at great speed with his hand near his hip and Elisa could hear the disc zipping across the room. He hit the same spot every single time. The knight was trying to calm his nerves but it drove Elisa crazy. After about one hundred throws, she almost snapped at Anderley.

The castle bells struck nine and her stomach churned. Elisa thought she may get ill but fought the feeling off and grabbed a few good luck charms. Sir Anderley stood up and went to the corner of Elisa's room. He gently moved a wooden box in which she stored her exotic perfumes and exposed a door in the floor.

"You're sure you know your way through these tunnels? If we end up in the wrong room, we will all die," Elisa said.

"Relax for a bit, I can hear you breathing from here. Breathe through your mouth too, if need be. Don't worry. Everyone in the Guard knows the tunnels," he said reassuringly as he grabbed a torch from the wall. The pair went into the dark tunnels. Elisa had to bend down to avoid hitting her head on the ceiling of the murky passage and saw that the diminutive Anderley easily navigated the tunnel in front of her. Her dress caught on the wall and ripped, causing her to almost fall. Anderley had the light and she could barely see anything.

Elisa Burke Wamhoff already knew it was too late to back out, but she started to lose it again. Her breathing became erratic and she felt like she would faint. Sweat poured from her underarms and dripped from her chin, even in this cooler inner labyrinth.

Can Anderley really do this or is this an elaborate hoax to frame me for the murder? I have always been used as disposable property. I've heard all the stories of the backstabbing, could this be how it works? Can I really trust all these wicked Wamhoffs I just met only months ago? They have known each other for many years. This has to be a set-up.

She wanted to turn and run but Elisa wouldn't get very far in these lightless tunnels. Anderley stopped and looked at her with his finger over his lips. Elisa wasn't going to say anything but assumed they must be close. She kept having trouble keeping it all together and a tremendous lump built up in her throat. Anderley pushed open a door above his head.

He whispered, "That opened far more easily than expected. Be on alert. Leave this here," he said, dropping the torch. He pulled a knife from his belt and hoisted himself through the door. The taller Elisa easily pulled herself into the King's room. She had never been in here but it smelled of a funk she didn't recognize. A few waning candles exposed an empty bed. Ali-Samuel had said the King would be in his bed. Fear struck Elisa like lightning. Images became trapped in her mind of the guards busting in and seizing her. Within a fortnight her head would be on a spike in front of the castle for regicide. All instincts told her to cry but she didn't. When they moved in closer Elisa almost screamed seeing a dead, blood soaked King, lying next to his bed. After a few moments of shock, Anderley spoke, "We must go now. I told you that snake is a liar."

They jumped back into the tunnel and Anderley led them to a door that took them outside the castle. It didn't appear anyone had seen them and she followed Anderley.

A man approached in the darkness. Anderley addressed him, "Sir Oliver, by chance have you seen the Queen?"

"I didn't think you had to watch her now that Ali-Samuel is her personal guard. Her highness and the good sir took off on horseback a while ago. You want me to continue on and tell you what they're probably doing?" Sir Oliver followed with a grin.

"No thank you, sir," Anderley sharply returned. The two walked around the castle and came upon a commotion. A man ran toward them, "Sir Anderley, it's your brother in the church," the excited man shouted and ran off.

"Come," Anderley firmly said and pushed Elisa by the small of her back to hurry the pace. On the brisk walk in the hot summer night, Elisa felt so lightheaded that she seemed to float in the skies. Her mind and breathing still raced in twenty different directions. She didn't fully understand what had just happened.

I should have known something was amiss when the plan suddenly changed at the last moment. I cannot believe the Queen has betrayed me. Us Bears have to stick together, she said. She's run off with Ali-Samuel and possibly Ali-Ster to leave me with the blame. I better get out of this Capitol. I was so close to being Queen and making those who pushed me around my entire life regret it. I was so close to my voice being heard for the very first time in my life. I was so close to happiness, safety and power. I was so close.

When she regained focus they were racing up the steps of the church and Anderley threw the doors open. He entered and looked left and right before sprinting through the benches in the worship hall and up to the huge marble altar.

Elisa caught up to see a naked Penrose Ellsworth lying on his side. The fallen knight had two cut wrists and a dagger plunged into his belly aimed up into his chest. Thick red liquid rolled off the sides of the white marble and flowed to the floor. Anderley held his little brother's blood drenched hand and knelt, "My sweet brother, why did I ever bring you to Falconhurst? Me...I killed my own brother." Tears streamed down Anderley's face.

He stood back up, "Run back to the castle if you must and gather only your most important items that you can carry and meet me by the apple tree in Kent Square in five minutes. I fear you're to be blamed for the King's murder. I can protect and take you to a place that is safe. If you even get a strange look or feeling from someone, anyone, run. I shall find us horses and salted beef. It will be a long journey and we won't be permitted to stay at inns, so be practical in your choices."

She nervously ran back to the castle to grab her only important item.

67
ALI-STER

ALI-STER PACED BACK and forth, peering out his window at the stars. Last night had proved to be a sleepless one. He had tossed and turned, thinking about the plan. The biggest decision of his life loomed. He never thought it would come down to killing his own father. He thought of Leimur for encouragement and stopped to look at the night sky. He wondered if Leimur was looking at the same stars right now. He kept going back and forth with his reasoning.

He is certainly bad for the kingdom but he has never shown aggression toward any of us. If anything, my father has tried to protect us. His work is not of deliberate intent. Ali-Samuel will understand.

He hadn't talked to Ali-Samuel, Elisa or his mother in days. He had exchanged greetings a few times but nothing further. His thoughts went back to Leimur. If he followed through with the plan he could have his way as king. He would order the council to mind their duties and rendezvous with the fair Queen of Goldenfield. He liked Elisa but she wasn't a warrior.

In the end, the super couple would conquer the world and Donegal would finally stand on its feet again. He thought about the great warrior children they would have and he moved closer to going through with the plan.

The castle bells struck nine. Ali-Samuel should be here any moment. Ali-Ster had to make a decision. He still waffled, trying to pick. Several minutes seemed to go by and Ali-Ster became even more anxious. It wasn't typical of his cousin to be late. After about five minutes his angst turned to worry.

Did something happen? Did someone figure out the plan? Is everything lost?

As time passed without any signs of Ali-Samuel, the Prince became increasingly concerned. His arms and face now matched his auburn hair as his body began to overheat. Ali-Ster heard a stir from outside the door.

They caught Ali-Samuel and he gave up our plan. They must be dragging him up here to confirm it and take me away. How did we botch this?

Men marched by and Ali-Ster became confused. He moved to the door and heard more men moving by. He opened the door, recognized Nevrone and pulled him in.

"What is the meaning of all this?" the Prince demanded. "They say Sir Penrose has killed the High Priest and then himself. We've come to tell the King," Nevrone reported.

"Alright, continue with your duty," said the Prince and Nevrone went on his way.

What in the name of all the Gods is happening? Sir Penrose? He seemed strong of mind. Why would he kill the High Priest?

Through the disbelief, Ali-Ster realized he didn't have to back out of the plan and look craven in front of his cousin. He felt great relief with the burden off his back. He went down to the banquet hall near the kitchens to find ladies crying as lords and guards paced around.

"Where is my father?" Ali-Ster questioned.

"My deepest condolences, my Prince, I would have thought you had already heard. Our King is dead. Eternal shall live our King in the heavens," Henley Moore dejectedly stated.

"Eternal shall live our King in the heavens," he repeated.

What the fuck is going on now? Did Penrose kill the two men closest to the Gods in Donegal?

Ali-Ster never swore, not even to himself but this was the maddest situation he had ever been involved in.

"What happened?" he asked. "Numerous deadly stab wounds to the back and neck, my Prince," Henley answered.

"Have we any suspects other than the obvious Sir Penrose?" Ali-Ster wanted to know. "Where is my mother and cousin? I don't see them." Ali-Ster looked around at the scattered people around the room.

"They are part of the suspect list, my Prince. Elisa Burke and her sister Telly are missing and so is Sir Anderley which can possibly put him in cahoots with Sir Penrose," Henley informed him.

Ali-Ster started to turn red again forced by anger and felt a strange hollow feeling.

I've been betrayed. Every conspirator has fled and I am left to hold the bloody knife. My mother, my cousin, my own blood has betrayed me. Death and deception are part of life.

Ali-Ster went up to his father's room to see the body. He got to the room and fought his way through the horde to see the ghastly sight. In strong light, the horrific-looking King could only solicit sympathy. Every part of his body from the waist up was completely covered in the liquid of life that had run through his body only hours ago. *Death is part of life.* Ali-Ster surmised either his father tried to run from an attacker or the killer made his move from behind. The anger he felt for himself shifted to sadness for his father. *No man deserves to go like this*, he thought as he spotted Count Silzeus attending to the King.

"Count Silzeus, how many wounds did my father suffer?"

"Sixteen, my Prince, with a rather wide blade it would seem," Count Silzeus told him. "Did you find any clues in the room?" Ali-Ster pressed.

"We did find the secret door to the tunnels slightly ajar and the table that had covered it on the ground, sideways. I sent Sir Oliver to investigate the tunnels," the feeble old man said. "Thank you, Count Silzeus," Ali-Ster replied.

"Of course, my Prince, if you should need to talk about this later, be sure to summon me," the dependable Count reminded him.

Whoever did this certainly got their money's worth. Sixteen times seems a bit harsh. I cannot believe the innocent looking Elisa was in on it too. I should have stayed on the war campaign and never come back to rotten Falconhurst. At war at least I know the rules unlike these shady dealings that take place in the Capitol. There is honor in killing on the battle-field. There is no honor in this. Betrayed by my own blood. Betrayed by my own blood.

Ali-Ster walked back into the hallway and saw his uncle Ryen. The dead King's brother came over and softly touched Ali-Ster's cheek with his palm. "Eternal shall live our King in the heavens. Are you alright, my nephew?"

"Eternal shall live our King in the heavens. This is quite shocking to say the least. I honestly don't know how I feel. I am confused," Ali-Ster unsurely said.

"Let's go to your quarters and talk in private," Ryen said with a reserved grin. He had taught Ali-Ster more about being a man than Ali-Stanley ever had. The two went to the Prince's room and sat down.

Ryen started, "It's fine to have mixed feelings about your father. Being king is a difficult battle to win but being a father and a king is an unwinnable battle. Kings are told to produce children, not raise them. It may seem like your father wasn't always there for you but even you have seen the demands of our King. He followed what our father did before him. Our father never paid attention to us and looked at his children as burdens. It has been pounded into Ali-Stanley's head that this is the way of the land. Before you fully judge him, wait until you have been burdened with some of the same responsibilities. Your father was a misunderstood man and he often told me that you were his pride and joy. He could seem like one man at the small meetings and a totally different person when he talked about you. He said he couldn't bring himself to tell you how proud he was of you. Ali-Stanley was our father's second choice to be king, I believe you know. He saw everything in you that made his twin brother the first pick to succeed our father. Resentment is difficult to shed and as freely as he could tell me how much delight you brought him and the family name, he just couldn't do the same with you."

Tears formed in the Prince's eyes and the sympathy expanded for his father. His anger faded concerning the bastard children and castaway brother. He felt a renewed pride in the Wamhoff name.

"I have trouble talking to girls as I have told you. Maybe it is similar to that?" Ali-Ster posed.

"Could be, but the message you should take is that your father loved you even if the words couldn't be expressed. I will be here for you whenever you need to deal with the grieving," Ryen assured him.

His uncle Ryen had always been there for him. He would go to his uncle rather than to his father on almost every occasion for help or advice. There were only a few people Ali-Ster could truly trust and that list shortened as time went on. He really believed he could trust Ryen and knew his uncle would help him get through the death of his father and former King of Donegal, Ali-Stanley Wamhoff.

The next morning, Ali-Ster and Ryen Wamhoff awoke before dawn to sneak off into the King's Woods. They had been going on early morning hunts for the past month to get away from the responsibilities of the realm. After only one night, Ali-Ster had already come to realize his mother, cousin and Elisa weren't coming back to the Capitol. Seething anger filled the Prince as the men rode into the dark forest. He still couldn't figure out who had killed his father as he moved away from a long tree branch. He'd brought his longbow, sword and several knives. Ali-Ster wondered why Ryen wasn't his father. His uncle had been more of a father to him over the years and Ryen was a warrior too.

A fog persisted after the sun pushed its way up to officially start the day. The men trotted along on horseback, but could only see a few feet ahead. Ali-Ster enjoyed these hunts with his uncle where the two men barely spoke. He needed to get away from the Capitol every now and then to clear his head. The two Wamhoffs never told anyone else about these secret hunts because everyone would want to tag along.

Ali-Ster couldn't wait for his brother to take over as King of Donegal and sanction his mission to create the super kingdom. *If the King gives an order, it must be carried out.* He didn't want to manipulate Ali-Varis like the vultures around Falconhurst, but he knew his plan would be best for the entire kingdom.

Ali-Ster remembered all the hunts Ryen had taken him on as a child. His father had only embarrassed himself on hunts and given up on them before Ali-Ster was born. He still didn't fully comprehend the fact that he had lost his mother and father on the same day.

The fog dissipated and the men drew their longbows as the stallions galloped deeper into the woods. Ali-Ster was truly happy away from the treacherous games of the nobles. He searched the camouflaged settings for movement. He pulled back on the reins and slowed the pace to a walk. He and his uncle spotted the menacing eyes of a wild woods fox in the thick bushes. The big beast took off when Ryen's horse stepped on a twig. The stallions instinctually followed, and Ali-Ster's pulse quickened. He squeezed his legs around the horse and pulled an arrow. He set the missile in the bowstring and saw the fox moving farther from the path. He loosed his arrow and just as it sank into the animal's side, another hit at the exact same time. The dying animal ran deeper into the woods, but Ali-Ster and Ryen tracked the trail of blood and found the beast. He stared at one of the biggest foxes he had ever seen. *My word is this thing huge. This animal would eat us if it had the chance.* The men slung the meat over the back of Ryen's black stallion and slowly trotted back toward the King's Castle.

The Wamhoffs came around a turn on the path to see two common men wearing tattered clothes and holding poorly constructed longbows. The men appeared to be in their forties and immediately realized they couldn't outrun the royal horses. They dropped to their knees and one man said, "Sorry, so sorry, my lords." The other pleaded, "Apologies, deepest apologies, my lords."

"We was starving and the other woods is over hunted, there's no food. So sorry," the first man explained with his head lowered. Neither man had looked up at the Wamhoffs since bowing on their knees. "Relax, fellow citizens. We just killed a woods fox and we don't really need the meat. We would be glad to share our game with you. Where are you men from?" Ali-Ster asked. "We live over in the Knot's Woods," the first man said.

Ryen and Ali-Ster showed true compassion by taking the men back to Knot's Woods. They gave the men the fox and their longbows, after which Ryen led the Prince in a different direction from the castle. The two went to the horse races to relax even more. They gambled for several hours and Ali-Ster lost his bets, but it was still a great day.

After the races, the two men went to the practice yard and squared off, toe to toe. Ryen's strength always impressed the larger Ali-Ster. His uncle had never gone light on Ali-Ster or let him win. He always made Ali-Ster earn a victory like he would have to on the battle field. A few sweaty hours of sparring really increased the men's hunger, and Ryen had another surprise for his nephew.

Ryen had arranged a small feast for the family with performers and musicians. His uncle prepared the event to help with the grieving of the entire Wamhoff family. Ali-Ster didn't usually drink much, but he got good and drunk tonight. The Prince was pleased with the day his uncle had put together for the two of them. The men who had been to war gathered around to tell stories. This made Ali-Ster feel back in his element, in battle. He put his arm around Ryen's neck and pulled him in for a gesture of thanks. They hadn't talked about his dead father, and that was exactly what Ali-Ster needed. Later on he even danced with most of the ladies, an activity he rarely took part in. Ali-Ster had his first entirely enjoyable day in the Capitol since returning just before spring.

68
THE TAKEOVER-THE MAN WITH THE GOLDEN SWORD

THE GLINTING GOLDEN blade of The Man's sword was dulled from fresh, dark blood as he approached the Etburn castle. The city walls weren't closed and his contingent had waved false flags of the Royal Army to confuse the enemy. Once inside the city walls, they had easily hacked their way through most of Elkridge on the way to the Duke's stronghold. Most men and women had yielded by lying on the ground, face down. The Man with the Golden Sword had already claimed eight lives but he wouldn't be satisfied until his men conquered the castle.

The Man watched the arrows flying from the embrasures. He hated the cowardly archers. Two arrows whizzed past his head and a large rock landed a few men away, opening a hole in his young soldier's unprotected head. He had warned the men without helms to wait until the castle was breeched. Undaunted, The Man with the Golden Sword helped the men push a ladder against the castle wall. He put away his sword, stuck a dagger in between his teeth and started to climb. He pulled the knife out for a moment and shouted, "Follow me, men, and let's take this castle."

A wild rumble exploded as more ladders and troops tried to get on the castle roof. The simple Etburn castle was a stacked stone building with four sides and a keep in the southeast corner with smaller towers in four other areas. Most of the noble dignitaries were probably stuffed in the keep unless they had already run. He was trying to get to the lower roof bailey. He thought that would make a perfect landing spot as his army attacked the north wall. He felt a rock hit his horned helm and when The Man regained the courage to look back up, he saw a member of the Etburn guard leaning over the crenellated parapet. His adversary grabbed the ladder and started to push The Man backward. He looked up to see the enemy's face over the wall and shifted the knife to his hand

and blindly flung it upward. Through pure luck, the knife embedded itself into the bottom of the soldier's chin, causing him to fall back. He pulled the ladder with him and laid it flush against the stone wall. The smoking sun sizzled overhead and the brightness hurt The Man's eyes as he looked up. A rush of tingles attacked his body and he felt a heavenly buzzing in his head from the near death experience. He became even more focused and grabbed a firm grip on the ladder. He rushed the rest of the way up, steadied himself on the merlon and heaved his body onto the parapet walk. The archers were unaware of their enemy's presence and The Man almost cut one in half with only a light swing of his sword. The Man took more pleasure in killing archers than swordsmen. He moved along the parapet walk, worked his way around a square tower and jumped down five feet onto the level rooftop bailey.

With the battlement breached, he searched the open, flat stone area to see forty Etburn knights but twice as many of his men had already invaded the roof. The enemy wore either boiled leather and mail or armor. More and more of them poured onto the roof and were ready for a fight but not a battle with The Man. The Etburn guard was old and had never expected anything like this. The Man readied his bloody sword and rushed into the melee. He exchanged swings with an extremely skilled older knight who couldn't keep up with The Man's speed. He quickly circled behind him, raised his sword with two hands and buried the blade through the knight's neck and down into his chest. The Man twisted his sword and screamed, "AAAAHHHH," sounding like a crazed man as he shook violently.

Suddenly, the fight got jammed into a tight space. People on every side kept bumping into The Man. His arms became so confined it rendered his sword almost useless. He grabbed an enemy by the left wrist with his left hand. He turned his sword down in his right and harshly shifted his forearm into the opponent's elbow. Bone busted through skin and bent the opponent's elbow backward as the soldier fell to the ground and yielded. The crafty usurper drew a dagger with his left hand and began poking around for the enemy. He stepped on a fallen body as the congested battle ground became even harder to navigate. He knew if he fell it meant certain death but looking down for dead bodies could also get him killed.

Suddenly a head-butt from an eagle shaped helm staggered The Man and rang his head. As he shook it off, the Etburn guard spat a bloody wad in his eyes before turning and running when he seemed to recognize The Man with the Golden Sword. The Man chased down the guard and pushed him against a tower wall. He dropped his sword, ripped the other man's head protection off and crushed him in the face with his own helm. The older man fell on his back and The Man pounced on top of him. He continued to use the eagle shaped helmet to bash his opponent's head into the ground. He methodically screamed at the guard, "You...don't...ever...spit...on...a...king." He poured down an anvil-like pounding until the skull popped with a bone-chilling thud. In the end, the enraged usurper just mashed blood and bone into the sun-soaked castle stone.

When he rose to his feet again he found his warriors had dispatched all of the Etburn soldiers on the rooftop bailey. He shouted, "Let's go inside."

They were outnumbered entering the tower but only for a few moments. The Man's allies quickly rushed in, crushing the most faithful of the Etburn knights, guards and family members. As he made his way down the steps and into a hall in the main castle, Etburn bodies were strewn everywhere. The Etburn eagle on most men's surcoats had been drenched in blood. He reached a staircase and went downstairs into the foyer of the castle. He saw his men looting and destroying anything with an eagle symbol.

The Crippler pushed an elderly man in his night robe toward The Man. "May I present the noble Duke of Waters Edge, Tyus Etburn."

The Man looked the old Duke up and down, "So noble that he leaves his men to be slaughtered like sheep following him into the blood ridden pastures. You really didn't believe you could defeat us, did you?"

Angrily but feebly, Tyus said, "I would have defeated you, had you only acted with honor. Breaching the city gates disguised as the King's army, hah."

The Man felt the anger boil up, "Honor...honor, what is it you know of honor?" he laughed and his men joined in.

"I know enough that when a bastard usurper attacks unannounced, it is cowardly," Duke Tyus Etburn struck back.

"Such tough talking for a man who stands defeated and couldn't even defend his own castle. I will strike a deal with you, Duke Etburn. I will give you one chance to retain Waters Edge. A man that spews as many strong words as yourself must be a menace with a sword. *Denys*," The Man called.

"Yes, my king," Denys answered.

"Hand the noble Duke your sword. If he can defeat only one man in a simple duel, he can have his region back. But that man is me."

"This should hardly be fair," muttered Tyus.

The Duke of Waters Edge struggled just to stay on his feet anymore. The eighty-two-year-old with a large round head could barely hold the sword. The frail man looked up and whispered a prayer to the heavens. The Man pulled his still-bloody sword and everyone crowded around, hooting and hollering. The Man tapped Tyus' sword and backed off quickly in defense, mocking the old man. As he approached, Duke Etburn courageously but slowly swung the sword. The usurper easily blocked the feeble attempt even though he was surprised and impressed with the old man's effort. He quickly returned a two-handed swing that separated the Duke's head from the rest of his body. The men moved in closer to get a look at the fallen Duke. They went wild as The Man grabbed the head and held it upright while buckets of blood poured down onto his shiny silver breastplate.

The Man's army suffered very few casualties and he was shocked with the ease at which he had taken Waters Edge.

How did they find out so late that an army of ten thousand was coming? I guess the disguise of the Royal Army and the bribes worked. The King surely had to send word when half his army went missing. I thought at least one person would sing to the eagles. They must have thought the royal army was simply passing through.

The Crippler dragged an old woman over to The Man and asked her, "Do you see it now?"

"As clear as a bright summer day. This man is a spitting image of my brother. Many years ago mind you, but it's as if he stands before us, young once again," the woman stated.

"Who's this?" The Man questioned. "Ali-Pari Wamhoff, sister of the King, or soon to be former King. She told me you have the precise looks of the King at a younger age," the Crippler informed him.

Now The Man with the Golden Sword started to really believe his prophesy to wear the crown. "She will live. Provide her with basic comforts," he ordered.

Later that night the Crippler and The Man sat in the former Duke's quarters that had been claimed by the usurper. The Crippler worked on a painting while The Man sat and drank.

"That came rather easy," The Man intimated.

"Getting to Falconhurst won't be anything like this. We need to make our rounds through Waters Edge to claim the citizens who could aid our cause," the Crippler said.

"They can come by pleasure or pain but bring any abled men or women who can help in all aspects of the war effort. We must also kill anyone who holds any sort of claim to the region. We need to find them and kill them," he told the Crippler. His mentor responded, "Apparently, the young blond woman I had working for us to tear apart the castle has died. Caroline something, I can't recall right now. If you remember, we were trying to convince her to kill her husband, the man who had the most sense in the Etburn family. Pretty little one. You would have liked her, maybe only for a night or two but you would have liked her."

He continued, "I think its due time that we strengthen your mind. Look at this." The Crippler showed The Man his painting. A crude red painting revealed a man on top of a castle with his arms raised in victory. The Crippler returned the wolf hair bristles of the paint brush to the red well of the overturned head of the former Duke.

The Man stood up and stripped off his clothes. "I found a better device for you to lie in," said the Crippler pointing at a contoured wooden bed with loose cushions. This had been their nightly ritual for the past several years. The nude Man lay on his back and closed his eyes. The Crippler massaged his head and eyelids, causing The Man to see spots.

The Crippler spoke in a soft tone. "Sleep away, sleep away, fade away," he kept repeating while continuing the massaging. After a few minutes, the Crippler lightly asked, "Can you hear me?" and clapped his hands in front of The Man's face who didn't budge.

The Crippler stated, "When I say the word 'trouble' you will be able to hear me. Trouble. Can you hear me?"

The Man responded, "I can hear you."

A sick smile came over the Crippler's face, "Repeat after me. It takes a hardened heart to rule a realm." The Man repeated the words.

"I will not let beauty or love blind me in my quest." The Man echoed the sentence.

"I shall give all credit to the Crippler when I am king." The Man said the statement without hesitation.

69
A MAGICAL PLACE—MARIAH

"I'M NOT ENTIRELY sure she is ready for this," Chopkins playfully said. "She's ready," Torvald stated. "Ready for what?" Mariah asked.

"Nothing, you should know not to let Chopkins tease you by now. It's only, when some people visit for the first time, they are a bit shocked," Torvald slowly worked his way through the statement.

The steepness of the mountain had tapered off after they left Housemont and moved upward toward Ridgetop. Mariah had grown up quite a lot since the ambush near Falconhurst. Her soul ached for her father and she still didn't know what had happened to the rest of her family. Torvald and his friends did their best to buoy up her spirits and keep her mind from the sadness. Mariah thought about how petty she had been to her mother and father the last time she saw them. She wished that she could talk to both of them one more time to tell them how sorry she was. She had committed to become more gracious in honor of her father who had always exuded class under pressure.

The images of her father flew out of her mind as the glimmer of gold came into view. The top of the steep mountain flattened out and a dirt path led them toward gold gilded houses on both sides of a street. Both sides of the road had gold hand railings and beautiful flowers of every color.

This is purely amazing. This must be a bittersweet dream.

She pinched herself and the pain proved that it was real. She kept walking down the street and saw stores and smithies. Despite the loud banging, some merchants employed singers, poets and jesters to attract clientele. Mariah was taken aback by the majestic scenery. She leaned down to Chopkins, "Maybe I wasn't ready?"

"Then brace yourself because it's about to get even more unbelievable," he cheerily told her.

Mariah almost passed out and her heart skipped several beats when she saw the golden castle. The entire castle was gold. Mariah's mind couldn't imagine how you could build an entire castle of gold. The singing and hammering faded and a newly laid road lined with rectangular silver stones led up to the enormous castle.

When the three were fifty feet away from the castle, they were greeted by pretty young girls on either side of the road. Wooden baskets attached to a rolling cart were filled with flowers. The young girls pulled them from the moving carts and threw the beautiful assortment in front of Mariah, Torvald and Chopkins as they walked along the road.

Ever the joker, Chopkins, sarcastically said, "Thank you, thank you. You shouldn't have troubled yourselves just for me." He leaned toward Mariah, "I told you they enjoyed life here and this is drab for the norm."

Mariah picked up a few flowers she had never seen before and smelled the freshness of summer. A smile flitted across her face in spite of her jumbled emotions, and they moved on as the shower of flowers continued. They walked slowly to let the girls keep up with the cart and by the end of the street, the baskets were empty except for torn petals and busted stems. The end of the road was lined only with petals and they walked through the open drawbridge. A wide moat surrounded the castle and Mariah heard the rushing waters underneath as they crossed it. She noticed some parts of the castle wall had peeled and the gold was actually painted on to gray stone. It looked twice as big as the castle she had grown up in and Mariah felt like she was floating on air as they crossed the drawbridge.

They went through the entrance gate and the portcullis slowly lifted. The latticed grill of red wood rose just enough for them to sneak under. She walked into a foyer and a singer came down the marble steps directly ahead. Rooms and hallways opened up on either side as she heard a song she recognized, "The Return of the Prince." The young singer worked his way down the steps while entertaining everyone. He moved off to the side and a stunning couple descended the white steps to stop directly in front of Mariah.

I look like a street beggar. They are going to tell me to leave. I wish I had a chance to present myself better. She's staring at me. I feel hideous.

The singer stopped and emphatically declared, "I proudly present the Duke and Duchess of Bottomfoot, Edword and Lucille Malik."

"It's an absolute honor to meet you," Mariah blurted.

Normally Mariah would panic about looking sloppy and saying something out of turn. In the past she would have thrown a fit if everything wasn't perfect when meeting a duke and duchess. Lucille Malik had dark brown hair braided into circles on the sides of her head. Mariah thought it was the neatest hairstyle she had ever seen. She imagined it must have taken days to make it look so exotic. Then she looked into the bluish-purple eyes of the Duchess of Bottomfoot. They were the eyes of angels and seemed to sparkle with moon dust. Firm in weight, Lucille carried it in upmost style. Every citizen along the way had asked about Duchess Lucille on her trip to Ridgetop. They all seemed to love her like a mother. Mariah immediately felt envious of her deep purple dress which hugged her ravishing figure and highlighted her mystical eyes.

"My sweet dear, I am so sorry to hear the terrible news of your family. Your father was a great man," Lucille consoled.

"Thank you so much. Do you…" Mariah stopped. "Go on and ask, child," Lucille said reassuringly.

"Do you know anything else about my family?" she erupted as if it had been bottled up the entire trip.

"Not much of good, I am afraid to say. It looks like the King got his fox claws into both of your parents. Your brothers Ryno and Krys are missing and Riceros is on a ship headed east with Sir Brehan Castaway. That is all my listeners have told me. I am soulfully sorry, my child," Lucille stated in a motherly, comforting tone.

The duchess hugged the weeping Mariah. She felt softness, warmth and love. Lucille spoke, "The other boys who travelled ahead from your group returned days ago and I had our gold smith make something for you." She held up a golden chain with a matching charm designed like a bull. The Duchess said, "It is, of course, a golden bull, just as your father was and always will be."

She handed the necklace to Torvald, "Place it on the lady."

Torvald moved behind Mariah and attached the clasp. The big chunk of gold that had been masterfully crafted into a bull rested on her chest.

"It shall stay near your heart, as I am sure, your father always will," Duchess Lucille said.

Tears freely streamed down Mariah and Lucille's faces as the Duchess hugged her tightly again. "Thank you so much, this means so much to me, I can't even put it into words," she blubbered.

"It's only a small token and although it will never cover up a large wound, you can think of him fondly when you wear this," Lucille soothed her.

Mariah couldn't believe the Duke and Duchess could be old enough to have Torvald. They looked to be only a few years older than him, and Mariah checked out the handsome duke. He looked like a slightly older version of Torvald. The Duke was taller and had thinning hair opposed to Torvald's thick mane. She noticed Edword's eyes were gray, not brown. Other than that father and son looked very similar.

Sir Bastion came up to the gathering. "My Duke, my Duchess, I have the troops ready to move."

Torvald jumped in, "Ready to move? What is going on?"

"Fox Chapel has invaded Bottomfoot. The time has come to strike," Edword said with confidence.

"I knew it. And we were worried about Burkeville. Lady Mariah, do you know the difference between a bucket full of shit and the Wamhoffs?" an angered Chopkins asked. Mariah shook her head and before she could speak, Chopkins revealed, "Only the bucket."

"Chopkins, watch the vulgarity in the presence of a proper lady," Lucille grinned at Mariah.

"All joking aside, we are sending two thousand men. They are reported to have no more than five hundred men split into two divisions. I need this new King and everyone else to understand the consequences of violating the trust of Bottomfoot. Our treaty strictly states that no armed soldiers from Fox Chapel will step on Bottomfoot land. Have you yet to hear about the death of King Ali-Stanley?" Edword asked.

"Are you serious?" Torvald posed back to his father. "Are twenty reported stab wounds to the back serious? We haven't sent word around Bottomfoot as of yet, but that's what the letter said," the Duke said.

Mariah felt numb. She thought it would make her happy to know the man who killed her father was dead. Instead she felt nothing. Just the emptiness of her fractured family persisted. This news didn't bring any more happiness or closure on this otherwise perfect summer day.

Shouldn't I be happy? He threatened to kill me too. He killed my mother and father but I cannot rejoice in the misery of others. Maybe Krys was right, I do have a soft heart.

"The clumsy King has fallen for good. Are they going to let Ali-Varis take the throne? He finally got what he deserved if you ask me," an irritated Chopkins said, looking around at everyone.

"No one has ever asked for you to opine, Chopkins, but that seems to rarely stop you. And Ali-Varis will only sit the throne in name. This will cause more struggles throughout the kingdom without absolute power. Personal agendas will be secretly sanctioned in the name of the king. This is detrimental for all of Donegal," Edword stated.

"Lady Mariah, let me take you to your chambers and we will get you cleaned up and properly fed. Sir Bastion, be safe and please return soon," Lucille told the knight and gave him a hug.

He backed up and said with a sweeping bow, "I shall be certain, my Duchess."

Lucille hooked her arm into Mariah's and led her up the marble stairs and off to the right. The stone blocks along the hallway walls were painted silver and a red carpet took them to another marble staircase. They stopped at the third floor and Lucille showed Mariah inside.

Fresh red, pink and white rose petals sprinkled the floor and a steaming bath looked refreshing to the dusty traveler.

"Here you are, my sweet dear. Now, I don't know what may happen with your family. They have told me that Ruxin is doing a fine job as Duke of Mattingly. I have put my listeners out to find more information on your family and you will be the first to hear about it when the words arrive. We can take you home to Riverfront if you wish but with a new King we know not what to expect. My sweet dear, from this day on, you will always have a home here in Ridgetop," Lucille promised.

"You are too kind, I appreciate everything, I truly do, Duchess Lucille. There's something I never got to ask Torvald. Why do they call it Bottomfoot when most of it is mountains?" she wanted to know.

"Bottom foot. Bottom foot. Listen to it. Doesn't sound pretty and what is worse than the bottom of one's foot? It just sounds ugly. In a region that begs for neutrality, it keeps people out. People won't look for gold in a place called Bottomfoot. No one wants to conquer a place called Bottomfoot, do they?" the Duchess posed to Mariah. "I suppose not," the seventeen-year-old answered.

"Well, I would guess that somebody wants to use Bottomfoot as Fox Chapel has shown." The Duchess helped Mariah into the bath. "I will send the handmaidens to give you a proper scrub. After your dirty adventure, I'll send the strong one," she smiled at Mariah, "Anything you wish, you only need ask, my sweet dear."

"Thank you again, I don't know quite what to say," Mariah fumbled for words.

"Say nothing, child, you have been through enough already," the loving Duchess said before she left.

The hot bath felt glorious and Mariah washed all the grime off her body. The two handmaidens corralled her into a purple robe that matched the color of the Duchess' dress from earlier. Mariah heard a racket outside. She walked out on the balcony and saw the Bottomfoot soldiers moving past the castle. The drummers set the pace for the organized march that looked very honorable and chivalrous to Mariah. She wished she could throw the rose petals to the men, but they were too far away. Mariah waited until every one of the brave soldiers had marched out of sight before going back into the room.

70
Surprises—Ali-Ster

"I FEEL THIS makes it even easier," said Ali-Ster. "How say?" Neron questioned.

"Ali-Varis can stay and rule. I go to Goldenfield in guise to meet the Queen. I will say I'm going to conquer Livingstone but I will really be saving everyone's lives. If we don't act fast we will have people attacking Falconhurst from every side. I am frankly surprised it hasn't happened yet," Ali-Ster told his cousin.

"This is madness. The council will want you to stay and rule," Neron objected.

"The council will want me out of the way so they can try to manipulate Ali-Varis. It would only be temporary and when we conquer the world, people will laugh when they look back on these times. I understand it's a muddy fight and boots will get dirty but it will be well worth it, I can promise," Ali-Ster hopefully stated with a stardust-like twinkle in his eyes.

"How can *you* make promises? Remove your head from the clouds. You must take care of Donegal first before conquering the world. I like the spirit, but you will die. It's that plain. It's that simple. It makes for a great story or song but you will die at the end of the song. We need you here," his cousin stressed, "You are the last hope for Donegal."

"I realize all that and more. Do you think I don't feel the pressure of the entire realm coming down on me? Everything I have done and will do is for Donegal," Ali-Ster said with force.

"You're out of your head if you plan to bring this up at a council meeting. Tell me you aren't, please" Neron said, hopefully.

"Not yet, but soon. Listen, you were pretty close to Sir Penrose. Do you think he could have done it?"

Neron's face became flushed and he bobbled the words a bit, "I cannot, no, I cannot believe it so. He talked with some disdain for the church, but never your father. The king had many enemies, but of that long list Penrose wasn't one of the names."

"I wouldn't think it was him, either. He *never* talked about being upset with my father, you say?" Ali-Ster pushed further.

"He was your father's personal guard. You know your father. Would you have said anything bad if you were in his position? He was ordered around like a kitchen wench by the king; of course he said some unkind words, but anyone would have. You can surely understand that," said Neron who seemed to get angry as the conversation went along.

"Of anyone, I surely can." *Neron makes perfect sense. Everyone had reason to talk ill of my father or even want to kill him. I came an hour away from almost doing it myself.*

"I must run, be well, good prince," Neron said and the husky youngster left the room. He had started to worry Ali-Ster a bit but he sincerely believed he could trust Neron to keep his secret. He did wish Neron had exhibited a better reaction about his vision of a super kingdom to conquer the world.

Neron's bright orange hair had shocked the royal family because all of Tersen Wamhoff's children had looked like albinos up to that point. He became the apple of his father's eye although extremely un-athletic and short. The crimson patch on his head was the only thing Neron Wamhoff's father cared about. Tersen desperately sought his king father's approval and the hair color was the only thing he cared about because his father stressed the importance of red hair among the true Wamhoffs. Most men believed Tersen had spoiled his son and made him soft. Ali-Ster would agree. One of the reasons he trusted Neron so much was because he believed Neron was threatened physically by him. Ali-Ster was a war hero at sixteen while Neron never performed his duty for the kingdom. Tersen had made excuses for his son and paid the military tribute to keep his son out of combat. His father had claimed he needed Neron to help him rule Cloverfoot. Tersen had said small rebellions kept erupting and his son was needed to quash the uprisings, but everyone knew there were no rebellions. Ali-Ster remembered when King Ali-Stanley had criticized Neron publicly for not serving military duty. The surrounding men had enjoyed a laugh over the King's hypocrisy as Ali-Stanley had never performed his service either. They had waited for the King to leave earshot but Ali-Ster overheard the men whispering, 'phony' and chuckled along.

Ali-Ster arrived at the council meeting. The musty room seemed emptier than usual. A stale breeze crawled through the window and moved lazily around the table. Ali-Varis still had to be officially crowned to name his full council. The king-in-waiting sat at the head of the table playing with his hands. He twisted and untangled them, much to his delight.

Protector of Donegal? Keeper of the Seal? This realm is in trouble if I don't save it. Queen Leimur would be silly not to agree with this plan. Should I bring it up in the meeting?

Dirk Eller, Jake Fielder, Derich Bonsfogger, Leo Braunshaur, Ryen and Tersen Wamhoff sat at the table with Ali-Ster. He took control of the meeting, "What is first?"

"The Man with the Golden Sword improves his hold on Waters Edge. He seems to have most of the region behind him now whether the people like it or not. Only a few small areas dispute his rule but those little battles can only help us. However, he stands as a serious threat," Leo Braunshaur started.

"How many men does he have?" Ali-Ster asked. "He came with ten thousand paid solders behind him and lost very few fighting Duke Etburn. Most are lifelong men of battle and extremely skilled. Our spies tell us another ten thousand traitors he conquered throughout Waters Edge have joined his cause. They say he is making the claim of being a bastard of King Ali-Stanley," Leo returned.

"Anything for a claim, I suppose. I am sure those *traitors* didn't have too many options. It was either die or join up. Have we sent men to guard the Blue Caps?" Ryen queried. His uncle didn't talk much, but he always knew the relevant questions to ask.

The Blue Cap Mountains were a huge range that ran along the northern Fox Chapel border, and The Man with the Golden Sword had to cross them to get to Falconhurst from Waters Edge. The only other way was by sea and the coastline remained well protected despite the financial troubles.

"Do we have men to send? Where are the men we pulled out of Bottomfoot?" Ali-Ster wanted to know.

A hush came over the room. Dirk Eller had the courage to break it,

"Your father wouldn't sanction your order to retreat. He said it would make the crown look cowardly. The men are still down there trying to find their way into Mattingly. And even if they reach Mattingly, are five hundred men going to capture the region?"

"He left us in quite a way. I am starting to think he may be the lucky one in all this mess. What else have we heard?" Ali-Ster questioned.

Ryen scratched his cheek and said, "We still haven't located your mother, cousin, Elisa or Telly Burke and Sir Anderley. The body of Sir Penrose somehow disappeared as well. Several men saw the nude corpse on the church altar only to return to find it vanished. Some are calling it heavenly intervention for killing the corrupt father and possibly freeing the church of Father Enroy's evil ways. He was much more hated than I had ever realized. Men really get the courage to speak up about a man after he is dead. Is Penrose still the prime suspect?"

Tersen jumped in with his shrill voice, "He would have to be. Seen in the castle. Leaves with blood soaked hands. Kills the Father and then himself. Sounds like a coordinated effort to remove the two most powerful men in Donegal."

Oh uncle, you want everyone to think that you are so wise. You have no idea how deep this runs. I cannot believe nobody suspects anything. He always was the black sheep of the family. Or the white sheep in this case. Ali-Ster started to laugh and caught himself by pretending to cough. *That must have been hard for the albino with all those normal brothers to live up to. I only have Ali-Varis and I could never be jealous of him.*

"So why did the others run like common criminals? Why leave the safety of the King's Castle ironically on the same night of his death?" Jake Fielder asked.

He and uncle Ryen are the only ones with true sense in this room.

Henley Moore rushed in late and took a spot at a corner of the huge wooden table by one of the lion supports. Count Silzeus came in after Henley, huffing, puffing and struggling to get to the table. Ali-Ster could hear his heavy breathing from down the table.

"They might have been killed and thrown into the Royal River for all we really know," Leo Braunshaur claimed.

"We can speculate either way all day and night but we must wait to see if the potential traitors turn up. *We* have spies all over the world, *we'll* find them if they run. Now what else?" Ali-Ster asked becoming annoyed with this meeting.

"The Tiger Queen of Goldenfield has returned to her Capitol. It would seem that she now has fifty tigers that loyally follow her around at all times. Wild beasts, they are. They say the tigers followed her out of the Animal Kingdom. I think it's high time we send assassins before she changes course and heads this way. She grows too powerful and the citizens love her. They will fight hard for their Warrior Queen. If we cannot get to her on the field of battle, we can try to cause some chaos until our ship is righted. I had the perfect Wamhoff in mind for the attempt but he has gone and disappeared," Dirk Eller reported.

Ali-Ster's heart sank. He had heard them mention an assassination plot for Queen Leimur when she first took rule but it had seemed to be forgotten. "Do we really want to risk being found out and starting an all-out war which we would lose? Without the support of Waters Edge, Mattingly, Bottomfoot and that compost pile called Burkeville, we are nothing. Burkeville is the only thing standing between death and us. How many of you feel safe about that? If our murder attempt is discovered, they will crush Burkeville with ease and the rest of you will watch Uncle Ryen and me die defending your Capitol. Look, Fox Chapel even stands divided. What is going on in Burkeville anyway?" Ali-Ster wanted to know. He became more animated and stern toward the end.

Jake Fielder spoke up, "Burkeville is in complete turmoil with at least ten men making claims for the Dukeship."

"There aren't even ten districts in Burkeville," Ryen contested.

"Four are lords in Arigold alone. It's a complete war right now. The death of Duke Burke has had the opposite effect than was intended. It has caused an incredible impact that nobody could have foreseen. Whom can we send to clean things up? Too bad the Grizzly Bear left the region. He was a murderously cruel man who strangely kept the peace through violence and the threat of it. Who's ruthless, with money, doesn't mind war and is greedy?" Jake Fielder asked.

Tersen immediately responded, "Ichibod Ellsworth, of course."

"And about one hundred more lords to match. Who is actually capable from within Burkeville? We need to back one man in this mess as much as we can. Right now we aren't receiving much in taxes from

Burkeville, so stability is necessary," Ryen said.

Count Silzeus spoke in his weary voice, "I nominate Lord Longway for the sacrifices he has endured in dealing with the constant border conflicts through all these years. We rest easy with our luxuries knowing he is defending our borders." *Anyone resting easy these days is a damn fool.*

Jake Fielder said, "Interestingly enough, Lord Longway hasn't staked a claim."

"Of course he hasn't," the Count argued. "He is a humble man who obeys our laws. He wouldn't stake claim to a title unless it were appointed by the king himself. He's not anything like these savages who sip on the still warm blood of Duke Burke and Etburn. We've lost three of our five dukes in less than a season and that is precisely why he should rule Burkeville. He will embrace the crown's honor and show utmost loyalty to the king."

"If he brought his men from Bear Gate and we moved in from the east, Arigold can be recaptured. But would that put an end to it? Can he hold Arigold?" Ryen wondered.

Ali-Ster's head began to ache. There were problems in every region including his own. When he was a boy, Ali-Ster dreamed that ruling a kingdom only revolved around dressing nice and talking fancy. Now he understood the phrase, "He who sits the throne shall never enjoy comfort." He daydreamed about how carefree life would be when he and Queen Leimur were on the battlefields conquering fresh realms for their kingdom. The mindless worries of ruling a kingdom made Ali-Ster glad his father had never named him heir.

"I have one more matter to bring to the council," Tersen winked at Ali-Ster. "I would like to call a King's moot."

He cannot be serious. He is going to try to snake the throne from Ali-Varis. He never said a word of this.

"And who is it you nominate?" Dirk Eller requested.

I can't believe he is going to do this. "Prince Ali-Ster Wamhoff. Now I take nothing from our Prince and heir but we can all agree this is the best choice for the kingdom we are sworn to protect. He has the proper claim and ability," Tersen proudly said.

Ali-Ster felt shock and anger all at once. His uncle had totally blindsided him with this.

Count Silzeus cleared his throat, "The words of the Rosewood Scrolls state that any candidate for the throne must receive over half the vote of the council. If they pass, it will then be voted on by the high lords of Donegal to establish our king. If there should be a unanimous vote in council, the candidate will take the crown from the heir. Simple rules really. I do not believe I have forgotten anything."

Ali-Ster's face burned with emotion. He felt ambushed by his uncle and wondered if everyone had been in on this. He knew something was awry when they let him control the meeting but couldn't have expected this.

"All those who choose Ali-Ster Wamhoff to be his king, raise your right hand and say aye," Count Silzeus ordered.

The prince closed his eyes. The ring of, "Aye," sounded with a couple more singular calls that followed. Ali-Ster opened his eyes to see every council member's hand in the air. "I vote nay," he quickly said, raising his hand.

"The candidate receives no vote, my apparent King," Count Silzeus informed.

My King? NO. I don't want to be King Ali-Ster. Tell me this isn't happening. "Ali-Varis is still falconer. He gets a vote, no?" Ali-Ster looked at his brother drooling onto his chest and almost sleeping.

"No, highness, both candidates are disqualified for previously obvious reasons. This is unprecedented. No candidate has ever tried to vote against himself," the count said with a chuckle.

Tersen smiled at everybody, "The coronation will go on as planned with only one small change." Tersen happily looked at Ali-Ster but his nephew wouldn't return the kindness. The new King of Donegal slumped down into a chair, stunned. He stared at the table and tried to fully comprehend matters.

"This stays within these walls until the coronation. I trust I will see everyone at King Ali-Stanley's funeral march on the morrow," Tersen said before leaving.

After everyone left, Ali-Ster sat back and lowered his head. He didn't even have a crown yet and his head already hung heavy. A thought hit him.

I am the King. These fools have to do as I command. This will make it much easier to unite kingdoms. I am the King.

The next day a bright and sunny sky greeted the funeral procession. Small puffy clouds floating along the blue background provided a little relief from the sun but Ali-Ster was already sweating. The procession was scheduled to go a half-mile up the Royal Road and return to the castle. The King lay atop a long marble slab on a beautifully crafted rolling cart made of wood and painted red. He was covered up to the neck with a huge Wamhoff flag. The former King's scepter and several jewels were laid out below the slab on a sub-platform. The funerary cart was surrounded by Ali-Ster, Ali-Varis, Tersen, Ryen, Dirk Eller and several guards. Every king had been paraded on this route after death, with or without a body. The citizens were out en masse today and extended almost out of Ali-Ster's vision on both sides of the Royal Road. King Ali-Stanley had been on display in the House of Eternal Light for nearly a fortnight and the body stunk fierce. They had dressed him in black and red silken robes soaked in perfume but it only worsened the strong scent of putrefaction. The crown wobbled on his head with the movement of the cart and Ali-Ster looked at his father's pale blue face with its sunken skin. He felt remorse for having plotted against the man. He looked so innocent now, not the evil man whom Ali-Ster saw the last few months of his life. *Death is part of life. Will I ever know who did this?*

The citizens had descended on the muggy Capitol and crowded onto the street to catch a glimpse of the regal body. Nobody really seemed to be mourning or crying. Many of the commoners had never seen the King in real life. This was the only chance to do so for many people even though this wasn't a very good representation of Ali-Stanley. The nobility had already paid respects at an earlier ceremony and they never mixed with the lowborn of Donegal except to have them as servants or workers in their castles. A scruffy old man with a long white beard and hair approached the cart.

"Can I pwease touch the King, pwease?" he humbly asked.

Tersen shoved him away, but the man persisted, "Pwease, my lowds and pwinces?"

Tersen looked to the side and said in a casual voice, "Sir Oliver, kill this man."

As soon as the words were out of his mouth, Sir Oliver Wedgeword had liberated the man's intestines from his abdomen. The old man crumpled into a messy heap. Most of the commoners erupted in rage when they saw the unnecessary slaughter and rushed the cart. Ali-Ster stared at Tersen in disgust and before he realized it, he was enveloped by the venomous mob. "Stay behind me," Sir Oliver instructed as pandemonium broke loose. Ali-Ster wished he had brought his sword with him. It was tradition for the family escorts not to be armed. Sir Oliver pushed some men away and killed a few with his sword but the great numbers of lowborn had the strong advantage over the armed guards. They overpowered the guards and Ali-Ster saw Sir Ranley Orton ripped to pieces by the incensed citizens. The blood sprayed Ali-Ster in the face when they tore off his arm at the elbow. The screaming and dying made it impossible for Ali-Ster to hear Sir Oliver only a few feet away. The angered commoners got to the cart. The jewels and crown disappeared fast but the citizens kept going after another prize. The crazed eyes of the citizens shocked the King-in-waiting. Ali-Ster stood in fear and watched as his barbaric men and women ripped patches of flesh, ears and other body parts from the rotting carcass of King Ali-Stanley Wamhoff. They claimed their trophies, held them in the air and shouted wildly. The maniacal, screaming citizens weren't even satisfied after that disgusting display. They pushed Ali-Ster and his uncles back against a storefront. There was nowhere left to run. The deafening chaos left Ali-Ster bewildered.

Ali-Ster thought about how safe life on the battlefield was compared to Falconhurst. He wished he had never come back from his service and got involved in this whole mess. Ali-Ster kept envisioning Leimur Leluc and his dreams of a super kingdom that he felt were being crushed under the pressure from the angry mob. Sir Oliver got dragged down and stomped upon as the people descended on their secretly chosen King. He hadn't even seen Ali-Varis with everything going on. Ali-Ster was being pulled in every direction. He wondered what part was going to come off first as the pressure increased to an unbearable level. He felt his shoulder stretching and making the sound of twisting ropes. *Death is part of life.* He felt it about to pop when a horn blared and the citizens started to scatter. The scratched and stretched Ali-Ster saw his backup guard rushing in to save the day. He also observed dead bodies as far as the eye could see.

He ran over and grabbed Tersen by his neck with one hand, "Why did you do that? What were you thinking?"

His uncle squirmed under his taut grip and Ali-Ster increased it. "He was a security risk," Tersen fought to say.

"You started a fucking riot." Ali-Ster only swore with the soldiers during his service, "You almost got everyone killed. Thank you for your duty, wise uncle." He let go of his throat and stormed back to the castle. Ali-Ster knew the one move he had to make right after they pronounced him king. He would have to repair the kingdom of Donegal and this move would be a huge help.

71

THE PRISONER

HE AWAKENED IN complete darkness yet again. Had it been months, years or even longer? Starving, his voracious appetite made him howl out loud, "If you're going to kill me, just end it already." He spoke, but the words sounded foreign when he heard them. He felt like he hadn't talked to anyone in years. His dry, scaly skin felt like demons were constantly tugging at it, pulling tighter and tighter. He entered the dungeon a husky man, and now was reduced to skin and bones. The flesh seemed to be suctioned out from his gaunt face and his dry tongue always stuck to the roof of his mouth. He had already sacrificed two fingers and two toes to starvation. The guard had given him water a few times but he still had to drink his own urine to survive. He couldn't remember the last time he ate something other than his own body. His confused head centered on a thought.

I am in the King's dungeons. He's the one who pokes me with that pole. What is going on?

The jailer came up with a candle. It barely lit the surrounding area and teased the prisoner's eyes. The flame appeared to be fading back and forth, leaving fiery trails like a comet. He closed his eyes and saw giant white spots that stung his sensitive vision.

"Here's your feed," the jailer said as he slid in a small metal tray that scraped on the stone ground.

"What is this?"

"I just told you, it's feed. Now eat it," the jailer scolded.

"Why? Why do you feed me now?" the cautious prisoner asked. The jailer got irritated, "Cause if they tried to hang you now you wouldn't have enough weight to die. Now, just eat the fuckin' feed or die."

The candle disappeared but not before the prisoner had his hand touching the tray. He attacked the food with the same vigor he had used in combat. He didn't even taste it and couldn't tell what it was but it seemed like the greatest meal of his life. After he finished, the hunger pains still lingered but he was confident he wouldn't die tonight from starvation. The prisoner promised himself that he would open his neck for the Gods before taking another appendage. Time had become extremely difficult to gauge in the constant dark environment. Another meal followed not long after the first. The prisoner devoured it again and although his entire body still ached, his stomach writhed as he digested real food and felt a buzz of energy course through his body.

More meals kept coming in what seemed to be the next couple of days until a fiery torch danced in front of the cell. A tall redheaded man in a black leather overcoat that prominently displayed the Wamhoff crest over his left breast came into view. He wore a glittering object on his head. The food had unscrambled the prisoner's mind a bit, but confusion still dominated.

"Duke Colbert, I am Ali-Ster Wamhoff..."

"Where is your father, the King?" the prisoner snapped.

"Dead, and currently scattered about the kingdom. I am the King of Donegal now," Ali-Ster softly said.

"So you came to finish his dying wish with your first order just like he did with my father. Well, get on with it," Jon defiantly stated.

Jon had sacrificed so much to get to this point. He didn't want his body to be paraded around like a trophy and thought he should have killed himself.

"I served my duty for Donegal. I only ask that you don't make a spectacle out of me, soldier's honor," Jon requested.

Ali-Ster pulled over a stool and sat in front of the cell. "I haven't come to kill you. My father was afraid of you. I remember the day of his ambush. Sir Penrose dragged you into the castle. A bloody mess you were but you still looked better than you do right now. My word, have they fed you recently?"

"They have," Jon replied, still adjusting to the torch light as his eyes watered from the brightness.

"Sir Penrose handed my father his sword, thinking that Jon Colbert's self-proclaimed arch-rival would want to finish the job. The look of terror on my father's face culminated in disaster when he dropped the sword and cut his hand trying to catch it. He then insisted we throw you in the dungeons until his hand healed and he could carry out the act. His hand healed several months ago and yet here you rot still. My father...he was afraid of you. I am not. I am not afraid of any man. I will not apologize for any of my father's actions as I am not responsible for his deeds but luckily for your sake I differ greatly from our former king. I cannot wash away the sins of my father but I have learned from them. If I condemn a man to die, I will only do so if I am willing to enforce the sentence myself. I will have the stomach to look a man in the eyes and sentence him, then send him to the Gods." Ali-Ster stared right into Jon's dilated pupils.

"That is an honorable quality. I don't remember seeing you at the ambush," Jon told the young King.

"My father sent me and my uncle away on a hunt. We would have been the only ones to put a stop to the matter so he got rid of us for the day. My father also hid behind bad decisions with excuses of unnecessary revenge and the good of the kingdom battle cry. I realize for Donegal to be successful I need you back at the helm in Mattingly to restore things to their former state. No silly grudges from here on," Ali-Ster finished.

Jon Colbert could only exhale until the air of life finally filled him again. He shook more than usual and breathed heavily as his stomach churned. His chest buzzed with anticipation as purpose filled the Duke once more. Jon felt like a crying baby with his erratic breathing but no tears came out. So many joyful emotions rocked Jon's exhausted body as they tore at his hollowed core. He had only experienced misery recently but that was swiftly swept aside with only a few words. He had to be sure, "Just like that, you will release me to my family?"

"Yes, but we need to speak on that as well. You weren't the only member of your family targeted by my father. As it stands, everyone other than your son Ruxin is dead or missing. However, your remaining son has done you proud, Duke Colbert. He has protected your home with ferocity and unbreakable determination. He may not equal the loss of your entire family but you can stand proud of him. He had my father on tenterhooks until his last day if it softens the wounds at all," Ali-Ster spoke in a soft, caring voice.

"It doesn't. Unlike your father, I don't take pleasure in the misery of others," Jon retorted.

"Nor do I. That's why I shall return in an hour and you will finally leave this rat infested hole. I will not force you to kneel or kiss my hand if you simply pledge your fealty to my rule and swear to never move against me. You have been embarrassed enough already, I won't disgrace you in a public ceremony."

"You have my word, my King," it stung to say that but he seemed a stark contrast from the evil king that Jon had known. "How long have I been down here?"

"Approximately three months. It's midsummer. I will send you a large meal. You will need enough strength to ride," Ali-Ster said.

Before leaving, Ali-Ster handed the torch to Jon and grabbed one from the wall on his way out. Just as promised, the large meal soon arrived. Jon's freedom was peppered with sorrow. Only Ruxin appeared to be alive.

My sweet dove. My loving children. Should I even go on? Jon clutched his shank and mentally wrestled with the urge to drive it into his neck. He shook like a dying man and raised the blade to his throat. *This will wash away the pain. I will never truly be happy without my family. I should do it.* He eventually dropped the shank. The confused man ate the meal and Ali-Ster returned. He handed Jon some ill-fitting clothes through the open cell door.

The nude prisoner got dressed and walked from the wretched cell. He tasted freedom once more, and swore never to be captured again.

Walking awkwardly, Jon followed Ali-Ster to the outer stables, drinking in the beauty of the stars and moonlight. The smell of fresh air quickly faded as the stink of human waste assailed Jon's nose. Even so, just being outside seemed luxurious to Jon. The dungeon smelled of death and doom.

"What happened with your father?" Jon asked. "Stabbed from behind in his bedchamber sixteen times."

"Who did it?" Jon probed. "Everyone has a theory but nobody truly knows. The only thing that may be certain is that it wasn't you. I should have let you, shouldn't I? The singers and poets would burn out their mouths with that story of redemption. But alas, I can only offer a horse and peace," Ali-Ster apologetically stated.

A beautiful white courser waited to take Jon Colbert home. It had an ornate saddle and platform stirrups. "You are a good man. I shall never raise arms against you, my King," Jon bowed his head only a bit.

"I hope you find the courage to forge on, Duke Colbert. You are a noble man indeed and we need you for Donegal to succeed," Ali-Ster concluded. The new King and the most powerful Duke in Donegal sealed the pact with a handshake. It took all of Jon's strength to get onto the horse. His rusty coordination was tested as he heeled the courser a bit too hard. The horse bolted with a soft spurt of speed, almost losing its rider. He pulled back to slow down the courser from a canter and regained control. Jon held on for his life and didn't plan to stop until he was safely inside Mattingly. He took off in darkness and couldn't wait to see the sun for the first time in three months. Thousands of thoughts jostled for attention inside Jon's head as he still couldn't fully process his newfound freedom. *I'll ride from dark until dawn or dark until death.*

Thank You for reading *Two Heads, Two Spikes*.

I am a new author seeking feedback to get better so I encourage everyone to leave a review but I respectfully understand if that's not your thing. Here are the Amazon and Goodreads links if you do wish to leave a review. I thank you in advance.

Amazon:

http://www.amazon.com/dp/B00L3FJOOE

Goodreads:

https://www.goodreads.com/book/show/22798853-two-heads-two-spikes

If you enjoyed the first volume, here is where you can find Volume 2—Fractured Families:

https://amzn.com/B017A86OXG

If you thoroughly enjoyed this book and would like to receive early release material, be an advanced reader or find out about the author's generous exclusive offers, I'd love to have you join Jason Paul Rice's mailing list. I love to regularly reward my readers, especially Jason Paul Rice's Roundtable of advanced readers. For an easy sign-up simply go to: http://jasonpaulricebooks.com

Jason Paul Rice Community:

Author Website: http://jasonpaulricebooks.com
Facebook: https://www.facebook.com/2heads2spikes/
Twitter: https://twitter.com/2Heads2Spikes

Goodreads:
https://www.goodreads.com/author/show/8199394.Jason_Paul_Rice

BookBub:
https://www.bookbub.com/authors/jason-paul-rice

Amazon:
https://www.amazon.com/Jason-Paul-Rice/e/B00L3JUJ6M

◇◇◇

www.ingramcontent.com/pod-product-compliance
Lightning Source LLC
Chambersburg PA
CBHW061301170626
46817CB00001B/5